TRAIL OF FATE

B.S. DANIELS

Buttercup Publishing

ISBN: 979-8-218-47008-1

CONTENTS

Prologue 1
1. Late 1800s - Colorado Foothills 3
2. Roan's Story 17
3. Two Forks, The Town 23
4. Welcome To Two Forks 34
5. Tate 59
6. Café 64
7. Reg 67
8. Remembering Dad's Story 75
9. Reg Recalls His Part Of The Story 81
10. Mom 83
11. Cherokee Woman 86
12. Reg 91
13. Back To The T Lazy 7 And Our Cows 94
14. Spence 100
15. Chelsea & Maggie 112
16. Delivering News 114
17. Digging For Bones 123
18. On The Trail 128
19. Reg 131
20. Tucker 139
21. Finally, The Truth 144
22. Ben 154
23. Meeting The Town Marshall 161
24. Reg Speaks At The Town Meeting 164
25. Time To Rest 171
26. Betty 176
27. Spence 179
28. Ben 185
29. Reg 192
30. Spence 200
31. Reg 205
32. Pinkie 209

33. Deputies   217
34. Tate   223
35. Tom   227
36. Reg   229
37. The Valley   235
38. Relief   243
39. Tucker   246
40. Relief Turns To Grief   253
41. Time To Fight   258
42. The Marshall   264
43. After The Smoke Cleared   271
44. The Day Of The Funeral   282
45. The Cattle Drive   296
46. Back At The Ranch   311
47. Preparing For The Return Trip   320
48. On The Trail Again   323
49. The End Of The Trail   326
50. The T Lazy 7 Ranch   332
51. The T Lazy 7 Ranch   339
52. A Woman On The Hunt   349
53. Life Goes On   361
54. Maggie's Ranch   365
55. At The T Lazy 7 Ranch   368
56. Damsel In Distress   376
57. Reg   385
58. Return To Two Forks   389
59. Reg Is On The Trail   393
60. Sunday   396
61. Zeke Brings A Gift   403
62. Back In Town   412

Acknowledgments   421
A Request To My Readers   422
About the Author   423

*This book is
dedicated to all those
who have crossed my path.
In one way or another, they helped
create who and what I am today.*

If there is no will,
There is no way.

If there is the will,
There is always a way.

PROLOGUE

THE TRAIL OF FATE

The sun rises. Is it fate?

The moon rises. Is it fate?

The people we meet and the places: where we travel. Is it fate?

All the many roads, twists, and turns, the people who come and go in our lives.

Fate … What does it have in store for you?

1

LATE 1800S - COLORADO FOOTHILLS

REG

The air was crisp and cool, carrying a hint of sage and the constant feel of prairie dust. I slept as all men on horseback do, using their well-worn saddle as a pillow and the stars as trail companions. The morning light began to reveal itself through the mist under a cloudless blue sky.

The small fire I built helped keep the morning chill at bay, and the smell of wood smoke and fresh coffee was a pleasant aroma.

I had a hundred memories of times gone by sitting around a fire with a pot of hot coffee, enjoying the fire by myself or with companions. New or old trail riders, ones from just over the hill or miles away in this vast country, we all had a story to share.

The one thing we had in common was the stories. We kept a few to ourselves, but there were others we gladly shared. Coffee and a campfire were the best ways to gather information, or maybe just by listening to a tall tale that would be passed on for many years. It was the cowboy way to keep a person's memory and legacy alive.

All my senses snapped into full alert when I heard the report of a gunshot in the distance. Another shot rang out as I strained to look through the early morning's dim light. Instantly, I determined it was shots from two separate guns.

Every gun carried a specific tune; some were short and snappy, while others played a smoother ring. The shots split the air only seconds apart and rang from what seemed south of my location. I figured the shots echoed up from the valley floor below me, and with the sound traveling uphill, I estimated it to be about two miles down the adjacent draw.

The air and the surrounding area were now as ghostly quiet as a graveyard. I thought about why the shots had occurred. I was in the middle of no man's land.

Chances were, whoever was stalking about would probably not be the most welcoming individual. Outlaws would be my guess, but it could be miners, trappers, or dwindling numbers of renegades who worked hard to remain hidden.

Perhaps someone was only hunting for their breakfast. In seconds, my mind played out several scenarios to determine whether this would be friend or foe. *Should I keep my distance or see if there was someone in need?*

About thirty minutes passed, and when I decided someone was probably hunting for food, two more shots rang out. I knew from the billowing sound that traveled across the valley that the shooter used a long gun, a rifle. Whoever was shooting sent the bullet a long distance before the dull thud indicated it hit its mark. I sat back on my haunches, sipped my coffee, and focused my eyes and ears on any noise or slight movement from down below.

The only sound I heard was from my mare, my new companion. Her ears pointed south at full tilt, eyes fixed in a southward direction, breathing calm and steady. I took a couple of pulls on my coffee, enjoying the hot, strong taste and aroma. I decided I would take a look-see around the draw to the south and determine who lurked in the distance. I didn't for a moment imagine it would be Indians.

When Indians attacked, and if it was a war party, they could be very vocal, filling the air with chanting, hollering, and speaking out to their ancient warriors as bullets, arrows, and spears flew. They painted their bodies and their sacred horses with symbols and shapes.

We understood very few, and those we did carried no meaning to us but meant great power for the rider and horse. If they were counting coup, their highest honor, gained by touching a war stick to an enemy, the war feather was eventually added to that warrior's coup stick. Counting coup was like a game to them. The greater the risk, the greater the coup, big medicine, and power.

On the other hand, if they were on a mission, they would be deadly silent, stealing horses, women, or supplies. They would sneak in and take what they could without anyone being any wiser.

My guess was outlaws. *But what or who would they be shooting at?* I kicked out the embers in the fire, doused it with the remaining coffee, and covered it with dirt to hide the scent and smoke. I saddled the roan as the mist was lifting and set off in a wide circle to scout the layout of the land. We made a wide loop around the area from where I felt the shots had been fired. I scanned the foreground, looking for tracks or clues left behind.

Roan, my mare, caught a scent before I saw anything. I peered through the brush for a glimpse of what lay ahead. The horse moved slowly, alert and calm, with her attention directed forward. Her eyes constantly searched, ears up, shifting from side to side, listening for the slightest noise. She heard or saw things long before I detected anything out of the ordinary. Her muscles under me twitched like she was stretching her muscles out for a fast bolt if need be.

She stopped, dead in her tracks, calm but alerting me to what lay directly ahead.

After dismounting, I sat back on my heels and peered out from under the cedar and piñon trees that provided us with cover.

Two men lay face down in the dirt, twenty feet apart, guns remaining in their holsters. The blood-soaked ground proved these two died earlier, never knowing what hit them. The dead men wore their guns low and tied down, dressed more like men suited to town life, and wore dusty but tailored clothing, unlike that of an outlaw or trapper.

Boots neatly kept, not worn down at the heel. *Unlike my outfit, my clothes should be burned. I don't know how they kept me in and presentable.* And I'm sure my odor was probably just as foul. It's funny how a man can smell everyone else but not himself. I'm sure he would be tormented night and day if he caught his own scent.

These men did not ride astride mountain-bred horses. They were not cowboys' workhorses. They were more like well-cared-for gentlemen's horses.

I walked over and stood next to the two bodies. My four-legged sidekick stood on guard. I squatted on my heels, reading signs. I sensed these two were shot quickly from a distance. Neither one drew iron. Their guns on their hips remained in their holsters. I looked at the bodies and roughly calculated the shots that ended them came from the gentle slope to the north. The rain and the trees gave me cover. I placed their hats over their eyes, bowed my head, and whispered a few words.

Surely, there must have been an ounce of goodness in them, even when carrying out the actions that led them down this path.

Bending down, I peered from under my horse and saw the outline of a figure lying on the slope under a cedar tree. I was behind the roan for protection, but I knew if the figure up the hill was the same person who shot these two, I would have been dead long ago if he wanted me to be. I moved along with the horse to block any shot aimed my way. From this position, I studied the body on the hill, steadily moving forward, creeping through the cedars to provide protection yet keeping a sharp eye on the body upwind from me.

As I grew closer, I saw it was a white man who appeared to be resting or feigning sleep with his legs crossed, hands folded in his lap, and his hat drawn over his eyes. I presumed he was dead. He looked too comfortable to have been in a shootout. The small cedar tree provided him with shade from the sun. *This was a strange sight. Calm and peaceful, not what I expected to find after viewing the two dead men down below.*

I felt at ease walking up the hill toward him. As I journeyed through life, time and again, I felt a sense of when there was danger, sadness, happiness, and right or wrong situations lurking before me. At this moment, I felt as though I was walking up to an old friend where I had nothing to fear.

I stopped as I neared and waited, looking at my surroundings. I watched his chest to see if it moved. The man never moved or showed any evidence that he was alive. His hands crossed over his lap, relaxed and still. *Was he peacefully resting, or was he dead?*

He looked like he had lived through rough times, dressed in old, worn, and tattered clothes, with his boots and heels worn down. Or maybe he didn't like to buy new clothes.

I could understand that. In time, I knew that new clothing would be welcomed, but at first, they felt stiff and scratchy. Kinda irritated a fella. This man presented a muscular barrel-chested build, broad shoulders, and muscled arms that showed years of hard work.

On his side lay his long gun, clean and well cared for. I was not familiar with this rifle; nothing like any other I had ever seen. It was a big bore rifle, longer than most, with pop-up peep sights for shooting long distances. His hog leg rested under his hands.

There were two blood stains on his shirt where two slugs had entered his body, one in the upper chest and one dead center. If he was not dead, he was close.

"Cowboy, you have any coffee?" said a muffled voice from under the tattered hat.

The voice startled me. I felt for sure the man lying before me was dead. I replied, "I never shared coffee with a dead man before."

"Son, I'm not at the Pearlies yet."

I reached over to move his hat and saw a man with a sky-blue, keen-eyed stare, very much aware of everything around him. He had untroubled eyes and a stern, no-nonsense face.

I looked around. The roan munched on tall, sweet grass, relaxing and enjoying the cool breeze. Her composure put me at ease. As I built a fire and made coffee, I examined the injured man's wounds.

"Don't fret, son. It will be over soon."

I knew he was right. I helped him sit and propped him up on the saddle I removed from my horse.

"My name is Clancy," he said by way of a formal greeting.

Nodding, I said, "Call me Reg."

As Clancy struggled to sip his coffee, he asked what brought me to this out of the way place.

"Bad luck," I said with a shake of my head. "What about you, Clancy?"

"Good luck," was Clancy's clever answer.

I smiled at his reply and said, "Dying in the dirt seemed a long way away from good luck."

"Well, the story's not over yet, son." He smiled with a full mouth of white shiny teeth. I could tell he appeared to be a man who attended to what was important and what was needed to survive and had something important to say.

Clancy went on with his story. "I was on my way to meet my wife and three daughters in Two Forks. I sent word to them six months ago, and I'm not sure if they received my wire or not. I paid for their stagecoach tickets, room, and food in town. I figured they should have arrived a month ago if they got the notice.

When I left Texas over a year ago, I traveled to this area with an old map I had been given in settlement of a debt. The young man had no money but owned this map, passed down from a family member who kept it for years. The family never knew of the fortune he handed over to me that day.

Those two hombres down below tried to follow me. I gave them the slip, but they must have been scouting or waiting for my return from the hills. They may have asked about me in town and discov-

9

ered that I was returning for my family. I made a big mistake. I paid my bills in gold."

Clancy pointed down the hill towards the two bushwhackers. "I saw them both, along with two other men, in the last place I stopped, and I knew in an instant they were not honorable men of good character, each with an air of deceit and death. The hair stood up on my neck as I walked by them."

"I was heading back to town this morning when I rode up on these two. I came down the pass, and they shot me. I rode back up the hill and waited, killing them while they searched for me below. I could tell they were not men of the wild country. They didn't know how to track or hunt, only kill."

I looked down the hill and said, "Nice shoo-tin Clancy, two shots, two kills."

"Young man, my horse is over behind the rocks. I cut her throat. I hated to do it, but I knew I was done for, and I didn't want her leading them back to my secret place.

"I figure I can size a man up pretty well, Reg. I believe you to be a young man who has seen hard work but has the intelligence to break down a situation. I'm not in a good position to bargain since I have little choice in the matter of what's to come."

"Reg, look here in my bag. I'm running low on time. I'm afraid my hourglass of sand is running out, and I'm down to my last grains."

He pulled the sturdy canvas cloth bag from his side and tried to toss it my way, but he was growing weaker and couldn't make the effort. I reached over and understood why he couldn't toss it. It was packed full and heavy.

"Reg, here's the deal I need to ask of you. My wife and daughters have been waiting for my return for a year. When I left to chase a mystery treasure, I left them on the ranch with nothing but miserable hard work. I'll ask you to deliver this to them. You can wait till I die and go your own way, or you can do the right thing and honor my request."

When I opened the pack, I saw riches I never thought possible or would never see again: gold nuggets, not mined gold, busted and rough pieces speckled in hard rock, but washed gold, shining river gold, pure nuggets.

When our eyes met, Clancy smiled and said, "Hell of a favor to ask a man you had never met or would never lay eyes on again."

I looked at Clancy and said," Gold like this brings out the worst in men. They would kill for one nugget, let alone hundreds of them."

"Yep, that's why I know I've made a good choice. A dishonest man would lie through his teeth to have this bundle or cut my throat to get on his way to riches and all the sin it would buy."

"Clancy, what's your wife's name?"

"Nancy Jo, she's coming from Texas. My daughters are Chelsea, Caty, and Callie. Named after my favorite mule, "C." I named Chelsea after her and felt obligated to carry on the tradition. I didn't want the other girls growing up saying I didn't name them after "C" and that I didn't love them as much. So, a tradition was set in place. You know young'uns are always competing against each other."

I nodded my head and grinned. "I have a younger brother, so I know what you're saying. Clancy, I'll do my best to honor what you ask. If they're not in town, I'll track them down and make sure they know your fate. I'll make sure they receive this bounty you entrusted to my care."

The moment I finished my sentence, my mare turned and reared.

I spun on my heels. My gun jumped into my hand. I could feel the air move as a shot flew by my head, and the man behind me fell back and died before he hit the ground. I was disgusted that I let someone move in that close and be unaware of his presence. *The gold had its effect. I hadn't thought about my surroundings.*

Clancy smiled as he set his revolver down. Earlier, I saw the results of his rifle expertise. Now, he showed that he also knew how to use a revolver.

"Clancy, you could've given me a sign. I think I wet myself."

"Been watching the snake slither up for a while, Reg. I wanted to see how close that rattler would get before he would strike." Clancy appeared to be enjoying himself as he laughed.

"Now there's one less varmint in the world. Keep an eye open, son. There were four in town, and there could be more. That horse saved your bacon. It looks like a wise and tough mount. Bet she's got some stories to tell."

Clancy grabbed hold of my arm. "Reg, I'm done. In my boot, there's a map to riches you'll never believe. You'll be awestruck even when you see them with your own two eyes. Take your share, son, and again be careful."

Clancy was gone.

I knew I would lose what I held dear if I let my guard down again. I saddled my mount, looked into her eyes, and tried to let her know she saved my hide. In a moment of what appeared to be pure understanding and respect, she stepped on my foot as if to say, *enough already.*

Before I buried Clancy, I removed his belt buckle. I wanted to carry it to his family as a token they would recognize and proof of our meeting when I told this story. I buried Clancy with a few kind words and an epitaph I carved into a log. "A good man, who loved his mule, "C.""

I picked up Clancy's revolver, a unique piece, custom-built, long barrel with glazed-over sights. Instinct and years of use by the shooter would hide his bullet in any target. It was designed for a fast draw, with no time to sight in, just pull and shoot. The grip was small in diameter, made for a man with smaller hands and short fingers, giving Clancy a good tight fit on the gun. The weapon was well balanced, always riding well in hand, not butt or muzzle heavy, and would stay level when the shooter placed a finger in the trigger guard.

The rifle was also custom built and longer than most rifles. A red tip mounted on the barrel end allowed for quick sighting, and the rear sights were designed to slide up, back, or pop up for whatever range the shooter needed. Clancy understood his weapons and knew how to stop whatever trouble came his way.

He most likely was caught off guard when he was shot, probably only a moment when his thoughts drifted elsewhere. Basically, the same as my thoughts had been by not paying attention to my surroundings earlier when the third outlaw could have killed us both if it wasn't for Clancy and my alert horse.

I carried his revolver and rifle to where Clancy said his horse lay. I removed the saddle and gear. I didn't want to leave his gear out to rust and rot away. I knew that if I carried his belongings into town, someone would surely recognize them.

When a stranger rides into town, the first thing men look at is the man, horse, saddle, gear, and guns he possesses, and then lastly, back to the man.

I would hang if I rode into town with the gold and Clancy's

outfit. No one would believe the story I would tell. I didn't believe it myself.

There was a rock shelf about thirty feet above me that would fit my needs perfectly. The massive rock was granite, hard, and smooth.

Spence, my younger brother, and I climbed all the mountains, hills, and rock outcroppings back home. We enjoyed climbing a jutting rock ledge and searching for stashes the Indians or mountain men hid.

Occasionally, we found old caches of dried wheat and grains, clothes, and ancient stone weapons. We liked to sit on the top of a massive rock, look out over the country, and wonder who else sat in this spot and which of us first witnessed the grand view below.

By removing my boots and socks, my bare feet helped keep me from slipping. I reached the rock shelf. If one looked up from below, the small cave was hidden from view. It would be perfect for concealing and keeping Clancy's goods dry.

Then, I reversed my steps to the bottom of the climb. I wrapped the gear and tied my lariat onto Clancy's possessions, working my way back up the rock face, hauling the other end of the lariat with me. I reached the ledge and pulled up Clancy's gear.

Removing my hat, I sat for a minute, taking in the vast valley below. What little breeze there was on the rock face felt cool as it gently blew across my sweat-soaked shirt.

Stowing the gear for later retrieval, I felt confident it would be safe in the cave. I would let his kin know of the location, and I felt sure they would want what belonged to him. It was odd at times like these what a person would cling onto. A knife, a piece of clothing, or a single possession was a meaningful connection to a loved one and often carried a special memory.

I moved and sat in the shadow of the overhang for a long while. I needed assurance that no one sat watching me or no men were visibly hunting Clancy or me. After convincing myself that the way was clear, I traversed off the ledge and worked for what felt like hours, concealing any clue to the location of the stashed goods and my presence there.

I tied my lariat to Clancy's horse and dragged her body away from the rock face. I covered and removed the tracks I had made using branches of sage as a brush to scatter the soil. I didn't want anyone looking around where I stashed his worldly possessions.

The sun hung high and sent scorching hot rays to the valley floor. The three bushwhackers were laid out in the dirt. I dragged the third man down to join the other two, turning him to face the direction which made it appear the hombre was killed with a bullet shot from down the hill as well.

A good tracker would figure it out quickly, but killers wouldn't have a clue. They only killed, assuming there were two men taking part in the shooting. After stripping them of their guns and rifles, I left them face down in the dirt. *No sense wasting my energy on these three buzzards. Worms gotta eat.*

About a quarter of a mile further down the trail, I hid their irons and gear in a separate lower rock crevasse, safely up off the ground and protected from rain and snow. I figured anyone stumbling upon the mystery stash might get the idea to look for other hidden stashes.

One day, I might be back this way, maybe with Clancy's wife helping her find the treasure using Clancy's treasure map. One never knew when extra guns might come in handy.

After rounding up the gunman's horses, I hoped to give the

impression that I found them roaming the hillside. Having a string of three horses was not easy to sneak across deadly country.

Apparently, the roan didn't care much for their company. She kept them back behind us with swift, short kicks.

Moving at a slow, leisurely pace, my parade crossed the ravine away from the direction of the nearest town and rode away from the draw.

2

ROAN'S STORY

A s I rode, my thoughts drifted back to how the roan and I became trail companions. We came across each other's path, or should I say, she walked straight into my path.

That day was cloudy, rainy, and bone-chilling cold, a sloppy mess. I was riding out in the most isolated part of the country a horseman could find when my horse broke her leg after stepping into a sinkhole. She stepped into the hole and couldn't regain her footing. We both went down, hard and fast. I received only a few bruises on my ribs and a egg sized bump to my head, but she snapped her leg.

After I slipped off the saddle, I brought her to the ground, tried to comfort her with soothing words and strokes to her head and muzzle, and not wanting her to suffer further or arouse suspicion with a gunshot, I cut her throat.

Without a horse, I wouldn't be able to move away quickly. Without a doubt, I would be a sitting duck for any evil person looking to gain favor from my bad luck. I pitched a camp under the overhang of rocks and downed piñon pine trees. I made a fire to dry myself out and devised a plan to cover miles of the country while packing a rifle, saddle bag, and saddle.

I knew it would take time to cross this isolated part of the country, but I wasn't about to leave my outfit behind. I knew I would probably end up stashing it along the way, but a fella grows attached to things, and I had to try, no matter how ridiculous it was. By packing my saddle and bags, I understood I would quickly outgrow my fondness for these items.

I started planning how to survive. I cut pieces of meat from the horse, ate some, heat-dried a portion, and made hardtack from the flour, water, and salt I carried in my pack.

In this part of the world, horses were a companion on lonely trails and a tool for labor, plowing, packing, or riding. But now, as sad as it was, it was a food source. I could shoot rabbits, squirrels, and birds, but I wasn't in a good way by not having a horse.

The following morning, I walked about five miles in the hours before breaking dawn, hot even at that early hour. I didn't notice the heat quite as bad when I rode horseback, but now I was the pack mule and felt the full effect of the sun's rays.

Setting my load down and wiping the sweat from my face was little to no help. Water ran off me like a dam had sprung a leak.

Missed that horse. I didn't think much about my saddle and belongings while on a horse's back, but it surely was on my mind in that blistering heat.

After three days of walking, tripping, cursing, and trying to keep a steady pace, a mirage of heat waves shimmered ahead on the horizon. Needing to refocus my eyes, I looked more than once at the mirage that continued to appear in the distance.

I've often witnessed strange things in places where they shouldn't have been. So, I propped my back against several boulders that provided a sparse shade, set my long rifle on a boulder, and waited.

I looked long and hard at the illusion created by the mirage while my vision continued to blur from the salty flow of sweat in my eyes. The shade was little help as the heat lifted off the sun-baked earth like a blast furnace.

The mirage advanced. *Surely, my eyes played tricks on my mind after so many days in the sun. Mirages do not walk.*

Was it an elk, deer, or bear? Well, hopefully, not a bear. Finally, I distinctly recognized a horse, truly a sight to behold, a strawberry roan, a beauty with a reddish tint to the coat.

A powerful horse walked directly to me as if I had called him. I assumed he was a husky stud due to his gait and proud carriage. Eagle feathers hung from the braided mane and tail, and war paint on his neck and flank gave clues of an untold story.

This treasured animal had seen many battles, a warrior's horse with scars from head to hooves. An Indian's horse, one who was undoubtedly a warrior also, and, I believed, a great honor to his people.

The horse never varied in his stride. He walked in a direct line to me as if I had willed him to my side. To my amazement, the mirage horse proved to be a mare, a strawberry roan mare, not a stud.

Never had I seen such head-to-hoof power in a female of the breed. Wearing scarred battle wounds with pride, this sturdy land animal had a way about her. She was every bit one of a kind, with a stocky build, a broad chest, a thick rear end, and extremely intelligent eyes and manner. I looked her over and instinctively knew she belonged to a warrior of great importance.

When I stood from where I rested, I half expected to be bitten, kicked, or run over. When she moved to where I sat, she glanced at me, tilted, and lowered her head. I understood her signal to me that she was here and ready to go. She remained calm, her head raised, attentive, and tranquil.

What are the odds of a horse walking up to a lone person in the middle of nowhere? It's like I ordered her from the store catalog, and they sent her to me.

Lady, I don't know who lost you or where you came from, but I'm damn glad to quit carrying this saddle. I scratched my chin and smiled to myself.

This may be where the party begins, or my story ends. Had anyone ever tried to put a saddle on an Indian's horse?

Indians were excellent riders and rode bareback. Grabbing a handful of a long, flowing mane, the brave swung up onto his mount. The rider commanded the horse by squeezing the horse's sides with strong, muscled legs and riding like the wind, shooting guns, arrows, or throwing spears. They were fierce warriors on foot but just as skilled and deadly on the back of a horse.

I picked up my saddle and stood back a foot or two to avoid harm in case her hooves flew. I placed it on her white-dusted red spine, keeping a firm grip on my gear as I didn't want my saddle disappearing should she decide to bolt. Tensing up, ready for what I anticipated would come next, the surprise shocked me when nothing happened. She appeared to think that I might be a bit dimwitted and needed help with my task.

In case she decided to argue, I secured my lariat around her neck. I tightened the cinches and placed the hackamore, a noseband bitless bridle, around her nose and watched her eyes, muscles, and stance every second, waiting for an angry reaction to the gear.

Probably before I could walk, my father had me sitting astride a horse, and I rode my whole life, broke a lot of mean stock, and was capable of doing so again. But I didn't know how willing I was to take on this challenge should it occur. I also didn't feel like carrying my gear again with a busted ass from being bucked off if this four-legged beast wasn't willing to cooperate. I looked into her eyes.

She was attentive and patient, but I wondered if the look she threw my way meant, *I'm here. Let's go, greenhorn if you are capable of riding and not falling off.*

"Partner, let's get this rodeo started." I threw my leg over her back and tried to relax but remained uneasy. She looked back over her shoulder. One pull of her head and off we went, like we had ridden together for years.

When I rode into the draw to investigate the shooting earlier that day, Roan and I had not been together long. I wasn't sure how she would react if trouble arose, but I had confidence in her.

She constantly moved her ears from side to side, trying to catch any sound, the rabbit under the sage, the birds in the cedars, never missing anything, all eyes, and ears.

Her keen sense of smell would warn of men ahead long before I saw them lying in wait. She was not uneasy but sure-footed, quiet, and slowly moved forward. After stopping, she lowered her head and peered beneath the cedar growth.

I dismounted and worked my way forward, keeping cover between myself and what lay ahead. After several minutes, she began grazing and pulling tufts of grass, basically alerting me that the path ahead remained safe.

From that day onward, she became my friend and confidant, and because of her beauty, I kept her name as Roan.

3

TWO FORKS, THE TOWN

After riding for endless days, a town was in sight, a small town with maybe a hundred residents. A Welcome to Two Forks sign .... a livery, blacksmith, the café, a general store, two saloons, and a handful of other small businesses fronted by a boardwalk made up this prairie village in the middle of nowhere. As I watched from a hillside overlooking the town, I removed the saddle from my companion and gave her free rein to graze.

The three outlaws' horses were staked for the night, and a small fire lit our camp. The taste of fresh coffee and horse meat was satisfying. Being close to a town and people felt peaceful, but I was ill at ease about the future. My thoughts wandered. *Was it possible that at least one outlaw from the group of four waited for his partners to return with pockets full of gold, or had he simply lit out from town to find me on his own?*

Then, there was the issue of Clancy's wife and daughters. *Would they be in town? What would I say? What would they say about their husband and father's demise? How would they react to seeing the gold and their whole life about to change before their eyes?*

I watched over the town. I thought more about Clancy and his calm manner. *Imagine. The trust he put in me, a stranger, a man who looked like he didn't have two cents to rub together, and he trusted me with a fortune.*

I grinned. It's funny how ideas or questions would pop up out of nowhere. All the questions I should have asked that dying man. I looked at a nugget I removed from the pack, smooth and shiny. Wherever it came from, it had years of water running over it, tumbling and polishing it. Rubbing the heavy stone, I thought, *I bet it had a unique history.*

I glanced at the outlaws' horses. I could release them, ride out at daylight, and be rich. But I knew once a man traveled down the trail of dishonesty and betrayal, it had a way of coming back on him.

As the sun bid me goodnight and the blackness closed around me and the horses, I moved slowly from camp and remained hidden in the willow brush, sitting for several hours and watching from a distance away from the glow of the fire.

Carrying the gold with me would be a problem, as I would be bringing this treasure into town with no one to trust or keep it safe. A change of plans was in order, so I dug a hole next to the fire, chuckling as I scooped up the soil. I placed the tote full of gold in the hole, covered it with several layers of dirt, and then put the fire coals on top of where I buried the gold, finally relighting it.

When Spence and I hunted or were out in the wild, we left clues under our fires. People never thought to look under the coals for clues. If Spence had to track me, he knew to always look below my fire remains.

The Roan would be my guard for the night. Feeling safe, I fell fast asleep. After coffee the following morning, I loaded up my gear and checked that my gun and rifle were clean and ready for any unwanted action that might cross my path.

Being aware that when I rode into town on the Indian's war horse and led the outlaws' horses, two things would happen.

Number one: I would be the center of attention. That's what I wanted, and the second would be that I intended to flush out the fourth outlaw.

When passing the livery, several men looked my way. Their eyes followed me while they mentally sized up my intentions. The curious, confused townspeople watched me pass, full of wonder and questions. They couldn't quite figure out if I was just another cowpuncher drifting through town or an Indian fighter. I needed to keep the outlaws' horses close where I could keep an eye on them, so I rode to the local watering hole.

When I pulled up to the saloon, all remained quiet, with a couple of old-timers sitting on the boardwalk playing checkers. Three patrons sat inside the saloon engaged in a card game, but I couldn't see the whole room from the street. *Well, anyone who wanted to find me would come lookin'.*

After tying the horses to the roughhewn hitching post at the saloon, I drifted across the street to Maggie's Café & Boarding House. I could tell it was owned or run by a woman just by the clean appearance and a neatly painted welcoming sign blowing in the mild wind out front.

Wanting Roan closer to me, I tied her in front of the café where I had a clear view of all the horses. Stepping onto the boardwalk, I turned to view the street and watched my horse remove the reins from the rail. S*o much for keeping her restricted.*

Using my hat, I knocked the trail dust off my dirty clothing and tried to finger brush my hair back. I needed to look like I belonged, but my feeble attempts didn't help much. I walked into Maggie's Café, where several groups of men and women were eating their meals, and immediately stopped to stare at me.

A lady with two small boys sat by the back wall. The young boys liked the look of their idea of a gun-toting outlaw. They whispered and poked at each other as small boys do. The woman smiled slightly and looked away.

I chose a wooden table that showed the scars of many a cowpoke's restless knife from years before I arrived to rest my bones in the same spot. I chose to sit next to the window with a good view of the street, pulled out a chair, placed my hat on the extra seat next to me, and made myself comfortable. Blue and white gingham checked curtains hung on the windows, and small pots of flowers lined the windowsills, filling the air with the scent of lavender.

An older woman, probably in her mid-forties, approached my table to take my order. She was a pleasant lady armed with a ready smile and dressed in a lovely green calico dress and a white apron.

"Cowboy, what's your name, and what can I do for you?"

"This appears to be a respectable establishment, and the food smells delicious," I said. "Coffee and a beef steak, please. Would you be Maggie? The owner? My name is Reg."

Chuckling, she said, "Well, that was a mouthful. Yes, I am. I'm the owner. Thank you for the compliment. Not many drifters notice much. They only want to be fed and be on their way."

After she left my table, I realized the woman with the two small boys had dropped her handkerchief. Reaching over, I placed it on the table next to her hand.

One of the boys spoke, his voice filled with wonder, and said, "Are you an outlaw? I'm Little Joe, and this is my little brother, Dan. I'm eight, and he's only four."

"Boys. Nice to make your acquaintance. Nah, I am not an outlaw. That meal you have there looks mighty good."

Disgusted, Little Joe answered, "I wanted steak, but I had to share my dinner with Dan. He doesn't like steak, so we had to eat chicken as usual."

"It's nice that you are looking after your younger brother, Little Joe. Ma'am, I noticed the beautiful triple-stitched handwork on your handkerchief."

The blushing woman took her handkerchief, smiled, and looked at me. "I'm Sara Carson," she said, "Thank you. It was my mother's, and it is all I have left to remember her by. I would have hated to have misplaced it. And you just met my two sons. Little Joe is named after his grandpa, owner of the livery."

"Well, it sure didn't take you but a minute to get acquainted," Maggie said upon returning with his meal. "Overheard your conversation with Sara and the boys. You know what a triple stitch is?"

"I have a mother who tried to teach me a little of the finer hand skills. I guess some stuck. Maggie, where would the marshal's office be located?"

She answered me with a hand on her hip and suspicion deepening by the sound of her voice. "There is no marshal here. He comes in from the next county every once in a while. We have had several, but they don't last long."

"One ranch owner here wants the town to run his way. The other ranchers are very respectable and hard-working families. Great assets to the town, but this one rancher is a whole different story, making it hard to keep a good marshal. He has men who do as they please with little resistance."

Frowning, Maggie then asked, "Are you in trouble, or are you looking for help?"

"Just looking for honest advice, Maggie."

"For that, go see Preacher Bill. He has been in this town for many years. Hear tell, he came in on the first wagon train to start the town twenty years ago. He knows everyone and everything that goes on here abouts and in the surrounding area. A good man, honest and honorable."

"How will I know him, Maggie?"

"You'll know him when you see him, trust me."

"It was nice to have a home-cooked meal. It had been a long time since I ate anything except trail food or meat tastier than a horse."

"Nice to meet you, but I still think you might be an outlaw," whispered Little Joe as he left the table while Dan lagged behind, busily stuffing a biscuit in his pocket.

"Boys!" Sara reprimanded.

"Sara, nice to meet you, and it's just nice to see boys with manners and curiosity."

"Thank you, Reg, and if you need any help, my husband, Bill, and I own the general store. Come by any time."

"I will. You boys stay out of trouble." Snickering at the words, they both ran outside.

The sun bid all a good night as dusk set in, and the town was busy with people heading home, last-minute shopping, or having a bite to eat.

The saloon was gaining popularity, but as I could tell, no one gave the hitched horses any notice. Roan moved away from them and stood in an empty lot between two buildings, content but always looking my way.

As I thought about leaving Maggie's, my stomach felt as plum full as a stuffed turkey, and I wondered if I could manage to walk. I ate too much and drank a whole pot of coffee. Before I stood to leave, Maggie offered a big slice of apple pie topped with cream.

"This is on the house. You finished your supper like a good boy, so you deserve a little treat."

"Well, I'll be." I lifted the pie to my nose and inhaled the incredible scent of apples and cinnamon, topped with a nicely browned pastry crust. "You are truly a talented cook."

"Well, Reg, thank you, but the credit goes to the young woman who helps around here. She is a wonder in the kitchen, a cook, and a baker, all in one package."

I ate the pie and savored every bite.

Maggie bid me a good night as she did to everyone in her place, making them all feel special. It was a place built around kindness. "Reg, where do you call home?"

"Long story. Maybe next visit." It would be nice to bathe and sleep under a roof away from the heat, dust, and bugs, so I inquired if she had a room open for several nights.

She assured me she did and would ready the bath water and, for extra measure, add bath salts to remove the outdoor aroma. She didn't try to hide her smile, which silently stated the obvious. *At least she didn't pinch her nose.*

I reached out for her hand, and she coyly smiled like I was going to take her dancing. Certainly, she was a fine woman in all ways, but she was an older gal, and I was only twenty-four with too many years between us to make a match.

I placed a small gold nugget in her hand, and she quickly closed her fist to hide what I gave her. "Maggie. I feel I can trust you to keep my secret."

"I'll run you a tab. This will cover you for a good spell."

The meal I ate with the coffee and pie came to about two bits. The gold nugget was probably worth a hundred dollars. I didn't like giving away Clancy's gold, but I had no pocket money then. It had been a long time since I traveled to a town where my family could wire money to me from home. The word of a drifter holding gold spreads like wildfire, but I trusted Maggie with my secret and possibly my life. I had the same feeling I had when I met Clancy. She was a person whom I could trust.

Stepping to the door, I ran headlong into a young lady rushing into Maggie's at a whirlwind pace. We nearly collided in the middle of the doorway. Her quick bit of footwork kept her from falling on her backside, but we glanced at each other, smiled, apologized to one another, and she continued on her way. In an instant, I witnessed a young woman who could turn a few heads on the dance floor, or for that matter, anywhere she went.

Roan was already on her way to greet me. I gathered the reins, walked across the dirt road to untie my string of horses, and strode along the street's edge toward the livery, feeling sure the man at the stable would know who these horses belonged to if they were from this area. They were fine horses, not ranch hands' mounts, so they should be easy to identify.

When I approached the barn, I noticed the stalls were mucked out, and the stabled horses nuzzled their noses in feed bags, completely ignoring me.

I smelled the caretaker long before I set foot inside the stables and shortly found an older man who didn't look dirty or untidy. He was blessed with a big smile, and a nod of his head was his way of saying hello.

But the pipe he smoked smelled like he packed it full of leftovers from the stall and then threw in a skunk. Roan tried to blow the smell from her nostrils, but it was useless. I stepped as close as my nose allowed.

He chuckled, "I can tell you and your horse don't care for my pipe makin's."

I tried my best to smile back, but my eyes burned, and it was hard to be pleasant. "You're right. That's pretty rough makins. I don't think anyone will ask for a puff from your pipe. Name's Reg."

"That's about right, son. I make it myself, and it smells worse than a week-old dead calf, but it carries a pretty good wallop." He knocked it out on the heel of his boot as he walked over.

Glad he put out that horrid smell, and bet Roan felt the same.

"You must be Joe. I just met a couple of boys, one named Little Joe, Dan, and their mama, Sara, at Maggie's Café."

"That's right. Little Joe and his brother Dan are my grandsons. Sara is my daughter. I'm Old Joe, but don't call me that. I may be long in the tooth, but I am not old. Just Joe will suit me fine."

"Sure enough," I laughed. *Hope Sara doesn't smoke a pipe like her father. I believe I like this rough old cob.*

" I came across these horses west of town when I rode in ten, maybe fifteen miles out." *I hated to lie. In truth, I was north of town,*

*eighty miles north. I wanted to trust Sara's pa, but at the moment, I
needed to keep my cards covered.*

Joe barely glanced and knew who all three horses belonged to.
He didn't seem to care much for them. Although he admired the
horse flesh, he wore a scowl and had a fierce look in his eyes
thinking of the owners.

"Fine animals, can't say the same for the owners."

"Can you put them up until someone comes to collect them?"

"Yep, son, can do. You want me to collect a finder's fee?"

Shaking my head, no, I said, "I hate to see anybody set afoot." I
thought back to when I was dragging my saddle and gear. I knew the
three riding these horses weren't doing any walking, but I needed it
to appear that I knew nothing about the riders or their whereabouts.

"Would be obliged if you could put the horses and gear in a stall
for safe keeping."

"Shore can. I run a clean barn, and nobody comes here a
snoopin'. Whatever you got is safe here."

"Much obliged."

Joe watched the mare as she also kept an eye on him. With her
ears bent back, she made it obvious that he should keep his distance.

He asked, "The mare, where did you come across her?"

"She came across me. My horse broke down. Roan walked to me
out in the wild country and acted like she knew me."

"I've seen that horse before. Roan was Eagle Soaring's war
horse. You can see his sign on the horse's neck and the eagle feathers
hanging from her mane and tail. It's well known that he was a
mighty warrior, one Indian you didn't want to battle with."

"The painting on her flanks also tells the many stories and battles
of these two mighty warriors together and the old spirits. In a

peaceful setting, the warrior was a quiet Indian, smart, thoughtful, and respectful. He knew our language and our ways. He was educated by a woman captured by his people many years ago."

"Eagle Soaring's horse was admired by everyone who saw her in action. The stories told about this horse were unbelievable but true. The Indians say she had been a war horse for over two hundred years, a great spirit, and she held the power of a hundred horses."

I would agree. "She's one hell of a horse."

"What happened to the Indian? You get the better of him?" asked Joe.

"No, sir, I never saw hide nor hair of him."

"I don't think this horse would have walked away unless Soaring Eagle was dead, but to be safe, I'd sleep with both eyes open."

"Joe, can I turn her out in your pasture?"

"Yep, but it's not fenced; you better hobble her."

"No, she'll be fine. I don't think anything will keep her in if she wants to run. Maybe tomorrow I'll rub off the war paint. I don't want some fool to shoot her, but I'll leave the feathers out of respect."

Joe nodded, and I headed out for a good night's rest.

4

WELCOME TO TWO FORKS

I sat in the tub soaking. It was comfortable, and it felt good to know the layers of grime and dirt that had built up over the last three months slowly slid off.

I felt like I had lost pounds of weight, and as I stood out of the wash basin and walked over to the long mirror in the room. I barely knew the man who stood before me.

I shaved off the growth of my chin hair, leaving my dark mustache. *Some people called it red, but I saw it as auburn...didn't care for red.*

I wasn't much for beards, but I did like a mustache, thinking it made me look older than I was.

I slicked back my hair, which had grown almost to my shoulder. It had been a long while since I took care of myself. Looking at the rags I called clothes, I dreaded the fact that I must put them back on.

Should have bought new gear before I took a bath. The feel of old clothes and boots that had a little traveling time and hard work in them just felt right. *I didn't relish the idea of putting on new store-bought clothes.*

After I had finished my soak and a shave, I rinsed my pile of garments the best I could and hung them out to dry, pulled on my extra pair of long handles for the night, and decided to pick up my necessary supplies in the morning. The room Maggie assigned to me was located in the back of her building, away from the noise of the town.

As I opened the door to my room, I smelled a fragrance I recognized as lilac, and it looked as clean as Ma would have made it with a soft bed covered in comfortable patchwork quilts. I laid back, propped up my pillow, and tried to relax, but my sleep was restless, and my thoughts drifted back to Clancy.

What type of man was he? What did he do, and how did his life's journey end on a grassy slope of a remote hillside? I thought about the outlaws, the lone one still out there, and the possibility of more.

More thoughts traveled to his wife and daughters. I even revisited Roan's journey and our meeting.

Sleep continued to escape me, so I peered out the window that overlooked the stillness of the town. Dogs barked in the distance, returning the bay of the coyotes calling from the prairie. As the moon dropped to the horizon and the sun was not quite up, I lit the lamp and retrieved the map Clancy placed in my care. I guess, in some way, we became silent partners.

The map was simply made and well-drawn, showing the country north of here, about thirty miles from where we met. The tea-stained colored map indicated a rock jam across the canyon floor and crude drawings of deer heads on the canyon walls. There was no explanation, just the drawings. I was unaware of any river in that area and was concerned that I had brought the wrong place to mind. I knew I wasn't wrong, but I remained mystified. I slid the map back into my boot.

Today, I will start the process of locating Clancy's kin. If they have not arrived, I will track them down in Texas. I went to the washroom, gathered up my clothes, or rags, I should say, and put them on, trying not to make any new holes. It was a battle, but I finally got all the patches in the right spots. The smell of fresh bread, bacon, and eggs filled the stairway at the back of the building. I decided to walk down to the livery to check on Roan, but to my surprise, she stood outside the café waiting for my return.

Well, girl, you must have missed me. I reached up to rub her ears, and she lowered her head and walked closer to me. *You like that, don't you, girl? A nice scratch to start the day.*

I left her there and hurried back to the café and straight into the kitchen, expecting to see Maggie in her cooking apron covered in baking flour. Instead, I saw the young lady who nearly knocked me over in the doorway last evening.

"I'm sorry, miss. I was expecting to see Maggie."

She wiped her hands on her apron and brushed her golden blonde hair away from her eyes with the back of her hand. "I know who you are. Maggie informed me of our guest who could eat us out of house and home. I'm Chelsea."

"I wondered if you would have any apple peels left over from the pies?"

"You are more than welcome to eat an apple if you would like. We don't need to serve you peels," she said, chuckling at her own wit.

"Thanks, Chelsea, that's nice of you to offer, but they are for my horse." I shook my head and grinned as she handed me three apples that were not quite acceptable for the pies, and I left to feed Roan. "Thanks. I'll be back for breakfast after I tend to my horse."

I placed an apple in the palm of my hand, and a grateful loud crunch followed from one greedy horse. All three disappeared in an instant. She looked at me and pushed me towards the door with her nose. *More?* I peeked over my shoulder, expecting her to turn the doorknob and follow me. I was surprised when she wasn't there.

I sat beside the window in the dining room, looking at a hard-packed dirt road. Chelsea arrived with a cup and a full pot of strong black coffee. "Reg, what can I get you? You're the first of the day. You get the best pickin's."

"How about eggs, ham steak, and pan-fried potatoes."

Unable to pass up a tease, she smiled and said, "What, no pancakes?"

"Sure, a couple would be good. I don't want to eat too much. I might have to go back upstairs and take a nap."

Again, she smiled shyly, shook her head, brushed her hair back from her face, and hurried into the kitchen.

I sipped my coffee and gazed around the room. It was nicely kept, with hand-woven rugs on the floor and bright, cheerful curtains covering the windows. Hand-drawn pictures hung on the wall, most likely made by the town's children. It had a comfortable feeling, a woman's touch, and the smells and sounds from the kitchen made me long for home.

"Here you go, your first go round." She filled my coffee and brought me hot syrup and butter for my cakes. "When you need more, let me know."

When the owner strolled in, she glanced at me, then over to the red-faced young lady who gave me a sheepish smile and walked into the kitchen. I wiped my plate clean with the last of my cakes.

Maggie returned, and she sat a spell while we talked. "Did you enjoy your bath? I think there was enough topsoil left in the tub to plant a flower garden on the front walk." She saw that it made me uncomfortable that I left a mess.

"Sorry. I guess it had been a while since I made an indoor mess. Don't tell my mom. She'll tan my hide good."

"It's okay. It was worth it. You look like a new man, clean and shaved. Better watch out. You may attract a girl, or is there someone at home?"

Smiling, I said, "No, there's no one back home. The girls back there are not to be fooled by a bath and a shave." I enjoyed the contentment I felt in Maggie's company and was interested in seeing more of Chelsea.

There couldn't be two females named Chelsea in this small town. If she were Clancy's little girl, she would be one who carried on the 'C' legacy. I needed to know more about her. Was her ma Nancy Jo, and did she have two sisters?

I ran the scenes over in my mind about how I would approach Nancy Jo and let her know her life was about to change forever. The loss of her husband and the fortune she would soon receive were heavy burdens to lay on a lady and her children.

The front door to the eating establishment swung open with a bang as three men pushed through the door. Directing their attention right at me, the leader asked, pointing a bone finger my way, "You the fella who brought in the horses belonging to our friends?"

Maggie leaped into the dining room from the back, followed in tow by Chelsea. "Gentleman, I would appreciate you not slamming my door and disrupting my customers. If you are here to eat, please be seated. If not, I would ask you to take your business outside."

I was impressed with Maggie. She had a tough streak in her with no backing down. Chelsea stood at her side with a rolling pin in her hand and held it with such a firm grip I could see her knuckles turning white.

There may have been a history behind these two women and the men. I could see the ladies wanted nothing to do with them except they wished to remove them from the café and out of their sight.

The man, who I assumed was the boss, spoke. "I would never wish to upset either of you women. We are here to get information from this horse thief on the whereabouts of our friends and how he stole their horses."

A fire was burning, and it was not in the kitchen. I felt my muscles tighten and my back stiffen. I was ready to defend the ladies and myself. I was sure their friends killed Chelsea's father if he was her father. I looked at Maggie. She no longer had a look of distaste but one of anger and genuine contempt.

I stood up. "Gentlemen, it's clear that you're not welcome here, and I don't take it kindly to being called a horse thief. Let's take this matter outside. Ladies, thank you for the fine meal and conversation. It was good as always, and I'll look forward to my next visit."

The four men left the café, and I could sense the guests behind me sizing me up, probably thinking, *dumb young drifter*. My clothes were worn, and my hair was long and unkempt. It would be settled by bare knuckles, which was fine by me.

I was raised by a father who taught us honor, pride, and integrity, sometimes with a loving but firm hand. At times, my brother and I got a lot of firm love. A warming of the britches would set us straight, or he would let us two brothers duke it out if necessary.

I was the oldest, and my brother Spence was younger by only a year. He was the jokester and the ladies' man. He was sure-footed, rugged, and aggressive when the call to fight arose, but I had the temper and the desire to fight.

If a fight arose, Spence would fight, but he would always try to resolve the matter with humor if he could. When he was around, there were usually a handful of young ladies whom he wanted to attend to. So, he didn't like to waste his time fighting if it wasn't necessary.

Spence and I settled plenty of arguments, toe to toe. And always following the fight, he would look over with a bloody shit-eating grin as if to say, "Kicked your ass!" Never the case, but it was always a battle.

Maggie reminded me so much of my mother, an attractive woman, not only by her looks but by her spirit, things I can't explain. My mom, always the light in the room, was only five foot two but tough.

When Spence and I started to battle, my mother would calmly say, "You better not cause damage to my house. I suggest you take it outside."

We knew from past brawls that if we fought in the house, Dad's belt would magically appear in her hand, and even though she was little, she could swing the belt with the vengeance of the Lord.

As we stood in the street, the three men, me and, of course, Roan, joined us, standing close by. That horse had the uncanny ability to know when I was coming. *She wanted an ear scratch? Now?*

She sniffed my hand as if to say, *"What, no apples?"* Her expression reminded me of Spence with that shit-eating grin of his. She walked between us and stood next to the rail, head cocked and keeping a watchful eye.

One of the three men smarted off as Roan passed him. "Looky-here, her mane is all braided up, probably with old crow feathers." It was a good thing that Roan kept walking past.

"My name is Reg. My mother taught us always to be polite, so may I please know your name? I want to know who is calling me a horse thief?"

The leader, a clean, well-dressed gent of slender build and a narrow jaw, spoke first. "I'm A. W. Tate. I'm the boss at the T Lazy 7 Ranch."

He reached behind his back to his pocket. I wasn't sure what he was doing. Then I saw a handkerchief in his hand. He took it out and wiped the sweat from his brow, folded it into a perfect square, and returned it to his pocket.

His companions were covered in trail dust and built-up grime on their skin and under their nails, but not him. He looked like he recently stepped out of the wash house, clean as a whistle.

I had just finished cleaning up with a bath, shave, and combed hair, and he was still cleaner than me and probably had ridden several hours on a dusty trail. *Mr. Tate*, I thought, and another name came to my mind for him. *A. W. . . . Ass Wipe, Ass Wipe Tate.*

"Who are these two?" I asked.

41

"These two work for me and are of no concern to you."

"Mr. Tate, I brought these horses to town, paid the livery for their keep, and asked Joe if he knew who owned them. Doesn't sound like a horse thief to me." I said this loud enough for the gathering crowd to make my point known.

Again, I spoke to Ass Wipe. "Mr. Tate, I just wanted these fellas' names to let the doctor know who I was sending his way."

He looked as if he was going to explode. I determined that he was not a man who would allow anyone to talk back to him or take the upper hand. He was not a fighter or a boss of working men. He was a paid thug, a gun hand.

He tied his well-cared-for gun down low. Even though the weapon was well kept, the holster showed wear from what appeared to be extensive use. I knew he wanted to pull iron but couldn't because I had no defense. Even with most outlaws, they would basically still fight somewhat fairly.

He gave a hand wave to his two hired no goods. The gesture said a lot, and Tate spoke sternly to his cowhands, "I want you two to teach him a lesson."

I was ready. These two were not men. They were cowards who would hide behind a woman's skirt. I squared off and was prepared to take on either one. "I'm ready, boys. Let's see who wants to lose his teeth first."

Not that either one had that many teeth to knock out. As I saw it, I would do them a favor by improving their looks if I knocked out what remained of their remaining choppers. I must have borrowed Spence's grin because one of the men said, "What are you grinning at?"

Then it happened. The man on the right stepped forward. I

adjusted my body to smash him in the mouth with a right-handed punch.

Roan, my watchful horse, let out a bellow, startling everyone. We all snapped our heads her way to see what happened. After whirling around, no longer facing the men, Roan balanced her body on her front legs. Releasing pent-up anger, she raised her back legs, driving her hooves into the on-comer's chest and sending him flying across the dirt street.

He let out a high-pitched, loud scream any schoolgirl would be proud of. When he hit the ground, he grabbed his chest and cried out for help. The crowd stood frozen in place. I've seen a horse kick, and I have been kicked, but never have I seen or ever heard of a horse waiting, taking aim, and protecting her companion in such a way.

Roan turned and now faced forward toward me. Her rear end was facing Ass Wipe and the remaining hired man to the left. Roan looked at me, and she sniffed my hand again. . . *Apples, please.*

As we all came to our senses, I looked at the man sprawled flat on his back in the middle of the street. "I guess she didn't like you talking about her hair and eagle feathers. Now, maybe you'll show a little respect," I said.

Tate stepped forward to his man on the ground to help him or chastise him. It was anyone's guess. At that moment, the most powerful hand I've ever seen pulled Tate by the shoulder and spun him around. As he turned, I could not see Ass Wipe's face, but I could tell by his stance that he had no fight in him.

Looking past him, I understood why. There stood a mountain of a man in front of him, easily six foot five inches, three hundred pounds of muscle. Even his ears had muscles. He spoke to Mr. Tate. "Enough, this fight is over. Pay this young man for tending to your horses, apologize for calling him a horse thief, and be on your way."

Tate backed up. "I'll leave when I get answers. I want to know about my friends and what happened to them."

The mountain gave him a menacing look. Tate threw some coins at my feet and stormed off. I bent over and picked up the coins.

"Thanks, Mr. A. W. Tate, for the money, and I'll be waiting for that apology."

Tate yelled at his hired man, "Pick up your companion. Take him to the doctor or the ranch but see that he shuts him up."

When the man-mountain turned my way, I saw it, the collar, Preacher Bill. When I stood next to this man, I looked like a youngster. I have never seen such power besides in a mule.

Preacher Bill grinned and stuck out his bear claw of a paw. I hesitated to grab it, believing my hand wouldn't fit around his. Plus, I felt nervous that he might not give my hand back.

When he spoke, he said, "Hello, Reg, nice to meet you. I'm Preacher Bill."

I reached my hand out and was struck speechless when I saw my hand swallowed up by this man's massive one. I looked up, and he beamed from ear to ear.

"I receive this reaction from people a lot," he said.

I hoped to cultivate this man's friendship. *If we were enemies, I'd probably just shoot myself.* "Preacher Bill, it's nice to meet you. I was looking forward to fixing that fella's teeth, though."

Preacher Bill said, "It would not have been a good fight."

I felt puzzled. *Did he not think I could pound that man?*

Preacher Bill put his hand on my shoulder. "Reg, always look at a fight and ask yourself, "Would it be a fight you'd be proud of, a good fight from a worthy opponent?' One you could walk away from and say to yourself, "That was a battle well worth it, win or lose."

"My son, you need to fight when it deems it, sometimes to the death. Sometimes, it's just to fix the opponent's teeth. And today, I'm sure you might have wanted to win a certain young lady's honor." He said this with a snicker as he looked over my shoulder.

As I turned, Chelsea shyly favored us with the most beautiful smile as she fed apples to Roan. "Preacher Bill, come in, and I'll fix you right up with hot coffee and a good breakfast to start the morning."

Preacher Bill nodded and greeted Maggie and Chelsea. "It's a fine morning with good clear skies, the smell of good cooking, and no one lost teeth. Thank you, Chelsea, but I need to visit with young Reg here if he doesn't mind."

Chelsea giggled and said, "Well, if you men are done playing around, maybe we can get back to taking care of our customers. Have a good day. Bye, Reg."

"Good day, Chelsea," answered both men together.

I walked towards the livery with Preacher Bill, who said he also wanted to visit with Joe. I glanced back to see Chelsea watching from the window as we walked away. She stepped back as she met my glance.

Most likely, she turned away to help a customer.

"Chelsea," Maggie said as she watched her sneak a peek through the window. "Don't worry, he's not going anywhere, but he may need someone to feed his horse later." Maggie was all chuckles as she suggested the idea.

Preacher Bill slapped Reg on the shoulder. "Son, for only being in town a couple of days, you sure gained a lot of attention, both male and female."

"I just have that magnetic personality, I guess."

We reached the livery and were greeted by Joe. He shook Preacher Bill's hand and slapped him on the arm. "Preacher Bill, I see you sent those no-goods on their way before the young pup here got into trouble."

"Wait a minute, Joe, I was fine. There were only three. I probably would not even have worked off my breakfast with the effort."

Joe laughed. " I guess we will have to watch the future. I'm sure you'll get another chance, probably sooner than you think. That is if your horse and the padre will let you be. It's hard to show off to the ladies when everyone keeps butting in."

"Joe, why does everyone keep talking about the ladies? I don't see how I'm showing off. Those hombres came at me. Roan decided to join in all on her own."

Hearing her name, she nuzzled between the clergyman, Joe, and me.

Preacher Bill laughed a loud, hearty laugh while he slapped his knee at my expense. "We better watch our step, or else Reg might sick his horse on us."

"Have a good laugh. Keep it up, and you'll join the other cowpoke at the doc's getting your teeth fixed, too."

Preacher Bill smiled a toothy grin, signaling that he wasn't the least bit worried.

Joe looked at me. "You need to be careful, Reg. Tate and his men came by looking at the horses you brought in. They wanted to know what happened to their companions and how you came across their horses. They also asked if you mentioned anyone else you came across in the backcountry."

Both men standing in the livery looked my way, expecting an answer, but I gave none.

Preacher Bill stood rubbing Roan's neck but stopped, stroking her. He placed his hand on my shoulder and said, "We all understand that you can handle yourself, but mark my words. There will be a time when you will need help. The old guy here and I will stand our ground alongside you. When the time comes, do what needs to be done, as long as you're on the right side of this matter. I'm talking about God's law and the law of man."

I nodded my head, appreciating his words and implications. The old one looked at me and casually asked, "What's your plan for that young lady?"

I let out a cackle of a chuckle and replied, "Maggie?" I tried to take the conversation away from Chelsea and me.

Preacher Bill belted out a sound more like thunder than a laugh. Joe shook his head and slapped his knee this time.

The churchman replied, "Boy, that's way too much woman for you."

I started to walk away. "See you later. I've got thinking to do." I waved goodbye and headed into town, comforted by the clip-clop sound beside me. I stopped at the telegraph office and sent a telegram to my young brother.

"Spence. Stop. If you're able. Stop. Come a-runnin.' Stop."

I knew a fight was coming and felt I could handle it. Plus, I had the help of my two new friends, but it would be nice to have my brother there. Spence knew my habits and could fill in wherever I needed it.

My next stop was the general store. Stepping onto the boardwalk in front of the store, I was met by the Carson boys hustling out of the double doors, fishing poles in their hands.

"Hello, boys, got some fishing to do?"

"Heading off to our favorite spot. You want to come along?"

I looked at those boys, and I traveled back in time to the days when Spence and I would go to our favorite fishing hole back home. "You ask your mama if it would be okay. I'd enjoy a little fishin'.'"

Pushing at each other to be the first to ask their ma, both turned and ran full tilt into the store, their fishing poles bending in the doorway as they forced their way through. At the top of their lungs, they yelled for her.

Sara ran from the back of the store as if it were on fire and scanned the two boys for broken bones or any sign of mischief.

At that exact moment, both boys shouted at her with unbridled excitement, "Reg wants to go fishing with us, Mama. Is it okay? We want to take him to Wandering Stream, our favorite fishing hole."

Sara placed her hand on their shoulders in an effort to calm them. "Boys, I can see you're excited, but you don't run into the store like wild Indians scaring me to death."

I walked in the door, "I'm sorry, missus. I forgot how excited we boys can get." I stood there with a smile and, in turn, held onto the boys with my hands clamped down on the top of their heads, trying to help control their movement.

Their mother looked at all of us. "Just call me Sara. No need for formalities here. That would be a nice outing, but now I will have to worry about three boys." She glanced to the other end of the store. "Why don't you three take the girls with you?"

Disgruntled, Little Joe looked down at his feet and replied, "Mama, girls can't fish."

Two young girls stocked shelves and dusted the prairie grit off the dirty items.

"And who are these young ladies?" I asked.

Sara introduced the two girls. "This is Caty and Callie. They are my little helpers, and this lady in the back room is their mother, Nancy Jo."

I could see where Chelsea got her looks. She was a beautiful woman. I knew why Clancy glowed when he spoke of her.

"Nancy Jo, please call me Reg. It's a pleasure to meet you and the young ladies. Right now, I was torn with guilt. *Should I take her and the three girls aside and let her know of the fate of her husband and the girls' father?* How would I start? *Nancy, I was with Clancy when he was ambushed, and he wanted me to give you this gold . . .* No, not yet. Timing's not right.

"A pleasure to meet you, Reg. But please call me Nancy. We have too many Joes around here already. You will understand soon enough." She laughed and nodded her head as she said those words.

Sara spoke to me. "We have all heard you are already acquainted with Chelsea, Nancy's eldest daughter."

"Yes, ma'am. I have met her."

Nancy spoke with a pleasant, calm, and cheerful voice. "I understand that she has taken a shine to your roan horse. She's a little unsure of you, though." She gave a tinkling laugh after that statement.

The room felt awfully warm, and I felt a need to run. The ladies enjoyed the fun at my expense. I did not know what to do. I felt like the room was on fire, closing in on me.

"Let's leave the young man alone, Sara, or we're going to send him off to the hills," said Nancy.

Little Joe was ready to go. "Mama, so can we go fishing with Reg? It would be fun." he said as he wriggled excitedly."

I looked down at the boys. The youngster was ready to go, while Dan remained clueless and played with the dust floating in the sunlight. "Boys, it would be nice to have the lady's company," I said. "What do you think?"

Joe and Dan looked at each other, and Joe said, "I guess it's okay, but they have to bait their own hooks. I'm not doing it for them."

Caty chimed in. "That will be the day, Little Joe, when you bait my hook. You're just worried I will catch more fish than you." Caty had Clancy's wit and sense of humor. She was quick-witted and carried his smile.

I was about to witness an argument and cut in on the conversation. "Boys and young ladies, if you would excuse me for a minute, I want to pick up my supplies. Why don't you find us more poles, and we will get this fishing trip underway."

All four scampered out the door while I looked for new clothes. I picked up two pairs of long handles, two pairs of pants, two shirts, and sturdy socks and placed them on the counter. The girls' mother glanced over at me. "If you need any help, let me know. What about a new pair of boots and a hat to round it all off?"

"No, my boots and hat are just starting to fit right."

Sara looked at his boots and said, "You may as well be going barefoot."

"Nope, there's still life left in them." *That's all I needed was a couple of women dressing me.* "Sara, I'm expecting a banknote in the next couple of days. Could I pick my supplies up then?"

"Your account is good with me. Maggie said you were covered. She vouched for you."

"Then, I'll have to thank her for standing up for me." *A man's name was the most important thing he owned. When you gave a handshake, it was binding and not to be taken lightly.*

Clancy trusted me to do the right thing, but I didn't know how to get the words out of my mouth without harming anyone in the room. "I guess I better get fishing. I can feel little eyes burning a hole in my back."

"I'm going over to see Chelsea later. I'll drop your supplies off at Maggie's," said Nancy.

"Thank you kindly. That would be real nice." I walked out the door and was greeted by a mob of two-legged gigglers. It was as if Christmas arrived early in Two Forks. I stepped off the boardwalk as Roan stood watching me and began her approach.

"Kids, you stay to the side of me." *I was not sure how Roan would do with these tiny terrors.*

Roan looked toward the little people carrying what could look like whips. I glanced to my left and saw the two boys and one girl, but Callie was gone. I looked at Roan, and Callie stood beside her with her arms stretched out, trying to touch the sky.

My heart jumped into my throat. I moved to grab Callie and watched the mare lower her head, crouch down onto her front legs, and then tuck her hind legs beneath her body. Callie grabbed a handful of her mane and climbed on.

I was stunned. The other three saw this and shouted with excitement. "We want to ride."

Roan remained motionless as the gang crawled onto her back. Callie wrapped her fingers in the mane as Dan clung to her and the longer strands of horsehair that he could reach. Then Little Joe and Caty sat at the rear. Roan gently rose to her feet carrying the younguns.

Looking at the boardwalk where Maggie, Chelsea, Sara, and Nancy loitered behind us, watching the giggling kids, I heaved a pent-up sigh of relief.

If they only knew that I thought Roan might send them flying to the wind, they would be heading my way with tar and feathers.

I waved their way, acting an 'all was well' confidence that I did not feel. My thoughts continued to whirl. *I secretly would have liked to have been a mouse in a pocket so I could hear what was said by the laughing women, knowing full well this would be another joke at my expense.*

"Reg," Maggie yelled out with a giggle, "have fun babysitting!"

Roan followed me down the road and across the open field to the river below. The kids giggled and squirmed all along the way as I carried the poles.

When we reached the stream's edge, the traveling four-legged carriage stood next to a fallen log so the children could dismount easily. Joe jumped off the smooth horsehide first, came to claim his pole, and headed off to his favorite fishing spot. Caty helped Dan off and attempted to remove Callie, but there was no pulling her off that horse.

I smiled at Roan and rubbed her ears. "Girl, I guess you'll have to babysit this one." Roan paid me no mind, walked over to a nice shady spot next to a large cottonwood tree, and once again laid down with Callie holding on to her mane. The little lass was very content on Roan's back and spoke to her in a language I surely could not understand.

Still, this clever animal understood every word. Callie was in the process of braiding the gentle beast's long, wild mane and fixing her eagle feathers. They both displayed ease and contentment with one another.

The other three were busy turning over rocks, looking for grubs or worms to bait their hooks. Dan was picking up pea-sized pebbles and looking for worms while Joe and Caty were turning over boulders half their body size. They would have made a gold miner proud.

Little Joe found one worm, baited his hook, and cast it into his special fishing hole, determined to catch the first fish. The competition was on, and he had no time to waste.

Caty pulled worms from the ground like a hungry robin tugging worms after a rainstorm. She had a handful of slimy wigglers trying to crawl out of her grubby hand, and she beamed with delight, showing me what she had gathered. She then placed the worms in her blouse pocket for safekeeping.

Caty took the time to help Dan with the amusing chore of putting a worm on his hook. He watched her and looked so happy that she had helped him. Caty then set him by the water's edge. "Now, Dan, let's cast your worm into that area where the water runs around that big rock and makes a pocket hole beside it."

Dan also let Caty do this as it appeared he might be afraid of making a mistake in front of her. When she handed him the pole, Dan said, "Boy, I got it in a good spot for sure."

Caty smiled and said with all the patience in the world, "Be real quiet, and you'll catch a big one." For a twelve-year-old, this young female had all the makings of a mother-to-be someday. She finally put her worm on her pole and walked to the spot she favored when the silence was broken by Dan letting everyone know.

"I got one!"

Caty set her pole down and rushed to help Dan once again. She turned and said, "Don't pull too hard, or you will lose him."

But to no avail, Dan ran away from the stream with his catch dragging behind. Caty helped Dan try to handle his catch. She was as excited as Dan, not for any other reason than she was happy for him. She held the line and sweetly spoke to Dan. "Boy, Dan, you caught the big one." Dan squirmed while he tried to grab onto his flopping prize.

Callie never looked up from her chosen chore.

Meanwhile, back at his favorite spot, Joe was fit to be tied. He had not had one bite and was upset that his little brother had already caught one.

Caty yelled out to Joe, "What do you think of Dan's fish?

Little Joe yelled back with an attitude, "I'm going to catch a bigger one if you two would be quiet."

Caty helped Dan place his fish on a stick in the water and helped him get his pole set up back in his special hole. Then she walked over, cast her line into the moving water, and let it drift to the spot where she was looking to catch her prize. This child knew how to fish a river, and a stream was easy pickin's. She had been taught well, and after several more casts, she belted out. "I've got one."

Dan dropped his pole and ran to Caty, yelling, "Don't pull too hard. You'll lose him." He was now a seasoned fisherman.

Caty gathered her catch and assured Dan, "Yours is bigger than mine, but mine's a keeper also."

Dan agreed, "Yep, I know mine is bigger, but yours is mighty nice."

Caty looked at me as I sat on a rock nearby, enjoying the fishing competition. I could tell at a glance Caty's fish was bigger than Dan's, but she wanted him to have his special day, so I gave her a wink of understanding.

Joe fumed. Being out fished by his little brother was terrible, but being out fished by a girl, too, made it unbearable. "I'm moving to my other special hole. How am I to catch the big one with you two making so much noise?" And off he stomped upstream.

Callie still sat on top of her guardian and had woven four or five braids along her neck. Roan had shifted her weight and lowered her head into the soft grass, giving Callie free rein to pull one strand over another and jabber away.

As the day ran on, Dan was content with his prize fish and turned to search for shining rocks, bugs, and sticks on the water's edge.

Meanwhile, Caty moved into Joe's old spot and caught two more nice rainbows. Soon, the little ones were losing steam and slowing down.

I hollered, "Okay, you three, we better be heading back. I'm sure your mamas are missing you by now." I knew full well, angels or not, the ladies were enjoying their free time, devoid of chasing after children.

"Yep, Reg," Joe said, "We may as well go. These two have scared all the big fish away. You and I will come back by ourselves and show them their little fish won't measure up to our big fish."

Joe took his pole and started walking towards home. He wanted nothing to do with the likes of his fishing companions.

Caty ran past the group. "I'll fetch the fish." Caty found a willow branch and stuck it through their gills to carry the catch home.

"I can carry them, Caty," Dan said. "I know they will be heavy with the big one I caught." Caty let him grab hold, but she carried the weight.

Roan stretched and stood, and Callie was ready to go. Amazingly, she stopped braiding and chattering. She hugged Roan's neck. Time for a nap. I lifted Dan up behind Callie and then put Caty up last so she could place her arms around the little ones.

"I'll hold onto these two." Caty giggled. "I'm sure they're both going to be sound asleep soon."

I carried the fish and the poles, and we started back, thinking about how this nice day reminded me of being at home on a lazy summer afternoon.

As we came into town, the women folk and a handful of town folks who stood on the boardwalk greeted us to view the fishermen's return.

I think they mainly wanted to see if I survived. I thought, *here come the jokes.*

Nancy was the first to speak, but she was polite. "Reg, we see sleepy kids and a handful of nice trout."

"Yep, we did good."

Caty interrupted, "I caught three, and Dan caught the biggest. Little Joe, well, he drowned some worms." Caty talked a mile a minute and was all smiles. She carried a glow with her everywhere she went. "Ma, can we have the fish for supper, and can Reg come and eat with us?"

"Sure, if he would like. He may be tired of kids and want peace and quiet, though."

"No, ma'am, that sounds good. After a good day of fishing, it would be nice to have a hot meal and adult conversation. I've been on the trail way too long, and it would be nice to sit and have a family conversation. Now, Roan listens well, but she is not great at carrying on a conversation."

Meanwhile, Caty located a pale of water. Then she pulled a folding knife from her pocket and started to clean the fish. This young lady cleaned our catch like a doctor working on her patient there. She was all business.

Little Joe took the poles and looked for a quiet place to consider the impossible fact that he hadn't caught a single fish. I think he was more upset about not catching something with me around. Not that he wanted to show off, but I suppose it would have been more like fishing with an older brother and gaining recognition if he had been successful.

I took my leave of the ladies to care for Roan and told them I would meet them later in the evening.

"Around seven," Maggie said. "Don't be late. You might upset the cook," as she glanced over Chelsea's way. It was futile to worry. Chelsea was busy and never heard a word.

My mind continued to wander back to thoughts of Clancy. I wished I had known this man in his earlier days. In the moments I shared with him, I instantly knew he was a man with a sense of humor, pride in his work and family, and as honest as the day was long.

He placed a task on my shoulders that I, for the first time in my life, didn't know if I could accomplish what he asked of me. Giving Nancy and the girls the gold and the map would be easy. I could leave it with a note and walk away. Or I could keep it. But I knew this would never be an option. I was not that man. Telling them was the hard part.

I was raised to recognize a man's hard work, blood, sweat, and tears, kindness to others in need, and willingness to defend those who could not protect themselves. I was raised learning to judge a man on his merits. Clancy was that kind of man, and his wife and children appeared to be cut from the same cloth. *Did he shape them, or did they shape him?*

I knew I must give his family the news and gold I held in trust. But I worried about the fourth outlaw who saw Clancy in town. What about A.W. Tate?

Were the four men working alone or acting as a group? Where was the fourth man on the day Clancy was murdered? I knew I had to find this man and determine if he was part of the group led by A.W. Tate. I felt it in my bones that they were all connected.

I knew I could not release the gold or tell Nancy Jo about her husband and the children's father until I learned who the remaining person or persons were."

This family would be in a bad way if word got out. Their lives, I was certain would be in jeopardy.

5

TATE

Tate gathered his wits and instructed his hired man to quiet the injured man's moaning. Get him to the doc. With the help of several bystanders, the cowpoke lifted the unlucky fella who had felt the wrath of the roan.

Another spectator who had witnessed the saddle tramp's comment and the roan's reaction stated, "I bet that fella will never make fun of a horse again."

"After you drop him at the doc's, you get your asses back to the ranch, along with the horses stabled at the livery," Tate angrily demanded of his hired help as he mounted his horse and headed to the T Lazy 7.

The boss could not contain his fury. He had no idea where the gold was and wanted to teach this Reg a painful lesson. Deep in his bones, he knew that Reg had the gold or knew where it was located, but he needed time alone with this no-account drifter to beat the secret location out of him, but he knew better than to sully his own hands.

When he returned to the ranch, he would gather other hired hands, not his gunmen but the bullies who could easily make their victim feel the pain and enjoy nothing more than damaging a man. As he rode onto the ranch, one of the buckboard drivers, a small-framed filthy, stable hand, ran out to Tate like a school child bursting with a secret to tell the pack's leader, trying to gain his favor. "Mr. Tate, your men were kilt. The men found their bodies and the grave of the gold miner.""Where did they find them?"

"They were up the Valley of the Five Draws. Our

men were shot and left in the dirt, and their horses were nowhere to be found."

Tate had no reason to talk with this scum about anything. He ignored the man, rode past him at a gallop, and headed to the main house.

Tate mumbled to himself, "I'll take care of Reg, so help me. I'll have him buried in the draw with the others."

He dismounted and walked into the main house to find Mr. Tucker, the ranch owner. Tucker came into this country ten years ago with hundreds of cattle and as many horses. He controlled a band of young cowhands who were more outlaws than cattlemen.

After arriving at the T Lazy 7, those who asked were told that he had purchased the ranch and that the owner and several of his hired hands had moved on. No one saw them leave or heard from them again. It smelled odd that the young men who worked the ranch dwindled off one by one. No one knew where they went or why.

Eventually, most of the original cowhands were replaced

primarily with outlaw gunmen. A handful of experienced cattlemen were hired to work cattle and the fields.

The original owner built the ranch with hard work, foresight, and determination. He cleared the land, developed hay meadows, and built stock ponds, barns, and corrals. There were high mountain meadows for summer pasture and streams of fresh running water.

No rancher would take years to build this paradise, sell out, and just walk away. The former owners had friends in this area who respected and admired them. There was no way they would have packed up and left without saying goodbye to those who worked and played with them side by side.

Tucker also acquired the small ranches around his property by intimidation and force when he took over this large spread. The small ranchers could not defend themselves against this kind of evil.

Tucker made it seem like he was doing the small ranchers a big favor by buying them out, saving them from the hard times to come. But in reality, they all knew their fate if they tried to hold on.

If time permitted, they could have grouped together to help each other, but Tucker worked fast at pushing them off.

The land baron filled his home with handcrafted furniture, pictures, and lavish furnishings sent in from across the country, all which Tate admired and coveted.

Tucker greeted Tate. "What do you have to tell me? What's new in town?"

Tate answered promptly, "I found the missing men's horses in town. They were brought in by a drifter kid named Reg. He said he found them west of town, ten to fifteen miles out. I know he is lying. I can read a lie a mile away. The boys found our men's bodies north of town eighty miles out, in the Five Draws."

"They also found the grave site of the gold miner Clancy," said Tucker, surprising Tate with his knowledge.

The horses never would've made it that far on their own. I don't know if our men were killed by this kid, Reg, or the gold miner, and then Reg found the bodies. I know he has information. I'm going back and beating the truth out of that kid. I'll find the gold."

Tate slammed his mighty fist into the tabletop. "I'll find the gold," he bellowed. This man had muscular strength, but he also had the power behind him that money provided. He was highly intelligent, a thinker, a planner, and a cunning killer with a fast temper.

"Send the boys back to the miner's grave and order them to dig the body up and look for the gold and map. Hopefully, he had a map and didn't die with the location in his head. Tate, when you left the ranch, I told you and the boys to locate the gold, look for the gold mine, and report back to me. I never told them or you two to have anyone beaten or killed. We can't get answers from a dead man now, can we?"

Tucker's voice echoed off the walls of the great room. "When you see this kid, Reg, you will apologize to him for your accusation."

"I will not," Tate heatedly responded.

Striking like a rattler, fast and with no warning, Tucker struck Tate in the chest with his fist. By taking away Tate's wind, the blow sent him staggering backward. "You will apologize and make it believable. I want him to stop thinking about us as his enemies. We need to gain his trust."

Tate reacted to the attack by reaching for his gun. Tired of taking orders, he intended to kill Tucker and whoever stood in the way. Tucker was rich and powerful due to the services he provided. As the hired gunman reached for his weapon, he came to see his boss possessed intelligence, cunning, money, and power. He soon realized that what Tucker said was correct. "Gain trust, then strike, and fast." He would wait to gain control of this ranch and the power.

Tate looked at Tucker. "You are right, Boss. I was too hasty." Tate turned away and spoke to Tucker as he walked away. "I'll get the men going."

Tate went out to the log cabin that housed the gun hands and picked four men who were loyal to him. He took them aside and gave them instructions the boss's instructions.

"Go dig up the gold miner, look for any information about the gold. Recheck our men's pockets and boots to ensure no map was tucked away. Look them all over from head to toe and report back to me. And me alone... If you run into this Reg, fella, be respectful, gain his trust, and I'll deal with him later. We want him to feel welcome."

6

CAFÉ

Maggie and her husband owned one of the smaller ranches. Maggie's husband stepped out to check on the cattle one early morning and disappeared. Tucker showed up two weeks later and offered concern about Maggie's husband abandoning her. Maggie knew this was not the case. Tucker killed her husband. She felt it in her soul. Tucker could quickly dispose of her, so she remained kind and thanked him for his sympathetic words.

When Tucker made an offer on the ranch, it was a fair price, more than she had expected, and she was torn between guilt and the idea of letting him take over the ranch they had built to raise their family.

No matter how tough she was, a single woman in this country would not last long. Maggie took the offer, moved to town, and opened her café. Over the years, Tucker tried to win her favor, but Maggie knew him as the snake he was, the sidewinder who she knew killed her husband. She vowed she would see his demise no matter how long it would take.

Chelsea stood behind Caty at Maggie's Café, twirling Caty's long hair. "Caty, why are you looking out the window? Reg will be along soon."

"I know, Chelsea, I wasn't looking for Reg. I was looking for Pa. He should have been here by now."

While she put her arms around her little sister, they both continued to gaze out the window. "I'm sure Pa is fine, Caty. He will be here soon. And I know he's excited to see us also. You know he gets busy, and time gets away from him. Caty, why don't you get the table set for supper and then help me finish icing the cake?" she suggested.

Caty hustled to the kitchen, happy to have a chore, but her sister continued looking out the window, knowing in her heart that there was a problem.

Pa was never late. I'm sure there was a reason he was not here, and I figure it won't be a good one, thought Chelsea.

Ma held up pretty well, hiding her concern. She was a woman of great moral character and would care for her family in any way possible, thinking things through and making plans. She was patient, kind, and highly protective when needed.

Pa and my Ma were two different individuals. Pa liked to just get it done. It will work out in the end. Which usually meant the project could take a couple of attempts to complete. He worried about things, but his philosophy matched his words.

. . .

"IF THERE IS NO WILL, THERE IS NO WAY…
IF THERE IS A WILL, THERE IS ALWAYS A WAY."

Pa always found a way, but Chelsea was truly scared this time.

7

REG

My soak wasn't as relaxing as I hoped, knowing the task I had in store for the evening, eating a sit down meal with a family I must soon tell of their loss. I shaved off the growth on my face, combed back my hair, put on new clothes, and felt like a new man. It had been a long time since I wore store bought clothes. As far as looking like a new man, I wasn't any better looking, just clean. Before heading to dinner, I stopped at the general store.

When I entered the café, clean and dressed up, the youngsters greeted me. The girls twirled in their Sunday best dresses, and their hair showed off braids twisted with many colored ribbons and bows to match. The boys were not as joyful as the girls. They tugged on their collars and wriggled around in their clothes. I covered my mouth to hide my grin.

"Come with me, Reg," Caty said as she grabbed my hand and led me off into a back room that she had set up earlier with a yellow patterned tablecloth on the square pine table and elegant China dishes with a gold rim that I was certain they used only for company. The women whisked brimming bowls and platters of food in and out of the kitchen.

I laughed and said, "Pretty nice set up here. I'm a little worried about sitting down. It looks so nice."

Chelsea entered the room, wearing a beautiful red and white pinstriped frock. Her hair glowed with the color of growing field wheat, and she smelled like rose water.

Little Joe pushed me and said, "It's not nice to stare."

"Leave him alone, Little Joe," Caty said. He wasn't staring. He was admiring."

"I'm glad you two are keeping an eye on me, but I have to say, Caty, that you and Callie are two of the most beautiful young ladies I've ever seen. Don't you agree, boys?" *Gotta poke the bear a little.*

"Oh, they look okay for girls," Little Joe managed to say with the known grumpy attitude he saved when girls were a topic of conversation. Dan nodded as if to follow the older boy's statement.

Dan spoke softly, "I think they look like girls in the order book, all grown up, ready for a dance."

At that, Callie swirled in a circle and flipped her dress to make it flounce around, and Caty was doing her best to look like a grown woman.

"Well, look at Reg, will you," Nancy said. "You look like a wealthy cattleman dressed up with a smooth shaved face, all cleaned up nice."

Sara, agreeing with Nancy, said, "What do you think, Chelsea?"

The young lady smiled and pulled her hair forward to frame her beautiful face. She had a smile and skin that was smooth and truly breathtaking! She couldn't help but tease a little. "He might pass for a townie after a couple more soakings."

"I've been called much worse," I said.

Caty grabbed my hand. "I helped with the fish and the cake. Chelsea did most of it. Mama doesn't like me cooking on the hot stove when we're grease cooking.

"You, young'uns. I picked up a few candies at the store. I want to share them with you with your mothers' permission. Therefore, that means only after dinner."

The children reached for the bag and enthusiastically looked at all the colors and wide varieties of sweets: chocolates, caramels, fudges, and many hard and soft candies.

They tried to decide which ones they would try first. The kids were eager to eat their supper and start on their candy treasures.

The ladies and their children sat around the table eating the rainbow trout the afternoon fishing trip produced, plus potatoes, greens, corn, even cornbread, and cider.

"Can we have the candy NOW?" said Dan, growing tired of eating and eager to get to the good stuff of the evening.

Wanting to tease them all a little, Sara dragged on with fish stories that continued to grow. We finished with cake and more cider before the candy spree began, and the pleasant evening started to wind down.

The little ones tried to fight off tiredness as the night wore on. They were allowed to taste a piece of each type of candy. Luckily, the women stopped their candy-eating spree and insisted they save the rest for another day, or they would have consumed every last peace.

I stood up from the table and stretched my legs and back. "I will help with the dishes. Then I'm off to bed. All that fishing has worn me down."

Chelsea shot out of her seat. "You're a guest. I will not have you doing dishes."

"I am more than willing. My ma taught me how to wash dishes and even how to dry them. I'd love to help."

"No sir, you better get your shuteye, or I should probably say your beauty sleep."

"Well, all right. I'll leave you to it. I don't want to offend the cook. I would never know what a person might do to my food."

Chelsea grinned. "That's right, cowboy. Making an enemy of the cook is not a good idea."

I bowed, took my leave, quickly stepped up the stairs, and dropped into bed. I fell asleep as soon as my head hit the pillow, but later, I woke up with too many unanswered questions and feelings of guilt for not telling Nancy and the girls about their husband and father yet. I knew it would turn their world upside down when I gave them the information.

Staring at the ceiling didn't help calm my mind, so I dressed in my old clothes and packed my saddle bags, intending to ride out, scout the country, and look at the T Lazy 7 outfit. I was careful to walk soundlessly, leaving the upstairs room, not wanting to wake anyone, but more so, I didn't want anyone to know what I had in mind. I recognized the familiar clip-clop gait when my four-legged friend waited by the hitching rail, giving me her familiar patient look.

I strapped my gun to my leg and carried the saddlebags. Roan was eager to go down the trail and perked up when I scratched her ears. The moon was crescent-shaped, so there was only a sliver of light as we walked to the livery.

Before I saw Joe leaning against the corral with that pipe sticking out his mouth, I smelled the foul stench of those weeds he smoked. He wore his long handles, boots, and a hat. "Joe, I'm glad you're not trying to sneak up on a guy. I smelled that tobacco even upwind."

"Didn't want you to be scared in the dark and pull that hog leg on me. You expecting trouble?"

"No, but it's always better to be prepared than be caught flat-footed. I hope nobody sneaks up now, heck of a sight, you in your night clothes."

Not caring about his nighttime appearance, the old man took a long pull on his pipe and laughed. "Got to give the girls something to talk about. Son, be careful out there. There's a lot of varmints over that hill."

As I mounted up and rode past Joe, my feisty horse snorted and threw a little kick his way. We both smiled and knew exactly what she was saying.

The moon barely lit the way this early, scarcely bright enough to see as we rode out. I liked to travel at night in a peaceful, cool, brisk air, with the moon's light guiding us. Plus, night sounds could be heard a long way off.

We traveled at a slow pace, viewing the countryside as we went. It was amazing how different things looked at night. The shadows in the moonlight gave a whole new view of the countryside.

Roaming out of the plains, I worked my way up the side hills. I wanted to keep down off the ridges so we would not be visible and not caught at the top of the ridge. I wouldn't call it sneaking, only cautious.

We rode for about two hours when we topped the ridge and gazed over a massive field of tall green grass, running creeks, and beaver ponds. Elk and deer grazed on their morning feed in the stands of good timber on the upper hillsides away from people. I was certain this was the T Lazy 7 Ranch. We rode off the ridge and followed the valley floor for about an hour, bypassing the grazing cattle roaming the valley. The glow of the new day was stretching outward, trying to find us as the sun started to peek over the ridges.

I could now see the ranch house, several smaller log structures, smoke billowing out of the chimneys, and lanterns burning inside. The main house was well built and designed for comfort but also as a fortress to hold off an attack. The walls were big, thick rock, and the windows were large, planked with shutters to enclose them in bad weather or for safety when an attempt is made by an enemy to gain access into the ranch house.

The roof was heavy timber with a thick sod roof. This would stop any attempt to set the roof ablaze. Port holes were visible on the sides of the building where a shooter could fire a long rifle to defend the occupants. The doors were thick and fastened with massive steel hinges and cross sections. If you weren't a welcomed guest, you would have to work mighty hard to get in.

Watching the area below me, I could see the ranch cowboys leaving to check on cattle or to begin the workday before the sun burned too hot. But curiously, four other riders rode out of the barn and did not join the morning work crew. The surrounding brush and pine trees made me nearly invisible should they travel my way.

The four stopped and talked to a man resembling Ass Wipe.

Outlaws would only leave this early to run away or were preparing to start trouble. They rode north in the direction where I left their dead friends lying in the dirt.

Ass Wipe returned to the main house. I watched the ranch for another couple of hours. Many of the hands were steady cattlemen, sitting comfortably in the saddle, moving the cattle to new grazing pastures, and working the water across their grass meadow fields.

Whoever planned this amazing piece of ground was an excellent cattleman who cared about the land. I assumed it was not the work of the current owner. If you employed scum, it would not be for the betterment of the land. Maybe they are more polished on the outside, but they would be what they are, regardless. As my old friend, Travis, used to say, "You can only polish a turd so much."

The occupant may be maintaining it, but I knew he didn't build it. There was too much hard work involved. I rode over the adjoining hill and viewed a repeat copy of the first valley I traveled through, only to find more thriving cattle. Out a distance, a couple of cows caught my eye. *Nubbed horns.*

Most cattlemen did not nub their calves or cow's horns. They dehorned when they were branded. Dehorning was a branding method that burned off the horn bud and the hair around it to stop the hair growth that formed the horn. Most cattlemen left the horns on so the cows could ward off coyotes, wolves, bears, and other cows or bulls.

My dad didn't like horns. He had been hooked several times and lost some good horses due to the older range cows with sharp horns goring them. We would let the calves develop their horns out a way as they grew. Then he would cut the horns off about three inches up from the head, giving them a little blunt horn, just enough to hurt but not do much damage.

Everyone branded their cattle with side brands burned into the hide or by cutting the ears in a certain way. We branded, and in addition, my dad would take a horseshoe nail, and mushroom out the top of the NAIL, and file grooves into the shaft. Then he would hammer this nail down into the horn stub. The grooves would keep it in place.

If someone rustled the cows and changed the brand, they would never think to look for a nail in the horn. Watching the cattle, I grew uneasy as these stubbed horn cows looked familiar to me. I rode up on one old cow and viewed the brand. It had been altered. *I knew there was a nail in her horn.* I wouldn't be sure unless I roped the cow, and for that, I needed help.

A burning rage blazed in me. Visions of my dad suffering from the misdeeds of the T Lazy 7 Ranch owner and his band of outlaws floated through my memory. These were the thieves and cowards I had searched for over the past months. I wasn't expecting to find our cows here, but now it made sense. My mount remained alert while I sat thinking, drifting back a year and a half to the story Dad told of his journey to find our cattle.

8

REMEMBERING DAD'S STORY

He traveled up into the high meadow on his dappled gray mare, Shadow. to check on our cows, and to his surprise, there were no cows. He saw an area where the cows had been rounded up and were being pushed north. By tracking their trail, four to five men appeared to be involved in the rustling of nearly a hundred head of cattle.

Returning home and riding into the barnyard, Dad shouted for my brother Spence to bring two rifles and guns and for Mom to round up a week's worth of trail grub. Rustlers had taken our cows, and Dad was determined to go after them. Spence and I grabbed the guns and shells and gathered our horses to help search for the animals.

"Boys, I know you want to help, but I want you to stay here, wrangle the remaining cows on the high line, and move them to the south meadow. Help your mother until I return."

Our father was a good man, stubborn and firm, yet capable of handling himself, but hunting rustlers alone was not rational. Dad was always ready to help anyone in need, but he would never ask for help, almost viewing it as a weakness on his part.

He gave Mom a big hug, a long kiss, and a grin, "I'll be okay. I'll be back soon. Reg, you ride over and let the neighbors know there's rustling going on and see if they're missing any cattle."

Then he mounted up, turned tail, and was off thinking the outlaws had about a five to six days head start on him. At ten miles a day, they would be about sixty miles ahead.

When Dad told the story, he said he reckoned they would go up the old Cherokee trail north, where sparse grass would be their wisest move. This direction would keep the cows moving between the water holes about every fifteen to twenty miles. The cows could be pushed toward water, but the men would not waste time letting them feed on tall grass along the trail. Thirsty cows move along faster.

As it turned out, a bad rainstorm hit with more than enough thunder and lightning to scatter the cows, making their trail easier to follow. It also took precious time for the rustlers to gather the cows back together, so the distance from the ranch was not as far out as Dad originally estimated. He rode nearly all day and night for several days to catch up with the rustlers.

When in sight of the herd, he felt the wisest move was to remain on the far ridge between him and the mix of nearly two hundred head of cattle.

Would anyone ever know how far the cows had been pushed and how many had been stolen before they even hit our place?

The cattle rustlers were good at stealing and moved the cows well. Even though he admired the skill, he knew he would have to kill these men.

Riding about two miles ahead, Dad picked a spot to wait on the rustlers and the herd while he set up his rifles.

The riders would be looking directly west into the setting sun, which helped to hide his presence until darkness set in, where he hid high up, waiting under cover and looking down on them in the valley.

Six mounted men moved the herd forward. My dad was an experienced hunter, taking his shots and changing his position as needed. When the rustlers were about four hundred yards out, he fired two quick shots, hitting exactly where he aimed, not the men but their horses.

With men being smaller targets, it was easier to hit the horses. A rustler without a horse was in a bad way. I knew my father felt terrible about shooting horses and would have preferred to shoot the riders, but he knew he must stop them quickly, which would also prevent them from coming after him.

Before the second shot hit its mark, Dad moved to his horse and rode down the slope toward the two on foot. He dismounted, crawled, laid flat on his belly, and rose to look over a hillock, watching the cows stampeding and running back the way they had traveled. He let go more shots, downing one more horse and wounding another.

Two of the six cowhands immediately left the area, leaving four companion rustlers without horses behind. The two on horseback split up, one racing up the hill at the far end of the draw, with the second trying to cut the hill in half from where the last shots rang out.

Dad remounted and rode toward the man on the upper end. When they met midway up the draw, the rustler and Dad both pulled their guns and charged, swapping lead as fast as they could pull the trigger.

Shadow went down as the two came closer to one another. No bullet met its mark on human flesh, but Dad thought his horse had surely been hit.

Shadow had thrown Dad, and he landed in the rocks below. His leg collided with a boulder and snapped below the knee. He knew he was in trouble but realized he must move to survive.

The second rider came over the hill and fired at where he thought my dad lay. But from where Shadow dropped him, and after brushing away his tracks with a broken piece of sagebrush, Dad had crawled about a hundred yards uphill to a rock ledge and rolled into a deep overhang. He reloaded his gun and waited. It was pitch dark now, and he felt blessed with a lucky break, but it would slow the hunting.

While waiting, he heard voices. The two men looked over the area where his horse now stood. His horse, being well trained, had stopped and waited for her rider. She had not been hit, only stumbled on the loose rock.

After a quick, unsuccessful search by the rustlers, Dad heard a gruff voice yell, "Get his horse. He must have been hit and fallen into the rocks below. He's no good without a horse, even if he is alive. I lost him when my horse damn near bucked me off. I think a bullet stung her. Let's move what cows we can and lite out."

"Okay, boss, what about the men?

"They are no good without horses either." The two rustlers then rode to gather the remains of the herd and found their cohorts. A volley of shooting echoed across the valley. The two on horseback shot the four men left afoot, leaving them dead on the trail. Then, one of the men killed the last standing horse. The horse was wounded but still upright.

The gravelly-voiced man with the commanding attitude, who appeared to be the boss, motioned for his companion to move along. His companion grabbed the reins of Dad's horse, and they started to push what cows they could forward and drove them out over the hill.

The bossman felt that, without a doubt, surely everyone, including my dad, was dead, but without seeing a body, he wanted to be sure that if my dad escaped death, he had no way of tracking them or finding help.

After a while, a commotion arose, with one of the two rustlers yelling. It seemed Shadow reared and bucked until she freed herself from the cattle thief's grasp. No amount of coaxing would make the well-trained mare leave her partner. Shadow was free and galloped back down the trail, passing the remaining cows.

After several hours, Dad could not hear the cows, horses, or men. He crawled out from the rock ledge and sat quietly, continuing to strain to listen for any movement while the world remained dark and silent around him.

He had examined his leg as he waited under the ledge and realized it was severely busted halfway down his calf. He cut away his trousers and stared at the bone protruding through his skin, barely attached by tendons and muscle. He cut a sturdy big sagebrush from the hill and stripped it clean until he had two pieces strong enough to make a splint. Then he fashioned a tourniquet above the break and winched it as tight as he could tolerate, understanding that he would probably lose the foot, but it would be essential to save his life. Torn strips from his shirt wrapped around his leg held the splint together.

Dragging himself out from the crevice and up to the ridge by the light of the moon, he witnessed an unbelievable sight. By the grace of God, he saw Shadow moving back in his direction. After hearing a familiar sharp whistle, the horse picked up her gate until she reached his side. He reached up to her as she lowered her head to greet him.

Remind me to give you a nice rubdown and extra grain when we get home . . . if we get home.

He dragged himself to a rock ledge, moved the horse under him, and fell onto her back. With excruciating pain, he settled into the saddle and headed down into the valley, with every step sending a knife-like searing pain up his body.

Upon reaching the bottom of the hill, unseen by the rustlers, about thirty head of cattle remained grazing close to two miles ahead. He let out a bellowing yell to get them running back to water and grass and a little closer to home.

Dad tied himself to the saddle rig so that if he passed out, he would not fall from the horse, knowing he would never get back on if he toppled off.

He chuckled, thinking to himself, *I'd probably break the other leg and then be in real trouble.* He fought the pain and drowsiness as long as he could, but as the sun rose higher in the sky, the heat and pain combined were more than he could bear, and he passed out.

9

REG RECALLS HIS PART OF THE STORY

My father rode out after the rustled cows. Spence and I got on the move to round up the cattle from the high meadows and moved them as we were told. I rode to the Patterson Ranch and let them know of the situation.

They wanted to help, but I asked them to wait and see what we found out. They understood my dad when it came to asking for help.

"This is nothing you want to handle alone if the time comes," Mr. Patterson tried to convince me, and I agreed with him but reminded them that my dad said he'd handle it.

I assured them, "I know you'll be there if we need you. Five days dragged by, and we were not giving up hope, but it was not looking promising. Spence and I decided we would leave the next morning, at first light, to search for him.

Before dawn, we quietly gathered our clothes to sneak out of the house unobserved, but Mom was up with packed food and water for us to carry. "You boys think you could sneak out, did ya? Go bring your father home." She was a good woman and always watched over the family in good times and bad.

We gave her a hug, kissed the top of her head, and headed out the door. After riding for about four hours, we spotted a lone rider in the distance and realized it was Dad. We rode hell-bent for leather to find he was in bad shape and out cold. We lowered him to the ground, built a fire, gave him water, and tried to dress the wound. His leg was not in a good way.

Spence looked at him, then at me. "What are we going to do? We can't fix this."

I tightened the tourniquet. I was concerned but remained steadfast in what we must do.

"Spence, let's get him on your horse. You ride double, and let's lite out for the house."

Spence knew the necessity of his task, but he felt Dad's pain. "His leg, Reg, won't stand the rough riding."

"Spence, put your leg straight out next to his. I'll strap it tight to yours. That will hold it up."

We started the horses at a walk. As we traveled, Dad would wake, moan, and fall unconscious again. Knowing the urgency, we picked up our pace each time Dad drifted into oblivion. *At least we knew he was alive.*

We barreled into the ranch yard at a faster pace. The horses were lathered in sweat and way past done in, but they did their job helping to save this man.

10

MOM

Mom stood watching from the porch when we rode in. She beat a fast trail to Dad, who remained tied to Spence and the horse. Once she understood the situation, she quickly firmed up a plan in her mind and squeezed his hand.

Dad groaned out a few words. "I told you I'd be back, Honey."

In the blink of an eye, Mom sprang into action as we carried him into the house. She spoke first. "Get the butchering knives and the bone saw."

Looking at each other and that gruesome leg, I can say that both his sons were scared as we laid him on the kitchen table.

Mom pushed her way in between us. "Boys, heat water, bring me the ointments we use to heal the cows, the laudanum from the cabinet, and towels from the dresser. She placed the knives in the stove fire and started to remove the splint and cut away his trousers, knowing the mangled mess of skin and bone had to come off.

She gave Dad a small drink of water, kissed him on the head, and whispered softly in his ear, "I love you."

With a steely-eyed look at her two sons, she said, "Tie your father down...tight." Then she doused him with laudanum for the pain, hoping to keep him in a dreamless sleep.

Mom took a deep breath and asked God to guide her hand, and she grabbed the sharp meat knife we used for butchering along with the bone saw and cleaned them with alcohol and hot water. Then, she threw them into the boiling water, continued sanitizing them until satisfied that no germs could possibly survive, and removed the tools to cool.

"Boys, keep him still. Reg, as I cut with the bone saw you pull the knife from the fire. It will glow red hot. I'll cut into good flesh below his knee, and you touch the knife to the leg just enough to stop the bleeding. Don't cook him. If the wound starts to bleed, touch it again."

We all took a deep breath and held it while Mom cut into his leg. *The courage! She showed she was steadfast and did not hesitate for a second. She did what needed to be done.*

As she cut, I touched him with the hot blade. *Thank goodness he was out cold.*

She made quick work of it, taking the bone saw and cutting the bone clean, and then, with several passes with a knife, the foot fell to the ground with a thud. I squeezed the ointment we used for cattle wounds from the tube after she washed the scorched portion of the leg several times.

We three looked at one another and were silenced by the aftermath, knowing we would never forget the sound of the foot hitting the floor, this day, or the smell of burning flesh.

"Mom," Spence asked, "Is that ointment going to be okay? It's for animals."

"Your dad's part mule and as stubborn as one, so it should work. I'm sure that's the least of our worries."

During this whole ordeal, my dad never moved. Every few moments like this, I wasn't sure if he was alive or dead. Mom finished dressing the wound, and we put the patient to bed.

Spence looked at Mom and asked, "Now, what do we do?"

"Pray, boys. We will need to watch for infection. He already has a bad fever. Spence, ride over to the Cherokee woman's place and tell her what's happened. Ask for her help."

She was an old woman who had seen years of battles and wounds but had knowledge of the old ways and had powers with spirits that we didn't understand.

I started cleaning up the mess while Mom tended to burning the bloody clothes. Spence launched out the front door, hoping to remove himself from the grizzly sight. Looking at me, he said, "What do we do with the foot?"

Mom actually laughed at us. "Boys, it won't bite you. Pick it up."

Spence grabbed the foot and headed out the door with it. I could tell he was mighty uncomfortable packing Dad's foot out the door.

He stood outside for a moment and took a deep breath. He lowered his head and, at that moment, said a few words to the man above. Then he headed to the barn and saddled two horses.

I listened as he rode away. He was riding full out, heading to the Cherokee women's place.

But where did Spence put Dad's foot?

11

CHEROKEE WOMAN

About an hour later, the door flew open, and Spence walked in with the old Cherokee woman close behind. This woman must have been two hundred years old. Her skin gave the appearance of brown cowhide leather. Her wrinkles were deeper than most ravines I'd ridden through. She stood just under five feet tall. Her hair was long and pure white, and It looked like a horse's tail after a major windstorm. She poked the stub of Dad's leg with a bony finger, making him groan.

"At least he's alive. . . would not have liked coming this far for a dead man . . . Coffee?"

What had she just asked Mom?

"Coffee?"

We all looked at her like, are you kidding me? He could be dying, and you want coffee?

She looked around the kitchen and said, "Biscuits, honey."

Then she made herself at home and sat at the table next to Dad.

The sight of a half leg dripping blood didn't seem to bother her in the least bit.

Mom made coffee and handed her the plate of fresh biscuits. We watched her, and without a word, she ate every biscuit on the plate, half a jar of honey, and drank a pot of coffee.

When she finished, she stood up and said, "Much to do. No sitting. Boy, get my bag."

I handed her the bag that sat at her feet. *Couldn't she bend over and get her own bag? I supposed she was too full.*

She laid out the bag's contents: chicken bones, feathers, and a few other mysterious items, plus small pouches of dried goods, flowers, and grass. *Who knew what else?*

She looked at the ointment, placed some on her finger, and licked it clean.

"Hum, that good will work." Then, she made a mixture of what looked like weeds and grass and added the dried items from the small leather pouches.

"Hot water, boy, in cup." Spence filled a cup, spilled some, and handed it to the old woman. She took it with steady hands. "Boy, you sit. You no help."

Spence looked weak in the knees and was going to pass out. He glanced at her and said, "Sounds good." Slumping into a nearby chair, he sighed.

Mom explained to her what she had done.

The Cherokee woman smiled a toothless grin and nodded as if saying *good job.* She showed my mom what to use and how to mix the concoction. She placed it in a small bag of what looked like an animal's gut. "Mix hot water, boy. Cool. Drink. No fever."

Spence started to stand, but I held him down. "I got it, Spence."

Then our visitor lit a white sage bundle, waved it over my dad and his leg, and chanted words in her native tongue, finishing with, "I go now. Give drink each moon."

She held up six fingers. She put on her tawny brown buckskin jacket with a rabbit fur collar, grabbed two more biscuits from the counter, strode soundlessly out the door, and walked into the night.

Over the next two weeks, we cleaned his wound and gave our patient the potent drink, breaking his fever. He took less laudanum and ate more daily as his appetite returned.

Early one morning, after we finished barn chores, Spence and I entered the folk's bedroom. Dad was sitting up, eager to crawl out of bed.

"I see you two handled yourselves well. I owe you one for searching for me. It doesn't sound like I would have made it."

"Well, Dad," Spence joked, "We really went out looking for the horse. She's a good one. That would have been a great loss."

"Here, we made you a couple of presents. We handed over a set of crutches we created out of walnut cut from an old piece of furniture so he could start hobbling around."

"Nice. They're going to come in real handy."

"I'll be back with the other gift in a minute." Spence left the room and returned with a package wrapped in burlap.

Dad reached to open it. "Why's it so cold, son?

"It was in the icehouse. We know you like to tinker around making unique things."

The bedridden man shook his head. He instantly knew what it was before he opened it. In the burlap lay his frozen foot in the boot, all cleaned and wrapped up pretty as you please.

Spence couldn't help himself. "Maybe you can make a lamp."

"What can I say? I'll use the crutches but go bury this foot by the old oak tree, and when I die, you can reunite me and my foot then."

Here was a man who always took whatever came his way, handled it the best way possible, and went on. Nothing stopped him. In the following weeks, he was moving about on his crutches and working in the barn, making a new peg leg.

As time passed, he was healing but so frustrated that he couldn't do the simplest things. One morning, he was alone in the kitchen and slammed a chair across the room. Mom ran in to see if he had fallen.

"No, I'm okay. I'm just tired of sitting around and not helping. This peg leg I built won't stop the pain, and I can't move around."

"You lost a leg, Jack. It's going to take time."

Spence and I walked into the room. I picked up the chair and looked sternly at him, "She is right. You have got to give it time," I said.

"Reg, stay out of it."

"No, I'm not going to. When I cut my leg years back, and it wouldn't heal, you told me to leave it alone. It takes time. Stop pushing it and whining."

Dad gave a deep belly laugh. "Look at who's the man of the house now."

I had never talked back to my dad like that before.

"Reg is right, Dad. It will take time. We're all here to help. Spence had jumped into the fire with both feet.

Dad hopped onto the chair and sat down. The room was silent. He looked up and somberly said, "You're right, boys, or I should say, men. Those days of you being my younguns are over. You all bent over backward for me. Mom has been watching over me day and night. You two have been doing the ranch work and caring for us all. It's time I quit whining and relaxed a little."

Spence reached down to Dad's shoulder. "That's right. Sit on the porch for a while. Reg and I will handle it. We've been doing most of the work for the last four to five years anyway. So, what's changed now?"

Dad let out another rare booming laugh and slapped his upper thigh. "You're right, Spence. Why did I have kids anyway? It wasn't to play games with. I had you to be my free labor."

The patriarch's sense of humor was intact, and it hadn't fallen far from the tree with the sons in the family either. We sat around and told old family stories, knowing all would be okay. It took a while, but he finally got the peg leg working. It wasn't easy, but he was almost as good as new.

12

REG

W hile still home on our ranch, practice sessions began with my hog leg and rifle. Always a decent shot, I could put meat on the table, but things were different now. I started to practice my shooting and marksmanship with the rifle. I shot faster with the rifle, and my aim gradually improved.

I could hit rabbits as far away as I could see. My aim was deadly. The only problem was that no rabbit was left on the other end. The rifle was powerful and didn't leave much meat to eat.

It had been a year of practicing, and I was the fastest and most accurate shot I'd ever been. The handgun work started slowly, first working on the aim and then the draw.

Spence continuously watched me. "Reg, I think you're as good as you're ever going to be. You're just wasting lead and powder now. You lookin' for a fight?"

"No. I'm ready to protect us and what is ours. I won't use the guns to start a fight, but I damn sure will end it." When we returned to the house, I sat with Dad and began a heart-to-heart conversation.

"The ranch is doing good. Spence handled the cows, I've finished the corrals, fixed the outbuildings, and the hay is up. I'm leaving in the morning. I'm going to look for our cows and the men responsible."

Dad looked me in the eye. "You're a grown man now. You keep out of harm's way. Don't start a fight, but if one starts, finish it."

Remember Reg . . .

It's easy to send a bullet.

But you can never call a bullet back.

"I taught you how to hunt, track, and survive in the wild. You bettered yourself with your firearms. What kind of man you want to be is now up to you."

"I understand, Dad, but I can't sit around and wait for more trouble. These men need to be held accountable for what they did to you and Mom. I'll tread lightly, and I'll remember what you have taught me and what you have shown me about being a man."

The next day, I loaded up my gear, hugged Mom, and slapped Dad on the back.

Spence looked out the front door and said, "When you get your back up against the wall, send a word, and I'll come and get you out of trouble."

"I'm sure you would be helpful if I run into a handful of lonely women. Not sure how long I'll be gone, but I will send a wire when I can. You know what signs to look for if I need ya."

I rode through some of the most beautiful countryside and also into places where a vulture wouldn't land. While traveling, I left signs for Spence with broken limbs, letting him know directions and miles traveled.

The signs we left were developed after years of tracking in the woods as young boys. Later, when I would ride into a town or outpost, I would send home a letter. As I rode by ranches, I looked for our cattle and tried to think where a rustler would head. I talked to ranchers and railroad agents at loading docks.

13

BACK TO THE T LAZY 7 AND OUR COWS

My thoughts eventually drifted away from the cattle and the family and turned back to the task at hand.

"Roan, I think we have looked long enough at this Lazy 7 Ranch. Let's visit this Tucker fella, face to face."

Riding toward the ranch house, I watched three cattle hands out in the fields. They waved and continued with the day's chores. One worker pointed my way, and shortly after, he climbed into the saddle and rode to greet me. I assumed he was the lead man.

"Hello, stranger. I'm Buck, ramrod here at the T Lazy 7. Can I help ya?"

I reached out my hand. "Call me Reg." I waited for a response to see if Buck recognized my name. If he did, he kept it to himself.

"Reg. what brings you to the T lazy 7, looking for work?"

"No, I was looking around the country and wanted to meet the owner. Nice spread he has here, but I'm not sure I'm welcome. I had words with your foreman in town the other day about horses I found on the trail."

"Yep, I heard." I understand Tate called you out as a horse thief."

I shifted weight in my saddle, wanting a better seat if our conversation ended in a fight.

"Relax, cowboy," Buck said, smirking at me and shaking his head. "Tate is the boss's hired man, not mine. Tate's no cattleman, and I don't really care what that sidewinder thinks." Buck wore a smile, but his attitude revealed one of pure disgust when he talked about Tate.

"Tate always has a way of trying to start a fight before he gets the facts. He may be the boss of his crew, but I manage the ranch. I don't care much for him and his type."

I understood what he meant. This man, Buck, was a cattleman, not an evil man.

Buck looked back toward the ranch. "I worked this ranch when the Anders owned it. Then, I left for a bit to stretch my legs. When I returned, I learned that the Anders had moved on." Buck looked over his shoulder to momentarily stare out over the lush landscape.

When he looked back my way, there were tears in his eyes...I knew there was more to this story. I looked away and let him have this moment. Buck took in a deep breath.

"I ride for the brand, but that doesn't mean I will bend the law when it comes down to the wire."

Buck spoke his mind softly but sternly. "I'm looking for answers! I see Tate is riding our way. Tread lightly with him and Tucker when you meet them. They both were cut from the same cloth."

Tate rode up beside us and spoke irritably to Buck, "I see you have met Reg."

"Yes, sir. He just said how much he admired the place and would like a visit with Mr. Tucker."

Tate's eyes flickered a glare but quickly replaced it with a slight upturn of the lips in case his boss happened to be watching. "Reg, first off, I apologize for the other day. I jumped to conclusions, and I was out of line. You did a good thing bringing those horses in, and we here at the ranch owe you one."

This apology felt like I had just been snake bit. I've been in scrapes before and have become good friends with the fellas I fought. This, I'm sure, would not be one of those times.

Buck shot me a look of disbelief. Tate moved his horse up alongside me. "Let's you and I ride up to the house, and I'll introduce you to Mr. Tucker, Buck's boss."

Tate tossed words over his shoulder to Buck. "I'm sure you have better things to do."

"You're right, Tate. There's always hard work to do. That's why Tucker hired me to make sure it gets done. Reg, thanks for the visit. Looking forward to seeing you again."

Tate rode alongside me and kept a watchful eye on the roan. She observed Tate as we moved toward the ranch. "That mare of yours actually lets you ride her? She has quite the temper and looks like she wants to take a bite out of me. You may want to teach her some manners."

A slight chuckle and a grin were the only responses I offered. I didn't say much as we rode.

Tate talked about the ranch and the cows. Aware that Tate didn't know horse shit from flowers in the field, I knew Buck was right. Tate was no cattleman.

I would soon find out what Tucker knew. It only took a minute to size most men up. Who was worthy, and who was not.

Upon arriving at the homestead, Tate slid easily from his horse. "Give me a minute, and I'll see if the boss is available."

I sat on Roan and waited as Tate went inside. Taking these moments to look around, I was amazed at the construction of the house and the details. This was truly a work of pride.

"Reg, how are you?" A voice rang out from the doorway. "Welcome to the ranch. I'm Mr. Tucker."

I answered back to the voice in the doorway as Tucker appeared. "Mr. Tucker, you sure have a beautiful ranch and home. It must have taken you a long time to accomplish all this."

Tucker smiled and politely responded, "I wish I could take the credit, but it was all built before I bought the place."

"I'm surprised someone would ever let this place go. It has everything a rancher would need. Where would one go next?"

"I'm sure the past owner had his reasons. Maybe it was too much for the old timer to keep running. I think he wanted to go back East and live an easier life. Who knows why folks do what they do?"

Reg nodded. "I guess. I noticed the cows as I rode in. You have quite a mix of breeds. Most cattlemen I've known prefer to stay with raising a certain breed of cattle."

Tate walked out to the end of the porch. "We like to mix them up, see which ones do the best, and sell off the ones that don't measure up. Now, Reg, Mr. Tate informed me you were the one that found our boys' horses and brought them back. I want to say thank you. Hated to lose such fine animals."

Reg agreed, "Yep, they are nice horses, but what about their riders? Did they finally show up sore-footed?"

"We haven't seen hide nor hair of them. They may have found trouble on the trail. I was told you found these horses north of here."

"No, Mr. Tucker, I found them west of town."

"I'll be. I thought it was north. The beasts looked like they had traveled far."

I answered slowly, with the tone of one who wasn't too concerned about the horses or riders. "I'm not sure."

As I said, "I found them grazing about ten miles out." I snickered then. "I bet your fellas show up sore-footed with a whopper of a story to tell."

Tucker was studying me. "Excuse me for a moment. I've got to talk to Mr. Tate."

I stood there looking at the reflection in the big window overlooking the herd, and upon Tucker's return, I asked him, "I noticed some cows in the field with cut-off horns. Why would you cut off the horns?"

"We didn't cut any off. Some durn fool had his reasons, I guess. I never met the cows' owner. The previous ranch owner bought them when they were moving the beef south. As I heard it, the outfit was in bad shape, and he needed the money to pay off his hands and probably bills back home, wherever that was."

I knew this whole conversation was a lie. *The previous owner of the T Lazy 7 was long gone or killed before our cattle were ever stolen.*

"Young man, are you a cattleman?"

"I've been around a couple of cows. We have a few head of cattle back home. I was more into the land and the buildings myself."

"Where do you hail from?" he asked me.

"Down south a good ways." I lied. *Our place was north and west of the T Lazy 7.*

"I cut the conversation off short. I was done talking. I saw and heard all I needed. I better be heading out. It's getting late, and I don't want to run into any varmints during the night. Thanks for the hospitality. I sure enjoyed looking over your place and your herd."

I mounted up, tipped my hat to say goodbye, and turned Roan down the road the same way we came. We were out of eyesight of Tate and Tucker by the time Buck greeted me on the other side of a small knoll.

"Reg, I kept an eye on you three from up in the cedars away from prying eyes. I didn't witness any gunplay as I might have expected. You all seemed pretty cozy."

Cozy isn't quite the word I would have used, but we were all searching in the dark for answers. "As far as gunplay . . ."

"Reg, like I said earlier, "We ride for the brand as long as it's fair play. Be careful out there."

I gave my horse a nudge and waved to Buck. I think we both knew we would be keeping a watchful eye out for each other.

14

SPENCE

"I guess you're going after your brother?" Dad said.

"Yes, sir. I convinced the Patterson boys to come over and babysit you and give me a break. They can sit with you on the porch and watch over the cows in the fields. Reg's letters have given me some direction. I will climb over the gap and see if I can backtrack ahead of him. I'll keep an eye out for our cows."

"Let us know where you're at, and when you find your brother, keep the fuel oil in the can, Spence. Don't be lighting no matches. Leave that to the other fellas you will run into."

"Now, Dad, you know Reg is the troublemaker. I'm the peaceful one."

"You bet, that's just what I was thinking," he snickered. "As I told your brother, walk carefully."

Spence knew his brother and could tell by his letters that he was zig-zaggin' across the flatlands, heading forward in a wide circle.

Reg was good with working folks; easy-tempered, polite, and soft-spoken.

Spence typically referred to himself as the throw gas-on-the-fire type. On most occasions, Reg helped untangle his baby brother from his messes, but they both knew together they were hell in boots or on horseback when needed.

Spence had been on the trail for several weeks and rode into small towns where his inquiries about Reg went unanswered. If he had come through, they would have remembered him, especially the older folks who were always drawn to him. Traversing an old Indian trail on a lower ridge, plain as day, he came across the marked trail his brother had left him.

As boys, they would go into the woods for days on end. Their custom was to split up and leave clues where each could be located on the trail. By turning over rocks and breaking several branches, the number of broken tree branches indicated to the other brother which direction he was traveling and how far. Turning the stones also told what day, week, or month it was. The trail could be weeks old by moving cows or hunting, but they could track, read the signs, and leave clues about where to meet.

Leaving notes under their fire was a tried-and-true tradition. They secured notes in a pit dug deep next to the fire and put the message into the new pocket in the earth. Then, when the fire burned out, they transferred the coals over to cover the hidden message. It would look as if the fire had burned out where the note was buried. The secret for saving information under a fire was three rocks in front of the fire pit.

Spence knew how Reg would cross the valleys and the draws, where he would sit and read the country. He rode past one of the clues but didn't catch it. His eyes didn't register it, but his mind must have.

A nagging feeling ran up his spine and to his brain. He turned around. He learned to always listen to that little man in his head, his guardian angels, or the spirit, as Mom would say.

Not listening usually hurt him or cost him money. Turning back, the lone cowboy came across several busted branch limbs next to a creek crossing. Under the busted limbs were a pile of rocks. It told Spence when Reg had been there, the direction he was going to travel, and the distance he felt he would ride until the next clue.

As Spence traveled, he found a trail easily marked for him to follow. It was plain as day to both of them, but an outsider would have difficulty following these clues.

Spence found the fire pit and the three rocks, indicating there was a note buried below. Spence took his time scouting the area for any more clues. He found none, so he built a fire next to the old fire pit and set up fixins of coffee and hard tack.

Spence waited until after dark. He didn't want anyone who happened to be watching to see what he was about to do. He dug down under the old fire and was expecting to find a note . . .

At sunrise, Spence made sure he left no evidence of what was hidden below. He saddled his horse, mounted up, and took his time looking about for any movement or evidence that someone may have been watching him. When he was sure it was safe to move on, he moved toward a small town below the hill's crest.

As Spence rode, he pondered the great mystery and what big

story Reg would have to tell. *The note was one thing, but the bag full of gold. . . well, that was just plain unbelievable.*

Spence laughed softly, thinking *I should pack up the fortune Reg laid out for me, forget the four-legged beasts, and go find true comfort.* He laughed again, knowing he could never leave Reg. No matter what fortune was to be had. He would die protecting or standing next to him in any battle.

As Spence grew closer to town, he saw it was a place people took pride in. It was clean and tidy. The streets were topped off with gravel. The buildings were painted and well kept. This was a place where a fella could be content.

Spence grinned ear to ear... *wonder how many single ladies are in town . . .* He giggled to himself and his four-legged companion. There were four places where Reg would stop for sure: the saloon, the local café, the livery, and the general store.

The young man figured to hit the saloon last, knowing good and well that he mustn't throw that gas on the fire in a new town. If he ruffled feathers here, he wouldn't be able to sweet talk his way out of the dilemma like back home.

Like Dad said, "Walk easy." *Hate to admit it, but he was right. Walk easy was sometimes harder than you would think.*

He sorely needed supplies, so he headed to the general store, and then he would go to the café to treat himself to a good meal.

When Spence entered the general store, a young girl was talking to a boy about her age.

"Caty, you don't know anything. I know I would have caught some fish, but you and Dan scared them all away. Reg and I would have hooked a handful of big trout."

"Excuse me, I'm sorry I was listening in, but it sounds like you're a great fisherman."

"Yes, sir, mister. I catch lots if no girls and little brothers are hanging around."

Caty held her ground. "You're just mad, Little Joe, because Dan and I caught the biggest and the most. You didn't catch nothing."

A woman's voice came from the back of the store. "Kids, you need to keep it down. You're going to scare off the customers."

"Don't worry, ma'am. I don't scare that easy."

"Then come on in. I'm Nancy, and these are two of the local terrors."

Little Joe, so that is your name?"

"Yep, my grandpa is Old Joe. He owns the livery. But he gets really red in the face and mad if you call him old," said the youngster, slapping his face lightly for emphasis.

"When I'm down at the livery, I'll remember to tell him I met his grandson, the fisherman. I heard you mention a friend called Reg. Is he a school buddy?"

"No, he's old like you, probably older. He is my best friend."

Caty had enough of this conversation, flapped her arms, and spoke to Little Joe. Reg is not your best friend. You have only known him a little while."

"Caty, he is too, my best friend. You're mad cause you're sweet on him."

"I'm not sweet on him. Chelsea is."

Little Joe yelled at her. "Every time I see Chelsea lookin' at Reg, she looks like she's going to throw up, and Caty, you get all girly-like."

"Little Joe, Chelsea's gonna marry him, for Pete's sake." Caty verbally jousted with the youngster.

Yep, Reg was in town.

Spence assumed Reg had been in town just a short while and, most likely, everyone he met would befriend him. Spence felt confident and smooth when it came to gaining attention from the local gals and could love-talk with the best of them, but big brother didn't even need to open his mouth.

The family joke was that if he ever went to a big city and charged a nickel for a kiss, he'd have enough money in a week to buy a ranch.

While the kids argued, Spence thought about their fishing buddy, Reg.

Nancy asked about his travels and where his journey would take Spence next.

"Kinda just been zig zaggin' across the country looking for trouble." He hadn't noticed a sheriff's office or a lawman walking around. The locals in most small towns, good or bad, usually handled their own problems.

"Well, ladies and gentlemen, it was nice meeting you, and I enjoyed you letting me in on your stories. Nothing better than going fishing with your friends."

Nancy, it was a pleasure meeting you as well. I'll come back later to get what I need. You have a nice store with an excellent selection of goods here."

"Well, thank you, Spence, but the store is not mine. It's Sara's and Ty's. Sara is Old Joe's daughter." Little Joe here is Sara's son, and Caty is my second daughter."

"I'll see you all soon. I smell some good cooking from across the road. It's been a while since I had a nice sit-down meal. I think I'll see what's on the menu."

Caty spoke up, "You will love the cooking. My older sister, Chelsea, is the best cook around for a hundred miles. Caty held open the door.

"Thank you, Caty, for holding the door for an old man."

Caty laughed. "You're not old; you're dang near a kid. Ma, I'm going to walk Spence over to Maggie's. He is so old he might get lost." The young lady turned into a bundle of giggles and face-splitting smiles.

Spence chuckled as well. *I like this little spitfire.*

"Ok, Caty, you walk him to the door, and that's it; you get right back here. You let Spence eat in peace.

"Can I introduce him to Ms. Maggie and Chelsea?"

"No, I think Spence can handle meeting women all on his own." Nancy cocked her head at a tilt, letting Spence know that she knew he was a young man who liked attention.

Spence and Caty walked out and started across the road. Nancy was at the door, "Caty, watch out for wagons and horses so you don't get trampled."

"I'll be ok, Ma. I'll watch."

"Well, Caty, is your older sister the one who likes this Reg fella, or is there another Chelsea in town?" "No, only one Chelsea. There's another Caty, spelled different than me. It's Katy, K.A.T.Y. Mine is Caty C.A.T.Y.

Spence tried to hide his grin. "Okay."

"Now, Spence, there is a Contessa, a Susie, a Hilda, and a. . ."

"Wow, girl, that's good, Caty. You can introduce me when we

see them. I like to put a face to a name. I can tell you're going to be a big help."

"Well, Spence, we made it. See ya later." She looked around to see that it was safe and off she ran back to the store.

Maggie's Café looked inviting and smelled wonderful as well. He removed his hat and sat at a table at the far wall where he could watch the door and the people moving around. A nicely shaped older gal finally looked his way.

"Coffee?" she asked.

"That would be nice, hot, and black, please."

"Newcomer, what can I get you to eat?"

"How about a big steak, please? Medium done."

"Boy, you're a polite one. Your momma must have taught you right."

"Ma'am, she tried, but I think the belt she chased me with did the real teaching."

"My name is Maggie. What do the ladies call you?"

"Spence, and I'm glad to meet you, Maggie. So, you the owner?"

"I'm the owner, cook, and bottle washer."

"Well then, let's see if you can cook." If Reg was here, he might have been trying to keep his business quiet, so asking nosy questions was not a good idea.

Maggie returned, holding half a beef on a plate.

"Now, that is what I call a steak! I usually eat the whole cow, but this will do just fine for now."

"You finish that, and I'll give you seconds for free."

"You gotta deal. Keep the skillet hot. Maggie, I ran across a passel of rascals and a nice woman, Nancy, at the general store this morning. I am curious about them. They were quite entertaining."

"Oh, the two girls are Nancy's, and the two boys are Sara's. The kids are always stuck together. Nancy's first and oldest daughter helps out here. She should be coming in soon."

"The kids were talking about a gal named Chelsea and that she was going to marry this guy named Reg. I understand he's new in town, also. You think there's time for me to put my name in the hat for this Chelsea girl?"

"Spence, that's a good one. Maybe Chelsea's a mean old gal with broad shoulders and big old hips. You sure you want to put your name in the hat without viewing what you're bidding on?"

"If this man is in the mix that fast, I'm sure she's a special girl."

"The café owner looked puzzled about how he would know what Reg liked. A stunning young girl with a single braid down her back and wearing a dusty rose-colored cotton working dress dashed through the door just about the time Maggie opened her mouth to ask that question.

"Sorry, I'm late. I was trying to get the kids fed."

"That's okay, Chelsea."

Spence eyed this girl with wonder. He whispered to himself and hoped no one overheard him. "I am not sure what Reg and this Chelsea girl had going on, but if there wasn't anything in the works, I will surely try to sweet talk this one."

"What was that, Spence?" asked Maggie, having a bit of fun with him, knowing she had heard him clearly. "Chelsea, this is Spence. We were just this minute talking about you."

"Is that so? Why would this one be concerned about me?"

"Nothing important," stated Maggie.

But, Spence wouldn't let this opportunity pass by, laid on the charm, smiled wide, and winked with a sparkling eye as blue as the breaking morning sky.

"Chelsea, I stopped into the general store, and according to your sister and Little Joe, you were getting hitched to a drifter named Reg."

She turned four shades of red, and the heat from her face would have melted ice.

"Well, I never," she said as she stomped into the kitchen.

Spence looked over to Maggie. "Hmm. Maggie. I think you're right. I may have to do more than sweet talking to get noticed by this one."

Finishing up his steak, he asked for his second free steak. Whether hungry or not, he wanted to stick around to catch another glimpse of the girl and see if his brother would show his face.

"You are kidding me, Spence. You ate it all, and you're still hungry?"

"No. I was just funnin' with ya. After another cup of coffee, I will head down to the livery to see if they have room for me and my horse. What does this Reg fellow look like? I may want to set a trap to cut him out of the competition."

"I think I'll just keep you guessing."

"Okay, be that way," he said, enjoying the teasing. "Chelsea, why don't you come out of that kitchen so we can have a proper goodbye?"

Spence heard, "Goodbye, Spence," from the back of the kitchen. "I hope the livery has room for you and your horse."

Man, if Reg doesn't chase that pretty filly down, I would try to steal a kiss someday.

Spence strolled down to the livery, chuckling the whole way before the worst smell imaginable assaulted his nose. He couldn't place it until he saw an older man puffing on his pipe.

"I've never smelled that blend, old timer. It must be from somewhere back East."

The liveryman watched him approach and took his pipe from his mouth. "You must be looking for Reg."

"I'm not sure about that. Who's this Reg person everyone seems to know?"

Joe puffed on his pipe. "I'd say he was a brother or a close relation. You have to be kin. Reg didn't care much for my pipe fixins either."

"I'm Spence. You must be Joe. See now, Joe, we're both psychic."

Joe was amused. "The way you walk and smile, it's easy to see you are related."

"Brothers. He's older. I'm just a lot better looking."

With that, Joe laughed. "I guess we will see about that. We might have to ask Chelsea for her opinion."

"You got a place for me and my horse to bunk for a while?"

"The horse can stay in the end corral. You can make a spot in the loft."

"As you can see, Reg and Roan aren't around. They rode out in the dark this morning. He said he was going for a look-see and didn't say when he would return. He'll show up when he finds what he was looking for."

"What? Reg has a roan? What happened to his horse?"

"Long story. I'll let him fill you in."

Looking puzzled, Spence said, "Joe, I'll be back later. I'm going to ride out and have a look-see as well."

"Be careful, son. Reg made friends fast in town, but I'm thinkin' he made enemies, too, maybe even faster."

"That's why I'm here. I'm here to keep him out of trouble."

"Hell, boy. Now, this ought to be good. You have trouble written all over you."

"Be a nice, old hand. I bruise easily," Spence quipped back as he tried to hide his wicked smile behind his hand as he turned to ride off. "Will you keep it under your hat about us being kin?"

The pipe smoker drew another pull on the pipe, nodded, and watched as his new friend rode away.

15

CHELSEA & MAGGIE

Chelsea asked, "Maggie, did you see Reg this morning?"

"I did. He rode out in the dark early on."

"He left town? Already?"

"I'm not sure he had his gear; he carried a rifle and wore his sidearm."

Chelsea ran up the stairs and knocked on his door, shaking like an aspen leaf on a fall morning. *He couldn't have just left without saying goodbye. I know it has only been a couple of weeks, but just up and leaving was unbelievable.* She turned the doorknob and found he hadn't locked it before he left.

"You asleep?" Chelsea asked loud enough for the entire building to hear. Since she received no reply, she leaned in and saw that the bed was made up properly, and neatly folded new clothes lay on the bed.

Her heart nearly stopped. *He hadn't gone.* Closing the door, she gathered her wits, slowly returned to the kitchen and found Maggie doubling over in giggles.

"He's coming back. A man wouldn't leave his brand-new store-bought clothes," Maggie said.

"How'd you know he left his clothes?"

"I peeked just like you did."

16

DELIVERING NEWS

I rode away from the T Lazy 7 Ranch and knew what to do. It was time to tell Nancy and her girls about their husband and father. *Come hell or high water, Tucker was going to pay.*

The sun prepared to kiss the ground goodnight by the time I rode over the bluff to town. It would be dark, but the moon and stars promised to light my way. I rode a wide arc away from the site where I buried the gold, not wanting to draw attention to the location or myself, but a burning fire up ahead did catch my attention.

Heart jumping a beat, I shook my head and silently laughed. "Well, little brother, I see you can still track."

"Of course, I can, and I see you packed more weight with ya along the way."

"Ah, so, you found it."

Spence drank his coffee and gave me a keen-

-eyed stare. There a story to tell?"

"It's a hard story to tell, and we both need to prepare for a battle.

Let me tell you, the battle will be much easier to manage than talking to those women about their father and husband, Clancy."

Filled with remorse, I took a deep breath and suggested, "I'm not ready to tell the story yet. Let's drink our coffee and sit for a while. I want to hear how you tracked me down and tell you how many clues you missed."

After many hours of talking, we loaded up and rode into town and directly to the livery. We will stay in the barn tonight, and I'll tell this tall tale tomorrow because that is what you think it will be, a tall tale."

The sun rose early in the light blue sky. The birds chirped, and Roan neighed her wake-up call. The brothers had ridden into town long before the locals would wake.

The two spent the morning cleaning tack and currying horses to pass the hours. Neither man looked forward to talking to the ladies.

Spence stood up from an old barrel where he had been whittling on a dry piece of scrap wood he found in the tack room.

"Reg, it's time. Let's go," he said without much enthusiasm.

"Spence, you don't need to come along. They don't need to have hard feelings against you."

"I don't think it's going to matter, Reg. If they're upset with you, I'm sure they won't be thrilled to see me, being your kin."

When we walked into the café, it was stone-cold silent.

Maggie greeted us, "Hello. I see you two have met."

I smiled. "Uh-huh, we have, about twenty-two years ago. Maggie, this is my little brother, Spence."

Maggie nodded. "I can see you're related, but Spence dresses nicer. What happened to your new clothes, Reg? Rubbed you the wrong way?" She couldn't help but chuckle at her wit.

"No, just didn't see the need to dress pretty like for where I was headed yesterday. Maggie, are Chelsea and Nancy around?"

They are over at the store."

"Thanks. We need to talk with them both." I looked over my shoulder as we left the café and met Maggie's eyes, knowing my own eyes reflected my state of mind: sad, lost, and confused. "Maggie, I hope we talk again."

The two men walked away, and Maggie mumbled, "Hope we talk again. What did he mean by that?"

"Um, Reg, I'll let you lead the way. I want to be closer to the door," said Spence, at a loss for proper words and knowing it wasn't time to joke, but he didn't know what else to say.

I looked up from under my hat brim and removed it when I saw Sara. "Good morning. Are Nancy and Chelsea around?"

"Yes, they are in the back putting up deliveries."

"Sara, this is my young brother, Spence. He has come to help me settle some matters."

She took his hand. "Nice to meet you. I've heard about the new charmer in town. I'm not sure this town can handle two good-looking brothers at the same time. I hope you two don't start fighting over the town's young ladies."

Spence was the first to grin. "No, Sara, I hear tell my big brother is spoken for according to what Caty says."

I immediately cut the conversation short. "Sara, can Nancy, Chelsea, and I talk privately somewhere?"

"You may use the side room. I'll run and fetch the ladies." The look Sara gave me after hearing my tone of voice alerted her that something was wrong.

Spence and Reg moved into the side room, a sitting area with small tables and chairs for Sara's customers to look over the store catalogs.

The store owner walked into the storeroom where Nancy and Chelsea were restocking. "Reg is in the catalog room with his brother Spence, and they would like to see you both."

Nancy frowned, her eyebrows nearly touching together and a puzzled look on her otherwise smooth-tanned face. "Reg's brother is in town, and they want to see us both," she repeated. "What could they want with us?"

Sara leaned in towards the women. "Maybe Reg or Spence have something to talk to Chelsea about. I've seen the glances at her, and they both act like schoolboys waiting to talk to the school marm after school."

Chelsea brushed her hair and straightened out her dress. Chelsea and her ma, Nancy, walked into the back room, and the women instantly knew they weren't there for courting talk. The look on their faces was somber and drained of color or emotion.

I had my hat in my hands and looked up with my face drawn and flushed. "Ladies, I have something serious to tell you and don't quite know how to start."

The women both took a chair, and I replayed the story about Clancy, the gold, and the map. Nancy didn't flinch, cry, or look away from me but remained resilient and steady, holding her daughter's hand as I spoke.

Chelsea did not utter a sound, remaining as silent as a frightened rabbit while told of her father's fate. The tears rolled down her cheeks, but she sat motionless and devastated. She never lowered her gaze from me or slumped over in the creaky wooden chair.

After the last of my words, I reached into my back pocket, pulled out Clancy's carefully wrapped belt buckle, and laid it in Nancy's lap. "I brought this for you as proof of my visit and a memento for you."

After what felt like forever, Nancy finally swallowed and spoke calmly but waveringly. "I know this was an overwhelming task my husband placed on you, and I'm grateful that it was you who he spent his final moments with. Thank you so much for having the foresight to bring us this buckle. It carries many memories with it."

"Clancy must have been drawn to you instantly. He had a good way with people and could judge a man's character in a second. Reg, for you to even try to locate us and to look after us knowing surely that danger was coming our way is unbelievable, not to mention bringing us what you say is a fortune in gold." Then, her tears began to fall.

"Yes, it is, and thank you. I would have been honored to have known Clancy. I also could tell he was a man I would have liked to ride the trail with. I wish I could do more. Ladies, I'll let you be alone now. I'm truly sorry."

A tremendous burden lifted from my shoulders, but although Spence did not feel the same obligation, I could tell he felt relieved that this ordeal was over for me. As we left, we both felt the deep emotion in the room and were saddened by the women's torment.

Pacing alongside Spence, we walked along the rustic wooden planks of the boardwalk.

Firmly placing my hat back on my head, I finally voiced my thoughts. "Brother, it's now time to get the answers about our cows and make certain if the stubbed horned cows did, in fact, belong to us."

"Then, we need to determine how Tucker came by them because Tucker didn't buy them with the ranch. Someone brought them in after he purchased the spread. An honest cattleman would have a note or a bill of sale. Time to see if the cows in question carried our hidden horn nails."

"Spence, we're going to ride out and have another look at the stubbed cows on the T Lazy 7 Ranch. If they are our cows, we're going to get some answers. Find a rope."

Chelsea was heartbroken. "Ma, I can't believe Pa is gone. I thought he was indestructible and would live forever."

Nancy reached for Chelsea's hand. "I know, Chelsea. He was one of a kind. A man who loved and lived hard. He experienced many brushes with death and still walked away, but this kind of evil that hides in the shadows is the hardest to defend yourself from."

Nancy had known there was something wrong since Clancy was never late. She felt it in her bones. To put off seeing his kids any longer than necessary was something he would never have done.

Nancy spoke softly to her eldest daughter, "I was close to asking Reg if he would go looking for Pa. Reg may look like a poor cowhand, but I assure you he's cut from the same cloth as your father. If you want a man in your life like your Pa, you needn't look any further than the man who just stood before us."

"Ma, I don't even know Reg."

"Yes, you do. The first minute you two spoke to one another, we all knew you took a liking to him. You need to tell that boy how you feel. He's heading into harm's way, and someone to care about is a powerful tool to help keep a body safe."

Chelsea ran to the window. "Is it too late, Ma? Has he already gone?" She could see Spence standing at the livery door but not Reg. "Ma, I will try."

"I know Chelsea," she said as they hugged each other around the neck.

"Go, now."

"Ma, what if he doesn't even like me?"

"**Enough**, Chelsea....go."

I was saddling Roan when I heard Spence call to me.

"Oh, brother dear, you got a visitor coming. You best get on out here."

I strode out from inside the barn, and my eyes fell upon the most troubling sight I had ever seen. Chelsea was running down the street, nearly tripping, tears rolling down her face, and her hair waving as she ran toward us.

I worried she was upset with me for bringing the news about her father and then leaving, but as I watched her, I realized she carried something in her hand. That gave me pause. *She could have a rolling pin or a gun. She surely didn't want to harm me.*

Roan walked past me to Chelsea, gave her a nudge with her nose, whinnied, and then started to eat the apples Chelsea carried for her.

Spence hooted. "That girl is in love with that horse, and here all this time, I thought she had a thing for you. Reg, what's the matter with you? You can't read signs? You just going to stand there all day?"

"I know you have never been a ladies' man like your little brother here, but there's no reason to take one more step looking for your mate. This is the one, and she's a keeper. Go, hold her hand, and tell her how you feel. Hug her, kiss her, and then give her another hug."

"Thanks for the love lesson. Next, you'll want to show me how it's done," I replied with as much sarcasm as I could muster at the moment.

"Take your gun off, and I surely will give you a love lesson. Remember, I've seen you practice with that weapon."

"I don't need a gun to stomp you, little brother."

Spence gave me a punch on the shoulder for good measure or maybe a good luck gesture.

Roan looked over our way, probably thinking, *What are you two doing? This girl has apples, and you two are over there playing around.*

Chelsea, looking sad, took a deep breath while mumbling to herself, "What if Reg doesn't want me? What if I'm not the girl he could care about?"

"Chelsea, I'm sorry."

She could feel her heart drop. *Oh, no.*

I reached over, took her hand, and hugged her tight. Then I backed away a little to gaze into those emerald green eyes, gave her a hesitant kiss on the cheek, hugged her again, and said, "I like you a lot, Chelsea."

"Well, I know I like you more, Reg."

Spence slapped his leg. "Looky there, brother, you did it."

Cheers, whistles, and clapping rose from the uninvited gawking onlookers gathered nearby. The local terrors ran down to greet their two favorite people. Caty scooped Callie as they ran, as the littlest of them all had been sidetracked by a floating butterfly.

Roan nudged us both and let out a neigh. Nancy and Maggie held each other, laughing and crying at the ridiculous spectacle we had made in the middle of the street.

Spence leaned on the livery post with Joe. Joe said, "Life certainly has a way of breaking you down and then giving you hope that it's all going to be okay."

Spence walked toward Joe. "Let's go into the barn. I want to try that tobacco to see if it tastes as bad as it smells."

I released my grip on Chelsea, "I'm so sorry our lives crossed this way, Chelsea. I wish your father could have been here."

Chelsea was both happy and sad, emotions all jumbled together. "My Pa would have said, "Make the best of the unusual situation.""

I remained silent, then spoke low and easy, "Chelsea, I guess we can't change the past, but we could work on a nice future."

Callie pulled Chelsea's hand. "Can I be in the wedding?"

"Let's not get carried away," Chelsea said.

Caty admired her big sister and was excited to see these two together. "I know Reg is too old for me, but one day, I'll find someone special, too." And then she looked at Dan.

Dan returned the look to Caty. "I guess we could go fishing some, but I'm not giving up my special hole to anybody. Especially a girl."

17

DIGGING FOR BONES

Tom and Poke, the hired hands who worked for Buck on the T Lazy 7 Ranch, rode up to Buck as he watched over the cattle.

Tom spoke quietly to Buck. "Who was that fellow who rode up to the ranch? Was he the one who found the horses?"

"Without a doubt, he's the one," Buck answered, chewing on a reed of hay.

" What do you think? Is he a horse thief?"

"No. I don't think Reg stole the horses. He was honest in bringing them to town. But I feel there's more to this story."

Poke asked Buck, "Why? What's sticking in your craw, Buck?"

"The way he looked over the ranch, he wasn't here for a ride in the sun. He was looking for something or someone."

"But what sticks in my mind is how Reg asked about the stubbed-horned cows," said Tom, wrinkling his face and appearing confused as if he were trying to figure out a complex puzzle. "Did you tell this Reg fella about the nail we found in the cow's horn?"

"No, I wanted to see if he leads us anywhere. I don't think he wanted to tip his hand just yet. And maybe he was just out for a ride and likes short-horned cows."

Buck shifted his weight in the saddle. "We all believe in staying true to the ranch and the owner, but I have never trusted Tucker. How he said Anders sold out and moved away to go back East can't be right."

"You two men didn't know them. I would have given my life for that couple. The mister was a good, honest man, and the missus was the most loving woman I ever met. You both would have cared for them the same way I did. The Anders were the salt of the earth, kind, and generous. There is no way they would have sold out and not said goodbye."

Buck's words rang true as he spoke, "I wasn't kin, but they always treated me so. I've stayed on here for one reason. I want answers. What happened to them both?" Buck's tone left no room for argument. "It's my time to get answers. You two don't need to ride along on this venture. I feel it's going to be a rocky stagecoach ride."

"Hell, Boss. I can't speak for Poke, but deal me a hand," said Tom.

Poke lifted his hat and agreed. "Hell, ya, we're all in. I will buy a ticket and see it through. We don't want to look for new jobs and train a new ramrod leader. We just got you where we like ya."

Buck gave a snicker. "Then let's sit tight for a while and see what comes our way."

Two of the hired men Tate sent to locate Clancy's grave spotted it by finding a carved marker standing over piled rocks.

The remaining two men rode the gullies and hillsides, looking for clues. They couldn't find any sign of a gold mine, camps, or trails. They were gunmen, not trackers or men from the wild country. If clues weren't marked on a rock wall, they would never find what they were looking for.

The men swapped words. "I'm sure the old timer covered his trail."

"And I'm just as sure he wouldn't leave us a pretty picture and lead us right to it."

Tate's hired men finally found one of the former ranch cowboy's bones spread across the hillside. The buzzards and coyotes had eaten well.

How quickly a body, clothes, and bones could disappear is amazing. A person soon became only a memory in a short time out in the elements.

The other hand pulled his horse around. "Let's ride back and see if the other two have dug up that body yet."

With their task finished and the buzzards fed, the men galloped back to where they had left the grave robbers. They saw the raiders had rolled the body out of the grave. The outspoken rider hollered, "You check his pockets?"

"I did the digging, and he smells like an old dead cow bloating in the sun, so I'll check his pockets, but I'm keepin' anything I find."

Lowering his bandana, one of the riders pressed his point, "Any gold nuggets and we are splittin' it."

"The hell you say." The man on the horse looked at the man in the hole. "We split it, or there will be two bodies in that hole."

"Out of luck. Nothing, just pockets full of dirt, dry as the bones."

"How about buried under him?"

Digging around, the one who checked the pockets found only hard red Colorado soil. "Nothing there. This ground is hard as a rock. No sense digging any deeper. That is obvious."

"Well, hell, no gold and no map. We need the map," said one of the men on a horse to the other three.

"Let's ride to the ranch and let Tate know. He'll want to track down this young fella and beat the map and gold out of him. Let's go." All four men had mounted by this time.

The fourth man watched and remained silent. "Wait, we can't just leave him. We need to bury him back in the ground."

"To hell with you, Ben. We knew you were a do-gooder all along." The men laughed, poked fun, and rode away. "You can be the do-goodie. We're ridin'."

Ben knew who he was. He had done a lot of vile deeds in his days and guessed he was rotten from day one, but the situation these men left him faced with now didn't sit well. He often told himself that his kind deserved to die rotting in the sun.

More than once, he thought to himself, *I'm sure that's how I'll end up, alone, bleached bones in the sun.* This man, he felt, deserved better. Ben climbed down from his horse, placed the man who had meant nothing to him back in the grave, and covered his body with his woolen blanket.

Not understanding why he felt this way, he was glad he did right by him. Then Ben removed his hat and tried to say a kind word or two. Lost in the effort, he still asked God to watch over this man's soul. Ben had never done this for any man or beast. Sinking to his knees, he cried, "Please, God, forgive me."

Gathering his emotions and drying his eyes, Ben mounted and rode toward the ranch. Not wanting to be near the other men or any part of their company, he rode above them on an upper trail with no intention of riding alongside them ever again.

Now, he figured, was the time to be on his own. For his entire life, he never cared about anyone or anything, as he did today. Ben was not going to be that scoundrel any longer. The days of killing, robbing, and chasing women were over.

18

ON THE TRAIL

"Chelsea, Spence, and I plan to ride to the T Lazy 7 Ranch. We want to look at the stubbed-horned cattle and see if what I'm thinking is true."

Chelsea grabbed my hand and talked to me privately and quietly. "Don't go. We have the gold for our needs."

"No, your ma has the gold. No part belongs to me. I can't let rustlers and possibly your pa's killers get away with what they did. They took what was valuable to you and your family."

"Reg, you could be riding into a hornet's nest. I don't want harm to come to you or Spence."

Spence put his hand on Chelsea's shoulder. "I'll watch out for him. We will ride soft. We're just going for a look-see."

"Besides Chelsea, from what I understand, Roan does all my brothers' fighting anyway."

"Speaking of which, Roan didn't like the smell of Joe's tobacco. She snorted up a storm, trying to get that smell out of her nose. She gave Joe and me a look, ample distance, and wandered over to the hay bin, trying to sniff for something sweet smelling.

Reg let go of Chelsea's hand. "We'll be back tomorrow. I'll have a better plan of what we need to do then."

"I just may be in love with you, Chels, so let's take our future steps slow and easy." I walked away, knowing now what it meant to have a purpose. *I love Mom, Dad, and Spence, but this was a new emotional feeling aside from pride and honor. Love. This young lady wanted me. I understood why a man would fight and hold his ground, but I tried to remain steadfast with my emotions before making a final commitment.*

I tried to find humor in every situation, and Roan proved me right today. I discovered her refusing to let my brother anywhere near her, turning her backside to him if he came close.

"I've heard how she kicks. Joe filled me in. He said she was a fighter but was gentle like a butterfly with those little ones."

"If you didn't smell so bad, she would probably let you be, but hell with that smell, I'd like to kick you, too."

"You are right, brother. It smells bad, but boy, it's got a wallop to it. I'll be up for days."

Chelsea returned to the café porch, surrounded by all those who cared for her, and she stayed on that porch until we had ridden far out of sight.

"Girl, it doesn't do any good to keep pacing and staring out that window. They just left," said Maggie.

"I know."

"You know, I looked out our windows for years, looking for your dad every time he left. It didn't do me any good. It only caused more heartache and misery," said Nancy.

"I know, Ma, but I'm so worried. I know I won't sleep a wink or even think straight."

"We both understand, child, but you must let it be. He's a good man, and he has his brother at his side. The two of them together would be a handful. Don't forget they have Roan. She's a heck of a babysitter. She'll keep an eye on them both."

Chelsea sat on the floor and cried her eyes out. Ma, we have lost a husband and a father. We have lost the best friend we ever had. We have lost a man who will never hold his grandbabies or walk us down the aisle. I am so torn for us all. I'm so sorry for being selfish and thinking only of me and Reg."

Her ma placed her arm around her daughter's shoulder. "Chelsea, your father, my husband, will always be with us. His stories will continue to be told for generations to come. We will cry, we will moan, but we will go on as he would force us to do if he was here."

"His life ended too soon, but there is nothing we can do but love each other and love deeply. Wipe your eyes, get up, and let's get your sisters and talk with them. Callie is so young that she will never know who he is, but Caty loves him so much. Her little heart will be broken. We know our hearts will heal, but she is going to suffer the hardest.

19

REG

From the concerned look on his face, Spence apparently wanted to speak to me. Firmly, he said, "Far be it from me to advise you, but I know you have never been in love, so I want you to stay focused on what we need to do. I don't want your emotions playing with your better senses."

I couldn't help but be amused. "Spence, what do you know about love? Kissing girls at the dance doesn't make you no expert."

"I can't say I have ever been in love, but at least you're right. I have kissed a girl or two. That's one or two more than you."

We rode side by side at a gentle pace to the T Lazy 7 Ranch, where we saw riders on the horizon. Those riders watched us, stopped, sat steady on their horses, talked for a minute, and then turned our way.

Spence murmured low to me so his voice wouldn't carry on the wind. "Reg, is that gun loaded and ready to play a tune?"

"It is, but that's Buck and his men. I don't think they're riding to find trouble, but I have a tune in mind if I'm mistaken."

Buck rode up first, leading the trio. "Hello, Reg. Out for another stroll, and you brought a friend this time?"

"Nope, Buck, He's no friend of mine. He's my baby brother."

Spence hated to be called my baby brother. Anyone could see it plainly by the grimace on his face.

"Hello. A pleasure to meet you." Spence winked at Buck. Give me a minute, Buck and you other two gents, while I knock my brother off that horse."

Buck found humor in the young man's words. "I understand, Spence. I'm a baby brother, too. Drives a guy crazy, don't it? Men, this here are Poke and Tom, top hands."

"We're gonna watch to see who's the tougher of you two boys," said Poke, "I haven't seen brotherly love since I left home."

"Me neither," said Tom, "But in my case, it was my older sister hitting me with a wooden spoon." The group of men chuckled and relaxed for a minute.

Spence finally broke the silence. "Hell of a fine ranch. This fancy Tucker dude built it up?"

"Hell, no," replied Buck. "It was old man Anders and his wife, the best people I ever met."

Reg stated. "I appreciate your tone and attitude, Buck. I know you said you rode for the brand. Whose brand?"

Buck shot back an answer so no one would ever mistake his loyalty. . . "Anders' is the only brand I see.

The only reason I'm still here is because I want answers and retribution for the Anders."

Buck held up a flat-headed nail. "What do you two brothers see here?"

I reached for the nail. "I see my dad's horn nail that came out of one of those stub-horned cows."

Everyone stiffened. *Did Buck and his men come to fight? Would we fight?* It was tense for a second.

Buck said, "Relax, don't want you sticking that attack horse on us." Three wary ranch hands nodded their heads in agreement. "I figured the nail is what you were looking for when you asked about the short-horned steers. What's the story?"

I turned the roan's rear toward the cautious trio. All three were backing their horses out of Roan's reach. Spence and I were the ones enjoying the antics now.

Buck laughed but kept his eye on her rear end.

"Fun times over, what's the story with the nail?" He looked at us with confusion and a complete lack of understanding.

"I've never seen a nail put in a horn before. I found it when we were doctoring a heifer. Thought a thorn was poking out of her horn. When I pulled it out, I was surprised to see it was a nail of some sort."

I retold the story about Dad, the nail, and the rustlers.

The trail boss shook his head and rubbed his chin whiskers. "I figured there was a tale to be told. There always is with a mystery. Tucker's a rustler. He was always showing up with cows showing new brands. That ornery cuss was pretty clever in how he re-branded cattle. Always said he bought them with a bill of sale, but I never saw anything in writing."

All five men sat briefly, not talking, just looking over the herd.

Tom finally broke into their thoughts, asking, "When Roan kicked one of Tate's boys, how bad was it?"

I know my hazel eyes twinkled and showed the delight I felt. "She sent him across the street, squealing like a pig. I'm sure he's healed up by now. How is he anyway?"

Poke shook his head and said, "Dead."

"What are you saying? …The…ay The kick killed him?"

"No, we think Tate did, or his hired help. That night, we heard a shot and never saw him again. Maybe they didn't want to take care of him, so someone put a bullet in him. Two horses and a single rider headed north that next morning. It looked like the other horse had something or someone draped over the saddle."

Spence cut short the story. "So, what we know is that Tucker's no cattleman. He stole cows, changed brands, owns no paper you have seen, and you're his cattle foreman."

Buck smirked, "Sounds about right." I spoke directly to Spence and the other three men. "I've only been here a short while, but I have gained a lot of respect for the town folk. What about Maggie and her place? Did Tucker and his men kill her husband?"

"I can't rightly say, but he was a good man, fair and honest as the day was long, and so is Maggie. I can't say, but if I were a gambling man, I'd bet my card hand that Tucker buried her man."

"Buck, you said a rider with two horses rode north, so how long was he gone?"

Buck looked north. "He was gone for about four hours, so if you had to dig a hole to bury a man, that doesn't leave much time for riding if you're only gone for four hours."

Buck looked north. He didn't point or gesture. "You never know who has eyes dropping in on your conversations. He probably rode into the big wash. It's about one and a half hours, easy riding."

"Ok, you three. Maybe Spence and I will ride back away from the ranch, work our way to that wash, and have a look-see if that's okay with you three?" I asked, looking directly at Buck, Tom, and Poke.

Buck answered, "Ride easy. We will keep our eyes and ears wide open on this end."

Spence turned his horse around and suggested, "Brother, it might be helpful if these hands came along should we find trouble."

"Not now, Spence, we're just riding easy like." Then I talked to the T Lazy 7 riders. "I think it might be a wise idea if you wranglers weren't seen with us all friendly-like for a while, especially in town."

"I think we're on the same page about Tucker and his hired gun, Tate, but it could be trouble for the three of you if they see you with us. Why don't you ride away and go back to work? And if anyone saw us ride up, you tell them Reg was showing his baby brother the countryside."

Buck turned his horse towards the hills. "Sounds good. We'll check the cows on the high ridge. If we see any rattlesnakes going your way, I will pop off two rounds at a rabbit on the run. From there, a rifle shot will carry sound a long way, giving you a heads up."

"Appreciate it. Be safe. We'll get word to you on what we find." We didn't wave goodbye as a friendly group would do. Never know who could be watchin'. Feeling the need to be on our way, we directed our horses back toward town while the cattlemen checked the yearling cattle stock from the ridge. Anyone watching would see them checking the grass and moving the irrigation water across the fields.

"Reg, it looks like we made new friends."

"You're right, Spence. I think we have some new good and trustworthy friends."

We rode wide and took a long time to get to the wash, making sure no one followed or watched our movement. We rode like two cowboys who enjoyed the countryside, not hunting signs, just riding. But our eyes never stopped watching the country for anything unusual.

As we rode along the hillside above the wash, Spence reined in his horse and said, "Let's have a pull of water under that tree over there."

"I'm alright. Let's keep moving. I'm not too fond of someone finding us out here.

Spence insisted, "No, get off your horse, Reg, easy like. Play with your saddle a minute, walk to the shade, and sit where no one can see us."

Spence was a hell of a tracker, and he made his point. He wasn't thirsty. He had something stuck in his craw.

I nonchalantly swung my leg over Roan's back, hit the solid ground, and loosened Roan's belly strap. I re-tightened it in case we had to ride. We sat under the shade tree; it gave us good cover. We both took a drink of water from the water bag. The master tracker picked up a stick and started to whittle.

As he looked down at the stick, Spence said, "Reg, look across the draw in the wash. What do you see?"

"Dirt, sagebrush. a hill."

"Oh, for crying out loud. Look closer."

There it was plain as day. I never saw it. The minor ledge on the bank had purposely been caved in over the bottom of the wash. It appeared to be a perfect place to tuck a body under the overhang of the hill and then collapse the ledge over the top of the corpse. A lazy man's graveyard.

"Want to ride down and take a look, Spence?"

"No, let's mount up and ride up a short way. That spot would only cover one body. Let's look farther up the ravine."

It wasn't long before Spence put his hand down along his knee and pointed to the wash. He did it so only I could see, kept moving, and didn't look back. We found half a dozen places caved over, some years old. Then we rode away from the wash and out into the flat lands with Spence riding in tandem with me.

"Can't say for certain, but I'd bet we found the graveyard. I guess we will have to do more digging to make sure. Let's return tonight."

"Agreed. We can hike back to those spots up the draw, but let's check the older ones first."

That night, we made camp, a small fire, and laid our bed rolls out in the shadows. We snuck away from the fire, looked over the country-side for an hour, and headed to the wash on foot, leaving our camp-site location about two miles behind.

We came out above the draw and worked our way back down, an easy walk under the light of a full moon. We found a spot and sat watching and waiting to ensure no one was tracking us.

After sitting quietly in a spot for at least two hours to be sure no one followed, we started to dig. It was long, muscle-straining work with only our bare hands and sticks as shovels. It wasn't long before we located a man and a woman, the Anders, we suspected.

Digging around the area a couple of feet, we unearthed another man. He wore a belt with a silver buckle etched with a cattle brand. The familiar brand Maggie and her husband used.

We returned these missing souls to their resting places and spent adequate time concealing our tracks. We planted sage over our dig to hide it from stray riders passing by.

With Roan as our constant watchdog back at the camp, all still looked in good order.

"Reg, looks like we found our murderers and thieves. Time to ride for the law," said Spence, voicing the words that plagued him since we found the bodies.

In my best older brother's commanding voice, I said, "No, we will handle it."

"Reg, you are my big brother, and I'll stand toe to toe with ya, but we need to do this right. You don't want to be the bad guy and ruin what you have here. We will get the law and stand with them, making sure justice is served," argued Spence.

Hating to give ground to him, I said, "You're right. Now that we have bodies, we need evidence of who killed them."

20

TUCKER

Tucker spoke sharply to Tate. "Have you seen our cattle riders lately?"

"No, Boss, I haven't. They haven't been around much, but they're probably out checking the herd. Buck watches over this place and the cows like they are his own."

"I know Tate, but he needs to check in. I'm the boss, and he rides for me, not for himself. Go to the bunkhouse and tell him I want to talk in the morning."

"I'll give him the message." As Tate walked away, he mumbled," Soon, I'll be the boss man giving the orders around here."

When he reached the bunkhouse, he swung the unlatched door open with a loud bang as it hit the wall, alarming all three men.

"What's eating you, Tate? You damn near gave me a heart attack. We're trying to beat Buck in cards, but he keeps cheating," Poke said, so startled he dropped his cards.

"I don't have to cheat to beat you greenhorns. I just have to show up. You two lose all by yourselves."

"Buck, the boss wants to see you in the morning. He wants to know what you have been up to."

All three players at the table looked at each other, wondering if the messenger knew they had met up with the wandering brothers.

"I've got cattle to check on in the morning. What's he need?"

"I guess you'll just have to go up and see," Tate growled. "I am only the errand boy." Tate walked out the door, leaving it wide open. Buck got up and walked through the doorway, wanting to make sure Tate was nowhere in sight, and nobody else was lurking outside.

"What do you think, Buck, think he saw us?"

"No, Tom, if he did, he would have been busting down our door, ready for gunplay. I guess we will know in the morning. You might want to clean your irons, though. We may not need them, but we better be ready."

After sunrise, the men were sure the boss had eaten breakfast, and all three rode to the ranch house for the meeting. They stood on the porch and waited for what came, but Buck went in to face the music alone.

Tucker strode into the parlor, glanced at Buck, and sat at the massive pine desk but did not invite his ramrod to sit. "I thought maybe you moved on. I haven't seen hide nor hair of you and the other two. You got girls in town that you are keeping a secret?"

"No girls, Mr. Tucker. If we had girls in town, we'd be gone for sure."

"Maybe I should just fire you and your boys if you don't appreciate the job I have given you."

"Just joking, Boss. What woman would have us anyway?"

"You better remember who the boss is around here and who gives the orders. Now, exactly where have you been?"

"We've been checking on the cows and the water situation, getting ready for fall."

Tucker looked at Buck and glanced down to Buck's side. "Why are you carrying your sidearm? Itching for a fight?"

"Yes, sir, a fight with a bear. I seen a couple. Don't want to get ate. Now we have a lot of cows to check. Anything else, Boss?"

Tucker snapped, "Get out!" Get to work. I'm the one paying you. I want to see you working."

Buck slowly left the great room, halting at the open door with enough time to give a wink to his two cowhands waiting for him.

Walking away from the open door, Tom gave Poke a crooked grin. They remained less than a foot outside the open door, but they heard every word the two men inside had spoken to one another just fine.

"I'd like to see him try to take you, Buck; he'd be in for a hell of a fight," Tom said.

"Boys, we may soon see. . .we may soon see," said Buck.

Decked out in his city-slicker clothes, Tucker sat behind his big desk drinking whiskey, imitating a man who believed he controlled a grand enterprise. He was still fuming over his meeting with Buck.

Tate stood in the hall doorway, impatiently waiting for the next command from the man who ruled his life.

"Tate, we know where the gold miner was buried, and there was no trace of the gold or a map in that grave. This cowboy has to have the answers."

"Boss, what if he just found the horses and knows nothing about that man and the gold?"

"Tate, if I've learned anything in this life, I believe most things are connected one way or another. A person with a conscience and one who cared about other men buried him and carved a grave marker. That's not us or the men we ride with. I would bet my last dollar it is that new man in Two Forks. Tate, get your men together. We need to ride to town, find the answers, and take care of this Reg and his brother, Spence."

By this time, Tate paced the room and swiveled his head towards Tucker. "What do you think they know, Boss?"

"I know for certain we need to gather up those snub-horned cows and make sure our doctoring of their brands is believable.

"Should we run the cows off?"

"No, I've forged enough bills of sale. I'm not worried about that. I want to make sure about those cows. Sure hope I killed their pa when I shot him."

"I thought you did. I saw him go down hard on that hill. Don't know how a man could live through a fall like that."

"A lesson learned: never leave until you make sure and put a bullet in the person's head who you don't want to talk."

"What about the bodies we buried in the slope of that rocky ravine?"

"No, I don't think we need to worry about that, but to be sure, let's send a couple of men out to check around. Keep our secrets safe and make sure no varmints pull out anything from the site. Let's load up for a fight, get the men going, and we will take care of those brothers before they get the town's folk riled up and armed."

Tate grinned. "Those town folk and ranchers, they don't have the blood for killing. We do."

Tucker was a man who didn't know the meaning of losing. He would not let some young bucks think he could ride in and take what was his. Those two are in for a lesson. Men like me take. We don't ask."

21

FINALLY, THE TRUTH

When Reg and Spence rode back into Two Forks, Chelsea's heart nearly leaped out of her chest, and she bolted out the café door with skirts flying before anyone could ask where she was off to.

Little Joe jumped to a wobbly chair by the window of the café, nearly knocking himself and the plants on the windowsill straight through the pane of glass.

"Look, Miz Nancy, it's the two brothers. I'm gonna go see them and ask if they want to go fishing."

"NO LITTLE JOE," Nancy said in a voice that meant business. Leave them alone. Chelsea wants to make sure Reg is okay."

"What about Spence? Chelsea doesn't care about him?"

"Sure, she does," Caty piped in, "But she wanted to kiss and hug Reg. Spence will be taking care of the horses."

"She missed him and was worried sick," Nancy added.

Chelsea nearly collided with me, making a spectacle of herself. As she leaped into my arms, she almost knocked me to the ground. Luckily, I saw her coming full tilt, so I leaned into the tornado about to land. We would both have gone tumbling if I had not prepared.

Spence let out a pent-up sigh and rolled his eyes. "No need for you to worry about me. I was only risking my life watching over your man."

"That's what worried me. Trouble watching over trouble," Chelsea quipped.

Spence beat the red Colorado soil from his shirt and pant legs. "How about a hug for me, Chelsea?" It looks like we're almost family, so it's a rule you have to hug brothers, too."

So, she wrapped him in a hug that just about cracked every bone in his back, then gave him a peck on the cheek and whispered in his ear. "He gets hurt. I'm going to make your life so miserable."

She pulled back, and they both laughed. "See, brother, I told ya. I think you better start worrying. I can tell she's thinking about switching beaus."

Roan marched straight to where the two stood and gave Spence an insistent shove with her nose that moved him away from Chelsea.

I laughed. "Spence, even my horse knows who the favored one is."

Seeming to understand those words, Roan stepped over to Chelsea and nudged her apron. The smart young lady removed the apple peels from her pockets, assuring the horse that, indeed, she had not forgotten her treat. "I carried them around, waiting for you to return. You are my favorite horse. I love you, Roan."

"Looks like the hugs are over," Spence grumbled as he walked away. "I'm going to visit with my smoking pal, and maybe he will give me a puff. Lovebird, you send the wire. We need to get ready."

"Exactly what did he mean by that?" Chelsea asked, raising her eyebrows. "About sending a wire?"

"I'll tell you, but we need to get your ma and Maggie. What we found will answer a lot of speculation, but it's going to be a sad day. Can you get your ma over to the café? Maggie's going to need her friends close."

"Oh, no, it's about her husband, isn't it?".

"It's what everyone was thinking, but nobody had the evidence to back it up. We found the evidence of foul play and the bodies to prove it, but we need to get confirmation of who murdered these folks and also who ordered the killings. I'll send the wire and meet you at Maggie's."

Walking into the telegraph office, a bespeckled small-boned man wearing a white shirt with rolled-up sleeves, a dark blue vest, and a small green billed cap greeted me. This was the wire master I sought, the one dedicated to receiving mail and sending wires.

After introducing myself, I said, "I need to send a wire to the nearest town with a marshal, and it needs to be kept quiet with no leaks."

The man looked at me with a stern, hard look. "I don't leak information, and I resent the accusation."

"I make no accusations, sir. The townspeople could be greatly hurt if this message isn't kept under our hats. You, my brother, and I are the only ones who know what will happen."

"Marshall. Stop. Have evidence of murders and buried bodies on a nearby ranch in Two Forks. Stop. Need immediate response. Stop. Reg Carter. Stop."

"Please send that and let me know as soon as they respond. You swore to be a wireman and be responsible for the mail. I'm sure you'll keep it quiet."

"Young man, I've been in charge of the wire and the mail for years, longer than you've been on this big rock. I am a man of my word and have friends here as well. I care about this town. My wife and children have roots here. There are ones here we care for and ones we do not care for. I can read between the lines, and I'm sure I know what the wire is about," said the wire master, both disgruntled at me for questioning his honesty yet understanding the necessity of my words.

"Well, sir, I'll hold you to it. Thanks. I will talk to the individuals this affects and wait until the marshall responds before I send word to the townspeople."

The man responded, "As soon as I have a reply back in hand, I will personally find you with the answer, as I know we will all need to stand up to help."

Hearing the clickety-clack of the Morse code as my foot hit the boardwalk outside the office, I felt relieved that this wire was on its way. Then, I headed for the café where I was to meet Chelsea, Maggie, and Nancy and thought hard about every step of the message I needed to deliver.

Spence had left the barn earlier and sat waiting on the café's porch. I could tell he had found the old codger. He was upwind, but I could still smell him even from this distance and could see his eyes were red as the devil.

"You sent the wire?"

"Yep. Now, I will talk to Maggie."

"I'm sure she already figured out what happened to the Anders couple and her husband."

"I know, but it will be hard when she hears the truth about all three. We need more evidence, put together a plan, and find proof that Tucker or Tate ordered or did the killings themselves."

Upon opening the door to the café, we watched Maggie bravely stand and meet us at the threshold. "Did you find anything on your adventure?"

"We did a bit of digging, Maggie," I answered.

She looked down at our hands, clothes, and boots. It was evident that I wasn't joking. We looked like we had been out digging or playing in the dirt.

"You are good young men, but you have no reason to be sticking your neck out for me or this town. We're all grateful, and we admire your strength in dealing with the matter of Clancy and getting word to Nancy. Now, you tell me straight out, what do you know?"

Spence started to speak. He looked at me as if to say, *you sit this one out. I'll take it from here.* "Maggie, we were given information from the cattle hands on the T Lazy 7 Ranch that led us to where they felt a hired hand was shot, taken away, and buried. We found the area and located the remains of what we feel are the bodies of the Anders couple, and I'm sad to say, your husband. We have proof they were murdered, but not by whom."

In their excitement, all three women reacted at the same time, blurting out their sentiments and creating a chaotic ruckus. "We all know who's behind these killings. We know it was Tucker."

Spence agreed. "I'm sure he did it or had it done. That's why we need evidence. We need the smoking gun. We need the right person to talk to: a hired gunman, his cattlemen, or Tucker himself. If we could put pressure on one of them, they might turn on Tucker, or if we could get Tucker to brag about it, we would have them all. What we need is to set a trap."

Maggie had taken a seat and sat quietly in her chair, staring at her left hand while nervously twisting the wedding band she still wore.

"My husband has been gone for many years now, but I always felt it was Tucker and Tate who did this, without a doubt. I knew it but could never prove it. My husband would never just walk away. I know he loved me. We fought from time to time, like all couples, but even if he wasn't happy with me, he would never have left me stranded. We would have worked it out. He was that kind of man."

"He loved the ranch, caring for the stock and working the fields. His favorite pastime was having coffee in the barn as the sun rose over the fields, taking in the smell of hay in the loft and the scent of the pine wood as the sun warmed up the building. He was a good man."

Spence reached for her hand. "I'm going to make sure we get the answer to his demise, Maggie."

She was sad, but she was ready. The fight was swelling up in her. "I'll inform the town members, Spence. And Reg, it's my turn to carry the load. One way or another, I'm taking care of the bastards who caused harm to us all," she said with a set jaw and firmness that surprised those present in the room.

Then, it was my turn to take Maggie's soft yet strong, firm hand. By the look of tiny scars and callouses and the feel of energy in her grip, it was apparent that she knew how to work hard and carry her share of the load, especially the current task at hand.

"Ladies," I said pointedly, directing my comments to Maggie and Nancy, "my brother and I are outsiders here. We carry no weight with the opinions or decisions of the Two Forks folks."

"Maggie, you are the person who should meet with your friends and neighbors. You know who we can trust and who will stand with us against the T Lazy 7. An important point to keep in mind is that we don't want the news to travel out Tucker's way. The upper hand belongs with the good people here, but what we know now must be kept a secret. This town's well-being is what's at risk."

"You all know as well as we do that Tucker is not one to run away. He will fight and fight dirty. Men like him will do whatever it takes to keep what they have stolen from honest folks.

"Reg, this isn't your fight. It's up to us to deal with this, and it's way overdue."

"I may be an outsider, but I have a stake in this town, with the people and the place where I may want to live and raise children.

To their surprise, Spence and I exited the café after presenting our case, it was like the devil summoned up my demons.

Sitting astride their horses were Tucker, Tate, and his men. They had ridden into town and faced us head-on outside the café.

Spence stiffened his spine and took the lead. "Hello, fellas. Pleasant day for a ride into town."

Tucker glared at Spence, then gave me the same unwavering hard look as he sat with his hands folded over the reins resting on the saddle horn of the expensive hand-tooled saddle. "Ah, Reg, you are the man I hoped to find. My men, the ones whose lost horses you found, well, it is like this, never turned up. You got anything else to say?"

I looked Tucker squarely in the eyes. "Nope, I think I filled your man in on how I came across the horses. Don't know what else I could answer for you."

Tucker leaned forward in his saddle, "Like I said, our men never did show back up, and I was wondering how you found their horses so far south of where they headed. Tate sent them north."

"Can't help you there, Tucker. I've been up north past your place. It's not good cattle country, just desert. Not sure what your boys would be looking for . . . cattle? Or something else? By the look of their horses, they were not cattlemen, that's for certain."

The air grew still as both sides had now laid out their cards.

Tucker didn't care for his hand. "What are you trying to say? What do you know about cattle and what it takes to run a ranch? You're nothing more than a saddle tramp."

"Hell, boys." Spence jumped into the game. "You have never met Mr. Reg Carver. He is part owner in a cattle operation west of here. I'm also part owner in that same operation. I'm his brother. We run, say, about twice as many cows as you run. We own about four times the land you are sitting your ass on."

"So, I guess when we're talking about ranching, I would say Reg is knowledgeable and understands what it takes to manage an outfit and what kind of people it takes to make a go of it."

Tate wasn't about to be left out of this game. "Looks like we have a couple of cattle barons on our hands. What brings you our way? You looking to expand?"

"No, we were looking for our cows and who stole them, oh, round about a year ago. You may have even seen some of our stock."

"A cow is a cow. Why would I know yours from any of the others?"

"Because ours stand out. Our dad cuts off the horns. He was tired of getting himself and his horses gored. Kind of a pet peeve of Dad's. That beef is easy to spot if they are ever misplaced. So, have you seen any cows like that, Tate? How about you, Tucker?" asked Spence.

I took a step forward, my attention remaining solely on Tucker. My hand rested next to my pistol with my eyes focused on him, and Tucker knew it.

Tucker wasn't accustomed to being pushed. I could see his eyes close to slits and his shoulders tense.

"Boys, I'll keep an eye out for those cows. You never know what's going to turn up. Cows have a way of moving around when they aren't taken care of."

Tucker made his point. He saw he didn't have the upper hand. "Let's go, men. We have a ranch to run, and I think there's a storm coming. We need to get everything organized."

Spence agreed. "Yep, it looks like it will be one hell of a blowout. If you need help, just let Reg and me know. We would be more than glad to pitch in. We're good at battling a storm."

The women had listened from just inside the café doors. Nancy looked dumbfounded at Chelsea and asked, "Did Reg ever tell you he came from a cattle ranch, and it sounds like a rather large one to boot?"

"No, Ma, never a word. I had no idea. I could tell he was a hard worker who could carry a heavy load because of those strong, calloused hands and muscled shoulders. As far as cattle knowledge, I'm sure he is capable, but I didn't know about his ranch."

"It seems that man is full of surprises, good- looking, a hard worker, honest, and from what I have seen, also kind to small children. Hmm. Looks like someone found a treasure, and I'm not talking about gold."

Chelsea beamed. "I agree, Ma. He would be a girl's dream come true."

22

BEN

Ben returned to the T Lazy 7 Ranch. He wanted nothing more to do with the men he rode, stole, killed, and lived with, their smell, talk, walk, or, for that matter, any part of himself.

He was no longer the man he once was, now feeling dirty and tormented by what he had become. While he sat thinking of his folks, his brother, and sisters, his thoughts took him back many years, knowing how they saw him . . . the disappointment.

Back at the bunkhouse where Ben used to call home, he threw his gear together, packed his time-worn leather saddlebags, and walked through the door for the final time.

One of the hands inside asked, "Ben, what in tarnation are you doing, and where are you going? Partner, you better go see Tate and tell him what you are up to."

Ben saddled his horse and rode past the ranch house without a pause to see Tate or collect his pay. He wanted to outrun who he had become, riding as fast and far as his horse would carry him.

Trying to ride to a new future where he was unknown by sight or reputation, Ben rode well into the night away from his past and into the next day as if the devil were on his tail. Knowing it was a fool's errand to continue pushing his mount and himself without rest, food, and water, he finally stopped that evening and slept, the sleep of the dead.

The traveler followed the orange ball in the sky as it rose on a promising new day. Eventually, the town he sought, Tall Peaks, which was unfamiliar to him, came into view on the far horizon.

This Sunday, the joyful sound of church bells ringing reached his ears. He saw folks who had just attended services leaving the building, visiting and chuckling with one another as they held the handrails while climbing down the well worn wooden steps.

The lone rider remained respectfully on his horse as the people exited the church and walked by. All eyes traveled from Ben's face to the gun on his hip, then back to his face again. Ladies bowed their heads as they passed, not rude but cautious, while the men greeted him with a friendly 'howdy' and a tip of the hat.

He was a drifter. This was easy to see: raggedy clothes, worn boots, bed roll, and that was it. The guns, saddle, and horse were the only things of value he ever owned, and they were all stolen. He never bought anything. He just stole what he needed.

When the church emptied, he dismounted and walked up the stairs to the open double doors, removing his hat and beating the dust off his clothing with the shabby, tattered hat. His brown eyes, the color of chestnuts, adjusted to the dark room while he focused on the silhouette of the man hanging from the cross.

Feeling at ease, for the first time in his memory, Ben breathed in the clean, fresh air of the church, gazed at the stained-glass windows, and finally sat down on one of the long benches worn smooth by the many souls who had warmed them. An indescribable feeling overcame him, like nothing he had ever experienced, wanting to be a better man, one people could trust.

Ma and Pa, I'm going to be a better man, one you would be proud to call your son, and my brother and sister would be proud to call me family.

Sitting motionless for what could have been hours, he felt alone while those thoughts continued to stay with him.

A man in a black shirt with a white collar approached him, placed a hand on Ben's shoulder, and asked, "My son, what may I do to help you? Could I pray for you or with you?"

"Mister, are you the owner of this church?"

"No, son. I work in the House of the Lord. I am a servant of God. I'm Father Douglas."

"Father Douglas, I've never been in a church, let alone prayed. I don't know what it means, but I know I need to be here. I rode day and night for several days and ended up here. I have never felt this way before and am at a loss for words."

"Son, talk to God."

"I don't know how. Talk to him as you would a father, a good friend, a person you admire."

"I don't know any good men. I'm an outlaw, and I only know evil men and bad deeds. I've only done bad things with my life."

"My son, do you remember your Ma and Pa?"

"Yes, sir, I certainly do."

"Were they bad people?"

"No, sir. They were good people, always trying to get me to do right, but they failed in their efforts to help me see the light."

"Talk to them like we are talking here. Tell them what you want them to know: your troubles, sorrows, and hopes for the future. God will be there with you. You can say it out loud or silently in your mind. God will hear you."

"If it's okay, I'll just talk in my head. I don't want anyone else to know what I've done."

"That is fine. I'll leave you alone now. I'm here to help if you need to talk about anything. It will always stay between you, me, and God."

He talked to himself for hours after the padre left and then cried with the heartbreaking sobs of one who needed the forgiveness he sought and wanted so badly to love and care for those around him.

Ben woke on the long bench in the church, hearing chirping birds and wagons rolling through town. The drifter couldn't remember the last time he slept so peacefully and woke, feeling his mind relaxed and as clear as a sparkling brook. Rising from the wooden bed, he bowed his head and spoke to the man on the cross, or God, because he wasn't sure about such things. "Thank you for listening."

Once stepping through the white double doors of the church and church steps, he located the outhouse and then felt the urgent need for food, with hunger pains cramping his stomach. *I am sure my stomach would touch my backbone if I waited much longer to eat.*

The priest must have moved the lone horse to the enclosed area at the rear of the church to graze overnight. Promising to repay the priest's kindness somehow, Ben retrieved his horse and walked into town, locating a small café.

Although he couldn't read, he was savvy enough to know what each establishment was without reading a sign. Before sitting for a meal, he found the livery and asked if they could board another horse, telling the man that he didn't have the funds to pay him but would like to sell his rifle if any interested parties in town offered it as security on the bill.

"Mister, I think the general store would give you a fair price for it. You take it over there, and we'll settle up later."

"Much obliged."

"Friend, what's your name?"

"Ben, Ben Baxter from Wade County, Texas." *Feels good speaking the truth. Been a long while.*

"Ben Baxter from Wade County, Texas, I'm Toby. Looks like you're worn down, and it seems like you had a long visit with the Almighty. Saw your horse tied on the church rail."

"You're right, Toby. I did a lot of talking. He's a pretty good listener."

"That he is, Ben. When you're finished with your doings, come back and see me. I've been where you're at. Trust me, I know. If you want a place to bunk and do some work around here until you get some answers from above, let me know, and we can visit a spell."

"Toby, thank you kindly. I'll be back."

Inside the general store, the variety of goods surprised me. *Maybe there is hope for a sale here.*

The store owner stiffened as Ben carried the rifle in, but he relaxed as his new customer peacefully placed it and the gun on the counter.

"I am new in town with no need for these weapons and wonder if you might be interested?"

Not knowing what a rifle and a gun were worth, the former outlaw had no idea whether he was treated fairly or cheated when the store owner paid him.

In his former life, Ben only knew the ways of a thief's life with little to no knowledge of what a person paid for his gear. Tipping his hat to the patrons, he left with a smile, a jingle in the pocket, and a bounce to his get-along.

As he sat quietly in the corner, able to keep a watch on the door and away from prying eyes, he observed how the folks surrounding him ate, used their clean-up rags, and drank their coffee or sarsaparilla.

Never experiencing this type of upbringing or at least not paying attention if he had one, he listened with keen interest to the civil talk they shared, polite and kind. Humiliation overtook him when the food girl reached his hideaway table to take the food order. Looking down at his unclean, unshaven face and torn clothes, he wondered what she must think of him.

"Stranger, looks like you have come a far piece. Welcome to town. Glad to have you."

He asked her to recommend a meal, and with a blink of an eye, she said, "Mister, I'll get your food going. I am ordering the house special of steak, mashed potatoes with gravy, and a new dish, a rhubarb pie."

He enjoyed the day's special and drank his coffee black, never realizing this kind of peace existed. Constantly checking over his shoulder, looking to start or stop a fight, ready to dodge a bullet or send one calling, was the normal tension filled life he had survived. Eating until he felt ready to bust, he paid his bill and stood to leave, receiving a charming smile from the serving girl that she aimed his way.

"Hope to see you again soon. Don't be a stranger, you hear?" she said with a wink and a smile. "I may not want to let you out of my sight."

"Yes, ma'am."

"By the way, cowboy, do you have a name?"

'Folks call me Ben, just plain ole Ben."

"Betty. That's my name, don't forget it." She whisked away as fast as a hummingbird flits.

Outdoors, the day turned clear and crisp, with the sky a pale shade of blue and home to sporadic wispy clouds. A slight breeze kept the dust down and the irritating bugs away.

Located across the street were the marshall's office and jail. Ben inhaled a deep breath and slowly released it. *It is now or never.* He opened the door, entered, and closed the heavy wooden door behind him.

"I need to talk to you, Marshall, about some murders and buried bodies."

23

MEETING THE TOWN MARSHALL

The town marshal slid his feet down from atop his desk, stood up, and put a hand on the side arm hanging from his hip. "Drifter, buried bodies and murders? That's a hell of an entrance."

Eyeing Ben for a moment to get a measure of the man, the marshall decided that since the drifter carried no weapons, he wouldn't be a threat.

"Have a seat. Coffee?"

"No, sir, I've had plenty. It's time I got these murders off my chest. I am guilty, Marshall, of years of evil doings, and I deserve whatever comes my way. I'm ready for whatever it be."

"Let's start from the beginning. I need to call you something, so what's your name?"

"Ben, Ben Baxter from down Wade County, Texas way."

"Ben, what do you want to discuss?"

"I was hired on at the T Lazy 7 Ranch out of Two Forks, a three-day ride from here. Mr. Tucker is the owner, or I should say the murderer of the former owners and thief of the ranch.

I was hired by a man named A.W. Tate. I think he was from Texas as well. He was Tucker's hired gun. He hired me to be an experienced hand to do whatever Mr. Tucker wanted, enabling him to keep what he had stolen."

"While I lived on the ranch, Tucker murdered Mr. and Mrs. Anders, took over their ranch, providing a faked bill of sale from them for the T Lazy 7 Ranch. He told anyone asking that the former owners wanted to move away, back east."

"Tate killed another ranch owner and took over his ranch by purchasing it from the widow, a woman named Maggie. Tucker made it out like her husband ran off and left the ranch and his wife."

"An additional three other men were murdered when they came looking for lost cattle. Tate shot one of the men in the gut at the ranch and listened to him scream in pain for an hour. He thought this was great fun. The man is as evil as they get."

"Finally, he ordered the remaining two men to be shot in the head. He didn't care to deal with their complaining and whining about their partner's pain any longer. They were all executed."

"That's a lot of murders, Ben. Did you kill any of these folks?"

"No, sir. I witnessed it all, so I am as guilty as Tate and Tucker. I just didn't pull the trigger."

"Now, Ben, I can't arrest someone based only on your word. I need proof, evidence, you know? Is there anyone able and willing to back up your story?"

"Probably not. The other hired guns wouldn't talk. They're bad, bad to the bone."

"I can look into it, but without proof, there's not going to be a lot I can do."

"Marshall, I can't come up with anyone who will talk, but I have plenty of bodies to show you. Can you wrangle a posse together so we can go grave digging?"

"I will need to get this down on paper and have you sign it, right and proper like. I'm going to wire the district judge to make it legal. We don't want any snakes slithering from under the rug. You understand I'm going to have to lock you up until we can get answers?"

"I'm ready, Marshall. I've done what I've done, and I'll put my fate in God's hands. I ask one favor, though. I'd like to write to my kinfolk, Ma, Pa, my sisters, and brother, to let them know what has happened and what I hope the future will bring," said Ben. "I can't write or read. I would need some help putting it on paper.

"That we can do," answered the marshall.

24

REG SPEAKS AT THE TOWN MEETING

The word spread fast as Maggie continued talking to everyone entering the town. This evening, I walked into the café and found it packed to standing room only. After the recent visit from Tucker, Tate, and his men, we knew it was only a matter of time before the lid blew off the cookpot.

Tucker controlled four hired thugs plus Tate and probably tried his best to round up more bottom feeders. From our conversation in the street, we realized that both sides understood what would happen.

The cattlemen who were true to the bone ranchers displayed good, honest character traits. They probably would fight to protect their town but simply needed to be grouped under a respected leader. This is where the bond between Maggie and her neighbors entered into play. Each family had a lot to lose, not only their jobs but their ranches and their lives.

Sunlight shone brightly into the late afternoon while Sara's husband, Ty, and several ranchers met for the anticipated town meeting. One voice talking over the top of another, making as much noise as a gaggle of geese, was all I heard. Luckily for me, Maggie saw my confusion and waved me over.

Meeting with the men of the town to discuss a plan of action gave me a chance to offer what knowledge I had gained. Twenty men were present, and surprisingly, the wives accompanied them. It was remarkable to witness the varied group of men there and understand their backgrounds. The ranchers appeared to be hard, fair men of character willing to protect what they needed to.

Maggie started the ball rolling at the café.

"Thank you all for coming. We all felt at one time or another that Tucker was not on the up and up. His recent actions made it apparent we would all have to pick a side.

"This is our town with good working folk. We have families, businesses, and a strong community, and we must stand together and fight to take back what has been taken from all of us. It's time to agree to keep what we have."

The room erupted with voices shouting comments and questions from every corner, and everyone wanted answers at the same time.

A voice rang out from the back of the room, "Maggie, I've lived in these parts for many years, and I'm not a big fan of Tucker. We all have thought the same thing about how he ended up with the Anders' place and your ranch, but we didn't have any proof."

Maggie waved her hand toward Spence and me.

"Hold on, ladies and gentlemen, that's where I'll turn this over to

Reg and Spence Carver. They're new to our community, and Reg has a stake in what's happening in this town, same as we all do," she said.

I waved to the men so I could speak. "As you know, my name is Reg Carver, and this is my brother Spence. I hope the marshall will show up shortly and take control using the rule of law. I am glad there are men here who want to stick up for their morals and the people who make this town what it is, but I don't believe there is a man here who actually wants to start any trouble. In the meantime, and for the purpose of this meeting, let me tell you what I know to be true."

"Spence and I are cattlemen from west of here. We have a large ranch that we operate with our mother and father. A year and a half ago, we had a mess of cattle stolen."

"Dad was wounded, tracking down the rustlers in a skirmish where he lost part of his leg and nearly died. After he recuperated, I started to track our cows where he left off."

"It all began when I found Clancy, Nancy's husband, who was shot twice by Tucker's men. Before he died, he asked me to get word to his wife Nancy and his three daughters, who were to meet him here in Two Forks."

"I buried Clancy where I found him and marked his grave. I brought word to Nancy and the girls and laid out what I knew. Clancy killed the three men who wounded him, which is how he later died from the wounds they inflicted upon him."

"But he felt one more scoundrel wasn't accounted for. That's why I brought the outlaw's horses to town to see who would claim them. Tucker's men were the ones who showed up and claimed the horses."

One of the town's merchants asked, "How do we know you didn't kill Clancy?

"You don't. I rode out to the T Lazy 7 Ranch, where I found my family's stolen cattle."

"How could you tell they were yours? Were they branded?"

"Yes, but we all know brands can be altered. My dad had a unique way of marking our cattle, which was undeniably better than a brand. He cut off the horns to a nub and drove a horseshoe nail into the horn. If you didn't know it was there, it would be mighty hard to spot."

"When I rode past their ranch, Buck and his hired hands, Tom and Poke, from the T Lazy 7 Ranch, met me out on the grazing fields. They eventually showed me a nail they had removed from a horn. Buck told me that Tucker said he had a bill of sale for these cows but never produced the paper."

"Now, I'm sure you all have heard the story of my roan mare kicking Tucker's hired man across the street. It seems that same man ended up being shot by Tate, Tucker's hired thug. They buried his body out aways on the T Lazy 7 Ranch."

"That all sounds like a hell of a story, but how do we know it's true?"

"Buck, the foreman, told me of a draw where he thought Tucker and Tate were disposing of the other bodies."

"Spence and I scouted that draw and found the Anders couple and Maggie's husband there, along with three other men. We assume they were cattlemen who came looking for their cows."

"I wired the marshall, and I received a reply. He's bringing us a witness to the killings at Two Forks. The marshall informed me that the witness worked for the T Lazy 7 Ranch, and this man also told him where the bodies lay buried on the ranch."

The room was stone cold quiet. Everyone there was at a loss for words, but I felt sure they must have had a hundred questions.

I continued my talk. "Spence and I had a run-in with Tucker and his men in front of Maggie's Café. They know I have proof regarding the cattle theft. I'm not sure if they suspect my knowledge about the killings."

"My brother and Joe consented to ride out to keep an eye on the grave sites as these are the only pieces of proof of the murders we have. They will let us know if anyone tries to move them." *Or Spence and Joe will add more bodies to the pile.*

"Ladies and gentlemen, it is of the utmost importance that we keep a tight lid on what we know, or as sure as I'm standing here, Tucker will start killing his ranch hands, you ranchers, and the townsfolk. Nothing leaves this room."

I could hear a pin drop. Those listening now remained agreeably quiet, nodding their heads, understanding the severity of the situation.

Sara's husband, Ty, owned the general store and worked as its clerk, but when I talked with him and looked at the six-shooter tied down to his thigh, I saw a man who was far more than a clerk.

He said, "These men and I have been mulling over where we may be headed. We are men with more to offer than what may meet the eye. This is the West, and most of us have left our untold stories and those lives behind us."

"Ty, I couldn't imagine a store clerk would even know how to use an iron, let alone tie it down. I can see, though, by the wear on that pistol and belt, you probably do have a few stories to tell."

Many of the townspeople were not eager to see a fight break out, preferring it would go away if they closed their eyes. I assured them we would let the law handle it, but if it came to it, they would have to defend what was important to them: family, friends, land, and homes.

"If you can't draw iron, you could help with the women or help supply the other men with what they may need."

Preacher Bill, the mountain-like man, was the calmest in the room. He talked softly about scripture and man's rights in God's eyes. He was powerful but so patient and mild-mannered in character. The men and women were at ease with his presence and breathed easier knowing he was there.

Once calm settled in, one of the ranchers talking with Ty reached over and shook my hand.

"Friend, the other men and I gathered here have made a grave mistake allowing this evil to creep into our town. Most of us here are men with a past that involved gunplay. Some fought Indian wars, some fought their own battles, and some were men from the wrong side of the law who later saw the light."

"It took a pup like you to stand up for us all. We have stood in the shadows far too long. We owe you for opening our eyes. You lead, we'll follow."

I shook this stranger's hand and said, "I'm a newcomer here, but I would like to settle down, start a family, and be part of this community. I do have a stake in this fight. They have our stolen cattle, and my father was crippled by these men. If you all agree, I will take my place alongside you and be on the right side of the fight. Spence and I will take back what's ours and help return what belongs to you."

Knowing the guests would soon like to wind up the meeting, I felt it best to exit first so my presence would not hinder the opportunity for discussion among the families. Spence and I stepped out of earshot for our talk.

"Spence, you and Joe ride out as early in the morning as possible, stake out your lookout point, wait, and watch to see if anything unusual happens. Send Joe with an alert to me if need be," I said.

25

TIME TO REST

With plenty of daylight still burning, I headed to the corral. I missed my companion's company. My partner stood in her usual spot outside of the corral, eating the meadow grass. One thing I knew for sure: this horse would never be corralled. She was a part of the wild, and she allowed me to ride her, but I would never own or control her.

Roan strolled up to me as I leaned against the fence rail, looking over the flatlands leading toward the tree-filled mountains above. A gentle nudge on my arm reminded me that someone needed her usual ear and neck caresses.

My mighty horse shadowed me and followed me into the barn with alert eyes that appeared to understand what I had in mind. Loving the familiar scent of a barn, the hay, the wet leather tack, and the smell of the weathered wood slats was the soothing solace I needed.

Roan remained standing before me, then crouched down and lay next to where I sat. Horses lie down to rest, roll in the dirt, or sometimes sleep. While on the ground, they are most vulnerable and cannot defend themselves from predators.

I felt a sense of relief and contentment at the moment. We lay in the dirt together, letting the sun's rays caress and warm us. Resting my head on her neck, I felt her breathing and body warmth like a child sleeping in a mother's arms.

"Chelsea, is Reg okay?" Caty asked.

"Look there, Reg and Roan are both asleep," Chelsea whispered to Caty and Little Joe.

"I'll be. I never would have believed this could have been possible if I hadn't seen it with my own two eyes," Caty said.

"Be quiet, you two. Let's sit over here in the hay and wait and see who wakes up first."

They sat quietly on a hay pile, giggling and whispering softly.

"Chelsea," Caty asked quietly. "You love Reg. don't you?"

"I believe so, Caty. From the first moment I ran into him in Maggie's doorway, I felt I had known him for a long time. It was only a second, but I also knew I wanted to really get to know him much better."

"Is that how love works, Chelsea? You just bump into it?"

"Caty, most likely, it's different for everyone. It could start as being friends or courting, but sometimes in the West, marriage comes fast out of necessity."

Chelsea looked at Little Joe, shaking her head at the sight of the small boy, and poked Caty. The two girls giggled at the youngster, who lay fast asleep in the hay beside his best friend, Reg.

"Do you think there's going to be trouble, Chelsea? Is Reg going to kill the men who stole his family's cattle?"

"Where did you hear that, Caty?"

"It's the buzz around town. Everyone is talking about stolen cattle and people who have already been killed. Did Mr. Tucker kill Miss Maggie's husband?"

"Caty, there's so much going on. Reg sent for the marshall, and we will sort it all out when he arrives. You shouldn't worry. It's all going to be okay."

Thoughts plagued the older girl's mind. *It wasn't going to be okay. People were going to be hurt and maybe even killed. Wouldn't it be so nice to lie down next to Reg, hold him tight, and let Roan protect them both?*

Roan was the first to wake, listen, and look before she moved a muscle. She tilted her head slightly to find the girls sitting in the hay. Snickered as if to say hello, she shook her head gently as a mother would do to warn off visitors from disturbing her babies.

I opened my eyes and saw the three spies in the hay. The girls' chins nestled in their hands with smiling faces and mischievous eyes, watching us two sleeping like little kids down for a nap.

Caty was the first to speak. "Did you have a good nap, all cozy-comfy-like?"

"I might have if there weren't gigglers waking me up. I was having a sweet dream about a certain girl I know."

Chelsea said, "Must have been a girl from back home, one that got away, maybe?"

"No, one right here in town. Her name is Callie, and she is quiet. Likes to ride." I looked at Little Joe. "I see someone else likes to sleep in the barn."

"It's a man thing. I guess," Caty said with a giggle and a smile. "Men always trying to get out of work, huh, Chelsea? Chels, you wouldn't want to end up with a lazy barn sleeper, now would ya?"

At that, I leaped up, grabbed a pile of hay, and covered the three, startling Little Joe, who woke wide-eyed.

The girls squealed, jumped to their feet, and threw hay back onto Roan and me. Then, in a surprise attack, I reached over, grabbed Chelsea by the arm, and kissed her soundly.

"Well, I'll be Reg, you like kissing girls?" moaned Little Joe, trying to pick the hay from his hair.

"They might be in love, little man. That's what you do when you're in love," said Caty.

"How would you know, Caty? You don't know nothin'?"

The disgruntled horse shook the loose hay from her head and neck while she rolled to her knees and came up with a thunder, not amused at the hay war.

She pushed Chelsea and me aside and leaned into Little Joe and Caty, giving them a kiss-nibble with her soft velvet nose. Then she stalked out the door, flashing her tail, and loped off to stretch her legs and find water.

The two younger ones ran after her, hoping she would stop and give them a ride.

"I sure needed that nap, and I guess Roan needed one, too."

"Reg, I've never seen a horse do what Roan did, making herself into a nice cozy pillow. If you ever get crossways of me, now I know you can find a cozy place to sleep in the barn," said Chelsea, flying out of the barn doors and down the street, running with me right on her heels. People who saw us just shook their heads and commented on the young couple enjoying a moment of fun.

26

BETTY

"B en, you awake? "

"I'm up. It's tough getting any sleep when all I dream about is a noose tightening around my neck."

"Ben, I received a wire. It looks like your story pans out. I received word from a man named Reg Carver. He tells stories of killings and bodies on the T Lazy 7 Ranch, owned or stolen by a Mr. Tucker."

"I need more information on this Tucker person. If you could describe this man for me, it would be helpful as I want to get a description out on the wire and see if we get any more details."

Marshall, "I'm a fair hand at drawing. I'll draw a picture for you if I can get some paper and a pencil."

"What, you're going to draw a stick figure with a cowboy hat?"

"I can do a lot better than that. I may not be good at much, but I'm a pretty good hand with a pencil."

"Time's a-wastin' then. Let's get on with it. I'll have supplies brought over. There's a young lady named Betty who wants to visit. Seems like you made an impression on her."

"My luck. A nice woman has eyes for me, and I'm heading to the gallows."

" I think if what you said is true, and you have turned over a new leaf, I'll put in a word with the judge. You'll have to do some time, but maybe we can get the rope off your neck."

He was at a loss for words, and tears welled up in his eyes. "It's the truth. For the first time ever, I know I'm heading down the right path. I'd surely like to see Betty, and I'll be on my best behavior."

"Okay, but we need that information quick. We're leaving as soon as I can get the details out on the wire. By the way, who is this Reg, and how does he figure into this story?"

"I'll tell you on the way. It will give us something to talk about. You'll like the part about his roan mare."

It wasn't long before Betty showed up with paper and pencil and a mouthwatering scent of a home cooked stew she brought. She wore a calico blue dress dotted with tiny yellow flowers and a blue ribbon holding back her hair. Stepping as softly as if strolling through rose petals, she greeted Ben with that welcoming smile.

Ben noticed her nervousness as the tray wobbled when she bent forward to place the food on a short table next to the bars and hand him the drawing supplies.

"Thank you for coming to visit me," he said, "I feel like an angel just walked through the door."

"I don't know about the angel part, but I think I'm enough of a woman to help get you back on track."

"You come here often to feed the criminals?"

"No, you're the first and hopefully the last. I made that special, so eat up."

"I will, but will you stay and talk as I eat and then make a drawing?"

"I'd love to. By the way, the marshall said you have been helpful, and he will try to help you."

"I'll do all I can. I sure would like to be around to enjoy some good meals and conversation." They sat for an hour while he ate, sketched, and talked. He may be in jail, but he savored every minute. *Probably as close to heaven as I would ever get,* he thought.

"I'm done drawing. What do you think?"

"Oh, my. It's like I'm looking right at that man. When you said you could draw, I had no idea. It's beautiful."

"Bet you were thinking it would be a stick figure with a cowboy hat, didn't ya?" he said, repeating the words the marshall spoke earlier.

They laughed together. It had been a long time since he had laughed. "When you leave Betty, can you deliver this to the marshall?"

"I will be happy to. I think he's over at the saloon."

"Again, I sure do thank you for the meal and the company."

Smiling, she said with conviction, " Ben, I'll see you soon."

27

SPENCE

From daylight to sundown, Spence and Joe watched over the ravine below from high on the ravine's ledge, giving them a view of the graves buried in the draw.

"Joe, if you don't mind me asking, how'd you end up here?"

"By foot," he replied.

"Didn't have a horse?"

"You know what I meant. Smart ass."

"I meant, why did you come here to this area of the country?"

"I knew what you meant. I was fresh out of the war and wanted to get as far away from trouble as I could. I understood the Indians and their ways, but we white men had different values. Most of it had to be on how to make a buck, no matter who it hurt."

"This here, where we are, was an outpost at the time. Nobody here but miners, trappers, buffalo skinners. Back east, my pa was a wainwright. He made and repaired wagons and taught me the trades of forging and blacksmithing."

"After the war, I made my living from that trade as I crossed the land to the west. I ended up here doing that and other odds and ends to scratch up a life for myself. As the town grew, I thought about leaving, but I had been writing to Sara and her husband, and they wanted to move west to open a general store and start a family. So that's why I'm here. Those little ones are what I have. Riches come in many ways besides paper or gold."

"What about you, Spencer? What are your plans? And what about Reg?"

"To start with, my name is just Spence, never took to Spencer, reminds me of an old spinster woman."

"Touchy there, young fella. I could call you worse names, you young pup."

"I'm sure you could, old timer. I probably wouldn't even know what you were calling me, using words I'd never heard before."

"Joe, I like this country. I'm glad we found our cows, and I'm looking forward to rounding them up and taking them home to Mom and Dad. Our family worked hard and built a hell of a nice place."

"After my dad was crippled, we were worried he wouldn't pull through. It would have been hard on Mom, but she would have continued. She's a tough little gal. I probably still have welts on my backside from when she took the strap to me."

"I'm not sure what Reg's plans are for the future. I don't know if he will stay in this country or travel back home. I know he's sweet on Chelsea, and we will all watch and see if it develops. He has never been a hound dog like me. We all knew there would only be one woman in his life. I like to try out the waters, and I always have my eyes looking over the next hill."

"You'll outgrow that someday. The right woman will twist you all up in knots, and you'll be head over hills. I can see it now . . . a whipped pup."

"We shall see, Old Joe."

Joe gave Spence that look, *don't push it. boy…*

"What do you think Pappy, can we puff the pipe, or do you think the smell will give us away?"

"We're a mile away up on this ledge, and the wind is blowing in our faces, so I think it will be okay."

"The law should be here soon. In the morning, Joe, why don't you ride for town and let Reg know what's going on here? I'll stay until you return with news. Maybe give it two days before you ride back? I'm sure your grandson misses you, and we will need more grub."

"Sounds good, but I don't like leaving you alone up here. You could get ambushed."

"Not hardly. When you pull out, I intend to move up to that rock ledge. See that crack in the wall? No one can sneak up on me there, and I'll have a bird's eye view of the valley. Just leave me some tobaccy when you pull out. It will keep me awake."

When the sun broke between the clouds the next morning, Joe left, and Spence moved back up to the rock ledge. Before posting themselves as lookouts, he had corralled his horse down the hill in a small box canyon with access to grass and water.

After Joe left, the lone cowboy took the time to build a corral fence on the hillside with old limbs and sage to keep her in. Spence had no concern about her running off. She was a pig for grass and would be content in the temporary home.

An hour or two passed, enough for the sun to begin warming the earth with its rays, when he heard two riders pop over the hill. They weren't scouting or traveling quietly but riding directly to the ravine.

Watching from his perch, he observed the duo ride to the high ground and dismount exactly where he and Reg had earlier located the bodies. Their conversation carried to the top of the hill plain as day. There was no mistaking their words.

They repeatedly reassured themselves that the spots where they buried the bodies looked perfectly fine. But they didn't spend much time scouting it out or digging in the dirt to know for certain.

Spence knew that he and his brother covered the bodies with a great deal of care and brushed over their tracks well. If these men were trackers, they might have seen signs of our previous presence, but being hired gunmen, they were not much for detective work. After a short time in the heat of the ravine, they rode over the hill back to the T Lazy 7.

As the trusted town lookout, he felt it necessary to wait several hours before returning to his horse, leveling the corral, and heading away from town.

On the odd chance a straggler saw him and took a notion to follow, he repeated Reg's tactic and rode for a couple of hours away from town before changing direction and heading back.

Joe met me at the livery. "Spence, you okay? I thought you were going to stay up on the ledge."

After filling him in on what he saw and heard, they both agreed that the town now held the upper hand in the card game.

"Let's find the brains of this outfit and update him on the new developments," said Joe.

"Sounds good, Joe. Any news from the marshall?"

"Yep, the lawman sent a wire to Reg. It seems he has a witness who dropped in to see him about the T Lazy 7 and the bodies. It's amazing how, at times, things come together like there was a plan. How could a witness just pop up out of nowhere?"

"The Almighty works in some pretty amazing ways. The marshall didn't say who it was but that he was bringing the man along. Things are falling together nice and easy like. I can see the noose getting tighter and tighter on Tucker's and Tate's necks," said Spence.

"The marshall should be here tomorrow. It looks like we're getting ready to start this party. Going to be a big event, I'm thinking."

"Joe, I bet Reg is at Maggie's. I don't know about you, old-timer, but I'm hungry, so let's go visit. I'm buying."

"Spence, you spend one night out away from town, and the first thing you want to do is go visiting."

"Yep, Joe, there might be a lonely gal I haven't met yet." He led the way, smiling from ear to ear.

Maggie was at the window of the café. "Reg. it looks like you have a couple of visitors."

He sat with Chelsea, enjoying a morning cup of stiff black

coffee. "What's he doing back in town? I don't see any blood, so his stay must have turned out okay."

I opened the door and leaned out. "What's the story, Spence?"

"That's a nice hello. I missed you, too, brother. How 'bout glad to see you're still in one piece. I was worried sick about your well-being."

"All right, little brother, glad you don't have any holes in ya. Sit down, and we'll get you fed. If that's okay with you? Then maybe you can fill us in if it's not too much trouble."

"Maybe when I eat, get some coffee and a piece of pie, but what I need first is a hug from that Chelsea girl."

"Spence, I thought you'd never ask. I don't know if I could have gone another minute without giving you a hug," Chelsea said with humor and a giggle. She leaned over and squeezed him tightly, giving me a wink at the same time.

She was a good hugger who made a guy feel special.

Spence couldn't fork in my first bite of food before I began to get itchy for answers. *I never had much patience for waiting.*

While Spence tried to chew his food, he dropped crumbs onto the plate and table. I continued to prod him along for every tiny detail, ignoring his need for food.

Nodding, Spence squeezed in a few words and said, "Joe here filled me in on the marshall and the mystery man with the information on the bodies and such."

I rubbed my chin between his forefinger and thumb, thinking for a minute.

Spence eventually finished the story and ate the remainder of a cold meal.

"So, now we wait."

28

BEN

"Ben, you ready to ride?" bellowed the marshall through the jail's front door. "We have a four-day trip. The weather looks good, so it shouldn't be a hardship."

"Marshall, I don't care if it rains, snows, or blows. I'm ready to ride and be out of this cell."

"Ben, am I going to have a problem with you trying to escape? If you give me your word, I'll keep the cuffs off ya."

"Marshall, I won't be a problem. I want to get this over with. There's only one thing. Can we stop for a minute so I can say goodbye to Betty?"

"I can do a little better than that. Betty is working in the café. Let's mosey on over, get some grub, and then head out. Remember, no cuffs, but Ben, if it comes to it, I will end our courtship. Understand?"

"Yes, sir, I got the message. I'll be a good boy."

Betty greeted the marshall and Ben as they grabbed a table close to a corner by the front window of the dining area. Betty gazed at the marshall and Ben with wide eyes, a smile, and a little giggle in her tone.

"Marshall, you letting the prisoner out for good behavior, or did you have to wrangle him in for his chow?"

"Not quite. He came of his own free will. I think he felt like he might run into a certain someone. We're getting a little breakfast, then we have some traveling to do."

"Are you taking Ben away to prison?" Betty grabbed her apron and started to wring the corner in her hand. Her face told the story. She was worried Ben would be leaving.

"No, as a matter of fact, he is helping me with an important case. Without him doing this good deed, I wouldn't have a case. If it plays out, it will make a world of difference in his outcome with the judge. Ben, you stay right where you are against the wall."

With a wink, the marshall said, "I'm going to sit over there." With his thumb, he motioned to a table across the room next to a pinewood sideboard that Maggie used for holding extra food for her parties. "I'll give you two a little privacy before we hit the trail. Both of you, what we are doing stays between us. I don't need anyone getting word, understood?"

"Got it, Marshall. I think Betty and I will have plenty to talk about anyway."

Ben sat against the wall facing the door and the window, looking over the street. *Nice listening to the conversations in the room, music to my ears, and the smell coming from the kitchen reminded me of home, a home long forgotten. The memories were filling his mind, like finding a long lost treasure.*

Before telling Betty his thoughts, he wanted to gather the right words to explain his past. He knew he wasted his life on cards, whiskey, loud saloons, and women who were not to be mentioned. *Amazing how much I took for granted and always thought I was free. I could travel when and where I wanted and do as I pleased.*

Now he realized that way of life wasn't freedom. Always on the lookout, tense, waiting on the bullet with his name on it had been no life. To enjoy the simple privileges was being able to sit, eat, and travel down the road free. He felt as if he had just been born or had been blind and now could see.

"Ben, what's the matter? You have tears running down your cheeks." Betty sat next to him and reached to hold his hand. "Is there bad news?"

"I'm better than okay. I know now what the preacher meant by being reborn. I'm alive and have only visited with you twice, but I know you are the one for me."

Feeling the burden lifting, he told her of the thoughts and memories that had just traveled through his mind, hoping she would understand when he explained them.

"I'm going with the marshall to take care of some wicked men. When I return, I'll pray for a miracle, do what time I need to, and hope we can be together."

"Well, now that's a mouthful. Let's get you fed. Then we can talk. I don't want you dying of starvation now that I know you will be back for me. I'm quite smitten with you too, Ben," she said, turning to go to the kitchen, trying to hide her tears.

Standing up to stretch and remove the tenseness in his muscles, he pulled Betty into a tight embrace, smelling her jasmine perfume. "I am experiencing feelings I have never felt before."

Betty returned the embrace and gave him a peck on the cheek.

Backing away, she said quietly away from curious ears, "I didn't think a hardened criminal could blush or be so soft. I see there's hope for you yet."

The room was so quiet we could hear a pin drop, and every eye in the place was looking at us. People smiled, giggled, a few sneered, and whispered under their breath. Ben fell onto his behind, glad the chair was there to catch him.

Betty whisked off to the kitchen, taking a moment to glance back over her shoulder. Ben didn't care what people thought of him, but he did care what they thought of her. He deserved the scrutiny and ill will. She did not. He vowed at that moment to do whatever was needed to make her proud and turn the thoughts of those doubters around.

The marshall and Ben had been on the trail for several hours before the lawman spoke. "I can see a different man in front of me now and truly say you are changing from what you have told me of your past."

"I have changed. Marshall, I'm glad we're on our way. I want to get back and put this behind me. I need to tell you all about what we're facing. If anything happens to me before I can tell the truth to the folks of Two Forks, you will have all the information you need to handle Tucker and his men and hopefully put them away."

"Now that you mention it. I sent wires across four states to see if there was any information regarding Tucker. By the way, your picture was a great help. It gave a clear view of what he looked like."

"Glad to help."

"You did more than that, son. I think we have a repeat killer there. There's more to this story than you know. Ben, it looks as though killing and robbing seem to be his handy work wherever he goes. Tucker was robbing banks and killing anyone who stepped in his way. He was able to steal a pretty good sum of money before he left the East. That's probably how he financed outfitting a ranch. Tucker would kill and take over ranches and cattle but still need money to build it up."

"Looks like we're going to have a fight on our hands. Do you have any more deputies coming?" asked Ben.

"I know this Tucker, Tate, and their outlaw companions won't go easy, especially with their deadly pasts. I've sent a wire to the man named Reg, and he'll meet us in town with members of the town. We will see what we're up against, and then I'll make a plan of attack.

"I reckon Reg will insist on being involved. He has made friends who will stand with him in town, and he dislikes Tate and Tucker. When the townspeople find out Tucker killed Maggie's husband and took over their ranch, I will bet there will be a crowd with ropes. Marshall, I'm hoping Reg's horse shows up. I want to see her in action."

"You mentioned a horse before. What's the story there?"

As he filled in all the details, Ben chuckled and enjoyed telling the tale about how Roan kicked Tucker's hired man across the street, sending him rolling.

"That's a hell of a story. I've known horses to kick, buck, and even protect a person from coyotes, wolves, or bears, but never to kick a man to defend its owner, especially with no rider aboard. Can't imagine it. In the middle of the street. I need to pin a star on that horse and deputize her. I could use good help."

. . .

The two men eventually rode into Two Forks with townsfolk watching and pointing their way, questioning their presence with curious gazes. It was just the way people were, always curious about who or what was coming into their town, wanting to be the first to carry a story.

The outlaw felt awkward and self-conscious, with so many eyes staring at him. *Hope they don't figure out my deal with the law, or things might get dicey.*

Not sure who might have hard feelings along the way and not want a revenge killer popping a shot in his direction, Ben played it safe and rode close by the marshall's side.

"Ben, I don't want you jack-rabbitting and running for the hills. Don't make me tell you twice."

"Don't worry. I'm not going anywhere. I might

want to ride double with you so nobody gets an itchy trigger finger."

"Laughing, the lawman said, "I think you are good, Ben, just don't do anything stupid."

"Ya, right. Nothing stupid like riding into a town where I am probably hated," Ben said with a hint of sarcasm.

Dismounting and standing on the elevated wooden walkway, the men resembled two lost puppies, only not as lovable. As luck would have it, Maggie happened to be escorting a patron out from the café and nearly collided with the trail-worn, weary men.

Recognizing Ben and not one to hold her tongue and her thoughts, she said, "Marshall, did you know this man rides with Tucker, the man we're going after? I hope you have enough sense to hold him as your prisoner."

"Ma'am, I'm Marshall Yates. This man's riding with me. I'm looking for Reg Carter. Is he around?"

"Behind you."

29

REG

Hay remained stuck to my hair from feeding the stock earlier. I walked from the stable with Spence and Joe by my side. Spence carried his rifle while Joe huffed along, puffing on his pipe and carrying his double-barrel shotgun over his shoulder. Both wore their sidearms for good measure.

"Marshall, I'm Reg Carter. I'm the one who sent the wire, and this mangy character beside me is my brother, Spence. Right there is the livery owner, Joe."

"Gentlemen, it's a pleasure. We've had a long journey. Missus, could we step inside for coffee and grub? This gentleman beside me is Ben Carson, and he has been a big help in this matter regarding the man you're concerned about," said the marshall.

"Yes, he did ride with Tucker, ma'am, but he's turned over a new leaf and has given me a great deal of helpful information. He's my prisoner, is not to be harmed, and will be treated with respect as my 'criminal deputy.'"

Not willing to put my trust in any situation or statement yet, I held my rifle casually in front of me, always at the ready. "Marshall, we understand, but we're going to keep an eye on this one anyway."

Ben spoke to the people gathered around him, "Perfectly understandable. I'm here to help and hold no ill will toward your feelings. I've given the marshall information, which you might find helpful. It's true, I'm a gunslinger, or should I say, ex-gunslinger. I am here to help because now, when I'm finished with my sentence, whatever that will be, I aim to earn my fair share of respect to make right for all my wrongdoings and be able to live in this or another community."

"I'd like to call someplace home and give the people there the respect they have earned. I hope to gain their trust and respect as well. I knew the details about the killings, but I had no hand in them. I came to Two Forks after that action took place. I'm sure the marshall will verify this with the evidence I provided."

Maggie looked at the men and offered an inviting gesture for all to enter the café. "Gentlemen, please come in. Let's go to the back room where we can talk freely." The marshall and Ben sat with their backs to the wall. Spence and I sat at the end of the table facing them but never took our eyes away from Ben. Maggie remained seated in the middle next to Joe.

"Chelsea, will you bring these men coffee and take their orders? After they eat, we will settle in for this meeting."

Chelsea pulled Maggie aside and whispered, "After I get them served up, I will run over to bring Ma back. She will want to be involved."

"Young lady, does this woman, your ma, have a family member who has been killed or has land or cattle stolen?" asked the marshall.

Chelsea hadn't intended for anyone to overhear her whisper to Maggie, but since this man had, she politely answered, "Yes sir, she's my mother, Nancy, and Tucker's men killed my father, Clancy. I know the townspeople also would like to know you are here and to be involved."

"I'm sure your concern has merit, but at this time, I would like to keep this matter solely with the individuals in the room, including your mother. We will have time to address the public once I dig up more vital information." His voice was kind but stern and to the point.

"Yes, sir," she said, her face reddened in embarrassment. "I understand. I think I was getting ahead of myself. I'm sorry."

"No, lass, your intentions were good, but let's see where this meeting leads us."

"Gentlemen, if you would excuse me, I'll get your food, find Ma, and return. I'll keep this meeting a secret."

Maggie motioned the girl over. "Thank you for understanding. And please serve our guests whatever they request."

Chelsea hustled in and out of the kitchen carrying overloaded trays of coffee, eggs, bacon, potatoes, and bread with honey. Her guests ate eagerly, enough to feed a small army.

From the window of the general store, Nancy had watched the lawman and his companion ride into town. She longed for Clancy each day, hour, and minute in her heart, craving one last hug, kiss, and smile from her beloved Clancy. Now, all she held in her heart were the memories and a desire for revenge.

Chelsea burst through the open door and grabbed her mother, beginning to blurt out the details of the conversations happening back at the café as fast as a coyote chasing a rabbit.

After Chelsea and her Ma were seated at the café, Nancy waited patiently while the men ate, but Chelsea remained a bundle of nerves, tapping her boots and wringing her hands. Nancy sighed and waved her hand to the girl to clear the table to keep her busy.

The marshall sat back in his chair, knowing he spoke for all when he thanked the ladies as they all appreciated the wonderful meal.

"Ladies and gentlemen, I would like each of you to tell me your story, and as we continue, we will also hear from Ben Baxter. I know you're concerned about him being a part of the Tucker bunch, but I'm sure you'll change your view of this man when you hear what he has to say."

Maggie started with information about her husband and their ranch.

Nancy spoke about her husband, Clancy, and the meeting place at Two Forks, and Chelsea told about his dreams and the type of man he was.

Spence and I gave detailed information about their father, the stolen cattle, Clancy, and the buried bodies.

Joe sat silently alongside Maggie and listened to all the heart wrenching stories.

Ben rose from his chair as the time came for him to speak his piece. Red veins crossed the white of his eyes like blood trails in the snow, and dark circles had grown beneath them, lending credence to his lack of sleep and the obvious burden he carried. His body looked as though the whole world was resting on his shoulders.

The truth in his statement would be hard for loved ones to hear, but his rare position made it possible to bring peace and justice to them. He paced the floor as he spoke, pausing to gather his emotions and gesturing to emphasize specific points in the story.

Everyone in the room was astonished that this man willingly gave the information he did. He voluntarily provided facts that would send him to prison or swing on the scaffold. Each person hearing this story remained deep in their thoughts. If indeed silence could be deafening, this was one of those times.

"Folks, thank you for listening to my words. I don't ask for forgiveness. I do not deserve it. I want to change my life. Whatever happens, whatever decision is made, I'm willing to take what punishment is due."

I spoke up first. "Ben, it takes a big man, a good man, to walk into a jail and offer the information you have. It's not like you had been caught and were spilling your guts in hopes of gaining favor. You did it of your own free will. I can't talk for others in this room, but I can say I'm impressed, and I'll stand beside you, but I will be watchful of your actions."

Hmm, I will be curious to hear what the others do. I Imagine I'm more willing to forgive as our loss was not the loss of life. Close, Damn close.

Maggie and Nancy stood up while Joe remained seated. Maggie went directly to the point as she spoke to Ben.

"Ben, by what you have told us here today, I do believe that you didn't have a hand in killing our husbands or friends, but you took part in the deceit of the whole ordeal. I can't talk for Nancy. I'm not sure I could forgive you, but I appreciate your coming forward and will try. Maybe when these men have been brought to justice or lay face down in the dirt. I'll be able to look you in the eye."

"That is all I could ever hope for, ma'am."

Nancy approached Ben and took his hand. "Thank you, Ben. The truth hurts, but it will help Chelsea and me heal . . . in time."

Nancy and Spence stuck out their hands, and Ben shook them. He nodded with pride, and a shimmer of moisture shone in his eyes.

Our words seemed to have touched him. Having heard what he needed and indicating that the meeting was at a close, the marshall gathered his paperwork and stuffed it in his satchel.

"I have all the information I need and will head to the T Lazy 7 Ranch tomorrow morning to visit Mr. Tucker. I am duty-bound to get a feel for the man. No one else is to do anything at this time. IS THAT UNDERSTOOD?"

"As hard as it may be to wait for answers, please go on with your day-to-day lives, acting as if nothing has changed. I promise I will have the answers, but this matter will be managed to my satisfaction and the letter of the law," he said with a clarity that no man would misunderstand.

I moved forward to interrupt the marshall. "I think you are riding headlong into a hornet's nest. Why don't you let Spence and me tag along?"

"I appreciate your concern, but your involvement will look suspicious and beg for a fight that way. That's exactly like hitting the hornet's nest with a stick with you two along." The room filled with laughter, breaking the built-up tension.

"I've been doing this a long time, and I've faced many a bandito, outlaw, Indian, and wild animals. I will do this my way, and this matter shall be handled by me and me alone. There may be a time when I may need assistance, and I will request it at that time, but it will not be tomorrow."

As the marshall and Ben left the room, we returned to our seats. Nancy sat hand in hand with Chelsea. Tears filled their eyes.

"I want to thank you all for the support you have given me and my children. You welcomed us into your town and watched over us. Reg and Spence, I don't have enough words to thank you. I want to get to the bottom of this and start our lives over. I'll always love my husband, Clancy, and I'll miss him so much, but you young men risk getting hurt or killed will only make things worse."

Still holding onto Chelsea's hand and squeezing it tightly, Nancy said, "Chelsea, I want you to have a full life, and I would love grand-kids. I hope there is romance and love in your life here, but the blessing you would typically have from Pa will now be my decision, and unless there is a period of courting and proper dating in the future, I will be hard pressed to grant it."

The three young adults stopped in their tracks, stunned at Nancy's words, wondering how that grit and spunk suddenly appeared.

Spence giggled. "Reg. I wouldn't be too concerned about Tucker. I'd keep an eye on Mama Bear over there."

I leaned over and gave Chelsea a peck on the check. "I will court you, Chelsea, but your mama's right. We might want to take a bit of time to learn about each other. I need to see if you fit my standards."

Spence nearly choked as he laughed. "You bet Mr. Romance, you, and your standards."

I shook my head. "All I can say is, if I have my way, I will want it to be a short courting process. Maggie, you know how to make a wedding cake?"

"I do, and I look forward to it with Mama Bear's permission."

Spence nudged me as we walked out the door. "You may want to visit Roan and let her know there's another woman in your life and see if she thinks Chelsea meets your standards."

My young brother laughed so hard that he almost tripped over his own two feet.

30

SPENCE

With the knowledge they gained at the meetings, Maggie, Chelsea, and Nancy began making lists of the supplies and tasks to be performed should problems arise in the near future. Busying themselves without alerting others and preparing the town women to be ready for the trouble required fancy footwork and creative reasons for doing so, but subterfuge won out. The idea of an upcoming street festival worked as their reason.

Chelsea and Caty performed bad weather drills and developed games that would help keep the children close to town. The general store's cellar became a new clubhouse, thrilled the children, and helped keep them occupied.

As the sun cracked open the horizon, bidding good

day to the moon, the marshall eased out of town alone, just as he promised.

Itching to mount up and ride to clear my mind, I determined today would be a good day to do just that.

When riding through the countryside, I always felt a sense of peace and used the time for reflection . . . enjoying the smell of sage, tall sweet grass, and the scent of the horse's sweat after a long ride was like a child enjoying a taste of candy.

Feeling rather unsure and edgy, Spence felt obliged to ask, "Reg, what do you think? Should we leave the marshall to do this alone, or should we follow to make sure he's okay?"

Joe spoke up from one of the stalls toward the back of the barn, "Spence, the marshall knows what he's doing and wants to get facts and information for his case. If you travel out there, you will surely stir the pot, and who knows where it will lead."

Spence just stared at the old goat while opening his mouth to argue the point. "I'm sure he can't handle all those fellas alone if a fight breaks out."

"I don't think there will be a fight, not yet anyway. Let the man do his job. He looks like one who can carry the load. When he asks for help, that's when we throw our hats into the ring."

"Okay, I'll wait as you command, old wise one."

Reg nodded in agreement. "I asked him to come to Two Forks and handle it by the rule of law. So that's how it is going to be. I'm going to saddle Roan and go out for a ride."

"Well, how exactly is that staying out of it, brother?"

"Don't worry, baby brother. I'm riding the other way. Looking at the scenery, spending some time thinking." I saddled up, packed my sidearm and long rifle, and headed in the opposite direction.

"Joe, how about you and I go out for a smoke? I'm feeling all hemmed in," said Spence loud enough for any little pitchers with big ears to hear and who might feel the need to tell their mamas where the men were.

The old man had been silently listening to the conversation, but Spence knew he was making plans. The silent ones are always the ones to watch.

"Best idea I've heard all morning."

Spence and Joe waited about ten minutes and partook in a smoke. Through the cloud of smoke, they walked back into the barn, saddled the horses, and followed in the direction Reg traveled. After riding several miles, they heard gunfire.

Joe asked, "You think he found trouble?"

"I don't think so. Shots are too even. It's his way of letting off steam, but to be sure, let's ride." They took off in a gallop and pulled up as they reached the top of the hill.

There stood the lone figure of his brother in the middle of an open field, shooting at old logs. As the two riders sat on the hill watching, Joe leaned in close so Spence could hear. "He's one hell of a shot. I'm glad he's on our side."

"Yes, siree, he can shoot alright and is deadly accurate."

After riding down the slope and dismounting, Spence said, "I see you're out killing trees. You feelin' better now?"

"Thought I'd make some kindling, winter's moving in."

Joe looked at me. "Don't use all your lead. You may need some."

"Not to worry. I'm toting plenty. If not, I'll take Spence's. He can't shoot."

With those words and the need to show off, Spence pulled his sidearm and made his own kindling.

Not to be left out of the word jousting, the aging town gent pulled his pipe tobacco and box of lucifers from his red plaid shirt. "I'm feeling safer by the minute. All I need now is my old shotgun. You boys just run 'em to me."

"Holy cow, you two stay downwind from me. I'd rather clean the stable than smell that mess you call tobacco."

"Give it a pull, Reg." When Chelsea gets you tied down, your chance will be gone."

"I think I'll survive without knowing the pleasure of smoking a bloated pole cat."

"Boys, thanks for the nice day, but some of us have to get work done. We can't just go plinking ammo and drinking coffee by the fire," said Joe.

"How about I give you a hand? I need to sweat a little. I'm gonna get too fat to ride or work the ranch when I go home," offered Spence.

"Any help would be appreciated."

"Reg, you going to go visit your gal?"

"I think I might, and then I'm going to send Mom and Dad a wire and let them know we're still kickin'."

"Tell Mom I'm keeping you safe and out of trouble."

"I'm sure she'll believe that."

The same gentleman who helped me on my previous visit greeted me inside the wire office, still sitting behind his tidy little desk. He peeked up from under the visored cap he wore. Apparently, it was part of his official attire.

"Hello again, young man. How can I help you today?"

"I need to send a wire home. If you could help me with that, I would be most grateful."

I wrote what I wanted to send, and the telegraph man proceeded to tap away on the telegraph. Figuring out what all the mysterious clanking and tapping meant was obviously a special talent, and he seemed sure someone on the other end would understand it.

I wrote... *Mom and Dad both doing fine. Stop. I found the cattle. Stop. The marshall came in. We'll see how he wants to proceed. Stop. I'm keeping my word. Walking soft. Stop.*

31

REG

When we rode back into town, we saw the marshall's horses standing, munching oats in their stalls. Apparently, he arrived long before we did.

"I guess his ride went well. I don't see any blood."

After visiting with the wireman, I chuckled at how I felt obliged to make sure my riding buddies weren't slackin'. I shifted my direction to the barn and found them covered in dirt, horse manure, and straw. They smelled like they belonged in the manure pile. To my surprise, they added a third helper, Ben, who was also as dirty as the other two.

"I see you all been taking it easy while I was gone," I said.

"You betcha," Ben shot back a quick response. "That's about right. And look who shows up when all the work is done."

"All great minds have a plan. Timing is everything. Didn't want to smell like you three."

Spence relaxed for a minute and arched his back. "Getting too old for this labor stuff."

"The marshall and Ben had stopped by. Ben pitched in to help. He was getting the jitters from sittin' around."

Chuckling, Ben tossed a shovel of manure over my way. "Marshall Yates wants to meet us at Maggie's at eight o'clock after the diners have pulled out. I told him we would be there."

I nodded my agreement. "Sounds good, I'm ready to round up our cows and move them back home."

As I turned to take my leave, I was hit in the back by a road apple. Without breaking my stride, I moved slightly to my right to be sure my brother heard my words and said, "Remember about paybacks, Spence."

Spence started to laugh and pointed at Joe. "He was the thrower."

Joe stared at Spence. "Bring it on pup, bring it on," he said, wiping his dirty hands on his even dirtier bib overalls.

Entering the corral, I tried to put a lasso rope around Roan's neck. She wanted no part of that idea, pulled her head away, turned her ass towards me, and I quickly backed away. She made her point loud and clear.

"I got the point, no rope. Well, follow me then. We're going to find some kids." After locating Chelsea, Nancy, Sara, and the kids at the market, I asked, "Anyone want to go for a ride?"

Caty grabbed Callie, Dan, and Little Joe, and they all ran out the door in a flash.

Using her wise horse sense, Roan understood the kids' excitement, stood patiently next to the boardwalk, and waited for them to mount up.

Caty hoisted Callie aboard, and the boys jumped on behind her.

Then I watched in horror as Caty walked up to the mare with my small piece of rope in her hand. Before I could stop her, she reached up with the rope, and Roan lowered her head to allow the gentle cowgirl to place the loop around her neck.

I rubbed Roan's nose and ears. "Pretty fickle there, aren't you? Just like a woman, you have to do it your way."

"What exactly is that supposed to mean, mister? Chelsea had snuck up behind me.

"I was just saying how sweet and gentle this beautiful horse is."

"That's not what I heard." Chelsea stood behind me, put her arms around my neck, and gave me a hug. I worried she was going to choke the life out of me.

Caty gently tugged the rope, and the roan shadowed her down the road with kids squealing.

Chelsea dashed away and returned with a bucket of apples. When the group returned from their travels down the lane, she divided the apples between the kids, and one by one, they treated their four-legged friend to a reward. The horse was as happy and content as the kids.

Chelsea sat down next to me on the boardwalk. "I'm concerned about what's going to happen with Tucker and that man, Tate. I don't want to see you or anyone else hurt. I want to do what's right, but we have the gold from my pa. We can buy what we need and live a good life."

"I understand, Chels. My dad worked hard for what he has. What if that was us? Would you want some low life snake stealing from us?"

"No, I know you're right. I just don't want you to get hurt or killed."

"We will all be okay. Let's see what the marshall says tonight and what action we're all going to take, but it's high time to finish this."

"I understand. The marshall returned, and he was unharmed. We're all meeting him tonight to get some answers. Ma and I had a good conversation about you. When this is all finished, we must talk about the gold and the gold mine," Chelsea said.

"That's up to you and your ma. I was just the messenger. I have no claim. . . "

She interrupted his intended speech, "I know my Pa gave you a split. He was always fair with the people he dealt with. He would have never just asked someone to take on this task and to do this amazing, good deed, free gratis."

"You have a claim. You better court me quick before I change my mind, and you're penniless."

"Hold on, little lady, whoever said I was penniless? I think you may have a little surprise in store."

32

PINKIE

Poke voiced his thoughts, "Buck, I can tell ya, I think the lid is about ready to boil off the pot. Tucker rounded up all the hired gunslingers to the main house. They have been in and out packing supplies from the storage barn for the last several days."

"I rode up to the main house this morning and wasn't greeted with smiles. They all have their guns tied on as usual, but I could see through the open door that rifles were propped up next to the door, with more lying on the floor across the room."

"They didn't even offer you coffee? How rude," said Buck, laughing at his own sense of humor. "Like you wanted to stay and mingle anyway. They ain't nothing but a bunch of roaches."

Buck pushed his boot heel into the floor. "And they're about to get squashed like the bugs they are."

"You got that right, Buck. I didn't plan on socializing, but they probably make better coffee than you do."

"No doubt 'bout that. My coffee is made for effect, not taste."

Tom sat his horse quietly, listening to the banter between the other two, and measured his words carefully before he spoke to his companions.

"One thing I can tell you. Those two brothers are not going to give up. They're in this card game until the end. Tucker can't run them off like he did the others."

Poke nodded his agreement. "Do you think they can gunfight? It takes a lot to pull iron and mean it to be able to fight."

"I've seen tough men walk away from gunplay. You see, those two are fighting for what's theirs and fighting for the people they care about."

"Spence is a lover of life. He wants to taste the fruits of the world. The kid plays hard and loves attention, but he cares for his brother the most. He'll walk down to Hell's gate to protect him."

"Now, Reg, on the other hand, is slower to act, a thinker, a studier of men. I've seen his type many times. When he goes into action, it will be well thought out and won't end till it's over. I don't think he's looking to put anyone in irons. He wants to stop them with lead, dead in their tracks."

Tom's observations made sense; the others always respected his wisdom.

"Boys, let's ride to the house and see what's up," suggested Buck.

"I like the sound of that, Boss,"

Buck talked slow and low as they rode. "Let's talk friendly and casual about cows and whiskey and pretty girls. Keep all the rest quiet."

They reached the main house and were met by the worst of the worst killers. These men had no feelings and no regret about killing. To them, it was like breathing, giving no thought to the act.

One of the men shouted to Buck, "Cowboys, you heading out to babysit your cows?

Buck looked away and told the jokester that his animals were all content, eating the tall grass and enjoying the sunny day. "I think we're doing a mighty good job keeping them fat and happy."

"How about you boys? Ya'll think you might leave the rocking chairs today and do a little honest work?"

Poke glanced sideways at Tom and whispered, "So much for going easy." These men didn't like people, especially the ones who called them lazy, even though it was true.

Tucker walked onto the porch. "Back down, men. They're just poking a little fun. I want you three to stay around the place for a while. Work on the barns and corrals. I may need you close by."

"If that's what you want, Boss. We aimed to check the upper fields in the mountains for two, three days to see how the cows were holding up."

I said, "You'll stay here. Get to work and be close by."

"All right, Boss, we'll get at it."

Tate walked out of the house as the cowhands rode off. "You know, Mr. Tucker, when it comes to a fight, those three will be useless and in our way."

"I know it, Tate. We can use them as pawns in this game. If a game comes up, you know pawns are the first to be taken out."

When we three rode away, Poke asked Buck, "We aren't going to check cows. What's up?"

"I got the answer I needed. They're getting ready for something. If they weren't, they wouldn't care what we did."

It was a warm day, and Buck's men were working on fences, lopsided barn doors, and hunting up odd chores to keep busy. There was always something to mend on a ranch, but Buck ran a tight ship, and the ranch and grounds of the homestead were already in good shape.

This foreman knew how to operate and maintain a ranch. For that matter, there was no slacking in Tom, or Poke either. They worked together like the well-oiled parts of a machine and labored hard with their blood, sweat, and good humor.

"You two," Tom yelled, "Look up there on the hill. There is a saddle horse with no rider working its way down the slope and heading to the ranch."

No rider?

The horse picked up its pace and started to trot to the barn. He entered the barnyard corral and drank thirstily from the water trough. The horse carried no clues about what happened to the rider, no note for help, no blood, just an empty saddle.

Surprised at the rare sight, the hands approached the horse. As the men inspected the horse, Ben pointed and spoke, "See there, up the hillside? There is a man following the trail left by the horse."

He was far off, his gait slow, and he appeared to be in no hurry. Poke asked. "Buck, does the rider look familiar?"

"Nope."

There was a lot one could learn about someone if a body paid attention and watched. Learning to study people, how they walked, talked, moved in a crowd, or sat on horseback was an art.

Buck instructed his men to keep their eyes on the rider, making no attempt to let him know they knew he was there. Several long minutes passed before the stranger entered the ranch yard. Then, he walked directly up to Poke and started to speak.

"I'm Marshall Yates. Who's in charge here?"

"Not me, I'm the one who gets the bad end of the cow. The ramrod is Buck. He's the one fixing that door hanging on its hinge. My name's Poke."

The man representing the arm of the law began to cross the yard to Buck, with Poke following close on his tail.

Tom came out of the back corral, leading the lawman's horse but not yet seen by the lawman. All four now stood at the barn.

Buck slanted his eyes to the right and glimpsed Tucker and his men, watching the foursome from the porch. They seemed to talk among themselves, trying to figure out who this lone man was.

"Buck, I'm Marshall Yates. Looks like you found my horse."

"It's more like he found us.

"Hello. Pinky," said Tom as he rounded the barn with the horse in tow.

"Well, as I live and breathe. Hello, Tom. Pleasant surprise seeing you here. Glad to see you're still alive and doing what looks to be honest work," said Marshall Yates.

"You, too, Pinkie, been a while. I thought you might have got tangled up with some bad hombres, and your bones were bleaching out in the sun somewhere."

"Nah, still upright on this side of the dirt."

"So, you two know each other?" Buck asked.

"You bet. Pinkie and I go way back. We both raised a little hell in our day, that's for sure. Tom, we sure did have a time, didn't we?"

"What's the story about the horse, Marshall?"

"Buck, I'll get to that. I see men watching us from over yonder on the porch. Is Tucker the fellow out front?"

"That would be him. The others are major trouble."

"Pinkie, you hunting here?"

"Tom, no, just setting traps."

Tom eyeballed Pinkie. "Pinkie or I guess, for now, I better call you Marshall. Marshall, Poke, and Buck are good, honest men. I think we know why you're here. You can count on us to stand by you if you have the need. Those on the porch are nothin' but trouble."

"Thanks. Tom. You other two men, let's keep my friendship with Tom under our hats."

All three nodded. "Will do, Marshall."

Tucker and two of his men marched straight to the barn from the main house. "What's going on here?"

Pinkie turned to watch the men's reaction to him.

Tucker and his men saw the star on the marshall's vest. They tensed, and their expressions showed caution, yet their darting eyes still showed their suspicion.

"Good morning, gentlemen. I was just thanking your men here for holding onto my stray horse."

Working the reins through his hands, he rubbed his horse's nose and asked, "You must be the ranch owner?" Marshall Yates stuck his hand out to greet Tucker. "I'm Marshall Yates."

"I'm Mr. Tucker." They shook hands and took a moment to size one another up, similar to fighters entering the ring.

"Pleasure meeting you. How about you other two? Got names?"

Neither answered. "We'll be on the porch, Mr. Tucker, if you need us."

Tucker looked at the marshall. "Apologies. You know, hired men sometimes forget to use their manners."

"Quite alright, Mr. Tucker. I've learned that men usually throw out a name to let everyone know who they are, either out of kindness, to intimidate others, or to see what they may know about them."

"They may not speak words, but their facial expressions could say a lot. Maybe they don't think it's warranted at the time, or they don't want to be known. Takes a minute to figure out what's what. I figure those two are trying to stay out of the limelight, but that's a matter for another time."

Tucker and the marshall delivered stern looks one to the other, both realizing the marshall made his point. Tucker forced his smile, one of dislike, not one of pleasure.

"Marshall, as you should understand, we're busy. What can I help you with?"

"Nothing today, Mr. Tucker. I'm just glad this runaway stopped. I wasn't looking forward to tracking him across the countryside."

As he remounted, he looked at Tucker and said, "I'm sure my prisoner would be a lot happier riding and not walking."

Buck spoke up. "Prisoner, Marshall? You caught you an honest-to-goodness bad man, did ya?"

"Hear tell, he was an ornery cuss once, but I think he's seen the error of his ways and now wants to make amends. You may have known him, Mr. Tucker. Name is Ben Carson. He was from around these parts."

Tucker looked like someone bashed him in the head with a rock. He was so dumbfounded.

Before Tucker could react, the Marshall backed his mount away and said, "Thanks again, gentlemen. Until we meet again."

The barnyard crew knew for sure what had happened. *Tucker had been called out.*

Buck shook his head and reminded his cowhands, "Let's get back to it. Like the boss said, we have a lot to do."

Tucker didn't move, didn't say a word. It was apparent to him that he was scared for the first time in a long time. He stole the cattle and killed them to build this ranch and the pleasures it provided. Now accustomed to being known as a man of means and comforts, the idea of losing that easy life wasn't acceptable.

The men returned to their chores, and Tucker finally returned to his senses. He felt as if he had fallen asleep standing up and now raised his voice loud enough to bring down the barn, "Tate, get the men."

Once out of Tucker's hearing range. Buck told Tom, "Your buddy, the marshall, just called out Tucker."

"Shore looks that way," said Tom. "Buck and Poke, we need to take a position. Pinkie is a good man, but he will not tolerate anyone who stands against the law, including me! When we were younger, he found being a lawman his calling."

"I wasn't an outlaw, but not the best of men. Just walked a thin, crooked line. He arrested me once and made it plain. Walk a straight line, or the outcome will be different the next time. He gave me a fine and escorted me out of town. That was the last time we were in each other's company. I headed west and left the past behind me. From then on, I rode a straight line."

33

DEPUTIES

It felt like I spent a good portion of my days in the barn, but taking a lazy walk there became routine. I knew friendship and a nuzzle from Roan would always greet me there.

My three buddies took turns taking a shower from an old bucket full of holes hanging in the barn that the men hurried to re-fill as it emptied. It didn't take long to clean up. The water was cold as ice, and we didn't spend much time soakin'. After we shaved, slicked our hair back, and put on clean clothes, we looked close to decent.

We cooked elk steaks over an open fire. Joe had saved the thick-cut steaks in the ice shed for just a night such as this. Time dragged by, and finally, we headed to Maggie's. The same group from our first meeting gathered again with the one addition of Preacher Bill.

Spence shook the marshall's hand. "Glad to see you're still in one piece, Marshall."

Reaching his hand toward Preacher Bill, he said, "I'm Spence. I'm the good brother." Spence failed to hide the mischievous grin.

"I'm glad, Preacher Bill, that you're a man of the cloth. You would be a darn scary bad man. Not that you're not intimidating as a good man."

Preacher Bill laughed at that and put his hand around the back of Spence's neck. "Yep, good and evil, now that's one fine line." He gave Spence's neck a little squeeze. Preacher Bill enjoyed seeing his prey squirm.

Spence backed away a couple of steps, nodded, and rubbed the back of his neck. "Thanks, Preacher, you fixed the aching kink in my neck."

I leaned over to the marshall and quietly asked, "How'd that look-see go?"

"I visited with the cowhands on the T Lazy 7 Ranch, and one of those fellas was an old friend named Tom. We grew up together, spending a lot of time trying to keep out of trouble. Some days didn't work out so well, but we had a good time."

"Tom is a good sort, same as Buck and Poke. I think we can trust those three to be of help," said Spence, adding his two bits to the conversation.

"I agree. I can't say for certain about the other two, but Tom is solid, and he will stand his ground. I'm sure if Tom is friends with the other two, they're good men."

"I also talked with Tucker and Tate. There were also four others there besides those two. You were right, they're gunmen, and they're preparing to battle. I could see their weapons were clean, and their temperament was on the edgy side."

"I put out a little trapping scent. I had a second horse with me. I let her run wild and pointed her toward the T Lazy 7 Ranch on the other side of the hill. Knew she'd run to the other horses, and I tracked her to the barn, where I met Buck, Tom, and Poke."

"After we talked for a minute, Tucker, Tate, and their cohorts came out to see what was what. We didn't let them in on the fact that Tom and I were friends."

"After a spell, I gave an adios and told them I needed to return to the prisoner who rode this mount. I explained that she had spooked when we stretched our legs and were watering some lilies. I asked Tucker if he knew the outlaw holed up in the area. When I told him the name, he turned silent and tried to act as if he didn't know who Ben Baxter was, but his face and body told a different story. I said my goodbyes and headed back."

"Marshall, now you poked the bear."

"You're right, young man. Now, we will see if he runs or wants to tangle. Fellas, I don't think he has any plans on moving from that fortress he has. I could try to bring more deputies here, but I think it would take too long for them to arrive, even with the fastest horses. If you men are willing, I'll deputize you, but we handle it my way."

Three men agreed, but Preacher Bill said, "I'm good, Marshall. I've been hired by a higher power. He will guide my hand."

Ben asked, "What about me, Marshall?"

"Ben, you're still an outlaw, but I feel you can be trusted. If you ride with us, I know it will go a long way with the judge, but if we see any notion of you turning your back on us, I'll drop you myself."

"Wouldn't expect anything less, sir. I'm in, if'n you'll have me. You others have a say in this. What do you say?"

"He's in," said Spence. "Reg, what do you think?"

"I trust these two, but you, Ben, I still don't know. I have been impressed by your actions so far, but I'm a little concerned about what may happen to your good intentions when you come face to face with the devil. I'm not scared of rattlers, but I'm damn sure not going to turn my back on one. So, you're in, but I wouldn't make any fast moves if I were you."

"Thanks, fellas, I'll carry the load. I won't give anyone a reason to doubt me. I want you to trust my word."

The marshall looked at Preacher Bill. "So, you're not tagging along?"

"No, I know my place; it's here. I'll keep an eye on the home front, watch the front door, and God will keep an eye on the rest."

"This meeting is over then. I'll deputize you, men, in the morning. Be ready to meet at first light. We're riding out to look for those bodies. I need the proof you say is there, then I'll meet Tucker, or he'll meet us. One way or another, tomorrow will give me the answers."

It was a sleepless night. I trekked up the worn wooden stairs to my room, organized, and cleaned my guns.

Spence still bunked in the barn. He enjoyed its peacefulness, listening to the animals chomping on grass, the barn creaking in the breeze, and the cool air moving through the loft.

He also loved the opportunity to visit and tell his stories to anyone willing to listen. They were all true, with a lot of color and spice added. Unfortunately for those around, he also enjoyed the chance to smoke.

I tossed and turned all night with thoughts about the folks back home and the cattle in the field. I missed Mom's smile and her sense of humor. Dad was a worker with not much use for lollygagging around. When it came to humor, what would be a knee jerker to anyone else, to Dad, it was a horse of a different color. His idea of a good laugh was evidenced by a slight smile and a nod.

"I wanted to get our cows home, but I knew Tucker wouldn't wrap a red bow on them and send them home for me. No doubt, someone would be hurt or killed soon. I thought about Dad telling me to 'ride easy' and that 'you can never take a bullet back."

I wished the cattle had never been stolen, but it did bring me here, to this small town and the girl I was coming to adore. We had only briefly known one another and had not even courted, but that short time felt like a lifetime.

Chelsea was everything I wanted in a gal. She was strikingly beautiful with a figure that took my breath away, that was for sure, but looks would fade and take their toll as the years played out.

She had so much more, a fun-loving, caring personality, yet strong enough to stand her ground, traits that would last a lifetime.

I instinctively knew that she would support me and protect our family if we were lucky enough to have a family. The West was sometimes harsh and brutal, yet its wonders were great enough to work through the hardships.

The night sky, the snowcapped mountains, the sweet grass on the plains, the water that ran free, clear, and swift. I loved it here and wanted to be a part of all it would bring my way, and I hoped she would, too.

Finally, in the wee hours before dawn, I dozed off but came fully awake within an hour or two by the floorboards creaking outside my door. Immediately alert, my hand was on my pistol before I realized it.

"Reg, are you awake? It's Chelsea."

I threw on my britches and a shirt, didn't want to open the door in my long handles. I opened the door, and there stood Chelsea, pretty as a picture, but her eyes were red and swollen from crying.

Why are you here? Is there a problem? What has happened?" I scattershot the questions so fast I barely had a moment to breathe. *Oh, Lord, please don't let anyone be dead.*

She threw her arms around my neck. "Hold me. Hold me, and never let me go."

She squeezed me so hard it was difficult to breathe. She would break a bone or two if she kept this up.

"I lost Pa, Reg. I don't want to lose you, too."

With a sigh of relief that my people were alive as far as I knew, I took a deep breath. "You're not going to lose me, but if you keep squeezing, you just might kill me."

She let loose a little and leaned back. "I made you breakfast. I'll wait for you downstairs."

So much for sleep. When she tried to move away from my embrace, I pulled her back to me. "Chels, it's all going to be okay. I promise you."

It better be, or there will be the devil to pay. I watched as she whisked away down the stairs.

Gathering my thoughts, I grabbed my gear and steered toward the delicious smells rising from the kitchen. *I was a lucky man. I was going to make this right.*

34

TATE

"Boss, you in here?" Tate yelled as he hesitantly walked down the hallway before entering the main room. He found it nearly as quiet as the woods in the backcountry. The fire burned, and the wood crackling echoed in the great room.

Tucker sat in a chair, bent over, staring at the fire. A whiskey bottle nearly empty of its contents sat on the table next to him. It was obvious he had been up all night.

"Boss, you okay?" The air remained deadly still.

"Tate, how well did you get to know Ben?" Tucker asked.

"Guess as well as anyone gets to know a drifter or a man running from his past. Why do you ask?"

"The marshall has him, and he knows our secrets. He could be trouble."

"Boss, I don't see it that way. Ben's as guilty as the rest of us. If he talked, he'd hang for sure. I think the marshall caught him in some act and used his name to draw us out."

Tucker never raised his eyes but aimed his words directly at Tate. "A man trapped in the corner will do anything to get away. If they push him, he'll squeal."

"Then he would hang, Boss. When your back is against the wall, you don't think straight. You think they'll show you kindness even as they put the rope around your neck."

"Get the boys, Tate. They have work to do."

"What are you thinking?" Are we going to bury more trouble?"

"No, we're going to dig up our old trouble, then we won't have any worries."

"Get the men now, I told you."

" Boss, It's early. They're not going to be up."

"Damn it. I said NOW." I don't want to repeat myself, understand? Tucker had his hand on the revolver resting on his desk. He was in a drunk's mean state of mind.

Tate backed away, cautiously backed out of the room, unwilling to be shot in the back, but he kept his eyes on the half-crazed Tucker just in case he took a notion to act out his distress.

Feeling himself gaining more courage and growing bolder, Tate soon knew this ranch would be his. He witnessed the weakness in Tucker, where he had never realized it before. Tucker held the loser's hand in this card game.

The boss's right-hand man strode over to the bunkhouse, not in a hurry nor dallying either, but continued with his mind full of anticipation.

"I'll be damned, Tucker, if you think you have trouble now, just wait and see. I'm going to take what's mine."

The overbearing ranch owner's time was running out. Tate would follow along, getting himself clear of trouble. *I will handle Tucker and give him his due.*

"Men wake up. It's time to move."

"Tate, what the hell? The house better be on fire?"

"No, but the boss is. He is red-hot, drunk, and ready to drop anyone who sparks his temper. Be mindful. Each of you, keep your mouth closed. Tucker's going to snarl like a rabid dog. Let him do so. Move on down to the house. I'll explain my plan later. Get moving with your guns and be saddled up. NOW."

The irritated gunslingers rolled out of their bunks, not in much of a hurry, not being early risers. They stayed up late, drinking and playing cards, and were uncomfortable taking orders or doing anything resembling work.

But they were also aware that the head honcho had a mean streak and could turn to violence at the drop of a hat. It wasn't a good sign that Tucker was up and moving.

The four gunmen guided their horses to the ranch house and prepared to stay where ordered for the remainder of the dark night. Stepping cautiously into the ranch house, they were met by Tucker and Tate, both standing by the fire.

Tucker's voice boomed in the open room, startling the men. "Tate, I gave orders for your men to move. I'm tired of waiting. Have two men bring the buckboard, shovels, and several tarps. I want you to head out to dig up those bodies. Wrap them up and tote them back here."

"What the hell, Tucker? We just planted them there. Now, you want us to dig them up?"

Tucker said, "We have no time to wait. Now. Ben is with the marshall, and if he talks, we're all going to hang."

"I want those bodies, and I want them faster than lightning, or I'll have Tate kill every single one of you, and you will take the fall."

"No one will be the wiser. Move. Do as I say. Bring the bodies here, and we'll burn the remains in the woodpile. There won't be anything left to identify, and I am not about to repeat myself."

Tucker was so full of rage that his actions clearly indicated his sanity was in jeopardy. He realized his authority was being tested, and he rested on his gun to remove any doubt about who ran this outfit. He was ready to bust at the seams.

Tate spoke to him in a calming voice, "Okay, Boss. We're going, anything you want. We were just a bit confused there for a minute."

The men were confused and talked to themselves as they walked out, fully aware that their lives were on the line if they followed this madman's orders. "We should just saddle up and ride out."

"Men, let me handle it," said Tate, trying to calm the rough waters. "Fellas, he's a rich cattleman. He'll hang this scheme on us and say he didn't know anything about the killings."

"Tate, he won't get away with it."

"Maybe not, but are you willing to bet your life on it? Play it his way, fellas, for now. I think we can swim out of this. Just keep your lips sealed and follow me."

"Tate, we will follow your lead, but you better fill us in on your plan first."

"Let's get the bodies back here, and then we'll talk."

With unanswered questions and worries on their minds, they still loaded the buckboard with shovels, tarps, and ropes. Tate rode with two men at his side while the other two managed the buckboard and hitched up the horses.

35

TOM

In his gut, Tom knew something was amiss on the ranch, and his thoughts made it impossible to sleep. He walked the floor in the bunkhouse for hours when he heard the distinct sound of men in the barn preparing horses and the wagon for an unknown mission.

"Buck, wake up."

"What's going on, Tom?"

"Tucker's men are on the move, and they loaded up the buckboard with shovels and tarps. I couldn't sleep, and I heard a disturbance in the barn. Poke, get up."

Poke sat up. "Now what? It's pitch dark out."

"Tucker's men are on the move.

They're heading towards the big ravine."

"Get dressed. Let's see what they're up to. Let's go out the back way to the barn and lead our horses out, real quiet like. We don't want Tucker to see that we're up."

"Buck, I figured this is what you might be wanting to do, so before you two were ready, I walked toward the barn to saddle up the horses and saw Tucker outside prowling the grounds, mumbling to himself. Maybe it is not so safe to ride out right now," said Tom.

36

REG

Chelsea made me, her beau, as she sometimes called me, a nice breakfast meal with plenty of hot coffee, and she was eager to refill my cup. Whether my cup needed a refill, or she only wanted to visit remained to be seen. Comfortable in each other's presence, we sat, and I ate with little to no conversation, only a pleasant silence.

Maggie soon scurried into the private area of the dining room, interrupting, "I see by the men gathering outside that it's time for you to be on your way. I want you all to be careful, watch your backs, and get home safe. Nothing is worth your life. What's done is done."

"We'll be okay, Maggie. We're just going for a look. Would you be kind enough to stay with Chelsea and Nancy today? I think you'll all need the comfort of each other's company."

"Turning to my favorite gal, I asked, "Chelsea, how about some pie tonight? I think the men would sure be ready for some of your baked pies when we return."

"Well, now that sounds like a good idea, but I think you forgot about your hard-working horse. She might like a treat, too. I'll make up something special for everyone, including MY favorite horse, and we will keep the kids active by churning some ice cream."

I hugged them both, gave the ladies a tip-of-the-hat nod, and as I trotted on my way, I turned and said to Maggie, "Better start making some baking plans. I keep hearing church bells ringing in my dreams," I teased to lessen the tension.

Even though it was dark, the sky was clear, with the stars twinkling like a sea of diamonds on dark velvet. As I walked to the stable, thinking about my girl, that sky was a sight to behold.

When I crossed the threshold of the open barn, I saw my saddle turned upside down in the dirt, and Spence sprawled on his backside next to it.

"Reg, I tried to saddle your horse, but that girl has quite the temper."

"I don't know if it's too early in the morning or she just has a thing for you," I said.

"She tried to kick my head off, so she made her point."

I picked up my saddle, brushed it off, and set it on Roan. I felt confident and hoped it showed, but I also hoped she wouldn't buck me off in a frenzy before the day ended.

I kept one eye on Roan and the other on the rail fence. The mare remained calm. "See, Spence, it's like this. You just don't have the touch with all women."

"You are right, brother. Some women just don't like a man who takes control."

When the marshall and Ben joined us, Spence, Joe, and I were saddled and ready to go. "Well, we saw somebody had quite the breakfast this morning. Thanks for waking us and inviting us to join you."

Spence was a little agitated, "What, YOU ate a meal and didn't invite me and the others? I am your only loving brother, you know?"

"Sorry boys, private party."

"Well, I see how we rate. Wait till I tell Mom that you were not a very good host. Guess we can eat hardtack."

Joe came to the rescue and announced, "Coffee's ready."

Spence rolled his eyes and gratefully grabbed a cup. "Thanks, at least somebody cares about others around here."

All five men stood together in silence, contemplating the tasks ahead and understanding that today would be the start of a hard road. The marshall would shortly have the answers he needed. He broke the silence then and spoke to the men.

"Time to ride. Let's get this started. Men, place your right hand in the air."

We all obeyed his order.

"Look at me. You're deputized."

We enjoyed a chuckle. "That's how easy it is to be a lawman?"

Nodding, the marshall answered with a grin and a hearty, "Yep."

We rode in a single file. Spence led the way, and the marshall was next, followed by Joe, Ben, and me.

We rounded the last bluff that led to the draw when Spence dropped from his horse and signaled with a closed fist for the rest of us to stop and dismount. He tied off his horse, crawled to the top of the hill, removed his hat, and peeked over the ridge.

Joe suggested that the others have a look as he moved the horses down the hill to keep them quiet. The remainder of this posse moved our way up the hill and crawled to the ledge to observe the five men below.

"From what I can tell, it appears we have grave robbers over the ridge. Five men with a buckboard, wrapping the bodies and throwing them into the wagon," Spence said.

"Marshall, there is Ass Wipe and four other men. Buck, Poke, and Tom are not with them."

"Agreed. I'm happy to know the ranch hands are not part of this group, but who is Ass Wipe?"

Spence whispered, "Reg gave A. W. Tate the nickname the first time they met. Ass Wipe for the A.W."

Pinkie grinned. "I think it fits him perfectly. Couldn't have picked a finer name myself!"

"I don't see Tucker anywhere," said Spence.

When I looked back over the ledge, I agreed. "It is possible the ranch hands may not have been invited, or they could have found trouble on the other end."

Pinkie barely nodded his head. "I bet they weren't invited. Tom is a sharp one. If there was trouble, normally, he could handle it himself. I think he would have gotten word to me if he thought things were going to be bad."

"What's the play?" I asked.

"We got the villains hands down. We're damn lucky we arrived when we did. If we were a day later, we wouldn't have any evidence. Damn lucky. They are all here except one, Tucker."

"Let's let them finish digging and loading the bodies into the buckboard. It looks like smelly, dirty work. They buried them. Let's let them dig the deceased up."

The marshall was insistent, and I could see he had worked out his plan while we waited.

"Spence, can you make your way back down the hill and find your way to the draw outcropping across from them?" he said in the lowest voice he could manage and still be heard.

"I can be there in about thirty minutes."

"Reg, can you move above us on that rock ledge?"

"Yes, I'll work my way back down this hill, then head up."

Spence moved downhill and signaled with his hand cupped to his ear as he walked by that he wanted to say something quietly to Reg since voices had a way of traveling when one least expected.

"There's a trail behind the hill with a cut in the rocks you can squeeze through. Go that way. That's where I sat when Joe and I watched that ravine before."

"Good call, baby brother."

The marshall leaned into Ben. "Ben, lets you and me go down into the draw."

"Right behind you, Marshall."

"Reg, when you see Spence is ready, signal Joe with a single arm wave. We will wait for Joe to signal with both arms when they have the bodies loaded in the buckboard."

"Then, Ben and I will ride up the draw and confront the grave robbers. Joe can move up here on the ridge when we head down. This is a matter of law, and I will handle this. That is an order. Do you all understand?" said the marshall.

He added, "Don't shoot. Wait, if at all possible. I want to get some answers, if I can."

"Marshall, I'm telling you again, you and Ben are riding into a hornet's nest."

"I realize that Reg, but you know they will not just lay down and respect our presence.

"Ben, you up to this, or do you want to stay with Joe? You have a choice."

"No, Marshall, I gave my word. I'm in."

" Ben, you let me lead the way. It's my show."

"Reg. I hear you're a deadeye shot with that long gun."

"I can hit any varmint if I need to."

"Deputy, I want your aim directed at Ben. I'll trust him to be straight up if there's a gun pointed his way."

The Marshall smiled at Ben and Reg, but we all knew he was dead serious. Ben would be put down if he were not acting like a loyal dog.

Ben lifted his eyes towards Reg. "Don't go getting trigger happy."

"Not to worry, Ben, if you are trouble, you'll never hear it coming."

They each crawled back off the hill and headed their separate ways. Joe moved up the ridge, keeping a watchful eye out as they all moved into position.

37

THE VALLEY

Spence moved across the valley and flattened himself on the ledge while I worked my way up to the rock outcrop and lay on my belly, watching over the valley. The marshall and Ben dropped from their horses and were in position at the mouth of the draw. The signal wave came from Joe, indicating that all the men were in place.

We waited several hours, watching the grave robbers digging up the bodies. These men weren't the kind who labored well, especially this kind of labor. The sun was straight up, and the temperature rose to the furnace heat on the valley floor.

The work was dirty and smelly, nothing compared to the rotting bodies in the heat. We could hear their unsavory conversations drifting up from below. It was a special treat. We watched cool and comfortable from the shade, and they were miserable. What a nice sight and feeling for once.

Finally, they finished this unwelcome task, the last body tossed on board and shovels thrown into the wagon. Tate and two others put a leg up to mount their horses, and the other two prepared to step up onto the buckboard.

Joe gave the signal wave to the marshall and Ben. They raced up the draw at a fast pace, wanting to surprise these men before they could escape.

"This is Marshall Yates. You're surrounded," he yelled as he neared the men. "You men raise your hands and don't move a muscle."

They caught the culprits red-handed. Tate spun his horse around, but the two men on the buckboard raised their hands. The two men who remained on their horses didn't move, leaving their hands on their saddle horns, remaining steadfast, keen-eyed, and calm. Each had lived through moments like this on many occasions.

The marshall rode up to the men, allowing himself enough distance to enable him to watch all five men.

Spence and I readied our rifles.

I pointed at the two, who rested their hands on the saddle horns. Spence was ready for the wagon riders. The angle of the rifles told me where they were aiming.

My brother and I had double-teamed on a lot of wild game, hunting the woods and fields. We knew from experience not to gang up on the same meat. Making that mistake once taught them a good lesson. Two on one meant little meat left after both had sent their lead flying at the same target while the second animal fled down the trail unscathed.

Tate and his two sidekicks scanned all directions to see who might surround them. The hiding spots we chose were well-hidden and not easy to spot. Our lookout kept a sharp eye out for any other riders we may have missed, but he saw none.

Tate decided it was time he spoke up. "I see, Marshall, that you have a rider traveling with you who is familiar to me."

"Hello, Ben. It looks like you're a bit confused. Forgot you had a hand in unsavory deeds on the ranch? You think you made a new friend?"

Ben's self-assurance remained. "Tate, it's over. It's time we all paid the fiddler."

"Ben, you got two choices. You can die with the marshall there or ride with us."

I could hear the conversation loud and clear, and my aim shifted to Ben.

Ben rubbed his chin. "As I see it, I feel my odds are a lot better on this side of the fight. Tate, I'd give up while you got a chance. Jail is better than dying."

"Ben, don't you mean hanging?"

"At this point, it's all the same, but I don't think I will do either today."

The two sitting silently on the horses sprang into action. Both fired as if they were one.

Spence and I let loose. One rider went down, toppling off the back of his horse. The other rider's horse lunged, and he flew over the top of his horse's neck.

During the crossfire, Ben had moved his horse up in front of the marshall, who was sitting in the direct line of fire. Ben took a bullet from one of the gunmen and slumped down in his saddle.

The marshall got off two shots, missing as he and his horse moved for cover.

At full gallop, Tate directed his horse to the trees. Spence didn't have an eye on him from his perch, but I threw lead as fast as I could move the lever action.

The two on the buckboard jumped to the ground and managed to grab the horses' reins from the two outlaws lying in the dirt. They mounted up and followed Tucker's retreat. Spence fired, hitting trees, but no rider.

Joe shouted at us. "They're heading back to the ranch."

We three in the upper area sprinted to their mounts and rode hell-bent to the marshall and Ben. When we reached them, Ben lay on the ground, his shirt and the dirt underneath him soaked in blood.

"Damn it, Ben. I ordered you to let me handle it."

"Sorry, Marshall. It was my turn to do something to help. It felt good for once."

"How is he, Marshall? Joe asked.

"Not good."

"Let me see." Joe moved in and ripped Ben's shirt away. Flipping Ben over, he saw where the bullet went clean through. He'd had many dealings with gunshot wounds in the wars and the Indian raids. His memory served him well.

"Get me some packing for the wound. I need to pack the wound on the back and the front and wrap him up tight. Pressure must be on the wound to stop the bleeding."

"Spence, build a good fire, heat water, and put your knife in the coals."

"Reg, you and the marshall keep an eye out. Don't want to see those three sneaking back on us."

We were, but the real watchdog was Roan, and she looked like a warrior, on guard at full alert, smelling, seeing, and hearing it all. There would be no need for us to watch with her present.

Spence quickly lit a fire and grabbed the coffee pot from his saddle bag. Luckily, a cowboy never traveled without his coffee pot and fixins. He placed the pot on the fire after he gathered water from a small spring rippling down the valley floor. He nestled his knife into the coals until the blade glowed red.

I watched Spence with a puzzled look. "Spence, what's up?" I could tell something was on Spence's mind.

"I was thinking of Dad's foot when you had to burn it. Gave me the willies. I feel like someone walked on a grave."

"Marshall, make sure to get ahold of my folks and Betty and let them know I did good and right. I want them to know."

Joe spoke up. "Save your breath. You'll tell them yourself. You're a long way from dead. Get him the whiskey off my horse and pour it down him."

Joe removed the wadding from his patient's back.

"Ben, drink all you can as fast as you can."

The makeshift field doctor cleaned the wound and reached for the knife, letting it cool for a minute. Looking at Ben, he said, "It's going to hurt like hell. All those bad things you done, well, we're going to burn them out of you now."

"Marshall, Reg, and Spence grab hold. Ben, bite down on your glove."

Jo grabbed Ben's arm. "It's going to sting a little."

Ben smiled and nodded. "Burn out the bad. Humph, I may be burning a while."

Joe worked fast. The pain was unbearable, and Ben tried with all his might to pull away from the hot knife, but we held him steady.

Joe wrapped the back wound up and stuck the knife back in the fire.

"I wish it were over, Ben, but you got one more side to do. Drink up."

Ben was half out of it, but we poured more whiskey down his throat. The marshall leaned over to the wounded man. "Ben, you took that bullet for me when you didn't need to. You could have just stayed out of the way."

The marshall barely heard Ben as he slurred his words, "I figured an old guy like you couldn't take much lead. I felt sorry for ya."

"Bet you don't feel sorry for me now."

"That's a fact."

"Steady yourself. We're almost done."

After Joe removed the temporary bandage and cleaned the wound, our stand-in doctor took the knife and pressed it to the open wound.

Ben immediately screamed and then passed out. Joe placed the hot knife on the open wound two more times to fully cauterize it. The smell of cooking flesh was overwhelming.

Spence looked at me and said, "I think when we burned Dad's wounds, he smelled a little sweeter."

I shook my head and took a deep breath. "Spence, that sense of humor will help you get out of trouble, and at times, I think it may cause you pain."

"Only you could joke at a time like this," Joe said.

Joe wrapped Ben back up and let him lay for a few minutes. "Reg, bring his horse. We must tie his legs to the saddle and wrap his hands around the horn. I will take him to town and ride hell-bent for leather to get there."

"Is he going to make it?" Spence asked.

"He's young. I think he has a girl to live for. It's up to him now. We burned the hole closed. If he can handle the ride, I think he will pull through. I've seen a lot worse, but you never know," said the marshall.

We all helped stand Ben onto his feet, lifted him onto his horse, and hog-tied him down. He may die, but he sure as hell wouldn't fall off. The injured man woke a bit tipsy and still in pain. "Thanks, men. I'll be waiting in the café when you get back to town," he said.

I held Ben steady as he babbled. "Just hold on there, partner. Chelsea is making us special pies and ice cream for our return, but don't you dare eat mine."

"I better tough it out then. I hear she's a hell of a cook."

Joe climbed aboard and grabbed the reins of Ben's horse.

"We three will trail behind you with the wagon. When you get Ben to the doctor, you might visit the ladies. Tell them we're all okay. Maggie, well, truth be told, she will have a hard time seeing what we are carrying home," I said, giving the horse a pat and a wave to Joe.

"Ride safe." The two took off at a pace that Ben could tolerate. "I'll be damned. He took that bullet for me. I am beholding. Thanks for the rifle fire cover. You sure earned your steak today. Sent a lot of lead their way. Did you get the other fellas?" asked the marshall.

"Two dead over here. They were the two on the horses. They weren't going peacefully, so they pulled iron first."

"Yates, Let's throw them over your horse and Spence's. You two drive the buckboard back. I'll ride alongside, shotgun. Don't want this scum next to these good folks."

"What about the others?" Yates asked.

Spence said, "The two on the wagon somehow grabbed up the horses and took out faster than jackrabbits to report back to Tucker at the ranch. We fired on them to give them a good escort out of here."

"Maybe you grazed them. It would make better evidence if they had wounds."

"I don't think they were marked with any bloody evidence, but I know I wounded a lot of trees. Them boys were riding like the devil was on their tail," said Spence.

38

RELIEF

We draped the outlaws over the horses. Spence and Yates drove the buckboard at a slow traveling pace while I rode ahead and watched for an ambush. Tucker would want these bodies. We had hanging evidence, and they knew it.

We arrived in town in the middle of the night, glad an ambush never came. It would have been a pleasant evening ride if it hadn't been for carrying the bodies of some good folks.

Slipping in through the back way of the livery, we tended to the horses and laid out the scum in empty stalls. "Should we do something to cover their bodies?" Spence asked.

"No, maybe the dogs will take care of them. Don't really care. Let's cover the wagon as best we can, and we will take care of these folks in the morning," said my riding buddy. *The "Marshall" title had worn itself thin. Yates was good, but I wondered if I could get away with calling him Pinkie?*

"Well, Pinkie? If you want to see how Ben is doing at the doc's,

Spence and I will check on the ladies. I see the lights are on at the café. I'm sure they're sitting up waiting for news."

"Pinkie, huh?" He smiled as he walked away. The room was packed. Maggie and all the children huddled in woolen blankets, sound asleep on the scuffed pine floor. Sara, her husband Ty, and the preacher sat quietly with Nancy. Their faces wore masks of worry and grief.

Maggie woke, stood up, rushed over to me and Spence, and wrapped her arms around us. "Joe told us what happened. You don't have to say a word. We all thank you and want to say it means the world to finally have answers. I don't have the words." She squeezed us even tighter and sobbed, soaking my shirt.

Jumping up from her sleeping position and unable to wait a minute longer, Chelsea ran over to Spence, hugged him tight, and kissed him on the cheek.

"Spence, thank you for keeping Reg safe. I will always have a special place for you in my heart."

What, a kiss for Spence? I couldn't help but chuckle. *Always the lady's man. Like he did all the work. Figures. That's Spence for ya.*

In the short distance from the chair where she had been sleeping waiting on our return, Caty became her sister's shadow and flew over to Spence, crying and hugging him fiercely. Surprising everyone, Caty blurted out, "Spence, I love you."

Not able to control his emotions, and with tears streaming down his face, Spence knelt and kissed her on the cheek. "I love you, too, little one."

Finally, realizing she hadn't paid attention to her beau, Chelsea hugged me and then kissed me on the cheek.

244

"Well, let's see now. Kisses for Spence first. I'm surprised you didn't feed Roan before you got around to me."

Nancy watched the display of affection and then approached me. "You are a good and kind man. All of you are. She took my hand and placed it in Chelsea's. If it is to be, I want you to be happy and to love each other. Clancy sent us the right man. I know he's smiling now and would want the same for you both."

Preacher Bill prayed over the entire gathering, saying comforting words to the women and the children. He was a giant man with the kindest heart I've ever seen.

It was a long night. We hugged, cried, talked, laughed, and shared the pain. The sun was cresting over the horizon, and a full day loomed.

This morning, identifying the bodies in the wagon and burying loved ones topped our priorities. After seeing our friends' needs, we would track Tucker and Tate and take back what belonged to us.

Marshall Yates stopped in to visit during the night and told us that our fill-in prairie doctor still sat at the bedside while Ben slept. It appeared Ben lost a lot of blood, but he was hanging on. The marshall was heading off to send a wire to Ben's folks and Betty.

39

TUCKER

Tucker had settled back in the ranch house when he heard the pounding of horse's hooves running at full gallop. Grabbing up his rifle and heading for the door, he watched Tate and two other riders race toward the ranch house. They dismounted on the run and leaped to the wrap-around porch of the massive home.

"What the hell? Tate, where are the other riders and the buckboard?"

"The marshall, Ben, and others jumped us, and then we were surrounded. I think it was Reg, his brother Spence, and I'm not sure about the others. There was gunplay everywhere."

"Where's the damn buckboard? Did they get to you before you dug up the bodies?"

"No, we had them all loaded up, and we were heading back to the ranch when they arrived."

Tucker was furious. "So, THEY have the bodies?"

"Yes, they have the buckboard and the bodies."

Tucker looked out the open door. "Appears they killed two of our men. I don't see them. Tate, did you bother to shoot back or just run?" he asked.

Tate grabbed a bottle of whiskey and gulped it down as fast as he could swallow. "We shot Ben, dodged lead, and rode for cover. I'm not sure about the marshall.

Tucker shook his head with disbelief. "Where's the damn wagon now?"

"Saw them taking it toward town with two bodies draped over their horses. I'm sure it was our two men they were packing since they were the first to go down. I'm not sure, but I think Ben was saddled and was being led to town, too. Looked like he was injured."

Tucker was red-faced, and the veins in his forehead looked ready to burst. "Tate, find our ranch hands. They're riding along with us to town in the morning. We're going to stop this and stop it now. All those men you saw today and whoever else is in my way will die, and we must stop them from getting the word out for help."

Tucker stood from the safety of his chair, moving around the room as he spouted his rant. "I'm riding to town and cutting the telegraph wire. Meet me at the ridge above town at first light. Make it very clear that the cowboys ride for me, and they will represent my brand, or they'll deal with me and the consequences. Have them ready to ride early with their rifles and irons packed and tell them we'll talk to the marshall about the attacks on my ranch. That's all they need to know."

Tucker went through the ranch house, gathering his side arms, rifles, and gear. He left the house and headed to the outskirts of town without his men.

Now Tate sat in the master's chair and took a swig or two from a bottle of liquid courage before he stood up and walked out the door.

"If Tucker thinks he's going to keep what is to be my ground, he's in for a surprise. His reign is ending," he said as he stomped to the bunkhouse where the three ranch hands greeted him.

"What's up, Tate?" Poke asked Tate as he crossed the bunkhouse doorway. "Why were you riding like the Devil had your tail?"

Tate jumped down the cattlemen's throat. "We're going to town. This outfit has business with the law."

"Where are the other riders?"

"That's my business, Buck, no concern of yours. You run cattle. I run, men. The boss told me to get our gear ready. We're heading out early. The ranch is under attack, and we're going to town to put an end to it. We're going to meet and talk to Marshall Yates in the morning. It's time you earn your keep and be part of the ranch and its brand."

Buck nodded and assured Tate they would be ready to ride.

"Like I said, "Pack your iron and rifles. We may need to do some persuading." Tate turned back to the main house and the comfort of the golden-brown liquid.

Buck directed his comments to Tom and Poke, saying, "You two do as you wish, but I ain't siding with Tucker and his outlaw bunch."

Disgusted, Poke loudly approved of the ramrod's decision. "I agree."

Tom added, "Me neither, boys, but they don't need to know that. Tate is ready for an argument, and I'm sure there will be more than words flying at that meeting."

"So, what if there is, Buck? He has no chance against the three of us, well, two anyway." Tom laughed. "Poke will still be hiding under the bed."

"Funny, Tom, I would have to push you out of the way first to get under the bed." They all knew they would fight, but Buck was right. *It was sure to be bloody, close quarters and all.*

Tate strolled into the great room, poured a glass of whiskey, sat by the fire, and was joined by his trusted gunslinging sidekicks. *The two whom he let believe they were his only trusted men.*

"Tate, this is bad. We'll have to kill Marshall Yates, Reg, his brother, and some town folk. I think we all agree on that point. We're all in for killing, but what's in it for us? We're not killing just to help the boss. We're paid to kill. We have killed for fun and at other times just for hell raisin', but trust me, we're not doing it for him," said the gunslinger standing beside Tate.

"Not to worry, we are not," Tate assured the rebellious men. We'll help get rid of the townies and the others. Then I'll deal with Tucker."

Tate made his point. The riders with him in the room knew if they lived through it all, Tucker would no longer be around to enjoy his cozy way of life.

"Give us a bottle, the good stuff. We're heading to our bunkhouse and getting ready for the hunting trip. We will see you in the morning."

Tate yelled as they walked away, "Don't go getting drunk and pass out, or I'll shoot you where you lay."

Tate sat in the boss's chair, drank his whiskey, and smoked his cigars. Sure thing, he was going to enjoy this place. He would take what he wanted and would kill to keep it.

As he left the ranch, Tucker rode through the dark night with only starlight to guide him to the far side of town, where he saw the loaded buckboard with the bodies and men sitting vigil in the barn. He watched their movements from his location on the hill. His task now was to cut the telegraph line so the marshall couldn't send for help.

Tomorrow, he would slaughter them all, followed by Tate and the other men right in line behind the dead town folk. Tucker understood the mind of an outlaw and knew Tate would be gunning for him and try to take what he always coveted, to be the man in charge.

A 'yes man' always held secrets close to the vest, and Tate had shown his colors and distrust of Tucker long enough. Knowing this day would eventually arrive, Tucker needed to eliminate those who knew of the past stealing and killings at the ranch.

On the outskirts of town, in the still of the night and long before the break of dawn, he threw his rope over the telegraph line and pulled until it crashed to the ground like a felled tree stirring up the dry red dust.

With this mission accomplished, he rode to the ravine and made an early camp. Tate and his other gunslingers would arrive in the morning and side with him until they completed the killing.

Buck and the cowhands were useless, but he would position them out front, using them as a sign of force and to block himself from flying rounds. They were valuable pawns in this game but also disposable.

Tucker's impatience grew as the nighttime hours dragged by, seeming to last forever. Finally, the sky cracked the horizon open, and a new day was born.Dreading the day, Tate and his fast draw riders half-heartedly saddled up and rode the trail to join the boss. The sounds of the horses' hooves and their heavy breathing deprived the morning of her stillness.

Upon reaching the ravine, Tucker waved them in, cowboys and gunmen alike. "Men, it's time I end this matter and keep my ranch. No one is going to take what's mine. I will give you all a thousand dollars each for sticking with me. That's more money than you'll make in years or at any one time. A good chunk for you to set your-selves up with. Plus, I'll give you boys a section of the ranch for your own. You will all have a stake in this."

Tom looked at Tucker, "That sounds like a good deal, Boss."

Buck and Poke nodded their heads in agreement. "Now we all have a stake in the game."

Tate looked at the gun hands, his trusted men. "What do you other two think about a gift of land and money?"

"I like the money. Don't want any land. I'll sell the land to you three cowboys."

The other rider agreed. "I'm in it for the money. I'll sell my section to the boys if they are interested."

Tucker shook hands with each of them, sealing the deal. "We're in agreement then. Let's finish this problem together."

"Buck, Tom, and Poke, when we get there, I want you three to ride up front. The townies and the two brothers like you. It will take any suspicious edge off us being in town. Tate and your two men will ride next to me. Remain on your horses, and I'll manage the conversation."

40

RELIEF TURNS TO GRIEF

The sound of a light tap on my door pulled me from my dreams. Surprised at how well I had slept, it took me a second to get my bearings.

"I'm up," I whispered.

"It's me, Pinkie. The telegraph wire is down, and there's trouble coming. I can feel it in my bones."

I opened the door while pulling on my boots, grabbed my shirt and gear, and we both bolted towards the stairs.

"Pinkie, did you talk to Spence?"

"The men are all waiting downstairs for us."

Once I was down the stairway, Joe patted me on the back. "Sleeping beauty, I'm glad you could join us. Get all your beauty sleep?"

"You bet you old codger, one of us needs to look good. I'm glad Pinkie woke me up. I was out of it, slept like a baby."

Nancy, Maggie, and Chelsea were there to serve the men food.

They had gathered around the table for coffee and biscuits, although no one had much appetite.

With the wires down today, those gathered in the café felt that Tucker cut the wire and was trying to keep us from bringing in outsiders. It may have been a coincidence, but they didn't think so.

Joe broke the silence. "I need to proceed to prepare your loved ones for burial. I know it will be hard, ladies, but you must identify the bodies we have in the barn." Nancy said, teary-eyed, "I'll go with you,. Maggie. Chelsea, you stay here."

"No, Ma, I want to be there for Maggie, too."

"No, young lady, you're not. You will do as I say," said Nancy while she hugged Chelsea.

Maggie understood Nancy's decision. She knew what lay ahead. The two ladies headed out through the door.

I held my hat in hand, following slowly behind the ladies and giving them room to gather their thoughts and emotions.

Considering the situation, Spence and Joe had removed the bodies from the wagon earlier and laid them out as best as possible. Joe lit a cedar fire in the barn to help with the smell of rotting flesh.

The marshall busied himself, trying to identify marks or pieces of clothing. He documented whatever he could. One body was dressed in what remained of a blue dress. He figured that it was Mrs. Anders. A man's body had a belt buckle with a T Lazy 7 outline, which we assumed was Mr. Anders.

The body shot in the back of the head was the outlaw Roan originally kicked, and he remained intact. Two other bodies were old and decayed, with little left to identify. From their boots, we figured they were maybe cattlemen passing through looking to find their herd.

Maggie's husband was the one we pondered over. We located

several bullet holes, busted ribs, and broken bones in this man's arms. If this was Maggie's husband, he went out fighting.

For the outlaws whom we shot, we threw them out in the dirt. We would bury them, but they weren't going to go pretty. A dirt hole, no box. They weren't worth the timber and nails.

The ladies walked into the barn, holding each other tight, and gazed at all the bodies before them.

Spence spoke. "I'm sorry, ladies, we tried to fix them proper like. I wish we could have done more."

The marshall talked to Maggie. "I need you to look at the bodies and see if you recognize anything that can help identify them. I know it's difficult and a terrible task, but we all need to know."

The widows fought back the tears. Maggie stepped forward. I saw the tension on their faces and the rigid way they walked. Maggie wished with all her heart that the bodies would not be their friends and her husband, but they all needed to know.

Maggie looked down at what was left of the human remains. "This woman is Mrs. Anders. I remember the pretty dress, blue with white lace. She wore it to church only on Sundays. They must have killed them on a Sunday, probably on the road."

"This is Mr. Anders. That belt buckle he is wearing was made in Denver. His wife gave it to him on their wedding anniversary. She ordered it special, made just for him." Maggie dropped to her knees, wept into her hands, and didn't speak for what felt like forever.

Nancy knelt with her and put her arms around the trembling woman.

Maggie pointed over to a body. "That's Jack. See his right hand. He's missing his little finger. It was cut off when the barn door slammed closed on it in a high wind. He looked for the finger for an hour. He wanted to save it, like some trophy he won at the fair. He joked he wanted to find it to make a necklace for me so he could always keep a hand on me. He had a twisted sense of humor, but that's why I loved him so much."

"He always made dumb jokes. The boots are his. He always wore down the outside heel of his left foot and needed to put more leather on it. I called him a penguin because he would walk with his feet pointing a little outward."

She reached over and held his boot. "I love you, Jack, and always will. Marshall, I don't know who the others are. I'm sorry I couldn't help more."

"You have answered a lot of questions for me, Maggie. It's enough to try to convict Tucker, Tate, and his men. Hopefully, they will all hang."

Maggie looked up. "What do you mean? Possibly hang? They did this."

"Maggie, unless we get more information that points towards them, we can't say they had anything to do with killing or burying these folks. We can only assume, and that's not evidence. I'm sure if we can get his remaining men to rat him out, we may have a case."

"What about Ben's story?"

"His testimony helps, but a good attorney would probably twist the facts and accuse Ben of lying to cover his hide."

"Joe, I'll help get these good folks ready to be buried," said Spence, hoping to change the conflict building between Maggie and the marshall.

"Appreciate it. Let's make some boxes and put them to rest."

Seeing that the ladies were worn out and near collapse, Spence and I gently took them by the arms and escorted them home.

Pinky spoke in a low tone that only the two could hear as they walked away. "Tomorrow, I'm riding out to the T Lazy 7 Ranch. I could use some help if you're still game."

"Marshall, we're riding with or without you. We're ready and willing, more now than ever."

41

TIME TO FIGHT

Tucker and his men rode to the bluff overlooking the town. Tucker stopped. "Men, some people wish to take what's mine and what will soon be yours. We're going to do whatever it takes to keep it."

Buck, Tom, and Poke nodded and rode off, traveling in advance of Tucker. They were far enough ahead when Poke finally spoke.

"Buck, we're not going to help Tucker, are we? I want money and land, but not this way."

"No. We're just playing our hand. When we get to town, we will lay down our cards. You two follow my lead. We're going to be on the right side of this fight. We just need Tucker to feel all cozy-like."

"Sounds good, Buck. Now, Poke, I've been around gunplay, and I know Tom, you have as well, but Poke, you haven't. You sit back a little and keep an eye out for any surprises. If you must shoot, aim dead center, and remember you're not killing good men, you're killing pure evil. There won't be a tear shed."

"The two hired men will wait for an opportunity. Tucker or Tate will probably start the fight. Tucker feels good now, but his boat is 'bout ready to take on a lot of water."

As Spence and I returned to the café, I turned and looked back at the barn. Roan let out a bellow and was bucking up with all fours. She was ready to fight. Her front feet pounded the dirt, and I could see why. Seven men rounded over the hill heading to town.

I was concerned by what I saw. Tom, Buck, and Poke rode forty yards in front of the bunch. Tucker and Ass Wipe followed with an additional two men.

Roan probably recalled the scent of the horses or riders from the first time they met.

I sent out a warning yell. "We got company. "Spence, get the ladies inside and clear the streets."

Hearing the uproar, the marshall rushed out of the barn with a rifle in hand. As I pointed to the hill, he checked the weapon on his hip and slid it back into his holster.

Spence did the same. They were ready. The lawman pointed for Joe to stay back. "Get your shotgun, and you watch the backdoor."

"You fellas, be careful. I'll be ready." Joe backed into the barn, and we knew he crouched out of sight behind the rain barrel on this side of the open barn door. They couldn't see him, but they would undoubtedly smell his tobacco.

Spence yelled at Joe. "You smoking at a time like this."

"You bet, may not get another opportunity. I also figured the wind blowing into their faces and the smell and the smoke ought to tear them up. I gave you a chance to join me, buckaroo," hollered back the old timer.

I think Joe was enjoying this moment, alive and helpful. Not the fact one of us could be hurt or killed, but I think he was living years gone by. He felt valuable out with his companions.

Spence gathered everyone inside and jumped down from the boardwalk, more than willing to help.

The marshall said, "It looks like the three front riders have made their stand with Tucker. Tom was my friend once, but if he's going to ride with outlaws, he'll take what's coming."

"I am not convinced." I removed my hat, rubbed my head, wiped the sweat out of my eyes, and returned the hat. "I don't believe they are riding with Tucker."

"As odd as it sounds, I agree with my brother," Spence said.

"Okay, Reg. You and Spence be watchful. If they make a play, don't hesitate." The lawman was livid. "I mean it. A pet dog can still bite," said the marshall.

I stood next to Spence. "You're my brother, Spence, and I know you can handle yourself. If it plays out, this is going to be up close and fast. Let Marshall Yates try to talk with them. Maybe they're here to surrender."

"Got it, I think I see a white flag in Ass Wipe's shirt pocket. Brother, I'll be fine. I'll just stand behind you and the main man over there. If you get shot, I'll take care of Chelsea."

"That would be a sight to see, Spence. She would surely whip you into shape."

Tate yelled at Tucker, "It looks like they spotted us. That damn horse. Think I'll shoot her first. We'll see how she handles a bullet."

Since Roan had sent Tucker's hired hand sprawling across the street, Tate had a pure hatred for the mare.

Tate was evil and he knew he would kill that horse when this was over. He was going to make dog food of her flesh and bone.

Tucker reined in. "When we get down to the men on the street, you three, Buck, Tom, and Poke, stay to my right up front. You other two, stay to my left."

Tucker knew where to place his pawns. If a man was right-handed and drew his iron out, it was easier for him to shoot to his left, faster, and more comfortable.

The three would be shot first, and that would allow Tucker to kill Reg, his brother, or the marshall. A split second was a lifetime in a gun battle.

"Tate, you're on my right. Ride in easy. I'll do the talking, lay down my law."

The marshall gave a wave and whistle to the remaining women and children who peeked out of the shop windows and doors to get clear. They realized what was coming after he pointed to the incoming riders on the hill.

In every doorway stood a man with a gun. The town was armed and ready. The intimidation was going to end today, one way or another.

The deputies all held their places as Yates had instructed. Ben let out a holler from the window above. "I'm ready, boys. I can't walk, but I can shoot."

"Ben, you hold off. Remember, I'm the law here. If they play dirty, then you other men, let your bullets fly."

"Ben stands as my witness. We have bodies, but I need to get Tucker to fess up that he ordered the murders, if I can. I'll try to get him to pump up and brag on the killings. If he pulls iron, y'all do what you need to. If he doesn't talk, I'll arrest him and try to get the others to give in."

Chelsea stood beside her mother and Maggie while watching out the café window. Caty and Callie stood behind the ladies' skirts but still tried to steal a glance.

Sara watched through the windowpanes at the general store. Dan and Little Joe were clamoring on top of each other, trying to get a front-row seat.

Ty, Sara's husband, had just entered through the side door. He took Sara's hand and said, "Sara, take the boys to the cellar and wait till I come for you."

Little Joe looked up wide-eyed. "Pa, we want to watch. We have never seen a gunfight."

"You're not going to see one now either. Go with your ma, or you'll see a fight right here, you two and me. Get going and listen to your ma."

"Okay, Pa," Dan mumbled from under his breath. "We never get to see anything. Come on, Joe. I'll race ya." They were off on a run, each pushing the other to be first to the cellar door.

Nancy grabbed Caty's arm. "Caty, you take Callie to the general store, help Sara with the boys, and be quick about it. I need you to do as you always do: help with the little ones."

"I will, Ma, I'll keep them out of the way. Ma is there going to be a fight? Will Spencer be okay?"

Nancy patted Caty on the behind. "You get a move on, young lady. Spencer will be fine."

Caty grabbed Callie and rushed toward the general store. As she passed Spence on the street, she sat Callie down and grabbed hold of Spence.

"Caty, you best pick up your little sister and get out of the street. It is dangerous out here," he scolded.

She reached out, gave Spence a quick hug. and whispered in his ear, "I'll be waiting on ya." Then she took off on the run to safety.

"Don't you two say a word," Spence warned his observers.

I slapped Spence on the back while Pinkie and I shook our heads. I smiled. "I think that young lady has her eyes set on the special boy of her dreams."

Little girl and little brother. I can see it now.

Spence smiled and watched her move across the street. "You know, fellas, if she weren't only twelve and were a much older gal, I would have to give courting a second thought. I always wanted a little sister, so this is just fine for now."

42

THE MARSHALL

The town was quiet. A lone dog barked in the distance, and not a soul stirred. The horses tied to the hitching rails stood lazily, swishing their tails. The sky was blue as robin's eggs, and there was a cool breeze. Time carried no weight this morning.

Spence leaned against the hitchin' rail. I stood at the street's edge while the marshall positioned himself in the middle of the road to ensure the rider's attention fell directly on him. He nodded to Ben in the window and then to Joe. Although he couldn't see either, he knew they had his back.

Down the road, the Two Fork's men were armed and ready should they be needed. But there had not been time to get word out to the ranchers. Ty and the preacher were on their own. The marshall stood and waited in the middle of that dusty dirt road. His mind wandered with his memories.

I have seen what the evil in men could do and witnessed what good men did every day. I can only pray that my talk is persuasive and direct and that my hand holds steady.

The riders were at the town's borderline. They rode slowly, their eyes roaming from end to end of the boardwalk, watching for any movement, indicating there were more than the three men on the road who might stand in their way.

Poke spoke up to Tom and Buck. "I don't like this. They have no idea that we're on the right side of this here fight. I don't feel like getting shot when Tucker and Tate should be eating dirt."

"Stop worrying. I know Pinkie. He's not going to shoot first and talk later. I'm guessing he's going to want information first."

Buck gave Tom the side eye. "Hell of a guess, Tom. What's the odds he shoots first?"

"Eighty-twenty."

"What ends the eighty on?"

Tom lifted his hands palms up in a motion of who knows. "Guess we're going to find out real soon. Keep your hands in sight, and don't move fast. Buck, you talk to the boys. Let them know how we stand without tipping our hand to Tucker and Tate. The boss may try to cut off the conversation, so keep it short," he said. "Deal. I'll do the talking to Pinkie," said Tom.

Cautiously, the three ranch hands walked their mounts into town close to sixty feet ahead of Tucker and Tate. His other men followed side by side behind them to the left with no sign of any member of the group slowing or turning back.

Tom spoke up and pulled his mount to a stop. "Good morning, Marshall. Out stretching your legs?"

Tom looked at Pinkie for possible directions.

"Today reminds me of the lazy days on the river waiting my turn to get my hands on the rope to swing out and drop into the cool water."

Marshall Yates stood silently with legs slightly spread, holding his ground while listening to Tom's words.

Spence looked at Buck and asked, "Are you gents going swimming today?"

"Nope, can't swim. We're just returning a nail to its owner."

With steely, hard eyes and features of chiseled stone, Tucker pulled his mount to a stop and stared directly at the law-abiding citizens facing him. The man was ready for cold-hearted revenge.

Tucker thought he would direct the conversation, but being the lawman and person he was, the marshall took the wind out of his sails before Tucker realized what was happening.

That scum would have to call me a liar or admit what he had done, and I was pretty sure I might have to call him out on it

"Tucker, you know my story. I'm the marshall, and I'm determined to get answers. We have bodies in the barn. Some are good folk, and three are your men, not worth discussing. What you got to say? You going to 'fess up to what you done, or you going to admit you're a coward and a liar?"

The sound of hooves beating the earth broke the silence. Roan ran full tilt from the back of the corral and between the general store and the saloon. Knowing she met these outlaws before, her outstanding intelligence remembered these riders by sight and smell. Keen senses and an excellent memory favored all horses, and she was an extreme example of good 'horse sense.'

Before any member on either side of the confrontation could draw a breath, Roan bolted into the street. She had stood in the corral, muscles twitching like fighters flexing and preparing for battle.

I moved forward in an effort to stop her, not wanting her to be in harm's way, hit by a stray bullet. I was well aware that she had seen many battles in her life. One only needed to see her scars to prove it, but this needn't be one of them.

She immediately headed in a straight line for Tucker and Tate. Lifting her head, she ran her chest into Tate's horse, directly hitting the other mare's midsection.

One horse fell sideways into the other, and both toppled onto their sides, taking Tate and Tucker down by the blow. The riders hit the ground hard, creating flying dust and a tangle of feet and hooves.

The two horses regained their upright position and footing, and Roan was all front hooves and teeth. She took this fight to the gunslinger's mounts. They lit out down the road like their tails were afire with Roan hot on their trail.

Spence and I jumped off the road as the half-crazed horses galloped by. Evidently, they had no idea what happened, but getting away from Roan was uppermost in their minds.

With the horse as protection, a rider had a better view of the surrounding area and portrayed the image of power.

Roan took this advantage away. Tucker and Tate were spooked and struggled to their feet without understanding what had just happened.

Tate rose and yelled, "I'm going to kill that horse."

I returned the verbal volley to Tate, "You pull, I'll drop you."

"That horse will get one in the head as soon as I finish with you."

Tucker was up and started to growl. "I've had enough. You're not going to run me out. I'll take over this town. I'll kill all of you as I killed all the others. You're going to have to deal with us seven."

Buck turned to Tucker as the three men began backing their horses away. "We're not your hired killers. We're cattlemen, not killers. You stole cattle and killed men and women, and we know you're a coward, a thief, and a murderer."

Ben spoke up from the window. "Tucker and Tate, you killed the Anders couple and the rancher Jack, Maggie's husband. I know it, and we have the bodies to prove it. Tate, you move, I'll kill you myself."

Tucker turned toward Spence and me. We both remained standing at the roadside, and he wanted a straight shot at us both.

Poke maintained his silence and backed his horse away from Buck. "If you don't drop 'em, Buck, Tom, and I will. They are rodents, and we need to clean them out," Poke said.

It was time for the marshall to lay down the law. "Tucker, you're under arrest for the murders of the Anders couple, Jack, your hired man, and two others I haven't yet identified. Your men ambushed Clancy and murdered him at your command."

"There are warrants out for you back east for murder and robbery. Put your hands up, and I'll make sure you hang and swing with a quick jerk of the rope."

Tucker was red hot, his face turning a vibrant, sickly color of red. He didn't like being told what to do or be caught flat-footed. Three men under Tucker's command had backed out of the fight, and he was fast losing control. No hired man had ever talked back to him and lived to tell the tale.

While Tate's mind raced, he remained silent, nerves overtaking him. It appeared that whatever he had in mind for the future was changing by the second. His plans to overtake the ranch and become the big boss were dwindling.

The three men in front of him refused to be bullied. Ben was in the window. That damn Roan. Tate couldn't stay focused, and he didn't know what to do to get out of this situation. He could push most men. They feared him and what he could do with a gun, but these men were steadfast. They wouldn't back down.

The lawman spoke loud and clear. "Tucker and your hired gunmen, drop your gun belts. You are all going to jail. Then, like I said, I'll see you swing. Drop them now."

Now, I stood next to the marshall. Spence had stepped away from the hitching rail, positioning himself tall and steady next to us, focusing on Tate and the other riders.

He knew I was gunning for Tucker, ready for him to make a wrong move. All he had to do was refuse to lay down his gun. This man tried to kill our dad, and big brother was out for blood.

There was no misunderstanding my words as they rang out. "Tucker, we're not going to dance all afternoon. Drop them or make your move."

"You're dead, you're all dead." Tucker spat and went for his gun, and as he did, a boom from a rifle split the air. Everyone was caught off guard by the unmistakable reverberating crack of the rifle shot coming from behind the three men on the street.

Blood spilled from Tucker's shirt pocket. His head jerked back, and the pristine hat he wore flew from his head. In quick succession, the snakeskin booted feet followed his head as he did a complete back roll onto his belly. He lay motionless as the red stain spread across his white shirt, tanned beige vest, and down his back.

Tate and the two riders went for their guns. They were all dead before they cleared leather. My gun came to life. I fired three shots, hitting all three where their hearts should have been. God only knows if they had a heart at all.

Tate looked down, fell to his knees in the welcoming red Colorado soil, and looked past me, a long, forlorn look, and then he collapsed face down. The other gunmen flew backward off their mounts and met their maker before they hit the ground.

Every deputy in the posse and the three ranch cowboys stared open-mouthed and wide-eyed at me in disbelief. I was fast, damn fast, and killed all three in a split second with my gun back in the holster before the others ever moved a muscle.

They all turned to see if Ben had shot Tucker, but it was Maggie who stood behind us with a rifle in her hands, smoke still drifting out of the barrel.

Maggie spoke with reverence, "Paybacks are another form of justice here in the West. Jack, I took care of him for you, honey. It's over."

My voice split the air clearly, "Spence, fellas, you all okay?"

"Kinda hard to get hurt, Reg, if you didn't let them enter the battle," said Yates.

I suppose I resembled a rock pillar, stern-faced, muscles like iron, but I had meant business. Regarding the pile of dead men, I said, "I happen to agree with Maggie about paybacks."

43

AFTER THE SMOKE CLEARED

S pence spoke up, "I guess Marshall Yates did his part, so what's next?"

Nancy and Chelsea hurried out of the café. Nancy reached Maggie first and took the rifle from her while Chelsea put her arm around Maggie's shaking shoulders.

"So, you can cook and shoot. It's a pretty good combination for a Western gal, I would say," Chelsea said, helping to ease the tension.

The marshall asked Tom, "What's your story?"

"Pinkie, I knew we weren't going to go along with this scheme of Tucker's, but I didn't want to have a shootout on the ranch. We could have handled it ourselves. I think, but one of us might have been killed. I figured we would ride to town and let you deal the cards, and we would back the play. The only thing I was concerned about was you shooting us beforehand. I hoped you would get my meaning when we rode up first."

"Yea," What were you two hiding with this story...swimming?" Spence asked.

Pinkie shook his head, chuckling, and began the short tale. "When Tom and I were kids, we would go down to the swimming hole, and there was a rope swing hanging from a tree limb over the water. Tom was younger and scared of the water. He was scared the water wouldn't break when he went in, so I would go first and break the water. As we got older, it was our joke, and I would always go first. So I got the point. Luckily for that story, you all dodged a bullet."

Poke scratched his head. "Hell, that was some good thinking. Tom, you could have let us in this, you know."

Pinkie asked Buck what his comment about returning a nail meant.

Buck glanced over at Spence for him to tell his tale. "Pinkie, my dad hates horns on cattle. He understood they were good for their protection, but he was tired of getting hooked and his horses scarred up, so he nubbed the horns. Dad made special barbed nails and pounded them into the horn, proving that they were his cows, his own little hidden brand. Buck found a nail, so Marshall, I understood when he said he was returning it."

"Hell, I guess everyone has a story."

I leaned over Tate, reached under his motionless body, and pulled the neatly folded handkerchief from his back pocket. I unfolded it and wiped the sweat and dirt from my face. Then, I kicked loose soil on the spotless man who lay in front of me. *Oh, that felt so good.*

"Tate," I said, "If women weren't present. I'd wipe something else." And I threw the handkerchief to the ground and turned my back on the scene.

Chelsea stepped off the boardwalk, watching me walk down the road, and began to walk toward me. Joe had walked over to her and was silent, watching, and listening.

Joe said, "Chelsea, sweetheart, I'd let him be. I know you want to make sure he's all right, but I know Reg, and right now, he needs a little time to reflect on what just happened. He has never killed a man before. He has a lot on his mind."

"You are probably right. I'll let him be for now."

By this time, the ladies had seen enough street action and hustled back to the café, where they hung the closed sign and sat down to rest. The marshall followed close on their heels, wanting a word with Maggie.

"I'm sorry I shot, but I wanted that man to die," she admitted.

"Maggie, you weren't alone. We all wanted this man to pay. He pulled, you fired. It's over. You settled in your mind now?"

"I will be. I want to get my husband buried proper. Spence. "Did you know your brother could shoot like that?"

"Maggie, I am not surprised. He spent a lot of time practicing before firing those bullets. He waited a long time to avenge my dad."

Buck pushed Spence's conversation further. "Roan, what the heck? Has anyone ever seen anything like that? That horse is amazing."

"Most likely, no one has ever seen anything like that. What a warrior." I bet those horses are still running. They are probably in Wyoming territory by now," said Spence.

I sat alone at the edge of town on a bench overlooking a small stream. Bending over, I held my head in my hands, worn out and tired to the bone. Roan silently walked up and stood over me.

"Girl, you never cease to amaze me. How in the world did you ever learn that trick?" I chuckled and nodded my head in thanks to my companion. In return, she shook her head in acknowledgment.

Pinkie looked down the road at where I had wandered off. "That's a good man we have here, fellas. Why don't we take these bodies to the barn, finish the others, and set the funeral for tomorrow?"

They skirted around the bodies in the street, knowing a long overdue burden had been removed. *For the time being, evil could no longer hold its fury over this town and good people.*

We could all smell that tobacco before the liveryman even got close. "Not again!" Spence yelled to Joe. The wind must have changed direction. "You better have brought enough tobacco for everyone."

Joe began a babble of words. "Plenty nuff to go around. I must have been dreaming. I've never seen a horse handle itself that way. And your brother, did anyone even see him twitch? Fast isn't the word. And Maggie shooting Tucker was an added bonus to the action, something you don't see every day. I'm glad I saw it all and lived to tell the tale. I'd never believe it if I didn't see it with my own eyes,"

Joe continued talking like a wind-up toy. "Spence, we could sell tickets, and people would come for miles to see that horse babysit your brother. Hell of a horse. Just a hell of a horse."

"All those deserving of a bullet are face down in the dirt. Let's carry this bunch to the barn. We'll strip off the valuable gear, sell it and their horses to pay the undertaker, maybe give what's left to the ladies," said the marshall.

Maggie and Nancy indicated they didn't want anything to do

with any leftover money. "Give anything remaining to Preacher Bill. He can use it in the church to help where needed."

The marshall nodded his head in agreement. "If that's what you ladies decided upon, I will make sure it goes that way. There's a bounty back east on Tucker and probably the other men, too. I will split that money from the bounty between all of you men. You earned it."

Poke laughed. "Tucker said he would give us all money for riding in with him, so I guess he stuck to his word."

One would think a town fiesta had begun out on the street as townspeople crowded the dusty road. Sara and all the children ran out of hiding and headed toward the gathering crowd.

Not wanting the children to witness such a sight, Spence stopped them all. "Caty, sweet pea, can you take the kids into Maggie's right now?"

"Sure, Spencer, are you doing all right?"

"Doing fine, all of us are fine. Please, take the young'uns in the back way so they don't see the results of this activity and have nightmares, and I'll see you in Maggie's in a little bit."

"Fine, I'll have food ready. I'm sure you're hungry."

The townspeople gawked and gathered around the bodies. Some celebrated with whistles and cheers, while others behaved more somberly.

Pinkie, Tom, Buck, Poke, and Joe grinned ear to ear, pointing directly at Spence while he spoke to Caty. He didn't miss the opportunity to glare back at the foolish men.

"Stop it. We have work to do. No joking about me and Caty, or I'll show you who's the fastest draw in the family."

Trying their best not to belly laugh at the lad's misfortune, the marshall and his helpers loaded the bodies into a wagon and headed for the barn.

I sat with Roan, standing watch close by late into the dark of the night. My mind moved like a runaway team eating up the miles as I clicked off the tasks that needed my attention.

Contact Dad and tell him we are fine and ready to move the cattle back home. Prepare to return Maggie's homestead to her. Locate any kin the Anders might have to claim or sell the T Lazy 7 Ranch. Help Clancy's family with his final wishes.

I second-guessed myself. *I knew it was right to stop the outlaws, but was I too eager to plant them in the ground? Should I have waited a little longer, directing the fight another way?"*

It's a fine line between caring and being a killer. Overall, I felt relieved that Tucker came to town and had a choice but turned it down.

"You did the right thing and are not a bad man."

The words startled me. I looked up towards the heavens.

"Not that high, son, just me."

I looked behind my back and saw Preacher Bill hovering above me. Wonderment filled my mind.

How? "Was I talking out loud? How did you know what I was feeling?"

Preacher Bill sat down next to me. "My son, knowing what a good man thinks is easy. Did I do right? Was I too hasty? Was I grudgeful? A good person always questions his actions. A sinful one never thinks about it. He just moves on."

"Reg, between you, me, and God, I have a bad past. You killed men with a gun. I've killed men with guns, knives, tree limbs, and bare hands. I felt life leave their bodies, and their souls haunt me today. Let it go, young man. You did the right thing. A power we can't understand guided your hand. We were lucky that good men were not harmed."

"Tomorrow, we will put our friends to rest. It's in God's hands now. You will have many more trials in your life. This is only one of them. How you solve it in your mind will guide your future. Reg, I'd like to keep our conversation between the three of us."

"Will do. Thanks, preacher. I'm just going to sit a little longer."

I watched the huge mountain of a man move away. I understood how the preacher's burden haunted him. For a man of God, it must have been overwhelming at times. I admired him greatly but was saddened by his comments and the weight on those shoulders.

My thoughts drifted to Chelsea. Everything moved so fast that I never had time to get to know her.

Was she in love, or was she just caught up with the man who was with her father when he passed and had brought his riches home to her?

Part of me simply wanted to gather the cattle and move them toward home. But I felt maybe I would enjoy courting Chelsea, and I certainly loved this town and the people.

The café had emptied at dusk, and the town had turned quiet and peaceful. For many of the townsfolk, a great evil and burden had lifted, and this small western town had a new beginning.

I walked in the shadows as I passed the barn. There was a fire, and the men stood, discussing the day's events. I walked on, talked out, and played out. I was just plain tired with only one desire: to rest.

I entered the café and placed my foot on the first stair step leading up to my room when he heard a voice, low and soft.

"Are you okay? I'm worried about you. Joe said I should leave you alone, but I can't stand it any longer."

Chelsea ran across the room, tears streaming down her face. Her red and puffy eyes bore witness that she had cried a long time. Stress, anger, hate, love, or relief all ran a foot race through her emotions.

"I was so scared I nearly died," she said.

I reached out and pulled her to my chest. Her shoulders were heaving, and she was breathing so fast I could feel her heart pounding.

"It's ok, Chels, I'm fine, we're fine. Everyone is far better off now, and there is a lot of pain with all the news, bodies, and all. Everyone can now start to heal and move forward. Chels, are Maggie and your ma okay?"

"They're sad and lonely, but they now feel some closure. The funeral will be tomorrow, so we can all say our goodbyes. I'm going to fix some food for you, Reg. You must be starving."

"I would really enjoy sitting with you and having a piece of your pie and a tall, cold glass of milk."

Chelsea guided me to a chair, hugged my neck, and kissed the back of his head.

"I care so much for you. Sit tight," she said and hustled off. She returned with a whole apple pie covered in ice cream, a cold pitcher of milk, and two spoons.

"You start, I'll be back."

She went into the kitchen, returned with a bag of apples, and ran out the door, finding Roan right there waiting for a visit, one girl to another.

Wrapping her arms around Roan's neck, she crooned, "I can't thank you enough, you beautiful, brave girl. I'll feed you apples forever."

Roan put her head on Chelsea's shoulder, and without waiting another minute, she bobbed for the bag of apples Chelsea had placed on the ground. "Eat up, girl, and I'll bring more tomorrow. I promise."

Inside, Ben sat with me. After resting in his room, he decided to seek me out. "Chelsea, I just wanted to talk with Reg for a minute, I know you two need some time. Reg, I'm at a loss for words. I've never seen anything like what happened today. It's a pleasure to be on this side of the law and hopefully be able to call you a friend."

"Ben, I was worried when we started this adventure. You were an outlaw and had a hand in the dealings on the ranch. Then you came forward, and this all came together because of you. I'm impressed that you took a bullet for the lawman Yates. You put your life in jeopardy for the ones around you. I will gladly ride the river with you any time."

And then I raised my glass of milk and said to him, "Here's to your health and good fortune."

"Thanks, partner. I know I've got a long road to travel, and I hope the law will take it all in, and maybe I can get out swingin'. Hoping to set my roots right here. Well, Reg, it's been my pleasure. God led me to you. I would like to talk again before I leave, but I'll leave you in this beautiful woman's hands for now. I'll leave you two to your pie," said Ben.

The emotional lass hugged Ben. "You need help getting back to bed? You need to relax."

"I'm healing in more ways than one. Eat up."

Even though I had eaten the melting ice cream, the pie remained untouched. Chelsea and I walked out to the bench by the creek and enjoyed the pie and each other's company while listening to the burbling waters.

Spence and Joe sat outside the barn, enjoying the warmth of a crackling fire. The two smoking outcasts enjoyed their tobacco and tried to persuade the other men there to partake, receiving resounding skepticism about the smell and their fear of trying it.

Spence placed his pipe on the sawn log beside him. "I suggest we talk to my brother in the morning. I'll give him one thing: He's the best person I've ever known for solving a problem. I'd lay money on the table; he's already thinking about this."

"Why would he care about what happens to us?" Poke asked.

"That's what he does. He's a worrier and a thinker. That's why I can sit around and smoke a pipe. He's the brainy one. I'm the one who smokes the pipe and waits for instructions. Don't tell him. He'll get a fat head. Pinkie, what about you? What's next for you?"

"I'll get all the information I can on these outlaws and see if any paper is posted on them and what rewards are up for grabs. Then, I'll head back home and see what's next on the list."

"Tom, that's where you come in. How about joining me as my new deputy? It's a good opportunity to learn the law. You can be trained and someday wear the badge in another town or take over for me. You're smart, Tom. I could see you entering the law profession and maybe becoming an attorney, a judge, or a politician."

"I've thought about just those things. I never wanted to be a cowhand. I just fell into it. It would be nice to start something new and avoid this lot. I know the smell would be better."

Poke laughed and threw a log into the fire. "It would be nice for us, too. Get somebody who could work. Yeah, and if we get into trouble, Tom could save our asses."

"Nah, not you, Poke. I'd let you go to jail or swing, but I'd save Buck," said Tom.

Maggie came out of the dark and startled everyone.

Pinkie spoke up, "Maggie, you scared the dog out of us all. You must be part Indian. Did you bring your rifle along?"

"No, Mr. Yates. I'm inviting you men up for food. I know you are all starving. It's on the house."

"No. Ma'am, the county can pay this tab," offered Pinkie. "And one hell of a tip."

"Sounds good." Poke added, "Food always tastes better when someone else is buying."

Buck laughed. "Sounds about right. Either Tom or I do the cooking and the cleaning, and you, Poke, you do the eating."

"What's wrong with that? I help where I can."

"Spence, you, and Joe come along but leave that damn tobaccy here. Love the company, just can't get over that smell."

"Guess we can oblige since we're sitting with a bunch of girlies and Pinkie's buying."

They escorted Maggie back to the cafe and enjoyed a nice, warm meal. The company was comfortable and full of good conversation and laughter.

44

THE DAY OF THE FUNERAL

The following day, I woke early and sat outdoors, watching the beautiful morning sky. The clouds parted slightly, making room for a slow-rising sun. The weather dropped during the night, leaving us with a cool morning.

As they staggered past me and entered the café, I greeted those who wished to attend the day's event. I'm sure they all were anticipating a long day. We had good people who we needed to have God's word spoken over them as we said our goodbyes. There might be a few words for the outlaws, too. We needed to let the troubled times go.

Preacher Bill would deliver the sermon, making people feel safe and secure. A powerful man with a heart that made everyone who came into contact with him feel welcome and easy to get along with. He could surely inflict some pain if he chose to. Good thing he was a man of God.

Visitors to the café offered their kind words and sympathies to all those whom the violence had touched. The women and men folk wanted to help in any way they could. The women present took over the kitchen duties and the serving while the men ate a hardy breakfast and then headed up to the cemetery to dig the graves. They appreciated the cool day, for the task of digging so many graves would be grueling.

Spence, Joe, and I went to the barn to build coffins. All three of us were good with our hands when it came to carpentry. Spence and I could turn our hands to just about anything our ranch needed, and Joe constructed not only his barn but his home and helped build many others.

The ladies who were not cooking helped the children gather flowers for the graves. Maggie, Nancy, and Chelsea dressed for the day. Caty, the childcare provider, took Callie for a walk, and they both fed Roan her favorite apple treats.

Upon returning home, Caty tried her best to clean and dress Callie. The four-year-old squirmed and argued about why she had to be clean and wear her good dress.

It wasn't Sunday, and Callie wanted to play and ride on her horse, Roan. Caty explained that they were going to a funeral, but this made no sense to the toddler. When Callie asked Caty why she was sad and had tears in her eyes, Caty said, "Callie, you'll understand someday."

Pinkie needed to inform the county and district judges of the news in his town. He also needed to let them know about Ben and his involvement. On his way to send the wire, he stopped at the barn. Spence went along to keep him company.

Spence sent word to his folks, letting them know Reg and he were safe and unharmed. He informed them he would be moving their cattle home and had hired help. He added that he had quite a story to tell when he got home.

When Spence returned, I left the men at the barn and began to search for Buck. I had questions regarding the Anders' place and whether they had any kin folk. Buck filled me in on what he knew, and I went back to send my own wire, this time to the Anders' nieces in Pennsylvania.

After finishing the final touches on the coffins, we wrapped the bodies, gently placed them inside, and sealed the lids. After loading the coffins in the wagon, we were ready to proceed to the cemetery.

In time, we figured we could check the brands on the cows and see if we could figure out who these two unknown cattlemen were. It would be nice to let their families know of their demise. Now that the individuals were all prepped and loaded, Spence and I went to see if the families were ready.

Maggie was dressed in a beautiful shirtwaist the color of newly sprouted green grass with white lace trim for the collar. Nancy and the three girls wore various shades of blue. *Apparently, blue was Clancy's favorite color.*

The lovely green and blues seemed fitting for the day, honoring their loved ones. They also reminded Maggie of Mrs. Anders. The ladies were beautiful. It was sad that they looked so lovely on one of the worst days of their lives. Surely, if their loved ones could look down from the heavens, they would be proud.

Preacher Bill took Maggie's arm. Spence took Chelsea's, and I walked with Clancy's widow. Caty was on Spence's other arm.

Spence stopped and put a pink wildflower in Caty's hair. Her pink cheeks told all around she was excited that he took the time to notice her. She held onto his arm and was pleased to be with him.

Spence was a lady's man. He knew how to make them feel wanted and always had the right words. It got him in trouble on more than one occasion, but today, he was what these ladies needed. The townsfolk fell into place as the mourners walked to the cemetery behind the wagon.

When the group reached the cemetery, it was evident that the men did a nice job preparing the burial ground. The ladies had flowers laid out around the graves. There were no markers yet, but they would be made in time. They had chosen a place for Clancy. There were flowers and an area prepared for his family to visit his gravesite when the need to talk arose.

Preacher Bill welcomed everyone and talked of God and the better place above. His words were heartfelt, putting everyone at ease with a short sermon and the kindness they all needed.

We lowered the caskets into the earth, and before long, a female alto voice began to sing "Amazing Grace," and the rest of the mourners joined in. Each person waited to say their tearful goodbyes to their friends and neighbors. Even the hardest of men felt the sorrow.

At Maggie's, the town ladies had made food and drinks and decorated the luncheon with more pretty flowers. I don't think there was a flower left in town.

Everyone listened to Maggie speak about her husband. Clancy's wife, Nancy, and girls, Chelsea and Caty, told stories of fond memories of Clancy. Buck talked of his time with the Anders. He surely loved them both.

In the following days, the whole town felt the pain of the losses and did all they could to help wherever possible.

Chelsea and I had time to walk and enjoy picnics along the river. We talked about our lives and the future, melding together and looking forward to it.

Spence had his hands full with Caty, shadowing him around town, playful and happy. They both went for rides to check the cattle and the ranch.

Tom continued to help and remained with Pinkie, collecting information on the outlaws. Buck and Poke returned to the ranch to keep things in line, waiting for a reply from the wire I sent to the Anders' nieces. Joe kept his word and sold the outlaws' outfits, horses, tack, and guns.

We buried the outlaws on the outskirts of the cemetery. Preacher Bill gave a quick-to-the-point service, asking for forgiveness and healing.

Roan was enjoying the attention from everyone who passed her, maybe adding a few pounds to her already large frame. The news spread, and people came from the surrounding area and countryside to see this mystic horse.

After several weeks of relaxation and simple living, Spence and I decided to round up the herd and move them home.

Pinkie tried to determine who owned the cattle left on the ranch. He, Tom, Buck, and Poke separated and sorted cattle and their calves.

Pinkie ordered the sale of some of the unbranded cattle to compensate the cowhands for their labor in caring for the cattle and the ranch's needs.

Spence and I prepared to move our cattle. I asked Chelsea and

Caty if they wanted to go help on this trail ride. The girls were excited and wanted to see the family ranch and meet our folks. Buck and Poke were also going.

The girls giggled and made a pact to tell the true story of what their sons did for their community. They knew Reg would say very little, and the embellisher, Spence, would say too much, always entertaining but adding more color and action than facts.

I rose early, ready to move, and set off to visit Pinkie in the room behind the telegraph office. Ben and Pinkie were enjoying their morning coffee when I arrived. "Any word from the Anders' kin?"

Pinkie lifted a paper. "Just got a wire. The two young ladies wanted to thank everyone for avenging their uncle's murder. They will be here in a month to take possession of the ranch."

Pinkie showed me the wire. "I also told them, Reg, that you wanted to talk with them about the ranch and their hired hand, Buck, telling them that he was a loyal hand and good friend to the Anders."

"That started the ball rolling. I think we're ready to start moving cattle. Buck and Poke will be going back to our ranch with us. Buck talked to the neighboring ranchers and asked them to watch the T Lazy 7 Ranch and cattle until we returned."

"Excellent idea, Reg."

Pinkie sold the Tucker mob's gear and tack and gave the proceeds to Preacher Bill to benefit the church's goodwill. It was a good amount of money. "I'm going to ride out and give the boys their due from the cattle money. I know they said they didn't want it, but they're getting their fair share of the profits from the sale of the cattle, the bounty on the heads of Tucker and Tate, and their outlaw bunch. They're going to be pleased. It's a fair amount of money, enough to get them a piece of ground and a good head start," said Pinkie with great pride.

"Here's your cut, Reg. I've already given Spence, Joe, and Ben theirs. Ben here wouldn't take his, so I threatened to arrest him again if he didn't."

Ben interrupted, "I don't feel I need to make a gain for taking the high road and doing what's right. It's funny, Marshall, you're going to arrest me again for not taking the money. What's my crime? Being mean to an old man?"

"That's right, Ben, and it carries a stiff penalty."

"What's worse than hanging?"

"I'm not sure, but I'll think on it a while."

I welcomed hearing this early morning banter.

"I guess I'll put it to good use. I could have you send it to my folks with a letter. They would never believe it was honest money if it came from me."

I asked Pinkie when they were heading out of town to see the judges. "In a couple of days, we will be back in time to greet the girls when they arrive from back east. I'm thankful you were here to help resolve this matter. It's one to remember for sure. I'm going to enjoy telling this story."

"Glad you have a new story to tell Pinkie. See you again, both of you, in a month. Ride safe. Ben, you all right with everything? Let me know if there's anything I can say to anyone to help you out. You're a good friend."

"Thanks, Reg." Ben looked with amusement at Reg. "How do you feel about jailbreaks?"

"Well, you have a pocket full of money. We could probably figure out something."

They all laughed, even Pinkie, and they knew it wasn't a bad idea but wouldn't say a word out loud. Just kidding. . . kinda," said Ben.

"Reg, can I talk to you for a minute outside?" asked Pinkie.

"Sure, Pinkie. Ben, good luck."

Standing on the silver-colored ironwood boardwalk, I asked Pinkie, "What is going on?"

"I talked to the judge about Ben. I told him how Ben came to me, turned himself in, and gave me information about the bodies and Tucker. The judge was amazed when I reported how he took a bullet to protect me. Ben is not going to hang. In fact, he's going to work for me as my deputy. He will be on probation for quite a spell but will be free if he holds up his end. So, Reg, he's going to be okay, and a girl named Betty back our way is waiting for him."

"Well, hallelujah! God has spoken and used you, Pinkie, as his tool here on earth. Again, Hallelujah!"

"He's not going to hang, but now that I think about it, working for you, he may rather go to prison. Good job, Pinkie."

I shook his hand and patted him on the back. "The last time I was this happy, Pinkie, was when Ass Wipe bit the dirt."

"I agree. Okay. Reg, keep it quiet. I haven't let Ben and the others in on it yet. I want to see him suffer a bit longer."

I laughed, a big, hearty laugh. "Be nice, Pinkie. He might end up shooting you if you make him suffer too long."

"I'm waiting for Betty, his gal. She's coming in on the noon stage."

"Alright, Pinkie, I'm not going to miss that. Right there is a great story to tell with a truly happy ending."

"Joe, where is that no good brother of mine?"

"You'll love this, Reg, come see."

We walked to the barn door and looked outside. Spence was walking away with Caty, Little Joe, and Dan. They were heading out to go fishing.

"Looks like that little brother of yours has found some new play friends his own age. Maybe the little ones will teach him something?"

I snickered. "I doubt it. He's beyond help."

"Joe, we're going to pull out in the morning. Meet me at the noon stage today."

"What's up?"

"You'll see, don't be late," I insisted.

I hollered at Spence, "Be back for the noon stage, and don't be late." He never looked back but waved. I was happy to see Spence enjoying the day. "Joe, when the babysitter returns, make sure he comes along. It's important."

Roan walked alongside Spence and carried the kids: Callie, Dan, Little Joe, and Caty. As usual, Caty rode on the tail end, holding onto the little ones.

"That horse is the best babysitter I've ever seen," Nancy said, exiting the mercantile with an armful of supplies for Chelsea and amused at the picture the horse and children made.

The stage finally rolled down the dusty road and pulled up to

Maggie's, the local stop where passengers unloaded. The driver dropped off the box of mail and several bags for the passengers. Then he hopped down off the coach box.

He opened the door, and two men and a woman stepped out of the covered coach. The men entered Maggie's Café while the woman stood outside in the midday sunshine. She was alone and was looking for a familiar face.

Spence, Joe, and I were sitting on the bench in front of the café. I stood up and said, "Excuse me, ma'am, I'm Reg. Are you Betty?"

"Yes, I am. I'm looking for Ben. Do you know him?"

"Sure, do. We all do. This is my brother, Spence, and our friend, Joe. If you look behind you, I think you'll recognize that fella."

She turned and smiled while the tears ran down her face. Then she leaped into Ben's arms. "I was so worried when the marshall wrote that you were shot."

"Betty, what are you doing here? I'm so happy to see you, but why have you come?"

"Because I am crazy about you, silly, and I know you feel the same about me. Do you love me?" Betty asked.

"You sure are right on that count. When did Marshall Yates write to you?"

"A week ago, he asked me to come."

"Ben, are you okay? The gunshot and all? The marshall told me that you saved his life."

"I'm not so sure about saving the marshall's bacon, but I did catch a bullet."

"Hope you had a good trip, Betty. Welcome to town," said a man's husky voice from behind her.

"Well, hello, Marshall Yates," she greeted him with a tight

hug. "Thank you for watching over Ben and only letting him get shot once. I might have worried a little if he had been shot twice."

The marshall shook Betty's hand. "My friends call me Pinkie. I'm sure glad you could make the trip. I want to talk to you both about Ben's upcoming trial."

"Why don't you two visit? Let's meet for dinner, my treat."

"Spence, please find our cowboys and Preacher Bill and invite them. I'll find the women folk and bring them along, too. Ben may need all our support."

Ben smiled until he heard that.

"Sounds good, Pinkie, like The Last Supper," said Ben.

Pinkie asked Ben, "What do you know about the Last Supper?"

"I've been reading up, trying to find a loophole to keep me from hanging."

Betty slapped Ben on the back of the head. "Hanging is not funny."

"I thought it was funny. . .a little. . . don't know what to say."

Ben took Betty's bag.

"Betty. Let's get you a room, and I'll let you get some rest, then we can talk."

"Ben, that can wait. Let's go for a walk. I saw a pretty spot by the river when we rolled in."

Ben glanced our way. "Fellas, I'd like to visit with you, but she's a lot prettier than you saddle tramps. I'll see you at supper."

"I see how we rate," said Spence, shaking his head.

"Spence, you're cute, but not that cute."

They walked off hand in hand. I turned to Joe and Spence. "Boy, his life is about to change."

"Reg, we need to do something. We can't let him hang. He's a good man. He's proven that."

"I know. We will talk to the marshall and let him know what we think. Maybe he has some sway with the judge. You in Joe?"

"Thinking a jailbreak and high tailin' him out of the county?"

I scowled at them both. "You think Pinkie would let it lay?"

"Probably not, but he might give us a head start. Ben did take a bullet for him."

That evening, a plentiful bounty was laid before us, with all our adult friends surrounding Ben and Betty. The women filled Betty in on what happened to Ben, taking a bullet and all. Visiting everyone was a special treat.

"Pinkie, I can't take it anymore." Spence looked Pinkie's way, then at Ben and Betty. "Ben is a good man. He's changed his ways and proven he's on the right road."

Ben said, "Spence, it's fine. He has his job to do. I'm the one who did the evil deeds. I deserve what I have coming."

Pinkie spoke up. "You're right. You do. Being a lawman is tough. Some things you must do are hard, but it's the law."

Joe stood up. "Pinkie, we older men here have all seen trouble. Some were our own doing, but that was a different time. We all came out without feeling the rope stretch around our neck."

Preacher Bill stood up and said, "Gentleman, let's let Pinkie talk. We all know God moves in mysterious ways."

The room went deadly quiet. The mountain had spoken, and only God could move this mountain.

Pinky stood up. "We all know Ben here is guilty of his crimes, and we know he came forward to help get to the truth. But the law is the law."

Ben stood up, watching Betty as she cried.

"Marshall, it's all okay. I know what's coming my way. I want to thank everyone. I do have feelings for this woman next to me. It's a shame that it's too little, too late."

"Ben, let me say my piece, please. Okay, everyone, I sent a wire to the judge and explained what happened. The judge agrees with me, and we both feel what needs to be done follows the law," said Pinkie.

"That's bull shit," bellowed Spence.

"Spence, sit back down," I said.

"No, Reg, I won't let this happen."

The preacher placed his powerful hands on Spence's shoulders, looked him in the eyes, and forcibly pushed him back into his chair. Then, the man of the cloth looked at Pinkie and said, "Go ahead."

"I'm sorry, but the judge and I talked. Your sentence is stiff and will be carried out to the letter of the sentence." Pinkie put his hand on Ben's shoulder. "The judge and I are giving you two years of working under me as a deputy. Then you're a free man."

We could hear the wind whistling outside; otherwise, no sound traveled through the room.

I broke into laughter. "See y'all, we don't need to break Ben out."

Spence and Joe gawked at me. "You knew?"

Betty screamed, "Ben, you're a free man. It's time for me to make an honest man of you. Will you marry me?"

With tears running down his face, Ben couldn't speak. He sat motionless.

"Ben?" Betty asked.

Spence gawked at Ben, but he stayed seated, then looked at Preacher Bill.

"Ben. You going to answer the lady?" asked the preacher.

Ben didn't say a word, but we all knew the answer when he took Betty's hand.

"Ben, you have a new job, or I can send you to the gallows. What's it going to be?"

"I'll think on it, Marshall."

Maggie slapped him lightly across the back of the head. Then again and again. "You're done thinking, answer the man."

"Well, I guess it can't be that bad. I think I can handle it, I guess," Ben said, beaming with a glow of happiness.

"Good to hear, but there is more," said Pinkie.

"What? Don't think my heart can take any more."

The Marshall reached into his shirt pocket and pulled out a banknote. "Here's a surprise wedding gift. Your cut of the cattle sale and bounty money. A fair piece of money and a good start for you two."

The room filled with hoots of congratulations, applause, and laughter. Ben cried and cried. He had never felt such fulfillment in his life. He looked skyward.

"Thank you. You did it all for me."

45

THE CATTLE DRIVE

W e had been on the trail, moving our cattle for several days, and it was going smoothly. Chelsea and Caty drove the wagon ahead of the herd, enjoying their trip together. They managed the cooking for the wranglers, the best grub any of the wranglers had ever tasted on a cattle drive.

Caty was a ball of fire, flitting from the grub line to sitting around the campfire, either listening to our stories or jumping in with those of her own, full of humor.

She became Spencer's shadow, never leaving his side. And he took a lot of ribbing on the trail, but we could see he enjoyed her company. She was now his little sister. She tried her best to win his heart. The first crush was always the hardest.

Chelsea worked long, hard hours, constantly rising before the rest of us stirred. She prepared hearty breakfasts with meat, beans, bread, hot coffee, and always pie at night. We all appreciated the fine meals we had on the trail and joked about taking the cows down to Texas so we could keep eatin' her cookin'.

She even thought to bring apples for the pie, and the peals went to Roan. *That was one spoiled horse. Of course, Roan was one of the family, so why not?*

Chelsea was a lot of fun around the fire. She kept our stories clean and kinda honest. Watching her, I knew this woman was more than I deserved.

Mom and Dad were going to fall in love with these two. I wished Callie could have come along, but she was too little for the journey. She would have loved to ride Roan and play in the wagon. Mom would not want to let these two go back home. She never said it, but we knew she always wanted a daughter.

We stopped at the river for a night to let the cattle feed on sweet grass and drink their fill of water. When we rested the cattle along the river, they were content and lazily walked the water's edge.

Riding back to the night camp, we were met by the ladies. They both held an armful of towels and plenty of soap.

"We could smell you a mile off. We think it's time for you all to bathe and soak those clothes." Caty pinched her nose and giggled so hard she could barely breathe.

"Reg, you need to talk to that gal of yours. Wranglers don't take baths in the middle of the drive."

"You're on your own, Buck," I said.

Caty sarcastically replied, "No bath...no food...your choice."

The other men didn't say a word. They inched their way close to the lady trail bosses and took the towels and the soap.

Poke smooth talked the females. "Ladies, I'll bathe every day if you keep cooking. Love those pies."

"Spencer," Caty asked with her hand on her hip, "What do you say? Bath or no food?"

"Listen here, Missy Smarty Pants, you better sleep with one eye open, or you may find a toad under your pillow."

Then, Chelsea threw the soap at Spence. "Maybe you should be sleeping with one eye open, or you may find a skillet coming your way."

I moved away from the line of fire, laughing with every step. "Spence, you're losing ground fast. I'd start moving towards the water if you get my drift."

We all stripped down to our long handles, and in we went. The water felt great. Nice to wash the trail dust off. We just didn't want the ladies to know that. After a long soak and a bit of horseplay, we ambled out and wrapped up in towels and blankets. We went to the fire and hung our clothes out to dry, but sitting around in our long handles in front of the females was very uncomfortable.

Buck pulled up his blanket around his neck and shoulders. "All we need is to be stripped down, and some varmint rides up to steal the cows, or worse, the animals start to stampede, and we're all riding naked. All hats and boots." *Funny, but not too funny.*

"It would be a hell of a sight, boys. Can you even imagine it?" Poke slapped his knee and bellowed out a great belly laugh.

"It's nice to be able to breathe, and I figured if you were eating pie, you wouldn't be telling lies around the fire," Caty teased as she offered a second piece of pie.

We waited for the girls to climb into the wagon for the night and then hustled to put on our clothes. Still damp, but it was far more comforting than sitting around with our manhood blowing in the breeze.

Buck laughed out loud from his bed roll. "I can see it now, Reg. We're going to have to take a bath before we come to visit ya. Towels and soap on the front porch."

Poke replied, "Yep, Buck and we will have to wash behind each other's ears."

"Not funny cowpokes, not funny at all," I said.

"Who's laughing Reg?" Spence now jumped into the middle of the tease. "I'm going to just send letters from home and sit around dirty."

"Like that's going to happen. Spence, as soon as we get home, Caty will tell Ma exactly who was boss on this trail, and your days of dirt are over."

"Women on a cattle drive, just not right, just not natural," Spence grumbled, shaking his head.

The drive with the cattle went easy. I signaled for the girls to pull the wagon to a stop while the men gathered around, taking in the breathtaking scenery before moving on to camp for the night. I wanted our companions to view this part of our ranch.

"Caty, this is part of our homeland. Mom and Dad carved out a nice piece of heaven here. It's twenty-two thousand acres, grass, water, mountains, and cows."

Chelsea looked in amazement, "Reg, this is unbelievable, and you hadn't said a word. All this time, we all thought you had a ranch, not a small country!"

Buck and Poke were amazed as well. "Your folks ranch makes the T Lazy 7 look like a petting zoo."

I smiled and waved to Spence and pointed north. "Let's get movin' the cattle to North Sparrow meadow before we get buried in niceness. We will set our camp there. Tomorrow, we will ride into the ranch and see the folks."

Chelsea said, "Why don't you ride ahead, you two? We can camp and meet you there tomorrow. It will give you time to visit."

"No, Chelsea, I don't want to listen to this story told five or six times. We all ride in together and show you two beauties off proper."

Chelsea told Caty, "I brought you a new dress, hair ribbon, and shoes so that you will be the center of attention."

"I'm excited to see Spencer's mama. I bet she's nice just like he is," said Caty.

I rolled my eyes. "Oh, yeah, she's sweet, just like Spence."

"Reg, you're just jealous because I inherited Mom's looks, brains, and smarts. What did you get?"

"Luckily, I have Mom's ability to tell the difference between B.S and the real truth when I hear it."

Buck threw down some firewood. "Reg, Poke, and I will stay with the cattle, so you will have plenty of time to visit with your folks," said Buck

"No, Buck, you and Poke are both coming along. Dad will want to hear the story of Tate, Tucker, and the T Lazy 7 Ranch. I'm sure I'll be talked out after a minute or two, and Spence will have told so many lies…"

"I don't lie, Reg, I embellish."

"Mm-hmm, Spence, a big fancy word for lying."

I pushed Spence on the shoulder as if to say 'love ya,' then grabbed up the reigns.

"Buck, why don't you and I go for a short ride? I've got something I want to talk over with you."

"Okay, I want to see this ranch land anyway." Buck looked over his shoulder to Poke, "I guess I'm his favorite since you're not invited," taunted Buck.

Poke snickered and said, "Maybe he's going to do away with you, so he doesn't have to pay you to ride back since we won't be pushing any cows. Reg knows who the good hand is."

The food was hot and ready when Buck and I returned to the camp.

"You piggies eat your fill. Caty and I are heading to the creek to wash up. It's going to be a big day tomorrow. Now, I'm taking a rifle, and if there's any peeking gentlemen, I'm a darn good shot. My daddy taught me. And I never miss."

Off they went hand in hand. Chelsea was nervous to meet my folks, but she hid it well. Tomorrow would be nerve-racking for any young lady in her position. She would find a place in their hearts, just as she found her way into mine.

And Caty so wanted to be grown up. She was a special young lady. I wished Spence were years younger. I worried about her heart being broken, but her time would come.

"Spence."

"Yea, Reg, what's up?"

"See that little girl, she loves you. Spence. You walk easy around her."

"I know, big brother, I would rather take a stick in the eye than see her heart broken. I'll just be my usual charming self and wait till she sees a boy who steals her away from me."

Spence stirred the fire with a long stick, sending sparks into the night. He said, "Buck, you and Poke are good to ride the trail with. The cattle moved easily, and you two are good company around the fire. What do you two intend to do with your bounty money, if you don't mind me asking?"

Buck looked deep into his coffee cup before answering. "I'd like to go back and try to start my own place, run some cattle, and try my hand at building myself a ranch like this place here."

"Me, too," said Poke. He continued to voice his thoughts, "I was hoping maybe I could throw in with Buck, and we could put our money together. He needs someone around to help him loosen up a bit."

Buck pointed to Poke, "Sounds good, partner. I need someone to boss around."

"Partners don't boss Buck. They speak respectful-like and learn to listen to all parties involved."

"Hell, Poke, I didn't think you had it in ya. Feel a little money in your pocket, and now you're a high falluten type."

"Pay attention, Buck, you might learn a bit."

As the sun rose the next morning, we waited on the girls until they finally popped out of the wagon. They were as pretty as ever, glowing, a sight to behold.

Spence took Caty by the arm and helped her into the front of the wagon. "Caty, I'll ride next to you. I want Mom to see the pretty girl I met on my travels. She'll never believe it."

"Alright, Spence, but be nice and make sure your mama likes me."

"Don't worry about that, Caty. She's going to eat you up."

Poke and Buck flattered the big sister with their suggestion. "Chelsea, you better ride with us. We need a pretty girl to ride in with."

"What about Reg?" Chelsea asked.

"Reg can push a cow. We just don't want Spence to be the only one riding next to a beautiful woman."

With those words, Caty turned every shade of red from pink to scarlet. She was also a happy young woman.

This homeward-bound gang rode into the ranch yard. Mom and Dad sat on the porch watching for us. Dad stayed there as always, stoic, watching from the outside.

Not so for Mom, who ran straight off the porch to give Spence a big hug and plenty of kisses, then reached over to tightly squeeze my hand. She started to cry as she said, "My babies are back home, and you brought me a house full of guests."

"Hello, ma'am, I'm Poke, and this fella next to me is Buck. Your sons roped us into this adventure. And we're glad it's over, so we don't have to listen to Spence talk anymore."

"I understand. He always had the gift of gab. He was usually talkin' when he was in trouble trying to squirm his way out of it."

"I see he hasn't changed much, ma'am," said Buck.

"Buck, you surely do know Spence," she said.

"Mom, enough already. I want to introduce you to the prettiest girl to drive cattle. Mom, this is Caty."

Mom approached the young lady and said, "You must have had quite the adventure traveling with this bunch. I want you to tell me all about it. You come here, show me that pretty dress, and let me look at that beautiful braided golden hair."

"Give me a hug. I'm a hugger. It's the best way to get to know someone's character." If they hug tight and straight on a full hug, they will be your friend for a lifetime."

"If they shoulder hug, you know, sideways to you, then there's not much hope you will become close. You may be civil to one another but probably never friends."

Caty met Mom head on, hugged tight, and giggled. She backed away and said, "See, we will be friends forever. I knew it."

Mom held onto her hand and would not let her go.

Then, Mom glanced Chelsea's way. "Son, who is this young lady here?"

"She's a hired hand. Our camp cook and she's in charge of the baths," I said.

"Chelsea, this is my mom." Chelsea and Caty are sisters, and they have a little sister back home named Little Callie, and she's quite a joy. She's only four, too young for the trail this time."

Chelsea walked proudly and steadily over and gave Mom a bear hug.

"Reg, she will fit in just fine. I believe she may be enough women to set you straight. "And, Chelsea, if he calls you a camp cook ever again, you crack him with the heaviest frying pan you can lay your hands on. As far as the baths, you must be able to stand your ground to get this bunch to clean up on a cattle drive," my mom said, laughing so hard she nearly lost her breath.

"I'll surely keep the frying pan in mind, Mrs. Carver."

"Nonsense, you all call me Jessie or whatever suits you. Let's sit out here on the porch, and you can meet the old grump up there."

"Now, Caty, don't you take any guff from that old man. He has a big heart deep down. He's like an onion. You gotta peel off the outer layers to get to the good part."

Caty giggled. "Okay. I'll start peeling." Caty ran up to the porch and stuck her hand out. "Hi, I'm Caty, and I rode with Spence to come see you. I can tell already that you and I will be good friends."

"Young lady. You think so?"

"Yes, sir, I do." She grabbed on and gave him a firm handshake and a big hug.

Caty looked at my dad. "You can tell a lot about someone's character by how they hug you."

Dad smiled. "Hmm, I've heard that somewhere before."

Chelsea nervously twisted her dress.

Dad smiled at Chelsea. "So, you're the one who stole my boy's heart. I can see he let the right one pick him."

At first, Chelsea looked puzzled at what to say, then the color drained from her face. Slowly, she regained her senses, realizing this man would soon be a relative, and she best learn to hold her ground.

Mom swatted at her husband. "Grumpy, you leave this girl be. Ladies, we are going inside to fix a nice meal and will get to know each other. You fellas chew the fat out here and let Spence do his talkin'."

"Sounds good, old woman. Boys, let's talk about that horse of yours over yonder."

Spence gaped at his father. "Dad, how'd you know about her?"

"Stories travel faster than a high wind across the plains, and we've heard many stories. Reg, grab the jug and let's allow Spence to do what he does best. Spin the tales."

"You bet, Dad. Let Buck and Poke judge the truth and substance of the story and what is just a plain fairy tale. Keep Spence on the level."

We all sat for hours, talkin', listenin', laughin', and trying to stop Mom and Chelsea from crying when Spence talked about the gunplay.

As always, Caty was a whirlwind, making sure everyone ate

plenty. She kept trying to hide the jug from Dad. She didn't have much luck, but she tried. We ate outside on the porch and enjoyed the oncoming night by firelight.

After a long while, Mom rose from the roaring fire. "Gentlemen, these gals are just plain tuckered out. They want to stay up and be with you all, but I can see they can't keep their eyes open much longer. They are sleeping in the house. You men bunk in the barn. We will see you in the morning."

Spence and I stayed up with Dad and talked into the wee hours of the night about cattle and our plans for the future.

Spence and I woke up late, glad to be back home and relaxing. The ladies were up and gone when we rolled out of the barn.

Poke, Buck, and Dad were nowhere to be found. We moseyed back into the house and noticed the cook stove was still warm. They all had eaten pancakes and bacon for breakfast without us.

"Spence, it looks like everyone abandoned us. They must have listened to enough of your stories."

As we sat on the porch drinking coffee and enjoying the morning sun, Caty ran over the top of the hill. Mom was hot on her trail, with the others not far behind. Caty left Mom in the dust and jumped up on the porch.

"Spence, you get enough sleep? Lazy bones."

"Nope, I'm thinking I might go take a nap. What has you so all fired up this morning? Where have you been, little lady?"

"We all went for a hike to look at the ranch. We moved the cows we herded here into the lower field. They look happy to be home with the other cows."

Chelsea came over and swatted me on the back. "Boy, I sure

hope you don't plan on sleeping late if you ever want to marry me, you lazy bag of bones."

"What? That's not sleeping late. That's just what we men do. I plan on getting up right before bedtime now that the cattle are back home. Need to save my strength."

Spence watched Buck. "What's up with you walkin'? Your horse run off?"

"Spence, I had to try this hikin' thing. Don't seem to care for it much. That's why God gave us horses to save our feet."

Spence stretched out on the porch. "Buck, I believe we need to start rounding up cattle by foot. It will be easier on our rears."

"Nope, my rear can handle it. My feet can't."

Buck sat on the porch, drinking a cup of hot coffee, and nearly choked on his coffee as he laughed at Poke after his pal finally reached the porch.

"Poke, you about croaked going up that hill. I thought you were dead for sure. I figured if an old one-legged guy could manage it, you'd be able to," teased my dad.

Spence's face cracked open in a wide, toothy grin. "Poke, that old man will out-walk you straight to your grave."

Dad grinned. "You young bucks are soft, not like when we were young."

"You got us, old man. We're just a bunch of lazy no goods."

We all worked hard during the next two weeks, sorting cattle, dehorning calves, putting up hay, and repairing pens.

Caty rode Roan, and Chelsea rode Mom's favorite horse, Peanuts. They explored every mile of the ranch and enjoyed wading in the creeks.

Mom was in heaven making several dresses for Caty and Chelsea and two for Callie as gifts when the travelers returned home. Mom enjoyed the special treat of having the two girls in the house.

The lovebirds were hard to find after the chores were finished for the day.

"Exploring," they said.

Buck and Poke enjoyed the time with Dad, worked hard, and talked nonstop about building a ranch.

Dad asked them both if they would stay in the area. But they both decided they would go back. They agreed a little about Spence's humor and that his stories went a long way. Dad knew they were only pokin' fun.

When the sun parted the clouds the next morning, I rode one of the ranch horses into town with Chelsea and Caty. I left Roan under a giant cottonwood, resting and enjoying the morning breeze.

The ladies drove the wagon as they wished to do some shopping. Chelsea had taught Caty how to handle the team on the cattle drive.

It was evident that Caty could master just about anything. She talked calmly to the team, controlling the reins with authority, and called out what she needed.

I preferred to keep a low profile but to no avail. Everyone who knew me stopped to talk and wanted to know about the gun battle and my Indian war horse.

I was content to sit on the walkway, chewing the fat with the passersby like it was old hometown week.

After a bit, I had all that excitement I could stand. I enjoyed the local gossip, and I would talk about my adventures another time.

I stood and said my goodbyes. I was polite but let the people know I was in town to help the girls buy supplies. *I wish Spence were here. He could have made a big impression with the local gals. They were pretty flirty.*

I found the smallest store away from the mob where I could shop for myself and hide away until the girls finished.

After making my purchases, all I wanted was to hightail it out of town. I found Chelsea and Caty down the road, strolling down the boardwalk without a care in the world. I realized the two sisters had other plans than returning to the ranch.

I trailed after the shoppers, lagging behind them for what felt like hours, waiting on those two. In reality, it had probably only been maybe a half hour at most.

When I went shopping, I was in and out. *Pants, shirts, underclothes, and socks. Same color and brand every time, but that is not the woman's way.*

No, not a woman. She looks for the latest style, size, color, and shape. What kind of fabric? How many yards? The list goes on and on. As I headed to the wagon, I was astonished.

"We should have brought the bigger wagon. You two must have bought up the whole town."

The eldest sister whispered, "I had gold I needed to spend, and I took that task very seriously. It took up too much space in my pocket. Remember, I am a girl of influence now. And for your information, Mr. Smarty Pants, there's nothing in this wagon for you or me. So be still. Tie your horse to the wagon and drive us home."

I guess she told me.

Caty crawled into the back of the wagon and made a comfy bed.

She said with her best southern drawl, "My kind sir, try to keep the speed steady, the bumps at a minimum, and proceed home."

I laughed so hard that the women thought I would fall off the wagon seat.

"Yes, my fair lady, I will do as you command." The royal one was out before we even started.

46

BACK AT THE RANCH

The wagon pulled into the ranch with our load. Those left at the ranch greeted us and launched into giving me grief.

"Hmm, musta bought the town out. Planning for the future?"

"Nope. I have been boldly informed that nothing in the wagon has my name on it."

"Christmas is coming early for someone. Jessie, may Caty and I fix up a special meal tonight? I'd like everyone here to be present, and I've got special gifts from Caty and me to give out."

"You surely may cook up a feast if you like. It's early, Chelsea. Do you want the boys to unload the wagon?"

"No, I'll do it, and no peeking from anyone."

After I unhitched the horses and put them out to pasture, I pulled a written paper from my pocket and announced there was news to tell.

"Before you all take off, I got a wire from Pinkie and the Anders' cousins. Two young ladies are coming from back East on the train and stage to see the family property. They will arrive in about a month. That means we're going to have to start back shortly. Let's make plans tonight."

Chelsea chimed in, "Oh, no, you don't. Absolutely not. Tonight's going to be a relaxing time. No planning."

"Big brother, I see who's wearing the pants."

Dad grumbled to Spence, "Whatever led anyone to question who's the boss when a woman is around. Just ask your mother."

Poke looked at Spence and Jessie and then at me. "Um, Reg, old boy, I can see a storm in your future. You better get some rules laid out if you are ever fixin' to say I do."

Chelsea giggled. "Poke, keep dreaming. You're a funny man."

Chelsea and Caty returned from the house with washcloths and soap.

Buck and Poke looked up.

Caty pinched her nose again.

"Chelsea, we just had a bath two weeks ago. My skin is still irritated from the soap last time."

"Buck, no wash, no gift. I'll take it back to the store."

Poke took his towel and the soap. "Chelsea, I love ya like a sister, but you sure can upset a fella's lifestyle."

Jessie grinned from ear to ear. "Oh, this is so good!" Laughing at this scene, she took a towel and soap and handed it to Sly.

"That means you too, old man, and wash that peg leg of yours clean as a whistle."

"Mother, if I clean up, you won't be able to smell me sneakin' up on ya."

"Honey, I'll just listen for that peg leg sound, like a kid hitting a hollow log with a stick."

They all went off to finish the chores and then headed to the creek. With the water turning cold, they didn't take much time bathing, but they managed to clean off at least one layer of travel dirt.

Jessie had set clothes out for Sly on the porch. When he climbed the porch steps, she yelled, "Take those rags off and burn them. I'm tired of trying to wash all the holes clean. There's not enough fabric left to hold the soap and water."

Dad grinned. "But, Jess, they fit right, damn first, a bath, and now I'm going to have to break in new clothes."

The sight and scent of the food were a pure delight for our eyes. Nothing could beat the smell of a freshly baked apple pie. We filled our bellies and then were treated to wild berries and apple pie for dessert. Mom made some whipped cream for the top in place of ice cream.

Chelsea stood up from the table, walked over, took me by the hand, and guided me to the sofa in the living room with the rest of the family following us. She truly was the most beautiful woman I had ever seen.

Caty elbowed Spencer in the ribs. "True love."

After we were all seated, Chelsea drew a deep breath and began to speak, "I would like to thank God for you men and what you have done for my ma, me, Caty, and our little sister Callie. We will never be able to thank you enough, but I would like to thank God for the blessings and the kindness we have been shown."

"Buck and Poke, I want to start with you two. You stood up for what was right and protected all of us, including the man I am so grateful to have found.

"Chelsea," Poke spoke up. "I think you need to be talking about

Roan. She deserves the praise." The room filled with joyous laughter at that sentiment.

"Why the tears, Chelsea? It's all over now," asked Caty.

"These are happy tears." Chelsea looked over to Buck and Poke. "You're on your way to being cattlemen. Caty and I want you to ride in high style."

Earlier, Chelsea instructed me to go outside and retrieve gifts, and now I returned looking like a pack mule, hauling two brand new saddles, one in each hand. I set them in front of Buck and Poke.

They looked down at the saddles, then at Chelsea.

Now, it was the men's turn for teary eyes. They had never been given such a gift or owned such excellent saddles. Poke remained so shaken he couldn't say a word.

Buck stood, hugged, kissed Chelsea, and leaned over to do the same for Caty.

We thought Caty would bust. She was so excited to see these men so emotional about these gifts.

Poke remained seated. "Ladies, I can't accept this. It's too much."

"This gift is from my whole family, and you can accept it. We want you to ride tall in that saddle for many years."

The two cowpokes, still speechless, inspected every square inch of the leather workmanship in their gifts.

"Now, Spencer, you are next. These gifts are from Caty." Caty walked in with an arm full of goods. She handed Spence a small package first.

"That's a pretty small saddle, Caty."

She grinned.

Spence opened it. It was a hand-carved pipe. It was cut from whalebone and beautiful beyond mere words.

"Now you can smoke in style with Joe. You'll still smell bad, but you'll look good."

Spence placed it between his teeth. "Well, now folks, don't I look fancy. I'm going to be the talk of the town," he said, trying to mimic a city slicker but falling short by a mile.

She handed him several more gifts. A new belt, silk neck scarves, and a pocket watch on a chain. Caty squirmed. "Open it, Spencer."

"Alright, already. Is there a little rattlesnake in here?"

Spence opened the pocket watch, which had a miniature picture of Caty inside and the inscribed words: "TO MY FRIEND SPENCER, CATY."

He grabbed up Caty, tears rolling down his cheek. "I'll always be your Spencer." Spencer was truly touched.

We all remained quiet. No one wanted to break this tender moment.

"We can change that picture when I grow up more, but it's good for now."

Spence was amazed at this little girl's heart. He wished she were years older, but twelve was still too young for courting. Spence reached out to Caty again.

"Caty, I hope I can grow up to be a man that you will always admire and respect. Little lady, you are a special gift to me. I will always hold this dear to my heart."

Mom and Chelsea blubbered like babies. Spence grabbed Caty and squeezed her so tight she thought she was going to bust apart.

"Spencer, you popped every bone in my back. You hugged me so tight."

"Not tight enough, young lady, not tight enough."

"Little brother, so it's official now," I said. Everyone looked puzzled. "Spencer sounds more dignified."

"Spence to you boys, but to Caty, Spencer, it is."

Chelsea spoke to Jessie and Sly. Now, the next gift is for you two. Jessie and Sly. I pray I'm not too forward, but maybe Reg and I will be married some time in the future.

Reg answered his parents' inquiring look, "In time."

Chelsea thoughtfully regarded Jessie. "I'd like to call you by a special name. My dad will always be Pa and mother, Ma, but Jessie, I would like a special name to use, hopefully for our children to call you by. I would be pleased to call you Marmee."

Chelsea explained her request to those present: "When Pa traveled overseas on the freighters, he made friends with a young Indian man. Pa heard this word and asked the meaning. The word in Indian means "shining." That's what I see when I look at you and your personality. Would that suit you?"

Mom was so happy to be given a special nickname the grandchildren would call her. "I love it. The name sets me apart from all others. The only thing we need to do now is to get you two married so I can have some grandbabies calling out my name."

Dad finally butted in, staring at Caty, "What's my new given name to be, young lady? Old man, peg leg, grumpy?"

Caty burst out in joyful giggles, trying to hide the laughter behind her hand. "I'll start with Papa."

She strutted around the room pretending to be him, thumbs in the shoulder straps of his overalls.

"The first time I saw you, you were all tough-like on the porch, but I could see you weren't. Like Marmie told me, you're like peeling an onion. At first, it brings tears to your eyes, but as you peel back the layers, you get to the good, sweet part. I haven't figured out Papa what I'll call you, but I'm thinking on it. We'll just start with Papa."

"Listen here, young lady, I'll latch on to Papa and wait on pins and needles for the next part. Now come over here so I can use Spencer's new belt to tan your hide."

Caty ran to Sly and leaped onto his lap. "You wouldn't spank me. I know you wouldn't."

"You're right, Caty. I am sure excited to meet your ma and that baby sister, Callie. I bet she's a handful like her two big sisters."

"No, Papa, Callie is so quiet you forget she's in the room. She likes to braid her hair and dress up fancy. She pretends she's getting ready to go out on the town. All grown up like."

"Well then, Caty, I'll have to take her to town and go shopping."

Mom almost choked on her cider. "I'd pay to see that. You never go shopping, you old fool."

"Marmie, I'm turning over a new peel."

"Papa, this is for you. Caty handed him a hand-carved walking cane with a nubbed horn cow's head on the top. It was cast in bronze. We saw it and had the blacksmith nub off the horns, special just for you."

"I'll be. What a gift. Now, I can walk in style and beat the children at the same time. What a practical gift."

Chelsea looked at Marmie. "We looked forever for a gift for you. We know you don't favor jewelry or fancy clothes, but you do love your family. We hope you enjoy this."

It was a leather-bound book with gold inlay on the blank pages., "We want you to have this book and to write down all the things we all do and all that hopefully your grandchildren will do. A book that will be passed down forever."

Mom was speechless. She would never have expected such a thoughtful gift. "Young ladies, I always wanted a little girl."

Laughing at the family joke, we knew what Mom referred to, but the others were clueless.

I had to spill the beans. "Mom would dress Spence like a baby girl when he was little."

Spence scowled and said, "Not funny. Not one bit. Was funny once but not so funny now."

Poke split a gut laughing. "It was funny when Reg told it, and it's still funny."

Buck took Spence's hat. "Maybe you can turn your hat in for a bonnet."

Spence grabbed Dad's cane and acted like he would pop Buck a good one. "One of these days, Buck, I'll get you."

Mom laughed and giggled at Spence's peril. "I always wanted some girls, so now the Lord has given me you two, and maybe I can win over baby Callie. I hope your ma, Nancy, has room in her heart for all of us."

Caty laughed right along with Jessie, "We know our mom. She will, Marmie, she surely will."

Chelsea decided to bring in more coffee, but I stepped into her path, stopping her.

"Wait a minute, Chels, there's one more gift to open."

No, I gave them all out.

No, Chels, you forgot one.

Caty reached out her hand to Chelsea. "Here, you didn't see this one. It's for you."

Who gave me a gift? Her frown gave away her puzzled thoughts, but nevertheless, she took the package, opened it, and burst into tears. Her legs gave way, and she crumpled right down to the floor. It wasn't hard to guess what just happened.

I kneeled beside her. "It's just a simple gold band, filled with the most valuable matter, a gift from God. It's hope and love in a never-ending circle. All you need to do is put your finger through the center, and I promise to give hope and love to you for all our days."

I took Chelsea's hand and placed the ring on her finger.

Chelsea could barely speak, her eyes running like a leaking dam.

"I love you, Reg."

"I love you, too, Chels. I wish your ma were here, but I couldn't hold out any longer."

"Reg, if it's alright with you, can we consider this an engagement and wait to get married until we return home? That way, Papa and Marmee can meet my family and see where we aim to raise their grandbabies."

I looked at Chelsea with love and compassion. "That's the plan. We need to start our new life with all the people we love right there beside us. I promised your ma I would court you first, though, and I aim to keep that promise. So don't go getting too eager to set that date. A promise is a promise."

47

PREPARING FOR THE RETURN TRIP

W e talked about the return trip over coffee at breakfast and decided to leave in a few days.

Chelsea asked me, "Are you sure you want to go back? This is your home."

"Chels, my home is with you, wherever and whenever that is. This here is my mom and dad's home. I have a big stake in it, but we're off on our own adventure now."

"Are you sure, Reg, or do you want to be with me for the gold in the bag and the hidden river of gold?" she asked with all the sincerity she could muster.

I paused, removed my hat, and rubbed my head. "The only gold I'm interested in is the gold on that finger of yours. And, I think that will be the last of this conversation."

Chelsea cast her eyes downward. She knew Reg was a good man. He never would have given Ma the bag of gold from Pa if all he wanted was gold. She was upset that she even considered asking that question.

Caty was sad when she heard we were all going to go back. She missed Ma, Callie, and the townspeople who had been so kind, but she was heartbroken about Spencer. Young love, a crush of the heart, was always hard to overcome.

Mom kept her busy with girl talk about the wedding and where the couple would live. Soon, Caty realized having them close by would be a blessing.

Before they left, the men rode the upper pastures of the ranch, checking the herd. When Sly was alone with his boys, he said, "Reg, I'm going to cut out two hundred head for you and Chelsea when you find yourself a home. You have two hundred head of your own and money in the bank from your years working here, plus the reward money to start your own spread. And I know you have money from Chelsea, the gold."

I immediately interrupted, "That's not my money, Dad, that's hers."

"No, son, if you love her, what's yours is hers, and what's hers is yours. It's not about pride. It's about a life together. If you're always keeping score, you've already lost. Time to grow up. Life is more than money."

"You two need to understand that money is like a gun. You can use it for good or evil. It's in your hands to make the choice."

I knew what Dad said held truth. It was hard to think about taking her money or help. It was all about pride, which at times was good, but not in this case. If we were going to make it, there would be hard times, and no amount of money would help.

After Sly's man-to-man visit, Spence returned to find Poke and Buck checking the cattle in a different location.

"Where are the new saddles?" he asked, his new pipe sticking out of his mouth. He was smoking Joe's backie, happy as could be.

Poke shifted in his saddle as they rode. "We can't quite get it in our minds to use the new saddles. We don't want them getting dirty or taking a chance of a horse rolling over on it."

"I guess you can take them back home and hang them on your rocking chairs next to the fire," teased Spence.

"Maybe we will try them out on the ride back home. We'll see," agreeing that they needed to get them broke in and use their fine gifts.

Poke coughed. "Wish you'd put that pipe away and quit smokin' that foul stuff. We would all enjoy your nice gift, lookin' all uptown, ifn it was home sittin' on the shelf."

"You're just jealous of a good pipe and smoke."

"We are going to have words with your Caty about her choice of gifts," said Poke.

"Speaking of Caty. What are you going to do when we pull out? You know she's going to be heartbroken," asked Buck.

"I will need your help with that when the time comes. You just go along with what I say, okay?"

"Anything you need. We sure like that little squirt."

48

ON THE TRAIL AGAIN

W hen the time came to leave, I sold the wagon in town. No sense in dragging it across the country unloaded. We bought pack stock and panniers instead. They would be needed in the future when we went gold hunting. Dad gave us two extra horses to carry Poke's and Buck's saddles and gear.

"Mr. Carver, you wanted to speak to me?" Chelsea asked.

"Young lady, It's Sly."

She replied all twinkly-eyed, "Okay then, Sly it is."

"Chelsea, I want to give you a bit of advice. I figure you and Reg could be a good match for each other. Marriage is a long journey. It's miles and miles of road, some easy and some hard. Together, two can smooth out the rough spots. Yes, it takes love, but more caring and patience. If you work hard together, you can make it."

"Sly, I've known your son for such a short time, but I knew he was the one for me the first time we met. Then I met Spence, you, and your wife, which helped me feel like part of your family. I miss my pa with all my heart, but I know he would be pleased. He was the one who sent Reg to me. I am willing to do what it takes to work hard and make him happy. I want to be part of your family if he is willing to have me."

"Then no more needs to be said."

Caty stood next to Roan with her little heart breaking. I could only watch the scene play out and hope for the best. Spence came out of the house wearing his pocket watch, new belt, hat, and blue neckerchief. He checked the time on his watch.

"Where's my Caty?" he yelled. "Caty, I need you to do me a favor."

She looked up, startled. "You bet, Spencer, what?"

You're heading back now, and I will be coming behind you soon." Now, he had her attention, and her eyes widened with excitement. "I need you to help the cowhands look over some range land for me. You have a good eye for such things and would know what I would be looking for. I trust your judgment."

Buck and Poke later explained that he would need to move his cows when she found the perfect piece of land, and she would be helpful in that task. In addition, they would all be much obliged if she also gave her opinion on grazing land for Buck and Poke.

"Caty, before I come along that way, Reg and I want to see what the Anders kin plan to do with their ranch. I would like you to send me a telegraph wire to let me know what's going on."

"I could do all of that, Spencer. I sure could."

Caty then looked at Chelsea and me. "Well, don't just stand there. We need to be going. I got land to look at."

Spence gave her a lift onto Roan. "You get back safe and get busy, young lady. My future may be in your hands."

We all said our goodbyes, and we started down the road. I passed Spence. "Little brother, that was some fine thinking. You going to be okay?"

He looked at his watch, shook his head, and silently headed to the barn. I think his heart broke, too. He sure loved that little gal, his little sister.

Dad was on the porch waving his new cane. Mom wrapped her arm firmly around his waist, happy and sad at the same time. Her boys were growing up, and the times would be changing.

Sly held onto Jessie's hand. "Mother, don't you fret none. I feel it in my bones, and there will be a wedding soon and a pack of grand-babies to love on."

"I know that you old fool. I just can't wait." Mom talked out loud to herself. "They're all grown up, but they still look like little children riding away. The time has gone by so fast, and tomorrow will be here and gone."

Goodbyes are hard, taking the wind right out of our emotional sails. We would be in for a long ride for a day or two, missing Spence's gift of gab and his quick sense of humor, but Poke could easily take over the duties.

I laughed to myself, tapped Chelsea on the leg, and pointed at the two men riding tall in those new saddles. Talking a mile a minute, Caty led the pack on Roan while we all enjoyed her purely innocent heart.

49

THE END OF THE TRAIL

The Marshall, Ben, and Tom eventually reached their destination, a small town now that would someday grow and become a big city.

Pinkie spoke to the two men. "It's been a hell of an adventure. Ben, I'm glad you're here. You'll be a fine deputy, and the future's a bright one for you. I'm willing to teach you all I can about the law and how to handle people and their problems, but you will have to face the backlash coming your way and hold your tongue. Ben, I foresee you taking over when I'm done, too."

"I know. I'll keep a stiff upper lip."

"Tom, on the other hand, I see your future in law practice, but it will be helpful if you see my side first. It will give you a better idea of the difference between the meaning of the law and its actual workings."

"I'm with ya on that count, Pinkie."

"Speaking of family, I need to find a preacher and get the ball rolling," said Ben.

"Who was speaking of family? Talk about impatient. Ben, you've only known this gal for such a short time. Why don't you get settled in and court the girl awhile?"

"Nope, when you know it's right, you know it's right, love at first sight. We both want to get it done."

"Alright, Ben. The preacher is down at the church. I'll see you later today. Tom, come with me. I may need someone for support."

"Tom and Pinkie, will you stand by me at the ceremony? I'd sure like that."

Tom looked at Ben and said, "It would be my honor, my friend. Single gals like best men, we look vulnerable. They also want to fix the busted ones that haven't been tamed yet."

Pinkie snorted. "I'll stand with ya, but I'm not the vulnerable type. The gals are all yours. Tom, you and Ben will be in charge when I head back to settle the T Lazy 7 Ranch ordeal. Tomorrow, we start introducing you to the town and its folks. There's a lot to take in, but I feel good about the future."

The minute the travelers hit town, Caty jumped from Roan and hit the ground running to greet her ma and baby sister. She picked up the toddler in her arms and teased, "I think you've grown a foot, Callie. I can barely hoist you up."

Callie squealed. She missed her sister and was overjoyed to have her friend back home.

Nancy moved quickly towards Caty. "Caty, it's been a burden, you not being here to help me with your sister."

"So, you only missed me because I was a good babysitter?"

"Missed that big smile too. Give me a hug, and let's get inside. Everyone wants to hear your story of the cattle drive. You must tell us all about Reg and Spence's kinfolk."

Everything would return to normal in a short while, but for now, it was a whirlwind of stories about their adventure.

Maggie and Sara were the first to offer a warm welcome. Most town ladies gathered around the two sisters, wanting to hear about the cattle drive. Caty was working her mouth on over time. She was talking so fast she could hardly breathe.

Nancy gave her a shake. "Breathe, child, breathe, we're not going anywhere."

Curious, Nancy then asked Chelsea, "Young lady, what do you have to say?"

"Nothing, Ma. I think Caty covered it all."

Maggie and Sara were up and cornered her in the blink of an eye, and Maggie grabbed Chelsea's hand. "I guess this is just some trinket you picked up on the way?"

The teenager gracefully blushed and reached down to feel the small gold band as she had done a thousand times already.

"Nancy looked into her daughter's eyes. "My little girl, tell us, are you a married woman or a bride-to-be? Which is it?"

"Ma, I would never get married without all of you there. The man who has my heart was kind enough to wait."

The women were so pleased and excited to see the simple gold band that they were soon all abuzz about how to prepare for a wedding. Caty and Callie had fallen asleep on the floor after finding themselves a snack in the kitchen.

Reg left the girls to revisit, and he proceeded to the wire office to see if any news had arrived on the Anders kin. I knew the family would be waiting for our news, so my next wire went home to let the family know we arrived safely. After finishing this task, I let Roan out on the hill and bid a good night to the gents. Feeling like the dried bottom of a rut in the road, I bathed and shaved, calling it a night.

Earlier in the evening, two dirty, tired cowhands walked their horses to the livery to gossip with Old Joe. He was excited to see them, and they stayed up a good part of the night by the fire, drinking some shine and talking about the trip.

I saw the hostler first thing in the morning. "Joe, you all talked out from last night?"

"The boys and I did a little talkin', but I think a lot more drinkin' than talkin.'" Joe was an old codger who lived an eventful life and had stored a wealth of information in his memories.

When we first met, I realized he was a man who remained stingy with his conversations. He studied me, deciding if I was worthy of his time and trust. I asked him questions, and he would answer with an "ah ha, yep" or only a nod. *I didn't believe he knew how to talk.*

But slowly, as he got to know me, he teased and talked a little more. Now, I couldn't shut the guy up. I figured this to be the way he considered us friends. If he didn't talk to someone, it didn't mean he didn't like them. He was just more reserved about what he shared.

When it came to me, our visits finally became more than a howdy-do moment.

I liked the old character, but when it came to him and Spence, it was a horse of a different color. They started out jokin' and cuttin' up, two matching souls from the get-go. I couldn't get a word in edgewise.

"Where are our sidekicks, Joe?

"They are outback, soapin' down those new saddles. That was a hell of a nice gift that gal of yours gave them. I know it touched them both greatly."

We walked to the back corral, watching the two from the corner of the barn, oiling up every square inch of those saddles.

I yelled, "I think you missed a spot."

They both grinned, and Poke threw his rag at me.

"I hope you two don't plan on riding with those saddles in the next month. You'll slide right off."

Buck laughed, "A rider like you, Reg, would have a problem staying on board. But two seasoned cowboys like us, well, it's easy money."

"How about you sling those saddles on the horses and ride with me to the T Lazy 7 to make sure all's well there? The Anders relatives, the two sisters, will be here at the end of the week."

"Two women," Poke scoffed, smirking with a laugh. "Probably two old maidens. Is Pinkie coming back to Two Forks as well, Reg?"

"Yep. he surely is."

I yelled to Joe. "You comin' old man?"

"You betcha. I'll ride. Let me get my pipe."

"Oh, hell, NO, Joe!" said Buck, coughing. You about killed us last night. "How about a break?"

"Sorry. Love me, love my smoke. You'll just have to stay upwind."

Buck gave Joe a backward look. "Upwind? We would need to pray for a tornado to blow that smell away."

Joe wrapped his arms around his sides, bent over, and laughed. "I sure miss Spence. He enjoyed this fine tobaccy."

50

THE T LAZY 7 RANCH

We all rode up to the T Lazy 7. The cow tenders we left in charge did a good job watching over the ranch. They moved the cows down from the high pastures in preparation for the early snow. The cows were putting on a winter coat, and the heavy growth of cones covered the pine trees.

Fewer cones, less snow, cones up high, deep snow. Bees' nests low to the ground meant a mild winter, but high up top anywhere meant heavy snow ground cover. The old timers kept track of the weather this way by watching nature.

But when anyone asked what I thought about the upcoming winter, I'd reply, "I'll tell you in the spring." I was right every time.

We stopped at the ranch house, curious about what would happen to the ranch. Cold and empty, the old girl needed love and a new beginning. No clue yet if the gals would keep it or sell her.

Buck asked me. "You're the deep thinker of the bunch. What do you figure they'll do with this place?"

"Your guess is as good as mine."

Buck knew that look on the cowboy's face. He was syphering for sure. A good friend could always see that brain turnin'.

Buck threw a rock he was carrying at Poke. "Poke, we got to have one person with a brain. I think you drew the short stick."

"Maybe so, but I was granted other gifts."

Poke walked out the door, chuckling and mumbling to himself. He needed to talk to his sidekicks, Buck, Joe, and me.

Joe walked around the house, admiring the building, the craftsmanship, and the hours spent on the detailed handiwork. Joe had finished taking his measure of the homestead and admiring the artistry.

"You know, the Anders were good people. I knew them from the start, the salt of the earth. I helped build this beautiful home. I surely miss those folks. I knew they just didn't up and walk away. I'm damn glad it's out of Tucker's hands. Whenever his name crosses my mind, I get the greatest joy thinking about sweet Maggie parting his chest. Just wish she would have parted his head from his shoulders. That would have been a lovely sight."

Poke looked like he had walked on someone's grave. "Heck, Mr. Happy, I hope you don't think of me often. It might be scary thinking about what's inside your mind. I surely agree with you, but you could have painted a less colorful picture."

Joe lifted his head and nodded. "I'm too old to care. Fair is fair," He patted one of the log walls in the house. "I hope the kin folk are good decent people. This house deserved good people."

The two ranch hands decided to run to town to restock food, retrieve their gear, and then move into the familiar bunkhouse.

Helping with the place until the Anders ladies arrived was a top priority. The old gals would probably need help.

After talking to the hired men, we rode back toward town. Roan was uneasy on the ranch. I think the smells of the place and the men who had been here bothered her. She was ready to go and loped away at a good pace, leaving the T Lazy 7 behind her in the dust.

We were all anxious to meet the ladies coming in from back east. The women folk were abuzz to see what they would wear, new dresses and hats. *Silly things to give a thought to.*

Poke and Buck bet on their looks. Both conjured up images of old schoolmarms from back east and would probably resemble the cattle in the fields.

A newcomer to Two Forks sat in the diner waiting for a meal. Maggie approached the starving soul with her cheerful howdy do, placed the menu and coffee down, and introduced herself. "Welcome to our town, stranger. Just passing through, or do you aim to stay on?"

"I am hopin' to find me a good job. I'm a mighty fine hand with a team, and I can plow with the best of 'em if I have a mind to. Oh, yes'm, sorry, my name is Bailey."

"Well, Bailey, I happened to hear not too long back that the stagecoach driver is looking to hire on a helper to apprentice so he can retire in his upcoming years. His old partner got hitched to a fine woman down South and quit. Would that be of interest to you?"

"Why, yes, it would, surely would. I am much obliged."

"The stage will be rolling in here any time now, and when it does, you put a fast step in your get-along and run out to see that old guy Zeke and tell him Maggie sent you. Just a warning to you. He has a mighty harsh bark, but mind yourself, and all will be fine," she said to the newcomer. *Another day in the life of the customers at my diner.*

The stage arrived two hours late when it rolled into town. The town's ladies were peeking from the corner of every window.

Buck and Poke were not about to hide behind a window. They sat on the porch of Maggie's Café beaming from ear to ear. They wanted a front-row look at these gals, whether beauties or beasts.

One man drove the team and pulled to a stop in front of the café to let the passengers out. The coach appeared to have traveled through a dust storm by the coating of dry soil on every available surface, including the driver's face and uncovered skin.

Before the driver could step down from his seat, Bailey rushed out the café door and introduced herself to Zeke.

"I already knows who you be. Here, let me hep ya with that there baggage, and then I want to hire on as your helper," Bailey said as she climbed to the top of the coach and began offloading the baggage.

Zeke looked like a rock, and a dust storm had been hurled at him, so he could only gape. "We can talk young 'un."

The first passengers to step out of the stage were two men dressed like bankers or attorneys in perfectly styled suits, proper from head to toe. Turning, they reached to help the ladies.

I looked along the boardwalk to see what my friends in the

windows and the people on the street were gawking at. *Looked like they were all trying to catch a glimpse of Santa Claus himself.*

Buck and Poke remained seated, watching with open mouths and bulging eyes.

I tried to hold back the chuckle.

Two women stepped off the stagecoach with the gentlemen's help. The females in town were not going to be pleased with the new competition. The two women were beautiful, but more striking was not the latest fashion we expected to see but their current manner of dress.

Who would have figured that they would be wearing riding clothes? Blue denim pants, deeply tanned brown leather boots, and soft blue chambray shirts were not a sight one sees on females in Two Forks.

Pinkie had arrived in town the night before. Once he caught his breath and found his voice, he asked, "Might you young ladies be the Anders kin?"

The two men who rode in with them moved toward the lawman. "We are the women's escorts, legal, and banking advisors. Our names are Josh Pratt and Dain Lewis. We are here to guide the women in these financial and legal matters. Allow me to introduce Miss Kylee Anders and her sister, Miss Kaylee Anders."

Pinkie greeted the first woman, his hat in hand. "Ladies, thank you for traveling this far. If you wish to settle in, we can meet in the morning to review the T Lazy 7 Ranch details."

"Thank you, sheriff. It's nice to see you are concerned about our comfort. How far is the ranch from town?" Miss Kaylee asked in a belittling tone.

"Now Kaylee, be nice. The sheriff was being quite polite."

"Kylee, I was polite, just to the point."

"Miss Kaylee, I am a marshall, not a sheriff, if you please. It's about a two-hour ride to the ranch house. The land is a large spread, and you will cross over a good portion before we reach the main house."

"Marshall, it is then. It's early. Would you mind finding two horses for us to ride and escorting us there in one hour? We didn't come all this way to sit around," said Miss Kaylee.

"That will be arranged, ladies."

"Also, marshall, is the man standing behind you, Reg Carter?"

"Yes, ma'am, that's me."

Kaylee walked past Pinkie and took my arm. "Reg, will you join us? We need to discuss what you have done here and details about the ranch."

"Yes, Miss Kaylee, I will join the marshall and escort you and your sister to your ranch."

"Please, call me Kaylee."

"Gentlemen, it's settled then. We shall enjoy a bite to eat and be prepared to ride in an hour."

The two ladies strolled over the worn boards in front of a storefront and entered Maggie's Café, passing Maggie and Chelsea on their way in.

Jetta peeked out from above the swinging kitchen doors. When Chelsea left to move cattle with me, Maggie hired Jetta to help with the cooking and such. She was a young little thing. She was of average height but had a slim build and was full of movement. This one couldn't stay still for a second. She was a whirlwind when it came to taking and moving orders. She was going to fit in just fine.

All the ladies raised their eyebrows, exchanged glances, and in a split second, unspoken and unpleasant thoughts appeared to cross the minds of each without a single word spoken.

Bailey ran through the glass doors, "He hired me, Miz Maggie. Thank you. Be seein' ya."

The last thing Maggie heard was a "Hiyah, gidyap there."

And the stagecoach took off with the reins in Bailey's hands and Zeke laughing. *I wonder if he realizes what mischief he has sitting under that floppy old hat his helper wears?*

51

THE T LAZY 7 RANCH

As we traversed the land to the ranch, both ladies were intent on attracting my attention.

These women magpies talked nonstop. They were asking for all the details concerning Tucker and the untimely deaths of their kin.

I answered the questions as simply as possible, talking about the country, the cows, and the weather. I tried to talk about the scenery and the peacefulness of it all.

Not being much of a talker, my thoughts relied heavily on the fact that maybe they would get the hint and stop talking. *Pointless.* They would be riding in my pocket if they tried to get any closer. *Wish the lady's man was here.*

They pretty much left Pinkie alone, and he remained quite amused at my predicament, covering his wicked grin when the women looked his way. He wisely rode behind us whenever possible.

I eyed Pinkie, who held his sides, as he tried hard not to rudely laugh where the ladies could hear him. He could feel my pain, which was ironic, two beautiful women giving you one hundred percent of their attention, and I wanted it to stop. I was a love-struck pup, but not for either of these two.

I knew Pinkie looked forward to the catfight, which would come sooner or later, either between these two or with the women back in town.

Our band of merry travelers rode up to the ranch house, where Buck and Poke greeted us. Riding ahead of us earlier seemed to be the best idea for those two at the time, but they missed out on the main attraction on the trail.

"Buck, Poke, this is Miss Kylee Anders and Miss Kaylee Anders."

Buck tipped his hat, "Ladies, it's nice to see you again. Did you enjoy your trip from town? I know it's a burden trying to keep up with Reg's banter and wit."

Pinkie choked out a cough on that one. It was great for him to see me in so much misery.

Miss Kaylee tittered with a simple laugh. "Our guide was a joy. We learned so much. His knowledge seems endless. Don't you agree, Kylee?"

"I most certainly do. I can't wait to light a fire, warm up, and get to know each other better."

My eyes rolled to the back of my head. At this point, Poke fidgeted and understood he needed to step in and help me out. *A battle I didn't know how to fight.*

Hat in hand, Poke motioned to me, pointing to the barn. "The hired hands need to see you, Reg. Down at the barn, seems important, something about our cattle's poor health. The boys think it's that tongue-tied disease. The one that chokes the heifers up for a spell."

Buck was so amused he nearly danced a jig. He helped the ladies dismount from their horses.

Pinkie was still trying not to laugh and suggested, "Buck, why don't you and Poke take the ladies inside and show them their ranch house, and Reg can meet with the hands in the barn? He may want to check the cows for hoof and mouth disease while he is there also."

Miss Kaylee spoke right up, "Reg, why don't you escort me and my sister?"

"Ladies, I need to attend to the cattle, and my horse seems to be off a step. I think I had better check the cows for dropsy, too. They may be suffering from jaw wag. We all know what jaw wag leads to. A cow that needs a workin' over." I smiled and turned to ride to the barn.

"Sir, I get the feeling you're not pleased with our company."

"No, Miss Kaylee, I would enjoy escorting you on the tour, but I don't want to walk back to town on a lame horse. Besides, Buck knows all about your kin and everything you need to know about the house, cattle, and land. He lived here on the ranch for years."

"Oh, don't worry if your horse comes up lame. You could always ride back with me."

Pinkie took a drink of water, and when she spoke, she caught him off guard. He choked and spat out his water.

"Marshall, you breathin' okay?"

"I believe the water just went down the wrong pipe." Pinkie knew I was in trouble and sinking fast.

The quicksand was swallowing me with every word spoken. *I couldn't make a move. The more I squirmed, the deeper I sank.*

Pinkie led his horse to me. "I'll help you in the barn. I need to go over some details with you."

Buck and Poke escorted the women into the house, and Buck gave them the lay of the land. Poor Poke was a fish out of water, even more so than I was. It was evident that these two city women felt he was below their standards. He may be the salt of the earth, but in their eyes, he was a lowly, hired man.

Pinkie walked alongside me and Roan. "You're in deep, buddy. I hate to see a guy have to fight off not only one pretty girl but two."

"Pinkie, this is not going to go over well back home. I felt holes burning in my back with the women in town, including Chelsea's staring fire at me when we rode out of town."

Shortly, we heard a noise down the road. We both had gone into the barn to talk and as we gazed out the barn door, we saw the banker and the lawyer bouncing along on a buckboard. They pulled up to the ranch house and went inside. After about an hour, they all came out the front door.

Ms. Kylee had latched onto Buck's arm and seemed quite content. Poke talked to the two men, pointing in all directions and describing the ranch and the land. Shortly after, they all moved our way to the barn, trapping me again.

"Kaylee and I wish to ride out onto the ranch land. We would like to see what's out there," said Kylee.

"Miss Kaylee, it's getting late, and we don't want to ride back in the dark," I said.

"Reg, I was thinking, why don't you stay here tonight? We could stay here in the big house. There's plenty of room and ample bed space. I'm sure we would be comfortable as easily here as back in town."

"Thanks, Miss Kaylee, but Buck and Poke are capable of watching over you tonight. I must return to town. I will ride out tomorrow."

"That would be acceptable if you make it snappy first thing in the morning. I don't want to be waiting long for your return. We have many details to discuss, such as the ranch and other things." The ladies and the two men retreated to the house after that command.

Pinkie sat on a bench in the barn laughing till his face turned bright red, and tears ran down his cheeks.

"You think this is funny? All of you! Buck and Poke don't say a word." I stomped through the barn, looking like a storm cloud ready to burst.

"Pinkie, there's probably going to be a murder in town. I'm glad you're here." Pinkie wiped the tears from his eyes.

"I am figuring on it, Reg. Chelsea surely will drop you, but one thing I've learned when it comes to women killing men is that men usually deserve it."

With as much disgust as I could muster, I mounted and said, "Come on, Pinkie, let's ride."

Pinkie walked past Buck and Poke. "I wish I were a younger man. I'd stay and show you how to win over a couple of hearts. You two watch yourselves. Those two will scare you for life."

"Hell, boys, I could use a couple of new scares. New stories to tell," said Poke. Buck and Poke were surely amused at my 'perdickiment.'

Pinkie and I enjoyed a nice ride to town, joking and laughing about the current situation. We both knew I had no interest in those two women. Sure, they were a sight to behold, and a man's mind might run wild with thoughts of the hidden possibilities, but I knew what I had, which was priceless in my eyes.

Joe hailed us from the open barn doors, puffing his pipe. "I see you came back missing a couple of women. Reg, you may want to sleep in the barn tonight. It won't be a pleasant welcome on the other end of town."

"Don't go there. It's not a good subject," I warned. Joe was as full of jokes as the rest of the gang.

Joe pointed his bony, crooked finger down the road. Chelsea stood on the café's porch with a dark frown. And I didn't believe for a minute that it was worry for my safe return.

"Pinkie, you going to walk to the café with Reg? There might be a hell of a tussle down yonder," warned Joe.

At a loss for words, Pinkie bellowed another hearty laugh. "My ribs and sides can't take much more of this laughter. I am all played out. You are on your own walk, son. Kill her with kindness."

I imagined it was like watching a little boy walking back to his mama when he had done something wrong. It was a long, slow walk.

"Hello, Chelsea. Glad to see you came out to greet me."

"Where are the Anders girls?"

"Kylee and Kaylee are staying at the ranch."

"Oh, it's Kylee and Kaylee, now is it?" she swished her dress around and stomped back into the café in a huff.

I looked back to the men watching me. I was in a bad way. I hustled back to the stable as if a fire licked at my heels. "Think I'm gonna sleep here. Joe, you got some grub, and I'm thinkin' maybe a bottle?"

We cooked up some tasty grub on the fire and pulled the cork. I felt bad but wasn't sure for what. If Chelsea was a man, we would have just gone to blows and settled it right there. But we would have been fighting for a reason.

Being a single man with no women ties was a sight easier and simpler.

Joe and Pinkie thought my neck in the noose was pretty darn funny. Joe puffed his pipe and stoked the fire.

"Reg, you can't win. She's mad you went, mad you came back, mad you called the women by their first names, and mad that you're down here with us. The storm's brewing. It's going to rain hellfire. All you can do is look for cover and ride out the storm."

After a restless night, I shuffled to the café early for breakfast. Maggie acted real quiet, taking my order and serving me coffee. Seemed like she was biting her tongue.

"Maggie, did you poison me?"

She tried not to grin, but it didn't work, so she came to sit with me.

"Reg, that girl loves you, but she's scared. Two beautiful women who own a ranch that wishful dreams are made of ride into town, and she's worried they'll steal your heart."

"Maggie, that's about the dumbest thing I've ever heard," I said as Chelsea walked in behind me and overheard my statement.

"So, now I'm stupid." She turned faster than a hummingbird left its flower and ran from the café.

Maggie was sympathetic but amused. "Give her time. Her ma and I will try to put out the fire. You can't win, but you do have to run the race. It's a rite of passage. Spence is coming in today, isn't he?"

"I think so. I hope so. I need his advice."

"No, you don't. That little brother of yours. . . all he sees is women's bosoms and all the curves. I'm telling you that you will be just fine. But here is a little advice: Always take Spence or one of the men with you to see those gals. Don't set yourself a trap. Those two are like wild tom cats on the hunt."

I finished my breakfast and watched the activity at the mercantile. I wished Chelsea would run out, wrap her arms around me, and give me a big hug. God knows I could use one. Lo and behold, I observed exactly what I needed.

Spence had arrived. "Going to get saddled up?"

"Yep, Spence, I am."

"You better pick some flowers for your new girlfriends. I hear they are smitten with ya," Spence said, mocking me about the ladies at the ranch.

The younger of the two men didn't see it coming. My gun was in my hand like magic. "If you weren't my brother, Spence, I'd drop you right there. I have had enough of this."

Spence turned his horse, and he was heading to the general store to see Caty before I could bat my eyes.

"Temper, temper! Better pick out a pretty one." He chuckled as he rode down the dirt street.

He dismounted at the store to see Caty. She flew out the door, eager to welcome Spencer. She giggled and started right in, telling him about the new women in town as they both re-entered the store.

"Spencer, I think you need to talk to your brother. He has a beautiful woman who loves him, and she is far prettier and nicer than those city girls."

"Caty, slow down a little. How are you?"

346

"I'm fine, Spencer, but those city ladies went to the ranch and made Reg go along. They're not nice ladies."

"Caty, I'm sure the lovebirds will be perfectly fine. Reg knows what he wants, and pretty ladies are not going to sway him."

"So, Chelsea's not pretty?"

"Caty, that's not what I said."

"You're just like your brother." She stomped her foot, glared at him, turned, and showed him her back as she walked around the corner of the store.

"What the hell? I think I just walked into a hornet's nest. Now, I really wish Reg would have shot me." He pushed off the boardwalk, took the horse's reins, and hustled to the stable.

I asked, "Spence, how did that go?"

"Reg, I think I'll pick the flowers. That little girl ripped into me a good one. I'm going with you to the ranch. Has to be safer than here."

Pinkie, Joe, and Spence rode with me to the ranch. The ride was full of good jokes and plenty of ribbing. This is where Spence was at his best. He could talk and tell stories and was a great trail companion. I wasn't pleased to be the butt of the jokes, but it was entertaining and far better than facing the wrath of a woman.

Pinkie and Joe were up front now, enjoying themselves. "What's so funny? You going to let me in on the joke?"

"We were just wondering who's going to get smacked with the frying pan first, you or Spence."

The hired hands were at the ranch, but there was no sign of the men I wanted to see or the Anders gals. The ranch hands informed us they left early, and all four rode to the upper mesa and were going to be at the cow camp in the box canyon. The cow camp was a small house used by the cowhands when they were out checking the cattle. The cowhands would stay there for up to a month.

I felt relieved that the place was empty, but Spence, on the other hand, was upset that the ladies were not there. He was all set on meeting these beautiful women who appeared to be the latest town gossip. Spence never said so, but most people could see it as plain as day that he had confidence in himself and would try to win one of these gals over.

I swung my leg over Roan, hit the ground, and readjusted the saddle. "Fellas, looks like we're alone here. Want to ride over and talk to the hands and do a little scouting around? Maybe Buck and Poke will show up."

"Maybe those gals will come a-runnin'," Joe said as he bit his pipe between his lips.

"Nah. I'm okay now. My protector here can handle the load."

"I got it covered. Two women. I can handle it. They'll be so busy with me they won't even know you boys are in the county," said Spence.

"Spence, those two are more than a pup like you can handle."

"I love a challenge." Spence pulled his hat down to shade his eyes as he scanned the horizon for his prey. "I'm ready. Let her buck."

52

A WOMAN ON THE HUNT

"Chelsea, you need to listen to me. I'm a woman with a handful of miles under her belt, just like your ma," said Maggie. "You're a young woman in love. Reg has done nothing for you to be upset about, and you know it."

"I know, Maggie. I am so scared one of those women will steal his heart with their looks, money, and womanly ways from the big city. I let my imagination run away with me."

"Chelsea, you need to walk over here," said her mother.

"Ma, I'm fine."

"Come over here, NOW," she said. "Look in the mirror. You're beautiful—a beautiful woman. You're smart, kind, and a hard worker —everything a man like Reg desires.

Plus, you have the love of a good man. We all see it, and you need to believe it. If you don't, then you'll be the one to blame, not the other woman.

"Now, if we were talking about Spence, you would have a problem. That young man is sowing his wild oats. And he's casting as much seed in the fields as he can. That's okay for him, but he's not Reg."

Caty jumped headlong into the conversation.

"Spencer is not going to like those girls. He has land to look at and will be too busy moving cattle. He won't have time for such nonsense."

Caty was confident she had Spencer all figured out. "Chelsea, Reg gave you a ring and kissed you, so he must marry you."

"You're right, Caty. I need to let Reg know that I'm the silly one. I'm going to ride to the ranch and tell him so."

"Chelsea." Maggie shook her head. "I think you need to let it be for a while. Let Reg think about the two of you. Wait until he returns to town, go for a nice walk, take the kids fishing, and let it come naturally."

"Maggie, I know you're right, but I can't wait."

Chelsea was out the door and went straight to the livery. "Joe, are you here?"

With no answer from the old man, Chelsea rounded up a horse she knew, saddled up, and quickly cantered out the barn door.

She guided her horse to the T Lazy 7 Ranch. The entire time she road, she focused on good, happy thoughts. But within a moment's notice, her world would turn dark with opposite beliefs.

When she finally arrived at the ranch, she found an empty barnyard, quiet and still, peaceful but eerie at the same time. In her present mood, it was not a good place to be, alone. . . all alone. . .

Thinking maybe Reg or Spence were at the big house, she headed in that direction and soon found it vacant as well. Feeling like she was visiting a ghost town, she sat on the porch for quite a spell, thinking of what she wanted to tell Reg.

Close to thirty minutes passed, and she saw trail dust flying on the horizon as three riders approached from the West. She walked off the porch thinking it was Reg, Spence, Joe, or maybe the marshall. She was not expecting to see the hired hands.

"Hello, Miss Chelsea."

"Good day, gentlemen. I'm looking for Reg. Have you seen him?"

"Yes, ma'am. He rode in, and we told him the
others had rode up to the mesa. The women were going to stay at the cow camp in the box canyon. I think he rode that way to scout around to locate the ladies."

Chelsea wanted to cry but held her composure. "If you see Reg, tell him I hope he's having a good time. I'm going back to town. I have better things to do than chase him around the country."

The cowhands were unsure of what was happening but were sure it wasn't good. "Okay, Miss Chelsea, will pass on the word if we see him."

Chelsea spoke as she rode away, "I'm sure you'll find him wherever you find those women." She rode away from the cowhands and that awful place, crying the whole way back to town. She knew she was losing the man she loved.

Spence pulled his horse to a stop and stood in the saddle. "Well, glory be, look who's coming, Buck and Poke. I don't see any women." Spence put his hands in the air. "Where's the gals?"

Buck and Poke looked at each other. Poke waved back. "It's good to see you too, Spence. Sorry, we ain't what you were looking for."

"You know I love you two, but I was hoping for something with some curves and soft spots."

Buck sat up in his saddle, turned, and put his hands on his hips. "I got curves."

Poke laughed. "And I got soft spots." The kids were back together.

I slapped Spence on the back of the head. "Wake up. Spence, you're dreaming."

Pinkie asked, "Where are the women? You two ladies' men wore them out and left them at the cow camp?"

Poke looked behind himself, turning in the saddle. "Will be riding back in a while. They wanted to look over the ranch, but we weren't on the invite list. That kinda tells you how last night went."

Spence came to life. "See, fellas, they probably heard I was in the area and wanted time to prepare."

I slapped him on the back of the head again. "Reg, slap me one more time, and I'm going to knock you off your bodyguard."

Joe smirked, "Hell, Spence, that horse won't even let you get close to Reg."

"Let's ride over to Maggie's former dwelling and take a gander at how it looks. We all started over the hill, looking like little kids playing silly games. We rode over the crest of the hill and looked down on Maggie's ranch, and I wanted to ask my two friends' opinions.

"What do you two think of this place?" I asked.

Buck sighed. "It's a nice spread. Maggie and her husband had a good eye."

I asked Buck, "What are your thoughts about Maggie? Do you think she'd let it go?"

"I imagine she might. I know she loved this place, but I bet she loved this place with her husband. All you need to do is talk to Maggie," Buck said.

Luckily, her mount knew the route home as Chelsea was blinded by her tears. Finally arriving at the general store, she jumped from her horse's back and ran straight through the doorway into her ma's arms.

"It's over, Ma, it's over!" Then she ran to the back room where they lived.Nancy followed her troubled daughter.

Sara waited in the store with Caty and the boys. The boys were concerned about Chelsea and wanted to know why she was crying. "Mama, did she fall off her horse?"

"No, boys, sometimes young ladies get their feelings hurt by simple things."

"Well then, what's she crying for? She's got the best man with a gun, and he has a great horse."

"That's all good. We know that, but when a girl has a boy on her mind, she doesn't think about guns and horses. It has more to do with feelings of the heart.

"Does Chelsea have a bad heart, Mama?"

"Boys go outside and play. I'll call you for supper," Sara

answered, shaking her head.

Caty spoke up, "Boys live in their own world. Miss Sara, Chelsea is not okay. I need to go see her."

"No, Caty, let her be. She needs her mama right now. There will be plenty of time later. Caty, would you watch the boys, take Callie out, and play with her?"

"I'll go. But if Chelsea needs me, just call me."

Caty grabbed Callie by the hand. "Let's go catch some bugs and chase the boys." She held onto Callie's hand, and they skipped out the door.

Nancywas concerned about Chelsea's mindset and wanted to comfort her, but Nancy knew she needed a firm hand.

"Chelsea, for the love of God, you have plainly made a mountain out of a molehill. As far as you know, Reg has done nothing that would cause you worry. If you want to lose him, you certainly are going about it the right way."

"Young lady, I love you and want you to be happy. But I won't sit here and watch you carry on about such nonsense. You need to sit quietly and think about someone besides yourself. That man deserves better than what you're giving him. A whole lot more. To tell the truth, I am disappointed in you."

When we wanderers returned from Maggie's ranch, we headed to the stable, setting our gear in the loft. Unaware of the female drama, we were ready to bunk for the night. We spent the evening reminiscing about our adventures with the older men, who mystified the us younger ones. We were like kids camping out with our buddies.

I woke early and spent time grooming my one-of-a-kind straw-berry-colored horse. Like most women, human or horseflesh, she was a mystery to me.

I moseyed on down to Maggie's after I gave Roan a good rub down with the curry brush and let her out to pasture. I found Maggie in the kitchen, and we talked privately for quite a while. I thanked her, bid her a good morning, and proceeded to load my camping gear behind my saddle.

Spence and Joe watched with curiosity. Men understood one another. A few brief words were all these men needed. With a nod of my head, I prepared for a peaceful jaunt out of town without any explanations.

I didn't visit Chelsea. She appeared to need a little distance from me, being upset by the slightest of things. *I was in a whole other world when it came to understanding women.*

Midmorning arrived, and the three sisters worked their way down to the stable, stopping along the way to satisfy Callie's curiosity as she chased after every small thing that caught her wandering eyes.

Ever faithful and thinking of their favorite horse, they carried apples for Roan, but she was nowhere to be seen. Thinking she might be in a stable, they found Spence and Joe shoeing horses inside the barn and inquired about the horse.

"Morning, Joe."

"Morning, Caty. What brought you lovely ladies here this morning?"

Always the lady's man, Spence picked up Callie and sat her on one of the horses. She loved these giants and felt right at home.

"Where's my horse?" she asked, holding out the apple in her hand.

"Roan?"

"Yes?" she answered, nodding, "She's my horse."

"Reg left this morning with her," answered Old Joe.

Callie took a bite of the apple, dropped it to the ground so the horse she was on could eat it, and began plaiting the horse's mane.

Confused, Chelsea asked, "What do you mean he left this morning? I thought he stayed at the ranch with the Anders girls."

Joe answered her. "We all rode out there yesterday, but they were at cow camp, so we returned."

"Why didn't he pay me a visit then?"

"I'm not sure. I guess he wasn't in a talkative mood," Spence added to the conversation.

Caty remained silent. Spence asked her, "Do you want to sit on the other horse?"

"No, Spencer, I'm fine." She looked down at the ground and was very quiet. "I'm sorry, Spencer."

"For what, Caty?"

"I was mean to you, and I shouldn't have been. I was upset about Chelsea."

Chelsea held Caty's hand. "What? Why were you upset about me, Caty? What was wrong?"

"You were mad at Reg, and you were crying. I was mad, too. I don't know why, but I was. Then, you rode to the T Lazy 7 Ranch and returned, still crying." Spence looked puzzled. "Chelsea, when did you go to the ranch?

"Yesterday, Spence, I went to find Reg. I thought he was with the Anders girls."

Joe walked over and took Caty's hand. "Little lady, you should never get mad at anyone, especially when you don't have all the facts."

"I understand, Joe. I'm sorry, Spencer."

Spence leaned down next to Caty. "If we're to be friends and if there's a problem, we need to sit awhile and talk it out. I don't want you to be upset with me, but if we are friends, there must be trust. Caty, are we friends again?"

"You bet, Spencer. I'm sorry I was unkind."

He lifted her onto the horse behind Callie. Callie took Caty's apple, ate another bite, and dropped it to the ground again for the horse.

Chelsea spoke in a whisper. "I guess that statement goes my way, too."

Spence said, "If the boot fits. Reg isn't like most fellas I know. He says what he means and means what he says."

"Spence, I guess I must learn to sit and talk a spell, too." As you said, "If the boot fits."

"When is Reg coming back, Spence?" asked Caty.

"I'm not sure. He packed up his gear and headed out first thing this morning."

"What do you mean he loaded up his gear?" Chelsea interrupted the conversation.

Joe walked over to the mystified girl. "Young lady. If he comes back, I'd surely pick my words real careful like."

"What do you mean **IF** he comes back?" Chelsea looked dumbstruck at Joe's words. Then she glanced at her hands and ring, knowing she had made the biggest mistake of her life. The thoughts and words she had spoken tormented her now.

Callie needed a horse ride, so her two sisters headed out the door for a brief walk around town, and Chelsea left them to it.

"I'll leave you all to it and let you get back to work."

After walking down the boardwalk, thinking about her recent conversation with the men, she turned, picked up her skirts, and hurried back to the barn, running through the barn door and headlong into Spence, who had been finishing his final horseshoe fitting. Hoping she could speak privately to the only person she felt would help her, she reached for his hand.

Spence was startled by her abrupt entrance since she had just left minutes ago. "Chelsea, are you okay? What's wrong?"

"Spence, I've driven Reg away." She burst into tears and fell to the ground in a heap of her cotton muslin dress and petticoats.

"Oh, good Lord, It's okay. Women. Reg hasn't left. He just had to go. There's a big difference."

"Then why is my heart breaking? I know I made him leave me. I was jealous for no reason. I saw the Anders girls and knew I would lose him to their beauty and city ways."

"Oh, for the love of Pete, you know him better than that. He has never been one for foolish and frilly ladies. Now, if it were me, you'd have something to worry about."

Spence kissed her on the top of her head. "Go home, wipe your tears away. He will be back soon. I'm sure you'll understand why he left, and I hope you'll let him know how you feel. I don't think he'll need to hear it, but I firmly believe you need to hear yourself say it."

He lifted her to her feet. "Let's go. You can walk me to the general store. I am in sore need of a visit with the young rascals. I've missed their company."

He walked her to the general store, dropped her off, and looked for the boys. Sara and Nancy greeted him at the front room door.

"Spence, how's she doing?" asked Nancy.

"She looks like a stampede of cows had run over her heart," said Sara.

"Nancy, she's pretty upset, a lovesick puppy who lost her way," said Spence.

"Not much more I can do for her. My daughter is at the end of her rope."

"It will work out, and I'm positive she'll appreciate this time away from him. She's going to be upset with us all for a while, but she'll get over it. Someday, she'll tell this story to her daughters when they make the same mistake," he said.

Chelsea needed to cry and have Ma tell her life would be fine. No one seemed to even act like they cared that her heart was breaking. Knowing that keeping busy would be her best medicine, she returned to the café to tidy the kitchen and restock supplies from breakfast.

Maggie understood a lovesick mood when she saw one. "Chelsea, why don't you go home? I'll take over. I know you've had a long couple of days."

"I'm fine, Maggie. If you don't mind, I'd like to stay and keep busy."

"If you say so. I'll go unpack supplies and leave you to it then," said Maggie as she shook her head and glanced back to watch the girl slide to the sink of dirty morning dishes as if her world had just ended.

53

LIFE GOES ON

"I'm leaving in the morning, heading out with another wagon load. I will see you girls on Sunday at high noon," Spence said to the ladies as he pushed open the door to the mercantile and went outside into the bright noonday sun.

The children played on a hard patch of dirt at the far end of town while the women organized the merchandise in the front window of the general store.

"Caty, you have a mess of marbles there. Guess I know who's winning," he said.

Little Joe was upset. "I lost my best shooters. Can't believe I'm losing." At least he didn't say a word about losing to a girl. "I guess if I gotta give them away. I'm glad Caty got them and not one of the other boys."

Caty glanced at young Joe and gave him 'the skeptic face look,' "Really? I don't think you gave them to me. I beat you fair and square."

"Yes, you did, Caty," Spence said. As he ambled away, deep in thought, he realized that he had lost his little girlfriend and had been replaced with a new man.

Caty yelled as she ran to catch him, "See you Sunday."

"Caty, not a word now, not a word."

The wire master came down the road waving a piece of paper. "Spence, I have a wire for your brother. Is he coming back to town?"

"I don't think it will be any time soon. I'm riding out to see him tomorrow. I can take the paper to him if you would like."

The wire master sternly replied, "I'm not supposed to let anyone else read another person's wire. It's not lawful."

"Why don't you fold it up all nice and tight, and I promise not to open it?"

"You give me your word, and I'll let you carry it to him. If you read it, I'll know."

"I give you my word. It's none of my business. If my brother wants me to be informed, he'll let me in on it."

"I'll trust you. Here you go."

Curiosity must have been written all over the young man's face, but it wasn't his business. After he shoved the message into his saddle bag for safe keeping, he instinctively glanced back at the telegraph operator, who remained looking at him.

Chelsea felt totally lost. Reg was gone, and now Ma, Sara, and Maggie were gone. They said they were going shopping in the next town over. They needed supplies for the café and the general store and wanted Ma to go along to help. So that left her with the girls and the boys to attend to and continue to remain in charge of the café.

The café was already in good hands. Caty and a young Jetta were willing to help. Jetta was a good cook and friendly with the customers and was always ready with a smile and a willingness to share her recipes and cooking skills. She had traveled to the West to find adventure and, if lucky, maybe a husband. *It might be worth a try though just to have someone to talk to other than family.*

Chelsea wasn't concerned about the work. Maybe Jetta would lend a friendly ear, but since she didn't seem ready for any courting yet, Chelsea wondered if she would even understand about a breaking heart.

Chelsea sat alone in the front of the café, and as luck would have it, the Anders ladies sauntered in to eat lunch. They had been on the ranch for several days and recently returned to town. They were seated with the banker and the attorney.

They did seem concerned about talking with a serving girl nearby. They placed their orders, keeping their conversation private. When she entered the room, they stopped talking and acted very secretive. Their actions did not help her worries about her future with Reg.

After finishing their meal, paying the bill, and sauntering upstairs, the only thing they requested of her was hot water for their baths. Before returning to the ranch, they wanted to clean off the ever-present prairie dirt.

Again, Chelsea felt empty of heart and mind, with no one to talk to. Torn, heartbroken, and understanding that it was her fault that the man she wanted had left, she desperately needed to find him. Jetta was about to get an earful of female woes.

"I think you may misunderstand me, Chelsea. I do understand you, a lot. I had a beau before I came here, and he did me wrong. I know how your heart feels right now," said Jetta.

"What did you do about it?"

"I gave myself a good talkin' to. First, I decided I needed to talk to him to see if what I had set in my mind was true. And I did just that." Jetta said tucking the loose strands of hair behind her ears.

"Yes, but then what? That is what I am so afraid of that he has set his eyes on one of these high society ladies.

"Then you have two choices. Believe what he says and go forward with him or call him out on it and go your separate way."

"But how will I know if he is telling me the truth?" Chelsea asked with raised eyebrows.

"Well, Chelsea, if you don't know him that well by now, you are not ready to be married and you will never trust him in the future."

54

MAGGIE'S RANCH

I rode out to Maggie's' old ranch. I didn't waste any time and started to work on cleaning the place. I had a project to complete and was driven to finish it. Joe and Spence brought out the wagon filled with tools and lumber. Joe, Spence, and I put in a week of hard labor. Maggie, Sara, and Nancy showed up and pitched in to help with my project.

The sun had decided to wake up and peek over the far hill when my visitors arrived at Maggie's ranch. Spence and Joe had rolled in early that morning, heavily loaded with the wagon full of items to finish today's chores. No one would have been the wiser seeing them leave town before sunrise if they rode out early.

Pinkie later rode in to ask Spence and me to return to town to meet with the Anders ladies. They wanted to talk about the ranch.

"Pinkie, can't Spence go alone? I don't need any more drama."

"No, Reg. Just stand up and be a man. Spence will protect you."

Spence removed his hat and combed his hair with his fingers, preening for us. With that long, curly hair, he looked more like a woman every day.

"He's right, Reg. They won't even know you are there. When those two see this smile and my gorgeous head of hair. I'm all they will be paying attention to."

"Pinkie, I absolutely will not go to town. I will meet them at the T lazy 7. We can do it there if they want to visit regarding the ranch."

"Okay, I'll get it lined up. Tomorrow, high noon, how's that?"

"That will work. Then I'm headed back here to finish up this work."

I aimed to whip Maggie's place into shape. Many moons had passed since her home looked this good. My helpers put in hours of hard labor, giving me a helping hand.

Offering me a cup of water from the pail he held, Buck said, "Reg, I hope it all goes well for you. I know this place means the world to you. You don't talk much, but what you have done here says it all."

"I hope others see it the way I do, my friend. I surely do. I would've never got it done without your help. Speaking of which, where is your sidekick? Never mind. I hear the snoring."

"Now, I think our work is finished here," Spence said.

"I believe you are right, little brother."

As an afterthought, Spence walked over to his saddle and removed the letter the wireman had given him. It was still folded nice and tight. "I have a letter for you. It came across the wire, and I was entrusted to make sure you got it. So here, my wire service job has been fulfilled. Make sure that you tell the wireman it was all folded, and I never opened it. He threatened me with my life if I did."

I took the letter, read it, and returned it to Spence to read. It was from the Anders gal's estate manager. I was pleased and knew my eyes revealed my sentiment.

I believe my life is coming together.

Joe climbed aboard the wagon, waving goodbye to us, and said, "Reg, I'll tell the women folk you're ready for them come Sunday morning, and I'll see you at high noon for the showdown."

I couldn't help but chuckle. "I hope there's no shooting, but we will soon find out."

55

AT THE T LAZY 7 RANCH

The ladies, banker, and attorney were at the ranch when Spence and I trotted in. Poke and Buck remained working out in the field. They waved when we rode by

but kept their distance, giving the women privacy.

Pinkie sat on the front porch drinking coffee. We dismounted and greeted him. I informed Pinkie that Spence would be accompanying me to their meeting.

"The ladies wanted to talk to you alone, son."

I tipped my hat back off my forehead, no longer shading my eyes. "Well, that's too bad."

After realizing I had arrived, the banker opened the front door, stepped outside onto the porch, and said, "Reg, the ladies are ready for you."

"That's nice. Please inform them that my brother Spence and Marshall Yates will join us."

The banker stiffened. His scowl showed that he wasn't accustomed to being told what to do by an underling, especially one he considered to be a saddle tramp.

"Wait here, gentlemen. I'll inform the ladies." Within minutes, he returned and said, "They would love to see you all. Please come in."

The two ladies were dressed nicely in tailored, form-fitting suits, enhancing their beauty. We walked in, and I introduced my brother to them both. They were very gracious and kind. Kaylee was pleasant but did not exhibit any exceptional goodwill toward Spence.

Kylee was genteel, asked Spence to sit with her, and thanked him for what he did for their family. She also thanked him for watching over the ranch and the cattle.

Spence was more reserved than usual for his personality. He listened and drank the offered coffee. Spence spoke kindly to Miss Kaylee and Miss Kylee.

"It's a pleasure to finally meet you both. I would have sincerely liked to have met your kinfolk. Please accept my deepest sympathy.

Buck speaks very highly of them. In my mind, Miss Anders, he's the one you should thank for watching over the ranch and the cattle. He always kept this place operating as if they were still here."

"Mrs. Anders is my mother, and she's long passed. You, Spence, will call me Kylee. It sounds more welcoming, if you know what I mean."

Spence said, "I will call you Kylee then. It would be far more welcoming, as you stated."

He was starting the ball rolling. I could feel the charm in the room. Pinkie and I glanced at each other. We both knew Spence was about to suck the air right from the room.

"Spence, we both agree with you. Buck is a good man, and we can tell as we rode with him that he truly cared for our family and this ranch."

Kaylee walked over to Spence and her sister and spoke to them both. "We know that Tucker and his men killed Maggie's husband, and Tucker paid her a small fee for her ranch and added this ranch to his T Lazy 7 holdings. Our attorney has drawn up the paperwork to ensure her property was no longer part of the T Lazy 7 Ranch. We all know it belongs to her and have no claim on it."

"Marshall, we would like you to assure us that this matter will be taken care of. I'm sure you will all watch over her interests. I feel certain no one will try to take advantage of her again. I heard she can handle a rifle quite well."

The attorney handed the paperwork over to Pinkie. "Please, Marshall, have her read these documents and sign them if she agrees. We have already signed."

Pinkie took the paperwork. "I will make sure she receives it. Maggie is an intelligent woman, and as you stated, Miss Kaylee, we all know who owns that ranch."

"Kylee and I talked to Buck and Poke about staying on and running the T Lazy 7 Ranch for the two of us. They were kind, but we could tell their hearts were not in it. They both want a place to call their own and fulfill their dreams. I think there could be a great opportunity for them at Maggie's place," the eldest of the sisters said.

I nodded and said, "I agree. I talked to them both about this very same thing. I think it would work out for all concerned if Maggie agreed."

"I think you're right. Kylee and I have discussed an opportunity for you two brothers to take over the T Lazy 7 Ranch operations. We offer you a paid position and ownership of the ranch. We have taken the liberty of drawing up a contract for you both."

The attorney handed Spence and me the paperwork to review. Spence looked thoughtfully at the ladies before he spoke. "Miss Kaylee and Miss Kylee, I appreciate the offer, but I have a place back home to manage, and I have no intention of leaving it," said Spence.

"Kaylee and I have talked with the two cowboys here about your family's ranch. They both said it was beautiful and well-run, a sight to behold. But, Spence, wouldn't you like to have a ranch to call your own?"

"Miss Kaylee, thank you. But that ranch is my place. My dad set the ranch up when we were quite young so we could buy our shares. We bought and sold cattle, bought land, and built the ranch together with those thoughts in mind. We all own the homestead, a one-third equal split. When Dad passes, the remainder will go to Reg and me as owners with equal shares. Our mother will live in the place until she passes away or decides to move to a smaller home. We both will take care of her, no questions asked. Ladies, I would never speak for my brother, but I decline the offer."

"You didn't even take a look at our offer. I think you would like to be part of this ranch. Please, at least, look at it. I think you and I could build something special here."

"Miss Kylee, I'm sure the ranch offer is more than enticing, and one I may have some sleepless nights over, but, again, I'll have to decline," said Spence.

Spence amused me with his antics. *I think he held his cards close to his vest pocket and, by now, played out his hand with the ladies. For a while, anyway. I knew why he was not interested in the land, but I wondered if Spence might hold out to see what played out personally with the young lady.*

"Miss Kylee." I began to take the heat off Spence. "Ladies, I also will have to decline. My thoughts follow the same path as my brother's. The ranch back home is a special place. I know he will keep it growing and developing it into a spread envied by other ranchers. That's why I'll turn over my stake in the ranch to Spence in future days. I'm looking to start my roots elsewhere. Hopefully, with a new bride and a dozen kids."

"So, neither of you will even look at our offers?"

"No, ma'am, we will not, but we are both grateful. I'm sure it is a very lucrative offer. Again, thank you," I said.

Kaylee was mystified. She dressed up and threw herself at them both, and neither saw what she offered them. "Blind?" she whispered to herself.

Kylee stood up and bent over to take Spence's coffee cup.

Spence glanced up as she did so, and it wasn't her eyes he was gazing at. This woman had some excellent property, that was for sure. When his eyes did reach her face, he saw the most beautiful smile he had ever seen and eyes as blue as the sky on a winter's day.

Yep, there would be some sleepless nights, and they wouldn't be about the ranch.

"Spence, I'm sure you can see what you are passing on, but truly, I think you have made a good choice, partly anyway. I hope we can be friends, and who knows what the future may bring our way."

Miss Kylee was amazing. She truly meant what she said. Now, on the other hand, Miss Kaylee was not amused.

I was ready to go. "Ladies, thank you. I'm sure my brother will keep in touch. I want to say this, though. You both are from back east, and I'm sure you are at home there. The ranch is beautiful, but it's not like where you are from. There are no gala events, theater, or the comforts of the city here."

"I would like to make an offer to buy the ranch, its cattle, and livestock and divide the property. I'll cut out the ranch house, barns, and two hundred acres you would both retain. The house is too grand for me. If you were interested, that would keep a section of the ranch for you two sisters to enjoy. I have put down some numbers of my own. Please let me know your thoughts once you have reviewed and reflected upon my proposal."

He handed the cyphered paper to the attorney. Miss Kylee graciously reached over and took the paper from her attorney. "I'll take a look at it. I know Kaylee will also, but she is just upset right now that you were not interested in her offers."

Spence picked up his hat and stood to leave. "Thank you for having us over. Ladies, I truly enjoyed the opportunity to meet you both and put a face to the names. It will always be a day I'll remember fondly."

"Kylee, I will look forward to our next meeting." I'm sure we will have a great deal to talk about in the future, and I look forward to enjoying many more cups of coffee with you," Spence said with a wink.

Everyone in the room was very much aware of what had just happened. Kylee smiled and batted those eyelashes to those beautiful blue eyes.

Spence tipped his hat, walking from the room with Pinkie following.

Miss Kylee walked with the marshall to the door. "Marshall, please tell Maggie we look forward to being neighbors."

"I shall do that very thing. Good day, ladies."

I said my goodbyes. "Please look at my offer. I didn't mean any disrespect. I just have a different vision of the future, like you two do."

Kylee looked at me. "Thank you. I'm happy for you. We both are."

Kaylee took her hand. "I am also happy for you, although I'm not as fast to forgive rejection as my sister appears to be."

"Thank you both. I truly wish you two sisters the best of luck. I know we will have years of working side by side with one another."

The three men rode off and were shortly met on the trail by Buck and Poke.

Poke asked, "You the new boss of the T Lazy 7?"

"No. Poke, I turned the ladies down and made them my offer to purchase the ranch. Time will tell."

Poke snickered at Spence. "What about you, Spence? You going to man up and handle the ranch or at least the ranch's women folk?"

This brought on laughter from them all, including Spence. Spence grinned and looked up, wiping the sweat from his forehead. "Not interested in the ranch, but one owner meets my standards."

Poke slapped him on the back of the head. "What's your main standard? That she is breathing?"

"Funny, fellas, I don't care if she's breathing. I just care that she's still warm," Spence said and rode away, showing that shit-eatin' grin. On the other hand, we didn't even know how to reply to that one.

I turned Roan away from town. "Men, I'll see you in a couple of days. Pinkie, you're heading back to town?"

Pinkie answered. "Yep, I'm going to visit with Maggie. I also need to send a wire to check up on Ben and Tom. Make sure they haven't run off. I'm looking forward to the future for you. See you soon."

I tipped my hat and rode toward Maggie's ranch. I was on a mission and wanted to get on with my life.

56

DAMSEL IN DISTRESS

C helsea assumed the ladies were out on a shopping tour to town and left the new girl, Haley, there to help Jetta in the kitchen on the odd chance Chelsea needed assistance. Even though Haley was a tiny bit of a young lady, she was a whirlwind in the kitchen. She would race through the orders with her long black braid flying while she sang a Spanish lullaby. Her dark brown eyes always had a mischievous twinkle to them, making her co-workers wonder what little ornery prank she was cooking up along with the beefsteaks.

But Chelsea had ideas of her own. After spending the evening thinking over what advice her ma, friends, and Spence gave her, she had a mission to carry out this morning.

She left the café in the girls' capable hands, and the determined lass strode down to the horse stables to borrow one of the horses Sly lent them for their journey home. Joe was nowhere to be seen, so she scribbled a note to him that she had taken Josie out for a ride to the ranch.

The morning dew lifted, and the fingers of a pink and purple sky lit up the horizon. A perfect day for the task at hand. Chelsea was an excellent rider, an out-of-doors woman but not one familiar with guiding a horse through this unfamiliar route she had chosen.

Caty looked out the front café window, hearing Sara, Maggie, and her ma drive the wagon back into town. Skipping out the front door to help unload the wagon, she found it empty and sitting in front of the café.

"Ma, where are the supplies?"

"We bought quite a lot, so they are delivering the goods to us. We sure had a relaxing trip, and so nice to have a day away. Don't say a word to your sister."

"Caty, speaking of getting away, how did the kids do? Did they run you ragged?

"No, Sara, the boys were good. They helped me a lot and kept my mind busy. No one asked me a single thing about Chelsea or Reg."

Before Chelsea was aware, a small prairie dog jumped from his burrow directly in front of her horse. As fate would have it, Josie reared.

Chelsea maintained her balance aboard Josie as the startled horse reared. As she settled back on all four legs, her right front hoof caught in the entrance to the prairie dog's burrow. With a crack of bone and an ear-splitting scream from Josie, the horse toppled over.

At this point, Chelsea flew over Josie's shoulder and landed in a heap against a mound of rocks. Upon landing, her ears rang, and her last vision was a confusing sight of sparkling silver stars on a shroud of black velvet darkness.

Little Joe sat playing out behind the livery when he spotted the horse running straight for town. "Grandpa, help! There is a man on a horse riding our way, and it looks like he has someone slumped over in front of him."

Old Joe rushed around the side of the building and immediately knew that something was terribly wrong. "Boy, run like the wind and fetch Doc Charlie. We got a big emergency here."

No sooner were the words out of his mouth than the horse flew by, and Joe recognized Reg holding Chelsea. She was flopped over in front of him, her head dripping blood, which made a trail down Roan's shoulder.

The old man ran down the street to the café to meet Reg as fast as his wobbly, arthritic legs could carry him. "Let me have her, Reg. I have sent for the doc. What happened?"

They both carefully lowered her down from the saddle. "I don't know. I was riding back here from Maggie's and found Josie with a broken leg and Chelsea out cold."

By now, the café had emptied of its patrons, and Maggie was first on the scene. "Quick, someone, run, get Nancy. Reg, carry her upstairs to one of the vacant rooms. Spence, wait for the doctor and show Nancy where we are."

Maggie helped to settle the patient in the single bed and mentally prepared herself to comfort Nancy should shock set in, but to her surprise, when the girl's ma arrived, she kept her emotions in check, showed a strength of will, only focusing on Reg's description of what he knew.

He explained about the accident as he understood it and told the ladies that Chelsea was unconscious when he found her. Apparently, she had fallen from her horse and had not roused on the ride back to town.

As the three in the room pondered that frightening thought, they heard Spence stomping up the stairs, making more noise than six children and being trailed by Doc Charlie.

"Um, Reg, this here's Doc Charlie," he said.

Although by nature I am the silent type, this situation caught me full to bursting with questions. I gaped and said, "You are Doc Charlie?"

"Why, yes, sir, I am."

"But you are a WOMAN."

"What great eyesight you have. You have a problem with that, mister?"

"I thought you would be a man. Charlie is a man's name."

Old Joe interrupted the conversation, "Oh, no, Reg! Doc Charlie's real name is Josephine, Jo for short. But if you call her that, she is liable to lay you out. Trust me on this one." Old Joe indicated by rubbing his jaw.

"I've never seen a woman doctor before other than the old Cherokee woman."

"Reg, shut your mouth while you are ahead. Just because she is a woman doesn't mean she can't be a doctor," scolded Maggie.

"Now, if we are done jawing over my name, let me see the patient. My nurse, Zoey, who also happens to be my younger sister, will be here in a few minutes, so please allow her passage."

Both men stepped back from the spitfire doctor and wisely remained silent. Spence took his cue to return to the lobby to await Nurse Zoey.

After examining Chelsea from head to toe, she explained to the waiting group, "I have determined that my patient has what is called a concussion. It was not unusual after a head injury for a patient to be unconscious for anywhere from a short period of time to days. Nothing can be done at this time but to keep her comfortable and wait. My nurse will help to change her clothing and dress the wound after I clean it. She will bruise and look mighty bad for a few days, so keep mirrors away from her when she wakes. Put ice on it to help the brain from swelling."

The stomping on the stairs sounded. And they all knew Spence was on his way again. Normally, and never at a loss for words, at this particular moment, his voice failed him. Waving his arms and pointing from the nurse to the doctor and the patient lying in bed was all he could manage.

I turned to see why my brother remained silent other than he didn't want to irritate the good doctor again. It was obvious that Nurse Zoey and Doc Charlie were sisters.

Doc Charlie had long strawberry blonde hair down to her waist. Nurse Zoey had long brown curly hair that was truly beautiful and most likely would touch the floor if not for the curls. Other than the difference in age and hair, they were nearly identical.

These two beauties stood before me. Together, they worked in a familiar routine, anticipating each other's needs.

Spence stared, the ladies smiled, and I understood. A vision of loveliness had entered that lady's man's world, and there remained no room in his mind for a clear thought or words.

It was wrong. Chelsea lying on the bed, knocked out and bloodied, and here I was, also smiling at two pretty girls. I truly was mentally unfit to be called a human being.

"I don't think you can play your cards close to the vest this time," I whispered to Spence.

"I have done all I can currently do. Watch her carefully for fever. Zoey will return hourly today to check on her progress. Alert her for any changes," said Doc Charlie. With that, she left the room, and still, no one spoke.

Day and night, family and close friends kept a steady vigil, watching over Chelsea. I took the night watch so the others could rest and still manage their daily chores. I held her hand and talked to her, even praying out loud, though I felt rather silly doing so.

Maybe if she could hear my voice, she would wake.

Still no change until the morning of the fifth day. As sunlight broke open the crack between earth and sky, the bedridden miss opened her eyes and said, "Go call Pa for breakfast."

"Ma, come quick!" Caty had just taken over the morning shift when she heard those words. Before two minutes passed, Nancy rushed into the room, breathless, with her nightdress on and her robe barely tied. "What is it?"

"Chelsea woke up and said to call Pa for breakfast." The child was in tears. "What is wrong with her? She knows Pa has passed."

"Run for the nurse like Doc said," instructed Nancy.

As she ran down the stairs, Caty barreled right into Spence and me as we prepared to sit down for a cup of coffee.

"Whaaat?" Spence yelped.

"No time to talk, move aside.... Nurse....Quick....Chelsea awake...."

"I'll go. I can get there faster, Caty," Spence said.

I raced up the stairs, hardly believing Caty's words, grabbed the door jamb, and flung myself into the room, nearly landing in Nancy's lap.

To my delight, Chelsea saw me but then let out a blood-curdling scream that could wake the dead. "Who is that man? Get that stranger out of my room, Ma!"

"Chelsea, it is me, Reg. What is wrong? Don't you recognize me?"

"Please move aside, Mr. Carter," said Nurse Zoey as she muscled past me and over to the bedridden patient. Nancy looked aghast at her daughter and me as she tried to understand what she had just heard.

"What is wrong with her, nurse?" asked Nancy.

"Would one of the people in the café hurry to fetch Doc Charlie for me? Without the doctor's opinion, I do not want to speculate about this young lady's condition."

Nurse Zoey also requested that I remain in the café until the doctor arrived and called for me, indicating this might bring some calm to the hysterical girl in her care.

Unaware of the drama taking place upstairs, luckily, Zeke happened to be sitting down for his morning meal before the early morning stagecoach run.

Old Zeke, the stagecoach driver, recognized that the breathless

Spence could use a helping hand since he nearly took the rails off the stairs on his way into the dining room. Zeke said as he jumped out of Spence's way, "Whoa, there, son. Can I hep ya?"

Knowing time was important, the only option for help at the moment was the stagecoach sitting empty in front of the cafe as no horses were at hand this early. Both men dashed out of the café and jumped on the stagecoach.

They rode through town to the Doc's house two miles from town. They both banged on the door, hollered, and woke the doctor. Nearly twenty minutes passed before Zeke and Spence delivered a bleary-eyed Doc Charlie to her patient.

Once the physician performed an examination, she nodded and murmured a few words to herself before addressing Nancy and Chelsea. She asked Nancy to step out into the hallway for a private word.

She asked Nancy to speak to Chelsea and explain in as few words as possible that she was the girl's mother and ask her what the last thing she remembered was.

"I believe your daughter has an ailment called 'amnesia.' It can be short-term, as in a few hours, or it could last for days or forever, depending on where she hit her head and how it affected her brain. She may have forgotten recent memories or those from quite some time ago."

"We must move slowly with our help in the healing process, and it is most important that we do not tell her what happened. She must remember facts by herself and not live the story we spoon-feed her until we absolutely must. I am now going downstairs to discuss this with her gentleman friend."

~

"Chelsea, do you know where you are and who I am?"

"Of course, I know who you are. You are my ma. Why would you ask me such a question?"

"Are you up to telling me the last thing you remember, Chelsea?"

"Well, I remember we moved here, and we are waiting for Pa to catch up to us as soon as he can."

"Yes, that is right. Anything else?"

"Apples and a beautiful horse. Ma, I am so tired. I think I shall rest now."

And with that, she fell deeply asleep once again.

57

REG

"By far, this is the hardest thing I have ever had to do. Acting like Chelsea doesn't know me? I feel like this is all a dream, and all I need to do is wake up," I said to Nancy and Spence as we strolled down to the stream for some privacy.

"It has been two months now, and there hasn't been any indication that she has regained much of her memory," said Nancy. "All we can do is wait, and you continue being a gentleman around her."

The three sat on the stream bank and tossed stones into the water. The sound of the water splashing over the rocks had a calming effect, helping to soothe our troubled minds. Luckily for the family, this community was tight-knit, and with the help of Preacher Bill, all who knew Chelsea allowed for her forgetful memory, introducing themselves when needed as if they were new acquaintances.

I stopped in the café occasionally when I knew she was working, and I tipped my hat or gave a cheerful hello if she waited on me. Today, I stopped at the back door to the dining hall and dropped off a load of kindling and firewood for the kitchen. The doctor had told us that seeing our faces might trigger a memory.

"Thank you, Reg. That certainly helps a lot when I don't have to carry it in from the wood pile myself," Chelsea said with that endearing smile.

"Anytime, Miss Chelsea."

The nightmares about not saving Chelsea from her accident and ultimately losing her in the future gave rise to sadness and a lack of interest in my surroundings. Even the young'uns couldn't rouse me to join them on a fishing trip.

At a loss for things to do around town, I rode out to Maggie's old place to make sure Buck and Poke were tending to the ranch with no problems. They were bunking in the small cabin there to help manage the property until Maggie decided whether to return to her home or sell.

"Howdy, Reg. Any news on Chelsea's recoverin'?" asked Buck.

"Funny thing, Buck, she remembers apples, Roan, and her new friendship with Jetta." She has retained some memories and has lost other memories altogether.

"Hmm, it sounds like all those things are comfortable memories for her. Maybe if you took some time to visit your folks to clear your mind, it would be less hurtful to you. I know it would be hard and nerve-racking, but there is the possibility she may never recall who we all are. You are in a bad spot, Reg, but I truly feel she will come around."

"That's a dandy idea! I would love to see Mom and Dad and Spence," I yelped and slapped my thigh.

The remainder of the day was spent with us three men riding the meadows, inspecting the growing herd, and counting the new additions since I was last here. That evening, we reminisced about our travels and my storytelling brother while we ate dinner around a campfire.

The visit with my folks and Spence turned out to be exactly what I needed. I took a hand in rounding up our newborn calves and their mamas and moving them to a new meadow.

Spence and I rebuilt the smokehouse and added an additional corral alongside the existing one. It appeared my brother had taken to the idea of expanding the number of horses on the property.

Mom and Dad were concerned about Chelsea but understood my need for space and time away from the memories she and I shared and the daily worries that haunted me about the loss of her memory.

Reluctant to return to Two Forks, I continued helping around the ranch, finding endless chores to keep me occupied.

A month had passed. I had been sending wires to Nancy, but there was no change in Chelsea's memory of our time together.

One morning, Dad pulled me aside. "Son, I believe the time has arrived for you and me to talk," said Sly.

I knew this would not be a pleasant talk, and I had been expecting it for a while now, so I let him speak his mind.

"Exactly what do you have in mind for your life now, son? Now that your heart is broken, and you can't see the future? Stay here and expect your ma and me to solve your problems?" Dad asked.

Always a man who got right to the point. He certainly hit this nail flush.

"Fear is a mighty, powerful enemy. If not tamed, it will eat you alive. A rest for the weary is exactly what you need, but hiding or running is not. Facing this fear of rejection or accepting the loss of the one you loved is the only way to move forward. You don't have to remain in Two Forks, but you will have to face your demons there."

Dad and I talked, or he said his piece, and I listened. Then, another month came and went after we spoke, and I turned his words over in my mind day after day before I decided to return to Two Forks. I reckoned I would have stayed there much longer if it hadn't been for my father's words of wisdom.

58

RETURN TO TWO FORKS

"Morning, Missus," I said to Sara as I reined in at the mercantile. Nancy hugged me tight, letting me loose when Sara edged her aside also to give me a warm hug welcome. It was a comfort to be back to where I hoped was home.

The hugs were as Mom always said, "A great way to learn about the huggies or the huggers." I felt truly loved and missed.

I helped them unload the supply wagon and stock the shelves. I knew there was no change, or it would have been a far different welcome home greeting.

"Well, Nancy, any changes? I needed to know.

"A few minor ones, but nothing major. She has been having dreams, though. The doctor thinks that is a good sign. Her dreams have flashes of people and places in them, like puzzle pieces she can't quite put together," she answered, knowing I wanted to know all about Chelsea's state of mind.

Guessing this time was as good as any, I walked Roan through the back fields behind the buildings and let her graze. I knew she would find me if she needed to. Taking a chance that Chelsea might be in the café's kitchen, I poked my head in to say hello. She knew I was a customer from months ago, so I knew she wouldn't be frightened.

I made a noise in the hallway and poked my head in the door. "Good morning, miss," I said in a low tone of voice, trying hard not to startle her. "Is there anything I could help you with this morning? Bringing in kindling or carrying water for you?"

"Well, good morning to you. Thanks for asking, but I am all set for the day," she said as Jetta watched wide-eyed from the wash sink.

"Then I will mosey on out to breakfast. Oh, yes. I wondered if you would have any apple peels left over from the pies?"

"You are more than welcome to eat an apple if you would like. We don't need to serve you peels," she said, chuckling at her own wit.

"Thanks, Chelsea, that's nice of you to offer, but they are for my horse."

Then she slowly put down her stirring spoon, turned to face me, and said, "Reg?"

I was so stunned I steadied myself on the doorframe. "Chelsea, what did you say?

"Reg? Why would you ask me for apple peels? You know I always feed them to Roan myself. You don't have to. I love that horse. I would never forget her."

"Chelsea, you remember me?" I asked as I stepped forward to look her in the eye.

Jetta took this opportunity to inch past me and scurry into the dining room. "Come quick, Maggie. It's Chelsea and Reg!" Jetta whispered to her. "Send for Miss Nancy!"

In a heartbeat, Maggie looked out the café door. Bailey was sitting on her perch on the stagecoach seat, waiting for the new passengers.

Maggie waved to Bailey to attract her attention. Run Bailey and get Miss Nancy. Then ride to find the doctor."

"I'm glad to oblige, ma'am, but I can't leave the team."

"Bailey, go now! Find Nancy, take the roan, and ride like you had wings. I said now!"

Bailey jumped from the stage, threw a leg up on the roan's stirrup, and threw her leg over her back.

She pulled the reins and yelled through the store's open door for Nancy as she sped past. Then she rode like the roan's tale was a'fire.

Those who saw the horse and rider looked on with amazement. The roan never balked at this little squirt of a rider. She just went where Bailey guided her.

Maggie didn't know what had happened in the kitchen, so she hesitated to enter until Nancy was there.

Nancy arrived within a few minutes with Caty trailing her. She looked like she had been through a windstorm, her hair unpinned and in disarray, dust smears covering her apron, and her eyes opened wide in alarm.

Taking a deep breath, then Maggie and Nancy peeked through the bat-wing café doors to the kitchen. Jetta, not wanting to be ignored, tried to poke her nose around or in between the two.

What the three women saw was Reg and Chelsea hooting up a storm at some funny story while Reg held her hand.

"Let's wait until they come back into the dining room," said Nancy. "I wouldn't interrupt this for anything in the world.

It wasn't too long before the couple entered the dining room. Reg sat at his favorite table, and Chelsea took his breakfast order as if nothing out of the ordinary was happening and then they both burst into laughter.

"She remembers me!" I said.

"It appears so," said Nancy.

"It was the apple peals that did it," said Chelsea, confusing the ladies and Caty.

And if that were not confusing enough, Bailey was back. She was sitting on Roan's back. Horse and rider walked right through the back door and the hallway to the dining room. Luckily, it was empty of customers by then.

"Doc is on the way." Bailey blurted to the amazed group. By this time, anything seemed natural.

Everyone was all tears and smiles.

Life in Two Forks soon returned to normal, and I began courting Chelsea just as I had promised her ma that I would.

59

REG IS ON THE TRAIL

"Joe, where are ya, ya old goat? I can hear ya up in the barn loft, or maybe it's a big smoking rat," yelled Spence.

"You guessed it, a big smoking rat. "Let's you and me head out in the morning with the wagon and get this ball rolling."

"Yep, pack a lot of smokin' tobaccy. I don't want to run back into town in the middle of the night. Whiskey, too. I'm starting to feel a powerful thirst."

"I'll have it all ready, don't you worry none."

"If you say so. I'm heading down to the café for a bite. You comin', old gray goat?"

"You will have to twist my arm, and then you're buying!"

The town was quiet, the worries had passed, and it was nice to walk carefree. As new settlers moved here, this small town was about to change. Once news spread about what happened here, the newcomers would feel safe.

The cattlemen were content, and the range was full of fat cattle. It was going to be a good year.

Both men walked into the café, and the scent of the cooked food made their mouths water as always.

Maggie was waiting on her customers. Chelsea was busy moving from table to table with arms heavy with food to deliver. Keeping busy, she was not her usual joyful self and looked as if she carried the weight of the world on her shoulders.

Maggie glanced up as the two men crossed the threshold. "Finally, here's two strangers waltzing through my doors. It's about time. My food not up to your standards lately?"

"No, siree, ma'am. Your food is the best around for miles."

"Not much of a compliment. I'm the only place around for miles."

"Well, then, guess you're safe being the best."

"One day, young man, you're going to step on that tongue, and I hope I'm still alive to see it."

Maggie bent low and whispered in Joe's ear, "I hear you've been busy helping to fix the place."

"Maggie, you keep your tongue. Don't need no loose lips," Joe said as he gave her a tilt of his head and a grimace, hoping to shush her.

"Then I'll rustle up your food. I surely don't want to be the one to spill the beans."

"Speaking of beans, bring me a load. I would like that," said Joe.

"Please and thank you might help," she said.

Spence pinched his nose.

"Of course, you would want beans. Nobody else will like it, but maybe it will help with that tobacco smell."

"Yep, fit right in with those skunks out in the barn," Maggie teased.

Chelsea kept her distance from the men, having difficulty looking their way, knowing they probably figured she was disgruntled. She was a sorry sight to see.

Reg would hate to see her like this. But Reg needed to be away from town. Chelsea didn't know why he needed more cows. But he told her he needed to make a living, and if it took being away from town from time to time, then so be it.

60

SUNDAY

Sunday rolled around. It was a beautiful day. A baby blue sky, billowing clouds, and a warm breeze filled the Sunday morning. The birds chirped their greeting, and an abundance of deer ran throughout the fields.

I had been out of town for two weeks on a cattle run. I knew Chelsea wasn't happy about being alone, but she understood cows and the adjustments that must be made by being a rancher. But cows were just an excuse.

Chelsea moved around the café, preparing to place the open sign out and welcome guests when Nancy, Sara, and Maggie came in. They were all dressed in their Sunday best.

"Ma, what's going on? Everyone is dressed so pretty. Wagons

and horses were going by the café, everyone was heading out of town, and all dressed for Sunday meeting," Chelsea said.

"We're all heading to church. You need to get yourself dressed and ready to go."

"I'm not in the visiting mood. I think I'll stay here and mind the café."

Maggie stepped over and looked Chelsea straight in the eyes. "Sorry, young lady, I'm closed for the day, and you need to get yourself ready for church services. You've been in this doom and gloom far too long."

Nancy looked sternly at Chelsea. "I laid out a new dress and ribbons for your hair. You need to get a move on."

The young woman was in no mood for travel, for people, or church, but she knew better than to argue with her ma. "I'll go, but I'm not going to enjoy it much."

"We will see Chelsea. It may do you some good to get out in the fresh air. The things you don't want to do often turn out to be the most fun."

Sara grabbed her arm, and all the ladies hurried across the street to get ready. The younger children were already in the wagon and were eager for a ride. Caty and Callie had dressed in new clothes with matching ribbons in their hair.

The boys were in long pants and suit jackets. They were not as pleased, but they were as handsome as could be.

"Ma, why is everyone in the wagon? The church is just down the road?"

"We're having church out in the country today. We all need fresh country air and beauty to lift our hearts."

Chelsea entered her room and found a beautiful dress, ribbons, and shoes spread out on her bed, all brand new.

"I bought these for you when I went to town the other day."

"Oh, they are so beautiful."

"I needed to spend some of the money your pa left us. This here is a new beginning. Now get dressed. Preacher Bill will surely start the service without us."

They were in the wagon heading out of town with the girls and boys giggling and squirming like a basket of new puppies. Chelsea gasped at the sight when racing over the hill to the T Lazy 7 valley. The whole town was there for worship.

Beautiful wildflowers were arranged and hanging from every fence pole, and roasting beef could be smelled cooking over an open fire pit. Tables were set with red and white checkered tablecloths; kegs of beer and whiskey bottles had a men's only place on the end of the table.

"Ma, I've never seen beer and whiskey at a church meeting. Everyone is dressed so nice, and the flowers there are beautiful."

The restless bunch of kids jumped from the wagon, and Caty yelled in a most unladylike fashion, "Spencer, you're here!"

Chelsea gazed in his direction, not recognizing him dressed in such fine clothes: new boots, pants, a shirt, a hat, and a long coat. He walked towards the adults in the wagon and reached out his hand to help Chelsea down from the wagon.

Then there stood Preacher Bill, all smiles. Poke, Buck, Tom, Ben, and Marshall Yates dressed just like Spence were drawn into her line of sight. Spence's parents stood in the background, surprising Chelsea even more when Sly walked forward to greet her.

Sly hugged Chelsea. "I'm glad you could make it. Hard to start this service without you."

Spence led the confused young lady up the path to the T LAZY 7 ranch house, and I stepped out of the front door. Tears rolled down her cheeks like a dam had broken.

"You are the most beautiful thing I've ever seen. We're all here, ready and waiting for the wedding," I said.

"What did you say?"

"Chelsea, will you marry me?"

Luckily, Spence had remained holding her tight around the waist as he felt her knees start to buckle. She began to faint right then and there.

Spence laughed and said, "Big brother, I think you made a fine impression on this lady. You better hold on to her. We don't need any more concussions."

My face did not show any amusement in that statement. I grabbed my bride-to-be with powerful hands and strong arms, feeling like I would never let go.

Chelsea was all tears. "I missed you terribly. You haven't left my side since the amnesia was over. You said you were moving cattle, and you didn't come back right away."

"I can't argue that fact, Chels. And I did move cattle from one pasture to another. I spent the rest of the time here, fixin' things for us if you will have me.

But I'm here now, you're here, and everyone who means anything to us is here. What do you say? We're going to have a party one way or another. We both will own this place if you say I DO."

Chelsea spoke softly, like a breeze from a butterfly's wings. "I'll marry you, Reg. I knew you were the one for me from the moment I first saw you."

I reached out for Chelsea's hand. "You have made me the happiest man in the world. First, before we say our vows, I would like you to step into the ranch house and meet a lady we have invited just for you.

Accepting the request, a bewildered Chelsea stepped into the foyer and was greeted by a charming olive-skinned young lady with intriguing mahogany colored eyes.

"My name is Jennifer. I am a seamstress and have recently begun to set up my shop in your town. I am honored to present you with this wedding gown, my first design as a milliner here."

Chelsea was stunned as the lady displayed a dress of the finest gown of lace, ruffles, and pearls she had ever seen, let alone been lucky enough to wear.

"This is close to the latest fashion in Paris, where they are breaking old traditions, and brides are now wearing white wedding dresses. I hope you will be pleased. I wanted to bring the tradition here."

"How, who?" Chelsea asked.

"Never mind. Let me help you dress, wear this gown, and enjoy this blessed day. The lovely dress you wore this morning will be right here for you to change back into to wear to your celebration party."

Taking a deep breath, Chelsea peeked out the front door, where she saw me waiting for her. Taking a deep breath, she stepped out onto the veranda and heard the congregation members give one audible collective sigh.

I reached for her hand, and we stepped down the steps and

walked to the altar made of elk antlers and wildflowers.

Preacher Bill opened the good book and read. "Fate has brought you two together by a father's love that ended too soon. Unknowingly, for these two here, it began hand in hand, with faith, love, and joy for a new beginning."

"Do you, Chelsea, take this man to love and honor for all your days?"

"Yes, I do." Tears choked her words. *A dream come true.*

"Reg, do you take this woman to love and honor for all your days?"

"I surely do."

"Before I pronounce you man and wife, I want you always to remember these words from 1 Corinthians 13:13."

Paul writes, "So now faith, hope, and love abide, these three; but the greatest of these is love."

"You are now, by the power entrusted in me by the holy word of God, 'man and wife.' Reg, you may now kiss your bride."

Time stood still. The air was crisp and cool. The birds chirped, and the deer in the field silently watched as they lazily stood in the meadow eating on the fresh grass. The guests let out a roar of whoops, cheers, applause, and clanging cowbells.

The happy couple heard nothing and saw nothing except each other.

Spencer raised Caty and kissed her, at which point she squealed with excitement. Callie picked the flowers up from the ground.

Nancy grinned from ear to ear while tears streamed down her rosy cheeks. She twisted the wedding band around her finger, looked over the field of wild grass, and knew Clancy was looking down upon them from the hillside riding his favorite mule, "C."

After the ceremony, Chelsea returned to the ranch house to change into the party clothes she had worn to the church, unaware that a wedding gown was waiting for her.

Once the happy couple rejoined their guests, they were introduced to a traveling musician tuning his guitar, preparing to entertain them.

"Howdy, my name is Andy, reaching out to shake hands. I will play anything from a polka to a waltz for you. Just holler out what you want to hear, your friends back here on the fiddle and banjo, and I will make it happen. Winking at the young ladies surrounding the impromptu stage, he gave an opening strum on the strings, and the fiddler joined in with a high-stepping tune to rouse the crowd.

During the month before the big day, Nancy Jo arranged for an artist to attend the festivities to sketch and paint a few of the wedding festivities.

The woman she hired was getting on in years and wore the craziest colored outfits. She made an impression on anyone who saw her, that was for sure.

She could memorize a scene and draw or paint it as if you were standing in the picture. She was a cup tipper and liked her fancy drinks loaded with whatever bottle was nearby.

She Might have been unable to walk at the night's end, but that artist could still move that pencil or paintbrush and always signed her name B.R.

Her work was recognized everywhere.

61

ZEKE BRINGS A GIFT

The celebration lasted through far into the night. The food was plentiful and was provided by those in attendance. There was beef, corn on the cob, fancy fruit salads, pies, and homemade ice cream. The children played until they passed out in the wagons.

The grownups danced and listened to the music, and mostly, the men drank until the fire glowed away to red-hot embers. Chelsea and I eventually disappeared into the stand-alone cabin on the property as man and wife.

The morning sun parted a few wispy clouds, and the sun opened with a painted soft, reddish glow, giving beauty to its peacefulness. The women were already awake and up, fixing a breakfast of coffee, eggs, pancakes, bacon, and spuds. The kids woke, rubbing the sleep from their eyes, but the men folk were not as eager to see the sun. They now understood why they quit drinking so many years ago.

As the men lingered in their sleeping areas, it gave the women folk plenty of time to talk about the wedding and the fun they had.

They were also taking time to poke fun at their husbands. There was talk of hell to pay for their behavior, but with enough sweet talk from the men, the women would most likely give them a pass this one time.

I woke early and was the first to exit the cabin. The joking started with those gathered around the morning fire. Later, Chelsea poked her head out of the cabin, dressed like the beauty she was, and the men started with their jibes again. They stopped the banter after receiving stern looks from their wives.

Chelsea walked over to her mother. "I'm a married woman now, Ma. It's a dream come true."

She received a giant hug from her mother as Nancy whispered in her ear, "I hope you didn't wear that boy out last night."

Chelsea turned bright red. "Ma!" All the women enjoyed their opportunity to poke a little fun.

Spence, Tom, and Poke rounded up all the little ones, and they headed to the fishing hole to catch trout, swim, and nap on the sunny bank.

The women enjoyed their coffee and the time away from their scamps.

The men drank coffee and tried not to move. Their heads ached, and they now tried to get food in their bellies to help with their hangovers.

Spence returned to camp, worn down from

dealing with the little ones. He enjoyed it but wasn't ready to have a handful of his own. Caty and Callie couldn't be happier.

Caty had Spencer's company. Callie loved the water and probably swam twenty miles. "I think you are half duck and the other half fish," he told her as he carried her on his shoulders back to the campsite.

The two young boys returned with their prize mess of fish and were excited to have the women cook up their bounty for a quick lunch for the boys.

The guests consumed lunch from the remainder of the food from the previous night's party. My buddies spent their leisure time sleeping under the trees in the cool grass, opening one eye to peer out to see if the kids were okay and then returning to their nap.

I had spent the morning visiting with my folks. They praised the beauty of the hills and talked about the availability of the water, the range, and cattle. Jessie, my mother, reminisced about family and grandchildren.

Her boys were grown, but her future had hopes of beloved grandchildren calling her by her special name, "Marmie."

"Not to worry, Ma. We will fill the house with grandbabies for you!" I said.

"Reg, hush!" Chelsea hollered as she heard what I said.

Maggie needed to return to her routine at the café, so she left first after lunch with the remainder of the folks from town.

Buck and Poke had cattle to tend to, and the lawmen surely would have mischief to straighten out back home, so off they all rode.

The remaining guests packed up to head back to town and their ranches, poking the last bit of fun at Chelsea and me. Laughter rang back to us from a distance away before it turned quiet again.

Chelsea, our kinfolk, and Preacher Bill were the only remaining guests at the ranch. We all stood waving to our friends as they traveled the dusty road back to their homes.

After about an hour's travel time and as strange as it seemed to be welcoming visitors after the wedding, the homebound travelers were surprised to see dust clouds forming on the road and heading their way.

The curious onlookers rode on, craning their necks to see who was rushing to the ranch at such a breakneck speed. The familiar stagecoach appeared with Zeke and Bailey sitting aboard the driver's box.

"Well, what in the world would Zeke be doing bringing the coach out here?" asked Nancy as she continued to clean tables and stack chairs. "It does seem strange. And he has Bailey with him. Let's wait here until he arrives and settles himself."

That was not to be.

As soon as the coach stopped, Bailey was first to jump down and head to the crowd. "You'uns ain't gonna be believin' this," she said, so out of breath, her words all ran together.

"Well, don't keep us in suspense. What happened?" I asked.

"Hey, ya'll. Let me tell it," huffed Zeke as he approached, limping along, struggling to carry a loaded basket.

"Hurry yoreself on up. I cain't keep this news in me foren ever, ya know!" Bailey whipped out the words.

After catching up to Bailey, Zeke set the basket down, thought better of it, and handed it to Chelsea, who was closest to him. The remaining family members gathered around.

Chelsea's new mother-in-law stood beside her, bent over, and lifted a large, square quilt. She could only gasp as she uncovered a baby and two baby bottles.

"A baby!" Caty yelled, looking around Jessie's side. "Scoot over, Marmee. Let me see better. Wait. There is a note. It says, "My name is Dakota. Please take care of me.""

"Zeke, what are you doing with a baby?" "Did you lose a passenger?" Spence joked.

"Not funny, Spence. Looks like this little guy lost his mama," Zeke said.

One person after another spoke over the words of the person next to them. During the confusion, Bailey tried to jump in the middle of the conversation with her version of the story.

Preacher Bill was finally able to bring some order to the chaos. With an ear splitting whistle, he calmed the crowd and asked Zeke to slowly tell the story.

"Well, here goes. Bailey and I unloaded our passengers at the High Rise Settlement like usual. While we was there, the wire man sent a boy with word that four people missed the coach at the Settlement and needed a ride into Two Forks later today."

"Now, you uns here all know not to be telling me what to do. I told the young feller I will get there when I get there."

"We were a fair piece out when I heard a squeal. I thought mebbe it were a wheel fixin' ta break, so I had Bailey pull up."

"While I looked around, I heard it again, only this time, it came from inside the coach. And this here basket is what I found."

"How could a passenger leave a baby behind?" asked Nancy.

"Well, I hardly would think it," interrupted Bailey. "All them passengers was men."

"Best I can figure it," Zeke continued, "is that when the men folk unloaded on one side and picked up their bags, someone opened the coach's side door on the other side and shoved the basket in, quiet as you please."

"Then off we went," Bailey said, needing to have the last word in that part of the story.

"I was plum out of ideas when Bailey 'membered the weddin'."

"I thought on it a mite and knew along the road and down south is Brian's Bluff, so I took the turn-off the cattlemen use when herding cattle down to the stockyards. It were a bit rough but doable. Then we high-tailed it out here."

"Zeke, since now you are a papa. What are you gonna do with a baby?" joked Spence.

"No way, son. No young 'uns in my life. I ain't the one holding the basket now."

Silence fell as each of us in the crowd turned their eyes to gawk at Chelsea and me.

Not a moment passed when a warm muzzle, a firm head, and a set of pointed ears poked her head between Chelsea and me. Roan carefully placed her nose down to sniff the baby, lifted her head, and gave a playful whinny.

Chelsea met my eyes, and we burst into laughter.

"Well, what are we waiting for? Let's get that baby out of the basket," said Jessie. The tiny guy giggled when he felt Marmee's hands lift him free of the beautiful hand-quilted blanket.

Chelsea gasped, "I've seen this work before. There is an old woman who travels from town to town selling her quilts. She is well known for her fancy handwork in the quilts but more so for her odd behavior.

She always wore a hat, each one different from the last. The strangest assortment you have ever seen. Where she found these outrageous hats and bonnets was a mystery in itself. No one knows her name or where she comes from. Locals call her The Crazy Hat Lady. She is an oddity. That is for sure."

"Look on the back. Maybe the quilter embroidered her name. Lots of quilters do that as a remembrance," Nancy offered.

Indeed, there was an inscription. A silence fell among the family members upon reading the finely embroidered words.

"Do not let your left hand know what your right hand is doing so that your giving may be in secret."

Preacher Bill stepped forward, saying, "It may be a secret message from the mother herself to whoever finds her baby."

"This is taken from Matthew 6:3-4 and can be interpreted in many different ways."

"Even though we can't take this at its literal meaning, I want to believe the mother is trusting her baby will be accepted into a loving home without question and her identity kept a secret."

By now, it was early evening, and we invited Zeke and Bailey to enjoy refreshments and a place to rest their heads for the night, which they gladly accepted. Discretely, they retired early to the ranch house.

Once the excitement decreased and all concerned caught a

collective breath, we warmed our backsides on the familiar chairs and sat around the tables to begin a family meeting.

After much discussion, Chelsea and I agreed to keep the baby under our careful watch until Dakota's future could be settled. Before that, discreetly searching for his real mama would only be the proper thing to do.

Zeke and Bailey had hitched up their team to the stagecoach and snuck away before the rest of us saw the thin light of day. Their obligation to the stagecoach line required that they pick up those last passengers regardless of the lateness of their arrival.

Nancy and the girls left first, and to Caty's delight, Nancy allowed her to show off her newly acquired expertise in guiding the horses in pulling the wagon.

Spence, Mom, and Dad pulled themselves into their buckboard and headed to town to catch tomorrow's stage. A thousand words were exchanged in the handshake I gave Dad.

Chelsea and I were finally alone, holding hands and carrying Dakota between us when they pulled away.

Spence reined in the buckboard and looked back. "They look like two little kids holding a picnic basket. Happy, but scared as hell."

I wrapped my arms around Chelsea's shoulders. "Mrs. Reg Carter, what do we do now?"

"I think I could use a bath in the creek and some help washing my back," my bride replied.

This time, I turned red. I wasn't exactly sure about the next move. "I'm game. I may need some directions, but I'm a real fast learner."

We headed back to the cabin to find towels and clean clothes. This time, we carried the baby basket between us, giggling down the length of the path.

Chelsea laid out a quilt, a snack for us, and a bottle of milk. She set the basket in the center of the patterned quilt.

Dakota was propped up in the basket happily gurgling and gazing at his surroundings. We knew he was safe. Roan watched over him, and we were only steps away.

Dropping our towels and stepping into the creek, we both anticipated a nice dip until Chelsea jumped up, bolted out of the water, rewrapped herself in her towel, and ran to the little boy's basket.

"What in the world, Chelsea? Did you step on something in the water?"

"Reg, I am in my birthday suit, totally naked. I don't want to scare the stuffing out of this little guy! It wouldn't be proper."

There stood Chelsea, turning the basket around so Dakota's back was facing us. Then, after Roan gave me a womanly stare down, shook her mane, and snorted, she also turned her back to me.

I laughed so hard that I fell backward into the creek, nearly drowning myself. *Women!*

62

BACK IN TOWN

When Maggie, Joe, Sara, and the kids pulled up in front of Maggie's Café in their wagon, there were twenty heavily armed men in front of her establishment. The man whom Maggie presumed to be the leader spoke first.

"Hello, ma'am. My name is Jake Samson. Ladies
and young men, if I may ask, where are all the people
in this town? We rode in, and this place looked like a ghost town, all closed down."

"Hello, I am Maggie, owner of the café. We had a wedding to attend, and we're all just now returning."

"It must have been a festive occasion and a special couple to draw everyone away. Maggie, will you be opening this evening? My men and I have been on a long trail. We could use some good food."

"If you gentlemen could give me an hour, I'll set up the place."

"Sure, we will wait, but you may have to build a bigger door for us all to rush through," he joked.

"We will watch to see who's the toughest or fastest to get seated first," said Maggie, chuckling.

After the ladies and kids climbed off the wagon, Maggie whispered to Sara, "Look at those men."

The women took a moment to glance over at the men Maggie pointed out. They were dismounting four at a time. The others turned their horses and watched the street in every direction. After those four men dismounted, they stood on the boardwalk, and another four repeated the same movements. This routine continued until all the men stood on the ground and took up sentry duties over the entire town. Their horses were trained, alert, and ready to stand where the men left them.

All the men carried a weapon tied down on their hips, a shoulder gun at their sides, and a long rifle. They had knives strapped to their boots. These men were professionals, hunters, killers, and possibly the law of the land.

The ladies were stunned and had no clue what to think. Jetta and Sara helped Maggie prepare the café. When everything was prepared the way she liked it, Maggie walked out to the porch and announced they were ready to serve their meal.

Two cowhands who had patiently waited decided to take the opportunity to scoot in ahead of these men or they might never be fed.

"Thank you, Miss Maggie. Boys, let's get fed."

The men politely smiled, removed their hats, and were very mannerly as they filed in. They entered as they had dismounted, four at a time. The first four went to the back of the dining area and sat looking forward with their backs to the walls and would see anyone entering. The following four sat across from the windows where they had a bird's eye view out front.

The remaining eight stood next to the windows divided in half by the hinged door. They could see every square inch of the inside and the outside.

Maggie walked around the room, writing everyone's orders on her notepad. The men were otherwise silent and aware of every movement in the room.

When Maggie took the order of the man she assumed was in charge, she peered at him over her scribbling. "I've never seen men and horses this well-behaved, organized, and disciplined. Are you a military troop if you are at liberty to answer?"

"No, ma'am, we're bounty men. We hunt the worst of the worst. We ride with the law, but we're given a lot of lead rope in doing so."

"Sir, I'm impressed."

Jetta and Sara fed the men and served never ending pots of hot black coffee. After their meal, the bounty men cleaned their tables, stacked the dishes, and returned chairs under the tables. Finally, the men left the same way they had entered, in perfect order.

Sara glanced at Jake. "I'm curious, Jake. Those two young men by the boardwalk. They haven't taken their eyes off you this entire time."

Jake smiled and looked toward the two young men. "Those two are quite the story. They are brothers. The older one with the big smile is Tyler, and the other is Cody. He is the silent one. I came across them several years back. They are trackers, best I've ever seen or heard of. I think they could track a bird in flight."

"The story goes that they were four and five years old and out on their own tracking lizards across hard rock. A band of Indians rode up and watched them track their prey. The warriors were amused but more so impressed at their skill."

"The boys looked up at the Indians and walked over to them, simple, friendly like. They reached up, and the Indians loaded them onto their horses and rode away."

Sara moaned. "The mother must have gone crazy worrying about them."

"No, Sara. She was a woman of, let's say, loose moral values. I guess she was the entertainer at a barn dance but a mite shy on mothering. I saw her a while back. She was a looker. That was for sure. I think her name was Kathy. Not sure."

"The boys were educated in the Indian way. As they got older, they went out on their own. Tracking for hire. Game or men, whatever paid. Tyler was, as I said, the talker. I heard tell he rode with a fella that killed hisself after he rode with Ty on a long cattle drive. He rode up on the hill and shot himself."

Sara and Maggie gasped at this pause in the tall tale. Jake smiled. "Yep, he couldn't take Ty's yawp'n no more."

The group of men laughed out loud and poked fun at Ty.

"Now Cody, he is the silent type. When he talks, you better listen. He is the brains of the two. Both boys have saved my bacon more than once. That is God's truth for sure."

"Maggie." He grasped Maggie's hand and gave her a tender handshake. Then he handed her a handful of silver coins.

Maggie looked at Jake and started to return some of the coins. "Jake, you overpaid double…

"No, it's yours, and please share with the other ladies for being so polite and thoughtful to a bunch of strangers."

"Jake, thank you. You said you were bounty men and go after the worst sort of men. Are you looking now?"

"Maggie, we're always looking. It's an endless task. Now that you mention it, I could use help in one little matter."

"Sure, Jake, how can I help?" Maggie said.

Jake looked at Maggie. "I'm looking for some answers. I'll be back this way in a month or so. As I said, my name is Jake Sampson. I believe you may have known my older brother as Tucker."

Maggie turned speechless.

"When I return, Maggie, I want to look up Reg Carver, who I have come to understand you may know." He looked Maggie straight in the eye as Sara stood silently beside her.

"Maggie, we will see you soon."

Jake mounted and turned his horse to leave. All the men turned in precise unison and rode behind him, leaving the women standing on the boardwalk gawking.

While Maggie spoke to the men outside the café, Haley brought the last dessert to the table where the two cowboys who first entered the café sat.

Not realizing Jetta was behind him, the young man stood from his chair whirling around as he bumped into her, and his blueberry pie first hit him in the chest and then tumbled to the floor.

Jetta gasped at the mess and bent to pick up the empty plate. Bending over to sit down on the floor, the cowboy snatched his fork from the table.

Blushing with a wink and a dimpled smile, he said, "Hi, my name is Adam, and you surely are a lot better cook than a waitress." He then stuck his fork in the pie on the floor and began to eat his dessert.

"You may as well pull up a piece of the floor and visit a spell until I finish. One gets used to eating a bit of dirt on the trail," Adam laughed, and Jetta couldn't help joining in as she stared at the tiny flecks of gold sparks in those hazel colored eyes.

Sara walked by on her way to the kitchen thinking, *Oh my, here we go again.*

Just as the bounty hunters left town, the stagecoach filled with passengers and luggage rolled to a stop directly in front of the ladies. The make-shift station inside the café was the regular drop-off point in Two Forks.

A clean-cut gentleman stepped out of the coach, waving away the road dust, and greeted the proprietor.

"Hello, I would like to introduce myself, my dear lady. My name is Mr. Asher Lionel," he said as he leaned on a black walking stick topped by a cut glass knob.

"My charges and I are passing through, and I hope to find a suitable establishment to settle in and rest our weary bones for a few days. Would you be kind enough to direct me and point out a fine eatery, as well?"

"Uncle, have we finally arrived after being delayed an extra day? And for a baby, no less!" said a young lady inside the coach. "I am parched and disheveled from riding in this awful conveyance."

"That would be my niece, Jaida," he said. "Well, then, alight and enjoy nature's bounty."

Mr. Asher put his hand forward to help Jaida out of the carriage. The teenage lass wore finery that suggested she was on her way to the debutant's ball in New York City. She flapped her arms and flounced her dress, fussing over the dust on her delicate slipper shoes.

Jetta covered her mouth so the girl wouldn't see her giggle while Sara poked her in the ribs.

"Oh, my goodness," Sara whispered.

"Uncle, may I get out of this cage, also?" said a boy looking out of the side window of the coach. "I don't want to miss watching a cowboy in a gunfight while stuck inside this box."

"And that voice belongs to her younger brother and my nephew, Chase," said the impeccable Mr. Asher.

And out of the carriage shot a young boy in a beige linen traveling suit smeared with sweat-dried dust around the collar and handprints on the trousers.

"Nephew, a bath for you before we dine!"

"Welcome to Two Forks," Maggie said. "My goodness, the dust is thick today," she continued, blaming her choking voice on the ever-present street dust. "Please step up onto the boardwalk and out of the street."

"Street? You call this a street?" said Jaida in the most sarcastic tone. "This looks more like a back alley in the slums."

"Jaida, your manners!"

Maggie stepped off the boardwalk to glance inside the coach to unload the baby, but no one seemed willing to help. *Baby, what baby? I thought I heard her say they were delayed because of a baby.*

Wanting to assure herself that it was empty, she glanced again and stepped away from the coach, shaking her head at the mysterious words Jaida had spoken.

"Watch yourselves! This here stuff ain't gonna unload its own self. Dern! Whacha totin' in them bags, rocks? Look out under me," said Bailey, Zeke's newly hired driver, as luggage pieces rained down off the coach.

"Missy, you best get ya some boots for stompin' here abouts. Ya getting' me, ya heah me? Rattlers and such bite mitey hard."

"My carpetbags are ruined!" Jaida moaned as she saw one had landed in a horse's road apple.

Interrupting the grumbling, Maggie welcomed the newcomers again and invited them inside the café for a meal.

Sara served Zeke and Bailey a glass of lemonade before they scrambled out the door to hit the trail.

"Ready to giddyap, Zeke?" Bailey asked.

"I believe I am ready to leave these city slickers in our dust, Bailey," replied Zeke with a shake of his head.

"Hiya, you girls! Giddyap, there!" Bailey called to the team.

Sara stood in the corner, gaping at the three sitting in the dining room. She had never witnessed people act like this anywhere, especially in Two Forks.

Gazing through the oversized café windows, Jaida's mouth worked like a guppy gasping for air as she watched Bailey's hat fly off her head, landing on her shoulders.

Luckily, Bailey wore a rawhide tie on her hat, or she would have lost it in her rush to get the team away from the depot.

"Why, Uncle, that was a girl who drove our stagecoach. How utterly uncivilized," remarked Jaida.

"What? A girl! Now this I gotta see," echoed Chase, knowing if this were true, he would have the first of many stories to tell his friends when they returned home.

"Looks like the town could have more excitement coming our way in the near future," Maggie said, nodding her head with a spring in her step.

No sooner were those words out of Maggie's mouth than Jaida's eyes opened wide, and she held her face between her hands.

"Here comes some sort of wagon with another girl driving it. Surely you DO NOT expect me to learn the ways of the dust-eating, uneducated, backwoods mountain girls while we are staying here?" she yelped while Maggie's customers stared at her in awe.

Maggie looked out the window and said, "Oh, look. It's Nancy back with the girls, and she let Caty drive the team. I wonder if they have any news from the ranch?"

THE END

ACKNOWLEDGMENTS

For every thought, every word, every meaning, I thank you, my God.

I thank and appreciate all those I have met on my journey and who have been an inspiration to me.

I humbly thank you, the reader, for taking the time to travel to the West with me in this story. Whether you purchased a physical book or downloaded a copy, I am grateful.

I want to thank Suzanne Minae for the cover art and formatting. I sincerely appreciate her skill and ability to know what I needed without me giving her an exact picture.

I also thank Catherine Townsend-Lyon with Lyon Media for her willingness to help me upload my debut manuscript and explain marketing details. Her knowledge of the publishing field and marketing is amazing.

Finally, I thank my collaborative helper, Barbara Daniels Dena, for helping with the rewrite. She earned her pay on this one. The check is in the mail.

During one of our many conversations, Barbara asked me when I learned to write in so many foreign languages.

I told her, "I didn't. I have a hard enough time writing in English."

She said, "You just made my point."

A REQUEST TO MY READERS

Reviews are important to an independent author. They are what help promote the sales of our books. My best buddy, Kinder, an English sheepdog, frowns at an empty food bowl.

If you enjoyed *Trail of Fate*, I would be thrilled to receive a rating and a kind note about my debut novel on Goodreads.com or Amazon.com. It is easy to do; a few words would mean so much.

Many thanks for considering my request.

B. S. Daniels

ABOUT THE AUTHOR

B. S. Daniels, or Scott, to his friends, calls Wyoming home after spending most of his life working in the Colorado mountains. An entrepreneur at heart, he loves a good challenge in making his way through life.

So, when the writing bug bit, he accepted the call, always with his special buddy, Kinder, an English sheepdog at his side.

www.ingramcontent.com/pod-product-compliance
Lightning Source LLC
Chambersburg PA
CBHW070901260626
47162CB00007B/2526